Selected praise for
CATHERINE ASARO

"Asaro has quickly gained a reputation as a writer of
very colorful space operas. Her novels are notable
for such typical space operatic virtues as (literally)
larger-than-life heroes and heroines, truly bad
villains, extravagant technology, star-spanning
empires, and action-filled plots. I hope that
description doesn't seem dismissive: On the contrary,
Asaro really does make virtues of each of these
characteristics. In addition, her novels feature
significant romance subplots...
first-rate rip-roaring adventures."
—*SF Site*

"Asaro's Saga of the Skolian Empire has quietly
become one of the most interesting, ambitious, and
popular science-fiction series since Dune,
captivating readers with its complex universe, its
diverse cast of sympathetic characters, and its
imaginative blend of hard SF, future history, military
SF, space opera, family saga, and romance."
—*Romantic Times*

"This latest installment blends dynastic intrigue
with theoretical physics to create a story
that will appeal to fans of hard SF
as well as grand-scale storytelling."
—*Library Journal* on *Spherical Harmonic*

"If you like romances, or if you think there's no way
anyone could blend them with science fiction, grab
this one. Asaro has done another very nice job."
—*Analog* magazine on *The Veiled Web*

THE CHARMED SPHERE

Catherine Asaro

LUNA

www.Luna-Books.com

LUNA

First edition February 2004

THE CHARMED SPHERE

ISBN 0-373-80203-X

Visit LUNA at www.Luna-Books.com

Printed in U.S.A.

CONTENTS

Acknowledgments

I would like to express my gratitude to the readers who gave me input on *The Charmed Sphere*. Their comments greatly helped the book. Any errors that remain are mine alone.

For reading the manuscript and giving me the benefit of their wisdom and insights: Doranna Durgin, Tricia Schwaab and Jeri Smith-Ready. To Aly's Writing Group, for their thorough and patient critiques of scenes: Aly Parsons, Simcha Kuritzky, Connie Warner, Al Carroll, Michael La Violette and J. G. Huckenpöler. To Mary-Theresa Hussey, my goddess of an editor, and all the fine people at LUNA who made this book possible; to Binnie Braunstein, for all her work and enthusiasm on my behalf; and to Eleanor Wood, my excellent and much appreciated agent.

A heartfelt thanks to the shining lights of my life, my husband, John Kendall Cannizzo, and my daughter, Cathy, whose love and support make it all worthwhile.

To my daughter, Cathy,
Whose luminous heart brightens the world,
With all my love

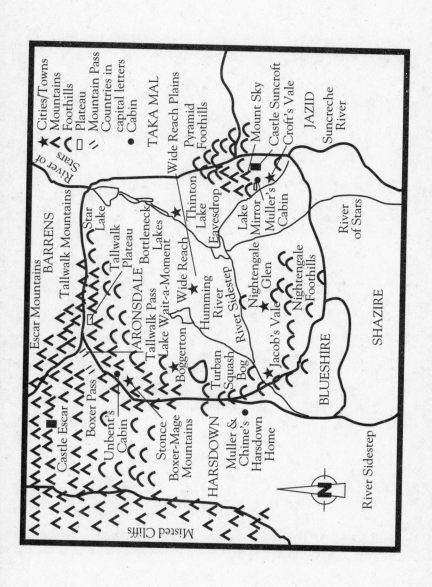

Jeweled Mages

Chime

Chime hid when the king came to town.

Everyone in Jacob's Vale knew the royal party would arrive today. Fast messengers traveling the country kept citizens apprised of the king's progress through the realm of Aronsdale. Chime had hoped he might skip a hamlet as small as Jacob's Vale, but apparently she wouldn't be so lucky.

A pack of boys raced into town, hair flying, yelling that King Daron was coming. So Chime hid. She ran to her family's orchard and climbed her favorite apple tree. At her age, almost eighteen, she was supposedly too mature for such pastimes, ready instead to settle down and bring a husband into the household. She had no wish to marry, however, and didn't care in the least about her supposed lack of interest in climbing trees. She scrambled up the trunk, dressed in tunic, leggings, and knee-boots, all the hue of yellow apples, her favorite color. She didn't stop until she was deep into the leafy cover of the branches, screened by spring foliage from curious eyes. Royal eyes.

Actually, it wasn't the king who inspired Chime to flee the town and stash herself in a tree. She feared a far more imposing person—Della No-Cozen, one of Daron's top advisors. Della served as the Mage Mistress for Castle Suncroft.

"Pah," Chime muttered. Although the idea of a castle being a croft for the sun appealed to her sense of whimsy, she had no wish to go there. She knew why Mistress No-Cozen was searching the countryside, visiting towns large and small. Oh, yes, she knew. They were looking for shape-mages, the adepts who used circles, cubes, spheres, and other shapes to create spells. Well, they wouldn't find any here, not if she had any say in the matter.

Although Chime's parents realized she carried the shape-mage gifts, neither had ever pressured her to reveal her talents. Besides, if she left Jacob's Vale and went to Suncroft, her family would have one less person to help in the orchards. Chime loved her family and she loved tending the trees, especially when they blossomed and brought forth fresh, succulent apples.

Thinking of fruit, Chime spotted a particularly juicy apple. She plucked it and settled herself more comfortably in the branches. Then she peered through the leaves at the dusty road beyond the trees, and past it to the hills. In the distance, the first riders of the king's party had appeared over a ridge outside the town. Taking a bite of her apple, she sat back to watch them arrive.

The stately procession crested the ridge like a wave of people. Chime had to admit they made an impressive sight. Warriors rode great horses with golden bridles. Their pennants snapped in the breeze, dyed the king's colors, indigo and gold on a white background, showing a castle silhouetted on the disk of the sun. An honor guard rode with them, officers in blue uniforms. As they drew nearer, riding at the edge of the trees and even under some of them, Chime saw the gold insignia of military officers.

Then King Daron appeared. At first Chime mistook him for a royal advisor. He made a spectacular sight, to be sure, tall on his great black charger, his gray hair swept up from his brow. And his chiseled features certainly had a kingly aspect. But he seemed so *old*. She had seen his image on the hexagonal coins people used to buy the apples, quinces, and pears her family grew. It made her expect a much younger man, one hale and hearty, full of vigor. This man's advanced age suggested his era of rule might end sooner than she, and most people, expected.

The thought perturbed Chime. King Daron had been a constant all her life, a good sovereign her parents said, steady and certain. He had no son to assume his crown; the prince had died years ago, lost in an orb-carriage accident with his wife and their young child, a boy named Jarid. Rumor claimed their loss had destroyed the king. He had been widowed himself years before, and he had never remarried. Instead he had chosen his nephew, the son of his brother, as his heir.

Chime took another bite of her apple, studying the king's retinue. Several nobles rode with him, the men in gold trousers and white shirts under brocaded vests; the women in pale tunics and leggings tucked into riding boots.

As the procession drew near, a woman looked up at the tree. Her full cheeks had a ruddy color and gray curls framed her lined face. Chime could see her eyes, gray perhaps, though she was too far away to be sure. What struck Chime most was their intelligence. The woman stared straight at her hiding place as if she saw the truant girl.

Chime held still, praying to escape notice. It seemed to work. The woman rode on with the king's party, passing below the tree with no more indication she knew someone was watching them. Chime hoped that were true, because she had no doubt who she had just seen—Della No-Cozen, Shape-Mage Mistress of Suncroft.

* * *

Chime climbed in a window at the back of her house, sneaking into her mother's workroom. It was here that Bell recorded the sale of fruit from their orchards, writing the numbers on parchments in beautiful inks with designs of vines around the edges. Bell had gone to the village earlier, so this entrance was safer for Chime than going in the front door, where someone might catch sight of her and prod her to go greet the king's party.

She was clambering over the sill onto a rickety wooden chair when a young voice said, "Hey!"

Chime jerked around and lost her balance. As she flailed her arms, she jumped off the chair and landed with a thump on the plank wood floor. Stumbling, she grabbed the wall shelves to keep from falling. Knickknacks rained over her, wooden harvest dolls that clattered all over the floor. She managed to avoid the ignoble fate of sprawling on the floor herself, but she winced at her undignified entrance.

Drummer, the younger of her two brothers, stood in the doorway smirking, his gold curls tousled over his ears and collar, his blue eyes full of delight at embarrassing her. Chime knew people thought she and Drummer resembled each other, both in appearance and behavior, but at this moment she had no doubt about the truth: imps had taken her true brother at birth and put this vexing creature in his place, leaving him to bedevil his poor sister.

Chime drew herself upright and brushed out her tunic. "Well, so why aren't you doing your chores?"

He stopped grinning long enough to glare. "Why aren't you doing yours?"

She spoke with dignity. "I was busy."

Drummer crossed his arms, for all the world resembling a nine-year-old version of their father, though Drummer had far less brawn. "Busy climbing trees?"

"Hah." She thought hard and fast for an excuse, or at least hard, anyway. Fast thinking had never been her forte. At a loss for good response, she fell back on sisterly disdain. "Little do you know."

Curiosity flashed in his gaze. "Know what?"

She brushed a leaf off her sleeve. "Oh, nothing."

"Chime!"

She had to relent, seeing his eyes bright with excitement. "The king's party has arrived."

"Hai!" With no more ado, he spun around and took off. After two steps, though, he skidded to a stop and swung back to her. "Well, come on!"

Chime smiled at his enthusiasm. He had always been that way, full of energy. "You go and see, Drummer. I really do have chores to finish."

"Mother and Father won't mind." His eyes were as round as the moon. "This is special."

"I'll come soon."

"See you there!" He whirled and dashed off. A crash came from somewhere, a chair falling over it sounded like, following by a breathless apology from Drummer, either to a person or the chair. The front door opened and slammed, and then it was quiet again.

Chime exhaled, relieved he hadn't pressed her to go with him. The news had excited him enough that he ignored her uncharacteristic desire to do her chores. Although she enjoyed working in the orchard, she loathed her duties around the house. Far better to be out in the sun, eating apples.

Pah. If necessary, she would hide in the cellar until the king left town and took Della No-Cozen with him. She went through the house, checking for her parents and her other brother, but she found no one. No doubt everyone had gone to the square to celebrate the king's arrival.

Chime found the chair Drummer had knocked over in the front parlor. She set it back on its feet. Her father's brother, a carpenter, had made it for them. His attention to detail and the beautiful carvings he created put his work in high demand throughout southern Aronsdale. With the income from the orchard, Chime's family was better off than most, so they could afford more of the pieces.

Her uncle would have given them his work for free, but Chime's father refused to let him, paying him with twelve-sided copper coins. For the best pieces he even paid a round copper coin worth twelve of the twelve-siders. Chime loved the shiny coins, which were made at Castle Suncroft. The perfect shapes gave her a sense of completion.

She soon reached the big kitchen in the part of the house built by her great-grandfather. An iron kettle hung over the embers of a fire in the hearth across the room, and the aroma of simmering broth drifted in the air. The dented metal door of the storeroom was closed, keeping in the cold air from the blocks of ice. Chime's father and her older brother had gone out hunting a few days ago, and brought back quail, hares, and a deer.

A rough wooden table that had been in the family for generations stood in the center of the room. Her slate lay there with a stick of white chalk. Chime winced. She was supposed to do sums today. She went over and peered at the slate on the off chance she might find the homework done. It wasn't, of course; her mother's neat writing covered the left half, but the right side where Chime was supposed to answer remained blank. Biting her lip, she picked up a cloth and dropped it over the slate, hiding the sums. She would do them later. Tonight. Really. She would.

Turning, she glimpsed a picture on the mantel of the hearth, a portrait her mother had painted last year. It showed Chime with hair as tousled as Drummer's, more actually, given that she had so much of it. Yellow curls tumbled over her shoulders and arms, and her cheeks were as red as apples. She had thought Drummer's eyes were wide and startled, but in the picture hers looked even more so, as if she had been caught misbehaving.

Chime tried to smooth her hair, which was as unruly today as on the morning her mother had done that portrait. Even as a young child, she had never liked being messy. It hadn't bothered her enough to stop her from climbing trees or chasing her brothers, but more and more often now, she wished she could spend time on her appearance, that she could have coiffed hair and beautiful clothes. She never would; although her family had a comfortable living, the garments she fantasized were too dear in price.

She sighed, disheartened by her impractical dreams. Fancy clothes would be wasted in an orchard. Besides, if she ever *did* have a life that included beautiful things, it would mean she had to fit that life, which would mean fitting in with the nobility. And never, ever could she adapt to their rarified existence.

Truth be told, she would rather be an orchard keeper. She loved it. Nor would anyone expect more than she had to give. No one would want her to do more with her life than she could achieve. She had a nightmare of finding herself in the middle of the royal court, unwashed and disheveled, surrounded by the sparkling elite of the land, all in gold-cloth and jewels, all staring at her with derision.

"Stop it," Chime muttered to herself. It made no difference that the king and his nobles had arrived in town. They would soon be off to another place, looking elsewhere for mages. Yes, soon they would be gone.

Soon she would be safe.

Muller

Muller Startower Heptacorn Dawnfield, Prince of Aronsdale, scowled at his valet. "Can't you fix the rip?"

His valet, Sam Threadman, wasn't the least fazed. Sam made no secret of the satisfaction he took in dressing the prince. Nor did he take Muller's grumbling seriously, though Muller constantly bade him to do so. In fact, Sam seemed to enjoy his company. Muller considered him a friend, though he never spoke of it aloud.

At the moment, Muller stood before a gilt-edged mirror in the bedroom of his suite at Castle Suncroft, surveying his appearance with a critical eye. The cream-colored trousers fit his legs without a single crease and tucked neatly into his finely tooled boots. His cream-hued tunic had gold stitching and tailored seams that accented his lean form. Unfortunately, a small rip marred one sleeve at his wrist.

"Your Most Estimable Highness," Sam told him. "I will see to the problem at once." With a flourish, he pulled off his sewing kit, which hung from his belt along with various other accouterments designed to make Prince Muller the most elegant man in Aronsdale. Sam prepared a needle with thread of exactly the right color and proceeded to repair the rip. He attacked the crisis with such expertise that when he finished, no sign of the tear remained even on close inspection.

"There." He beamed at his prince. "That should do."

"Thank you." Muller straightened his tunic, turning this way and that in front of the mirror, checking all aspects of his appearance, just as he did each morning before venturing out of his suite. It pleased him that Sam had done such a fine job making him presentable.

Unfortunately, the garments never helped. He enjoyed clothes, but no matter how carefully he dressed, nothing added authority to his demeanor. He had the leggy aspect of a gazelle rather than the muscular brawn he wanted. The straight gold hair that swept to his shoulders glistened in the light. And his face. What a disaster. His eyes were too large, his lashes too long, his features too beautiful. Who took seriously a man with pretty eyelashes? He was never going to strike fear into his enemies looking like this. Not that he had any wish to fight a war, but he was far more proficient with a sword than anyone believed.

Muller glowered at his reflection. "I am too thin."

Sam drew up to his full height, which although average for a man of the realm, left him looking up at Muller. "Sir, you are known far and wide for your incomparable elegance."

Muller cocked an eyebrow at him. "What a legacy that will be. 'He was the best dressed king we ever had.'"

"You will be remembered for leadership and wisdom," Sam assured him. Then he grinned. "But also for your style, eh?"

"Ah, well, I suppose one could do worse." Muller thought of the King's Advisors, the three elders who served as counsels to his uncle, King Daron. He seriously doubted they expected anyone to remember him for leadership. They seemed more worried that he would bolt before they could put a crown on him.

At times, Muller wasn't so sure he wouldn't do exactly that. He had never wanted the crown; he had expected it would go to his cousin Aron, the only child of King Daron. But Aron had died thirteen years ago, killed with his wife and their son Jarid when their carriage went over a cliff. It had left the grief-stricken Muller with the onerous and unwanted responsibility of becoming heir to the realm.

Muller wished his uncle would remarry and sire another heir. When King Daron had lost his beloved wife several decades ago, he had sworn on her death that he would never take another bride. He seemed determined to stay on that course even after his son died.

Which left Muller to become the most reluctant, albeit best dressed, king in the history of Aronsdale.

A knock came at the door.

Chime lifted her head from the book she was reading. Perhaps whoever had come to visit would go away. She didn't expect her family back from the town square for another few hours.

She wanted to finish her story. It was rare to find a book here in southern Aronsdale, especially a volume with such beautiful calligraphy and pictures inked in gold, silver, and bright colors. Her aunt Maize, one of the few people who encouraged her to read, had brought it back from Croft's Vale, the largest town in Aronsdale. Chime enjoyed the tale, an adventure about a young woman who rescued her beloved from a dragon. The idea of rescuing a handsome fellow appealed to her as long as she didn't have to go out and tackle the task herself.

The knock came again.

"Pah," Chime grumbled. She set the book on the table next to her chair and stood up, stretching her arms. Sunshine slanted through the diamond-shaped windows in the parlor. The air smelled fresh, though a bit dusty, probably because Chime hadn't yet cleaned in here as she was supposed to do today. Motes danced in the rays of sunlight. She smiled at the familiar scene she so loved. Then she went to open the door.

It was a bad decision.

As soon as Chime saw the gray-haired woman outside, she closed the door. Then she froze, horrified at herself. Good graces, she had just shut out one of the most important people in Aronsdale, the Shape-Mage Mistress of Castle Suncroft.

Another knock.

With her face burning, Chime opened the door. Della No-Cozen stood on the front step, her forehead furrowed.

"My greetings," Chime said meekly.

Della scowled at her. "And mine." Then she waited.

Chime cleared her throat. "Uh—would you like to come in?"

"Thank you, yes." Della started forward, then paused, her head tilted.

Mortified, Chime realized she was standing in Della's way. Moving aside, she invited her guest into the house. She ushered Della into the front parlor and offered her a high-backed chair with finely made blue cushions. Chime had embroidered them herself in gold thread.

"May I get you anything?" she asked. "We have excellent apple cider."

Della settled herself, obviously relieved to sit. "No, no, please don't bother." She motioned to the chair next to her. "Come, child, talk to me."

Chime sat down, wishing she could hide under the table between their chairs. "It is kind of you to visit, Mistress No-Cozen."

Della considered her. "So you know me."

"Everyone knows the great shape-mistress of Suncroft, ma'am." Chime wished she didn't, but that was another story. "You honor our home with your regal presence."

Della gave a very unregal snort. "Hardly."

Chime flushed. "What brings you to visit, ma'am?"

"I think you know."

Desperate now, Chime tried to think of an escape, but nothing came to mind. So she said, "I do?"

Della indicated the clock on the mantel across the room, one of the few luxuries in the house. Not many people had such a fancy mechanism. "What do you see?"

Confused, Chime said, "A clock."

"What is special about it?"

Chime had no idea what the mage mistress was about. Nothing looked unusual about the clock, which had a round face with two hands and numbers engraved into the wood. Right now it read slightly after the fourth hour in the afternoon.

The clock began to chime.

"Ah!" Horrified, Chime tried to forget the clock, but of course that only made her think about it more. Its chimes turned into clangs, as if an imp were whacking away on its bells with a tiny hammer.

Chime swore in a most unladylike manner and jumped up from her chair. She strode out of the room, into the entrance area of the house. The front door stood to her left and stairs to her right went up to the second story. She came up against a round table by the wall and set her palms on its unfinished surface, trying to steady herself. But instead of offering support, the table began to spin.

Chime jerked away from the table. "No! Stop!"

The steadying pressure of Della's hand settled onto her shoulder. "Breathe. Slowly."

Chime drew in a ragged breath. "I—I didn't do that." She turned to the mage mistress. "I don't know what happened. Really."

Della raised her eyebrows. "Don't you?"

"No, ma'am."

The mage mistress spoke quietly. "You've a gift. I felt it when I rode under the tree where you were hiding today, though I couldn't see you and had never met you before in my life. The power of your gift brought me to your home."

Chime stared at her in horror. "Ma'am, no! Surely you cannot feel such."

"But I can. It is why I am the Shape-Mage Mistress of Suncroft. I recognize mage gifts." Della's face gentled. "It is so strong in you, it glows."

This was even worse than Chime had feared. "No. You are wrong."

"Why does it frighten you?"

"I'm not frightened. I just know you are wrong."

"Indeed." Della put her hand on her hip. "You claim to know more than I? You surely are a powerful mage."

"I'm not!"

"Then you acknowledge I know more of mage powers?"

Chime hesitated, confused. "Of course."

"So if I say you are a mage, I must know this."

"I cannot be a mage."

Della's voice gentled. "Why? It is an honor."

"No!" Chime backed toward the door. Perhaps she could get outside and run to the orchard.

Della frowned at her. "And what is this, young woman? You find mages so offensive, you must close your front door on them and flee at the horrendous thought that you might be one?" She crossed her arms. "It seems Jacob's Vale teaches the art of giving insults."

"Mistress No-Cozen, no! I am sorry I closed the door. I was—" She swallowed. Terrified hardly seemed a prudent word right now. "Overawed."

"Overawed?"

"Yes, ma'am."

"And why is that?"

"Why?" Wasn't it obvious? Della was among the most powerful figures in the realm. "You are a King's Advisor."

"I'm aware of that." Della waited.

Chime squinted at her. "You've an imposing presence, ma'am. I fear I shall be incinerated by your disapproval."

Della gave a startled laugh. "Ah, well, you wouldn't be the first to think such." She came closer. "My point is this, Chime Headwind. You say you are overawed, yet it is I who came to see you. Does that mean nothing to you?"

Chime turned toward the door. "Ma'am, I love my home. I've no wish to leave."

"But, Chime, think of it as an adventure!" Della set a hand on her shoulder. "It is hard to find anyone with mage talents at all, let alone with your power. You drew so easily on the shapes of that clock and the table here." She spoke in a kind but firm voice. "Aronsdale has need of you."

Chime couldn't look at her. "If I went to Castle Suncroft, I would be like a bird trapped in a cage."

"Many would welcome the chance to live there."

As Chime turned to her, Della dropped her hand. Chime shook her head. "You want to tear me away from everything that matters to me."

"I won't force you to come," Della said. "But think about it, please. Give it a chance." She rubbed her chin. "I need to do tests. But if I am right, you are the strongest shape-mage I've found in your generation."

"I am sorry," Chime whispered. "I cannot go with you."

Della gave her a stern look. "Without mages, Aronsdale becomes weak. We have little else to protect us from Harsdown. We are farmers here."

"Harsdown?" Chime knew almost nothing about the country north of the mountains at their borders.

"They would like to conquer Aronsdale."

"King Daron has an army."

"A small one, yes. It is not enough."

Chime squinted at her. "I don't see what I could do."

"With training, a great deal." Della studied her. "You have hidden your talents, yes?"

"I don't want to be a mage." Chime willed her to accept those words. "I don't want anyone thinking I can use shapes and colors to make spells."

"Why not?"

Why not? Because it would terrify her to have the ruler of Aronsdale expect so much more from her than she was capable of giving. "I'm not even sure what mages do."

"I advise the king," Della said, as if this were a perfectly mundane activity. "I train mages. I teach them to soothe pain and harsh emotions." When she spoke of her work, her voice softened. "We heal. We bring light, not only that of a candle or oil lamp, but also into people's lives." Strength came into her words. "We also help the army. Mages can predict enemy strategies and heal wounds, both physical and of the emotions." Now a shadow seemed to come over her face. "But Aronsdale hasn't enough of us. We don't know why so few are born."

Listening to her, Chime felt inspired to say yes. Then her pragmatic sense of reality reasserted itself; she would be committing herself to far more than she could handle. "I wish I could help. But I cannot."

"Coming with me would have compensations."

"It would?"

"Haven't you wondered why King Daron never remarried?"

"He grieves for his wife."

Sorrow touched Della's voice. "He loved her greatly. But that is only part of it. The king leads our people as monarch. The queen leads as shape-mage. She must be a powerful mage."

Chime stared at her, aghast. "Ma'am! Surely you do not suggest I marry the king." In truth, she knew Della didn't imply such; to entertain such a thought would be a presumption so outrageous, the sky itself would collapse. King Daron would never pick his bride from among the rough country girls of Jacob's Vale. Saying it aloud would make Della see the absurdity of sending such a girl to Suncroft for any reason, including to become a mage.

"King Daron is not looking for a wife," Della said.

Chime nodded sagely. "Of course not, ma'am."

"Of course not." Della beamed at her. "You would marry his heir—Prince Muller Dawnfield."

Anvil the Forged

Hills bordered Aronsdale on all three sides. In the north and west they rose into rocky, foreboding mountains where few people lived, indeed, where few could survive.

The country of Harsdown lay to the northwest, beyond those mountains.

A tall man, gaunt and dark-haired, rode through the mountains of Harsdown. His cloak billowed out behind him like black wings. The Tallwalk peaks towered to the southeast, looming above the bleak landscape, a barrier that separated Harsdown from the fertile hills and meadows of Aronsdale.

The man, Anvil the Forged, rode to the Escar Mountains, home to the castle of Varqelle the Cowled, King of Harsdown. Anvil had heard much of Castle Escar. Made of blue marble, it stood high in the Escars, inaccessible except for one road that wound up the cliffs.

Anvil thought of Aronsdale. The time for my revenge comes, he thought. Soon.

Flight of the Bells

"It is the most absurd suggestion I have ever heard."

Muller Dawnfield stood with the king's top advisor, Lord Brant Firestoke. He should have been suspicious when Brant requested they meet here, on the Star Walk that ran along the top of the great wall surrounding Castle Suncroft. Brant's valet had once confided to Muller's valet, Sam Threadman, that Lord Firestoke came up here whenever he needed to brood about what he considered the dire future of Aronsdale when Muller became king.

They stood now looking out at the rolling hills and lush forests, wind blowing their hair. The crenellations in the wall had geometric shapes: circles, diamonds, hexagons, and most of all, stars. None of the figures bothered Muller: only flawed shapes caused him problems. These were all perfect.

Lord Firestoke, however, had given him a new and truly fearsome source of dread.

"I have no desire to marry anyone," Muller repeated. "Certainly not some country girl."

Brant pushed his hand through his shoulder-length gray hair, pulling it back from his face, accenting the widow's peak on his forehead and his deeply set gray eyes. His austere features made Muller feel insubstantial. At least he dressed better than Brant. The advisor's tunic, leggings, and boots were well made, but they lacked style. Really, Brant ought to find a better tailor.

"The king's message says this girl is the strongest mage Della has located. It is your duty to marry her."

Muller crossed his arms, taking care not to crease the sleeves of his tunic. The embroidered designs on its hems consisted of perfect circles and ovals, nary a flaw in any of them. That made them safe. He kept everything around him as perfectly shaped as possible.

"It is bad enough I must someday be king." Muller scowled at Brant. "I should at least marry a woman of the nobility."

"This one is the strongest mage." Brant made a visible effort to be civil. "Della's letter says Chime is pleasant."

"And?"

"And what?"

"That is all she said? 'Pleasant'?"

"What is wrong with that?"

"Has this girl no personality?"

"I am sure she is a fine young woman."

"Does she have a brain? Manners? Is she pretty? Is her background gentle? Does she comport herself well?" Muller peered at his tormentor. "How does she dress?"

Brant made an exasperated noise. "In clothes, no doubt."

Muller could well imagine. She probably ran around the countryside in a rough tunic and leggings with her hair wild and unbound. What an appalling thought. "I will not see her."

"It may be difficult to avoid." Brant regarded him steadily. "She and King Daron arrive here tomorrow."

Chime waited until the darkest hour of the night, when she was certain everyone in the camp had gone to sleep.

Then she ran.

She had been planning her escape for ten days, since she had left Jacob's Vale, riding with the king's party. Her parents had been so flabbergasted by her supposed good fortune that they insisted she go with Della. After ten days of dreading her future, Chime had already had enough. She couldn't go through with this. They had reached the king's lands and would be at Suncroft tomorrow; if she didn't leave now, she wouldn't have another chance.

She had talked very little to anyone during the trip, having no idea what to say to members of a royal party. Della had given her a beautiful riding cape, but Chime still felt a mess with her country ways and clothes.

Her family had accompanied them the first few days, discussing Prince Muller with the king and Della. They seemed delighted and overwhelmed, so happy for Chime that she hadn't the heart to tell them she couldn't face this marriage. After they had returned home, needing to tend to the orchards, Chime missed them terribly. If she stayed at Suncroft, she wouldn't see them again until they came for the wedding.

Each night, Chime had withdrawn to the tent she shared with Della, dined quickly, and gone to sleep. Or pretended to sleep. She feared if she became sociable, Della would ask questions about her mage abilities. Although Chime had managed to avoid giving any more sign of them, she doubted she fooled Della. The time had come to flee.

Chime didn't feel right about taking their gift, so she left the riding cape on her pallet. She snuck out in her yellow tunic and old leggings, with sturdy boots to protect her feet. On this lovely spring night, the Rose Moon was full, shedding a blush of moonlight over the land. She easily crept through the camp, though she had to stop often, lest a sentry see her. She had spent days planning; she knew when and where the guards patrolled and which ones fell asleep.

So it was that Chime Headwind, the recalcitrant betrothed of Muller Dawnfield, skulked away from the royal camp and her unwelcome future.

Muller stalked through the woods by an idyllic lake, glaring at any bird that dared to chirp. He was so angry, he didn't even stop to remove the leaf caught on his boot.

"Outrageous." He paced down to the shore, remembering Brant's talk with him yesterday. "Impossible." How could they condemn him to marriage with some rude country girl?

After a while he began to calm down. He stopped to brush the leaf off his boot, along with some grains of sand. Taking a deep breath, he straightened up and sighed. He ought to arrange a hunting trip and be gone when his uncle's party arrived at the castle this afternoon.

He was wandering through the woods, deep in thought, when a rustling disturbed his concentration. Puzzled, he looked around. Trees and lush foliage surrounded him and sunlight dappled the ground. Roses, skybells, and purple royal-buds grew in profusion, providing a bright cover where an intruder might hide.

Muller wanted solitude. He had told his staff he didn't wish to be disturbed. No one could enter these woods without permission except the royal family. That meant his uncle the king— and he was off gamboling through the countryside, gathering brides for his nephew.

"Who is there?" Muller demanded. "Show yourself!"

Silence.

"These are my woods," he said crossly. "You are trespassing."

More silence.

In his side vision, he glimpsed leaves swaying. He whirled just as a girl bolted from a royal shrub, showering purple buds everywhere. She raced through the woods, away from him, her yellow hair flying out behind her.

"Come back here," Muller bellowed. Then he took off after her.

They thrashed among the trees, Muller tripping on roots, vines, and wild shrubs. The girl moved like a sprite. Although he had longer legs and surely more endurance than one skinny girl, she easily outran him. Of course he had to slow down to avoid stepping anywhere that might muck up his boots.

It outraged him that this wild person had invaded his privacy. With all this tearing about the woods, no doubt she had bugs in her boots. Her coarse garments appalled him. He certainly didn't notice how well they fit her graceful curves. And she had leaves in her hair. Disgraceful. The fact that the glossy tresses glowed, as yellow as the sun, certainly had no effect on him. None. He didn't notice their beauty at all.

As she drew ahead, Muller gave up trying to preserve his appearance and broke loose in his run, eating up distance with his long legs. Branches and bushes lashed at his hair and he dreaded the condition of his trousers. But this had become a matter of pride.

As he closed in on the girl, she glanced over her shoulder and he saw her eyes, as blue as sea stones. Lovely eyes.

No. They were atrocious. Much too large. No doubt she had long eyelashes, too, just like him. It was mortifying for a man, which added to his irritation at her, even though he knew, logically, that her eyelashes had nothing to do with him. He ran harder, gritting his teeth.

There! Muller grabbed for the girl. He caught a length of her hair, but it whipped out of his hands. He lunged again, caught her around the waist—and tripped on a gnarled root.

Muller flew forward into a mass of foliage, sprawling on top the stranger. They landed in a tangle of limbs and weeds, sliding through the bushes and digging a trench in the mud underneath their leafy cover.

"You bog-warted son of a piss frog!" She pummeled him with her fists. "Get off me!"

Muller blinked, stunned motionless by her language. Then he sat up, futilely brushing mud off his tunic. The woman was sitting in a tangle of vines and twigs, with roses in her hair and mud all over her tunic and leggings, a truly appalling mess.

She was beautiful.

Saints almighty. She had an angel's face. A muddy angel's face, but exquisite. And she did indeed have eyelashes as long and curly as his own, though on her they looked far more fetching.

The girl glared at him. "You are a vulgar pig."

She suddenly stopped looking angelic. He crossed his arms. "I am not the one intruding without permission."

Her magnificent eyes flashed. "You are not only a vulgar pig, you are rude as well."

"This is unbelievable." Muller was so astonished by her tart words, he forgot to be angry. "I have never been called such in my entire life."

She didn't deign to answer.

"Who are you, anyway?" he added.

"Uh—Telli Tinner." Now she looked evasive. "I live in, um, Tintown."

Muller smirked. "No such place exists."

"And how would you know that?"

"I know all the towns around here."

She waved her hand as if dismissing his words, not to mention his intellect. "I didn't say it was around here."

"You are trespassing," he said, irate. "These woods belong to my uncle."

"I hope this uncle has better manners than you."

It finally sunk into Muller that she didn't recognize him. He didn't recognize her, either, but really, she ought to realize she was talking to the heir of Aronsdale. He opened his mouth, intending to let her know in no uncertain terms just whom she had offended.

Then he paused. He never interacted with people except as Muller Dawnfield, nephew and heir of the king. He always had to be on his royal best. He had no wish for a crown; he would have preferred the life his father led, a country gentleman who entertained the local gentry.

For this moment, he could be anyone. It gave him an incredible sense of freedom. He could do anything and no one would care. Maybe for just a little while, with this stranger, he wouldn't have to bend under the weight of a role he had never wanted. He hadn't realized how much he craved freedom until he saw it within his grasp.

Besides, if she didn't know his identity, he wouldn't be so mortified by his scruffy condition. He grinned at her. "My uncle has far better manners than you, Goodwoman Telli."

She blinked at him. "What?"

"I said he has better manners." Belatedly he realized what had confused her. It made him laugh. "Ah. You forgot. You claimed your name was Telli."

She reddened. "It is. Telli. Telli Tanner."

"I thought it was Tinner."

She glared at him, then harrumphed and rose to her feet, brushing rose petals off her skirt. "My name," she told him with great dignity, "is not your business."

He stood up next to her, picking twigs out of his hair. "I need to change my clothes."

"Are you going to a party?"

"Party?" He squinted at her. "No. Just walking."

"Those are fancy clothes just to walk in."

Muller silently swore. He would give himself away if he wasn't careful. "I was supposed to meet my relatives for dinner tonight. But, uh—I don't get along with my cousin. So I came out here instead."

"Oh." She eyed him doubtfully, but she didn't dispute his story. "Well, and who are you, Goodman——" She let the title hang exactly the same way he had with her. And she called him Goodman instead of Lord, which meant she took him for gentry, not noble or royal. His relief was followed by annoyance. Surely it was obvious he was of royal birth. Then again, most princes didn't slide around in the mud.

"Goodman Miller," he said. The name was close enough to Muller that he would respond to it even if he forgot he had given her an alias.

She bowed, more teasing than respectful. "Do you mill grains?"

"My family does." It was true; the Dawnfield line had many mills tended by families in Croft's Vale, the village that Castle Suncroft overlooked and protected.

Telli brushed at her tunic, which under all the leaves and dirt looked as if it had once been yellow. Muller reminded himself that he didn't notice the way it clung to her willowy curves when she slid her hands over the cloth.

"I need to change, too," she said.

"I have a cottage near here." He and his friends used it when they went on hunts. Its homey feel might convince her that it belonged to a man of respectable but not extensive means.

She hesitated. "I've nothing to change into."

"My sister has some clothes that might fit you." In truth, one of his friends had bought the outfits for a girl the fellow liked, but Telli had no way to know that.

Muller offered her his hand, then saw the dirt under his nails and started to drop his arm. At the same time, she reached to take his hand. The ring on her index finger must have broken and bent during their escapade. It slid off her finger and he grabbed it in reflex—catching the imperfect circle.

The moment his hand touched the damaged ring, power sparked within him. Light and heat flared in his palm; with a gasp, he dropped the ring. It hit the muddy foliage and sizzled, sending up wisps of smoke.

"Saints above." Telli gaped at her ring, which now lay in a charred circle of weeds. "What happened?"

"I've no idea," Muller lied. "Was that a flint?"

She gave him a strange look. "No."

"Odd." He bent to pick up the ring, but when he focused on the broken circle, it glowed again. He jerked back, stumbling in the bushes.

Telli laughed, her melodic voice chiming like bells. "You must be the clumsiest man I've ever met."

That annoyed him even more. People called him many things, including athletic, which he liked, and graceful, which he hated, but they had stopped calling him accident prone years ago. He glowered at her. "I thought I was the rudest, crudest man you had ever met."

She laughed softly, her face aglow. Saints, but she was lovely. Damned if he could make himself care that she had intruded on his privacy when she shone that way, with sunlight on her hair and her face full of mischief.

"I will tell you what," she decided. "We will say you are the most unique man I have ever met."

"All right." He couldn't help but smile. "I've certainly never met anyone like you."

"Well, then." She offered her arm. "Now that we have decided we are each one of a kind, let us go to your cottage and make ourselves uniquely presentable."

Muller grinned. "Yes, indeed. Let us go."

The Cowled King

The audience chamber of Varqelle the Cowled, King of Harsdown, had blue marble walls without adornment. No rugs softened the marble floors, and the spare marble ceiling vaulted high overhead.

On a raised dais at the end of the hall, Varqelle sat on his throne. A tall man with long limbs, he wore a blue tunic and leggings, and dark boots. Sapphire studs glinted in his ears. His presence dominated the starkly beautiful hall. No queen sat on the throne next to him; no advisors stood in the hall; no servants moved anywhere. He remained alone, except for one other person—the man walking toward him down that long hall, his dark riding cape billowing out behind him.

Varqelle nodded with satisfaction. Perhaps this Anvil the Forged could be useful to him. They both wanted the same thing.

Aronsdale.

6

The Hidden Cottage

Miller fascinated Chime.

She didn't know what to think. Despite his behavior, he seemed gently born, above her station. For a member of the royal court, which she was supposed to join, it wasn't appropriate to go to a man's home by herself. Customs in the country were more sensible; girls made their own decisions about such matters. Chime had even stolen a kiss from a boy she teased into chasing her in the orchard. Perhaps if she stole one from this annoying but handsome fellow, it would make her unacceptable to her groom.

Miller kept trying to clean off his shirt and smooth the wrinkles. She had never seen a man fuss so much with his clothes. He had the grace and beauty of a long-legged animal, an effect heightened by his mane of golden hair. If he cleaned himself up, he would be beautiful. Compared to the strapping, brawny youths in Jacob's Vale, he seemed fragile, but she suspected that impression was deceptive. Lean muscles rippled under his clothes as he walked, a truly enjoyable sight.

"Why are you staring at me that way?" Miller asked.

She flushed. "I, uh, I thought, that is, I wondered how far it was to your cottage."

"Not far." He motioned ahead, ducking his head under a branch. "Do you see?"

She peered where he indicated. Moss-draped trees blocked the way, hiding whatever waited for them. They picked their way through rosebushes and pulled aside loops of vine heavy with gold box-blossoms.

Then they pushed into a small clearing. On its other side stood one of the loveliest cottages Chime had ever seen. It leaned against a hill, and trees shaded it on every side except where a chimney rose from its thatched roof. Carvings graced the window frame with shape-designs: half spheres, cubes within cubes, spiraling tubes. The shapes beckoned to her. She walked forward, vaguely aware she had extended her arms, palms upward to the sky. Well being spread through her, but it wasn't until light glowed within her cupped palms, gold and warm, that she realized what she was doing.

Hai! Dismayed, she dropped her arms and smothered her awareness of the shapes. Her panic sparked; Miller would realize she was a mage and reveal her to the king. She swung around—and saw him several paces behind, cleaning grass off his leggings. She bit her lip, holding back her laugh. He hadn't even noticed what she had done.

Chime went over to him. "Miller?"

He straightened with a start, his face reddening. "Ah, yes." He cleared his throat. "Do you like my house?"

"It's lovely. Can we go in?"

"Yes. Of course. Certainly."

As they crossed the clearing, she noted the good care he took of his home. The gardens were well tended, with rosebushes and skybell shrubs everywhere, their flowers bright in the sunshine.

As they reached the front porch, she glanced at him. "Do you have more than one house?"

He froze in the process of reaching for the knob. "Why do you ask that?"

She wondered at his response. "You said you were a farmer. I just wondered why your house was in the woods instead of on your farm."

"Ah." He nodded. "My family has a house there, too. But this is mine."

Chime dimpled. "A fine house it is."

With a flourish, he opened the door. "Enter, if you dare."

He felt positively wicked. Prince Muller Dawnfield would never behave this way, bringing home a sensual trespasser he found in the royal woods. But Miller No-name could do as he pleased.

As he opened the door, his anticipation plummeted. Golden light filled the house, which could only mean his friends had showed up without letting him know. It wouldn't be the first time. Oddly enough, it didn't make him angry. He felt unaccountably peaceful. Soothed. Strange, that.

As he stepped inside, he realized his mistake; the cottage was empty after all. The light came from sunshine that slanted past open shutters on a window. His sense of well being also faded, though, leaving him feeling inexplicably bereft.

The room looked exactly as it had during his last visit a few months ago. His staff tended to its upkeep when he was gone. Comfortable sofas, chairs, and tables were scattered about, none elegant or expensive, all well-worn. He knew he should replace the circular rugs, which were growing tattered, but they hadn't yet reached the stage where their imperfections hurt him.

He smiled at his guest. "Here it is."

Telli walked inside. "It's lovely." She sounded like she meant it, which made him wonder at her background, that she thought so much of this tiny cottage. He wished she were a noble-woman, so it wouldn't be such an outrage if he spent time with her. Then again, he could never bring a noblewoman to an isolated cottage with no chaperone.

Not that it mattered, given that he was supposed to marry some blasted girl Della No-Cozen had dug up. He dreaded his unwanted bride. This might be his last chance to enjoy himself before his uncle and the King's Advisors shackled him in marriage.

Telli walked through the cottage studying the tables. The round tables. Just having her in here brightened the room; she seemed to bring light wherever she went. His good mood returned. When she stopped by a window, he closed the door and joined her. Together, they looked out into the woods, toward the lake, though right now the bountiful foliage of spring hid the water. Breezes ruffled the skybells and royal-buds.

"It's pretty," Telli said.

"That it is." Muller opened the window, using that as an excuse to lean closer to her. The glass had almost no imperfections, no bubbles or ripples, which was rare except for the most expensive panes, which only the wealthy could afford. If Telli noticed anything unusual though, she gave no sign. Instead she inhaled deeply and lifted her face to the breezes. Her gold hair stirred around her face, shoulders, and body. "So beautiful."

"Yes." He continued to look at her. "Beautiful."

She glanced at him. "You mentioned clean clothes...?"

"Clothes?" He was having trouble concentrating. Her air of mischief mixed with innocence drew him. The room had become rather hot. Before he realized what he was doing, he brushed his fingertips across her cheek. "I can help you change."

Telli stared at him like a deer hypnotized by a night lamp. "I was right—you are a rogue." She sounded nowhere near as definite in that assessment as before.

He smiled lazily. "But a fine one, eh?"

She gave him an imperious look that somehow worked despite the flower petals in her hair. "You, sir, should learn modesty."

"I would say you should as well," he murmured, "but you look so very fine in that immodest state."

Her face reddened. "If you keep this up, I shall leave."

"Don't do that." He endeavored to sound contrite. "I will behave."

Her lips quirked upward. "I don't believe you."

"Ah, well." He trailed his finger down her jaw. "Good behavior is terribly boring."

She moved his hand away from her face. "Is it now?"

"Very." Sliding his hand behind her neck, he drew her forward. For one glorious moment, she molded to him, her curves pressed along his strong muscles.

Then she stiffened and put her hands on his shoulders, pushing him away. "Stop that, you scoundrel."

"Come back." He tried to pull her close again.

"Rogue." Telli whacked him on the head.

"Hey!" He jerked back, raising his arm to defend himself. "Are you always so violent to your suitors?"

She quirked one of her perfect eyebrows at him. "So. You are a suitor? And when did you plan to propose, Your Royal Muddiness?"

Muller didn't know whether to be appalled or laugh. "And what would you do if I was royal, hmm? Continue to insult me?"

Telli looked unimpressed. "It wouldn't make a whit of difference. For all you know, I am of royal blood myself."

"Oh, are you now?" Muller knew she wasn't one of his relatives. "And just how would that be?"

She waved at him, a gesture so imperious, it made him want to laugh. He had never seen a woman among his kin do that.

"Telli, listen. Let's have a wonderful afternoon. I have to go back to my duties soon, and when that happens, my life gets dark. But you bring light." He faltered, surprised to hear himself admit so much.

She blinked, pushing a tendril of hair out of her eyes, and the room brightened. Joy rushed through him, a surge of emotion too extreme for this moment, yet he felt it. He had scraped his arm when he fell in the woods, but the twinges of pain from the gash suddenly stopped bothering him. The injury remained, but it no longer hurt. Even his anger about his upcoming nuptials receded. He felt good. And somehow, it all came from Telli.

"Come look," he said. He took her hand and indicated the window. "Do you see the sparkle through the trees?"

She peered where he indicated. "Just barely."

"A river there feeds a lake. It is packed with fish. If you like, we could go fishing."

She smiled. "It is true, I am hungry."

"Well, then!" He took her other hand so they were facing each other with their fingers clasped. "I will make you some fish to eat."

"I would like that." Her voice had an odd quality, tentative, uncertain. In that softer tone, she added, "It is true, we often have duties that darken our lives. Perhaps we can enjoy some light today, before the storm comes."

"Are you sad?" He wondered what made her so wistful. "Tell me what is wrong. Perhaps I can help."

The corner of her mouth lifted with a hint of mischief. Then she stepped forward, putting her arms around his waist—and kissed him.

Muller was so startled, he froze, rather than doing what he really wanted, which was kiss her back. In the past, he had always been the one to initiate amorous procedures with a woman.

Telli wasn't fazed by his reaction. In fact, she was full of misbehavior. She pushed him against the wall as if she were a pirate who had captured him, holding his wrists against the wood panel. It took a moment more to gather his wits. Then he wrested his hands free, wrapped his arms around her waist, and kissed her soundly.

Ah, yes. This felt right.

If only he didn't have to marry. If only Telli was a noblewoman rather than a country girl. Many nobles would prefer her common birth because a lord could more easily have her as a mistress that way. But as much as Muller might have liked such an arrangement with her, he would never ask for one. One didn't compromise a woman's honor. Besides, Telli was more innocent than she pretended. Her kiss also had a desperate edge to it, though why, he had no idea.

After a moment, they paused for air. She regarded him with dreamy eyes the color of a skybell. "You could take over Aronsdale single-handedly," she murmured. "Just by stealing its women from its men."

He smiled, slow and languorous. "You think so?"

"I do." Closing her eyes, she laid her head against his shoulder. With a sigh, he ran his hand down her back. For the first time, he noticed a well-washed pattern along the collar of her tunic, a design of squashed spheres.

Imperfect spheres.

Before he could stop it, mage power surged in Muller. Sparks leapt up from his hands, scorching her tunic.

"Hai!" Telli jumped back so fast, Muller almost lost his balance. He *felt* her emotions, but with flawed awareness. He didn't know if she realized what had just happened; he could tell only that it bewildered her. His fractured ability to sense her moods receded as she moved away, taking her imperfect circles with her.

Telli spoke in a low voice. "What did you do?"

"Do?" He tried to tease. "I kissed you. Surely it wasn't all that bad."

She craned her neck to look over her shoulder—and stiffened. He knew the back of her tunic must be burned.

A pounding came at the door.

"Ah, hell," Muller muttered. Who could be here?

Telli looked around frantically. "I must hide!"

His annoyance turned to curiosity. "Why?"

She ran toward the kitchen. "Do you have a cellar?"

Another knock.

Muller followed her. "I should answer the door."

"No!" She whirled to him. "You must not!"

He was thoroughly intrigued now. "And why is that, Telli? If your name really is Telli."

"Of course it is!"

"Your Highness!" a deep voice called. "We must speak to you."

Muller swore under his breath.

"Your Highness?" Telli asked. "Why the blazes would someone come to your cottage, pound on the door, and yell 'Your Highness'?"

"I've no idea." Muller tried to appear sincere. He forgot his discomfort, though, when he saw her terror.

"What is it?" he asked. Had she committed a crime? Suddenly it made sense; she had stolen something from the castle and hidden here in his woods. His men had come to warn him. "I won't reveal you to them."

The clink of keys came from outside. Muller knew if he didn't answer, they would break into his house to make sure he wasn't lying in a pool of blood, attacked by this ferocious vagabond with her gold hair and skybell eyes.

He pushed her toward the archway into the kitchen. "The door to the cellar is in the Prism Closet. Hide there."

"Thank you!" She spun around and ran into the kitchen.

As Muller strode across his living room, the door burst open and slammed against the wall. A formation of soldiers strode inside. As soon as they saw him, they stopped, the hexagon soldiers in the back bumping into the heptagon soldiers in front.

"Why are you bursting into my house?" Muller asked.

"Our apologies, Your Highness." The leader bowed, a burly man with the insignia of a cube-captain on his shoulder. "We had warning an intruder had entered the woods. And no one had seen you for several hours. Your uncle was concerned." He and the other guards were staring at him with undisguised astonishment.

Muller glowered, mortified to be caught in disarray. He had to make a conscious effort to keep from straightening his clothes and hair. "As you see, I am fine. I am relaxing. An anomalous concept, you would think from listening to my advisors, but nevertheless something I need to do now and then. Alone."

"Uh—yes. Yes, of course, Your Highness. We will be on duty outside." The captain bowed and the guards made a quick retreat, closing the door.

Muller swore. He didn't want them hulking outside, either. How would he smuggle Telli out without anyone seeing her? He didn't mind so much if they knew he had a beautiful woman in here, but it obviously bothered Telli, who might be in trouble. He didn't want to hurt her.

A rustle came from the kitchen. Turning, he saw her in the doorway. She had an odd look, as if she couldn't decide whether to be furious or shocked.

"What is it?" he asked.

"Your Highness?" She pushed back a straggle of hair. "Your Royal Highness?"

So. She had heard. He lifted his chin. "It is not a crime, you know."

"Your name isn't Miller." She spoke slowly, as if testing each word for the pox. "It is Muller."

"As in mulled wine, yes. My parents named me after the spirits they make from their vineyards." He crossed his arms. "You have a problem with this?"

"You lied to me."

Muller was growing angry. "Whereas of course you have told me the complete truth, Telli who can't even remember her last name properly from one moment to the next."

"My name isn't Telli."

"I didn't think so." He walked over to her, trying to look intimidating. "What is it?"

She didn't look the least intimidated. Furious was a better description. "My name is Chime. Chime Headwind."

And then she said, "I'm your bride."

Dawnfield Legacy

Tonight King Varqelle dined in the Horizon Chamber, at a crescent-shaped table with guests on either side, nobles from the elite of Harsdown. The floors and lower walls were made from the rare blue marble made here in the Escar Mountains. It shaded from dark into light blues up the walls, the stone cleverly blended in polished tiles that showed no seam, then into rose marble at the top and across the ceiling, like a sunset. Lamps in gold claws burned on the walls. Varqelle sat in a high-backed chair inlaid with sapphires and upholstered in blue cushions with rose brocade. His gray tunic and leggings clothed him like fog. Sun topazes glittered in his ears.

A tall man with dark eyes and hair occupied the seat of honor to Varqelle's left. Anvil the Forged. He had arrived at Escar with nothing more than his riding clothes and horse, but Varqelle welcomed him, for the realm had no other like this man. It wasn't only that Anvil was a mage of great power; he had also sworn fealty to Harsdown.

Varqelle needed mages. Even in Aronsdale, such adepts were rare. Harsdown had none. He had long sought to annex Aronsdale to his realms, but her people resisted too well. Her army was small but clever. They always seemed to anticipate the moves of Harsdown, no doubt because of mind tricks played by their mages.

Harsdown and Aronsdale had fought no declared war for generations, but their warriors constantly skirmished on the borders. Aronsdale fighters proved remarkably hard to kill. They recovered from injuries faster than normal men and kept going long after Varqelle's men would have given up. No doubt mage trickery was involved, though how, he didn't know.

He intended to find out.

King Daron was clearly irate.

Chime wished she could disappear. The king paced in front of her and Muller, his boots ringing on the parquetry floor, his face stern, his gray hair brushed back from his face. Chime could see Muller's resemblance to him, but the king had a severity and sense of authority unlike anyone else she had ever encountered.

They stood in the Receiving Hall with Della and the guards who had brought them here. The room stretched out, long and elegant, more beautiful than anything Chime could have imagined, drenched in sunlight from many tall windows. The walls gleamed with mosaics in lovely tessellated patterns of squares, circles, and stars. She did her best to ignore them, lest they stir the power everyone insisted she possessed, despite her adamant denials.

"Your behavior is appalling." Daron stopped in front of Muller and looked over his muddy nephew. "Though I must say, it is refreshing to see you forget this preoccupation of yours with clothes."

Muller crossed his arms and glowered.

"And you." Daron turned to Chime. "You ought to be ashamed of your behavior."

The only reason Chime felt ashamed was because she had let herself be caught by the very groom she had intended to evade. Even worse, she had kissed the scoundrel. She could hardly say that to the king of Aronsdale, though. So she said only, "I am terribly sorry, Your Majesty."

He snorted, his expression making it clear he had a good guess about how she truly felt. "No one will force you into marriage if you find Muller so repugnant."

Her face flamed. "I never meant—" She stopped when Daron held up his hand.

"Four weeks," he said. "Give this idea of a betrothal that long. If at the end of that time you wish to leave, you may do so. Is that acceptable?"

Chime nodded, her face hot. It was a fair request. "Yes, Your Majesty."

The king motioned to Della No-Cozen, who was standing nearby. The mage mistress came forward and bowed.

Daron indicated Chime. "Please go clean her up."

"Certainly, Your Majesty." Della cocked an eyebrow at her unwilling ward, making Chime want to squirm. Then she led Chime off, mercifully away from the king's displeasure.

Della didn't speak until they were walking down a hall with mosaics on the ceiling, walls, and floors. Then, incredibly, she laughed.

Chime glared at her. "You think it is funny the king despises me?"

"Actually, he quite likes you." Della couldn't stop laughing. "Never, *never,* have I seen Muller in such a state." She beamed at Chime. "You shall be good for him."

Chime tried not to think of his appealing qualities, that kiss of his and his charmingly roguish smile. "I don't think he shall be good for me."

"What do you fear? Is it truly so terrible to have such responsibilities?"

"I never asked for them."

"Neither did Muller. Nevertheless, you have them."

"It's unfair!" Chime declared. "I don't want to be a mage. I don't want to marry that vain fop."

"That 'vain fop' is the heir to the throne."

Chime just grunted.

After they walked a bit more, Chime snuck a glance at the jade pendant Della wore around her neck, a pyramid with four sides and a bottom. Despite her apprehension, she couldn't help but be curious about mages. During the ride from Jacob's Vale, Della had said that the five-sided shape represented the highest order she could draw on, with jade-green as her highest color. Chime had no idea what that meant; no one in her village had known much about mages and Chime had diligently avoided the subject. She made spells by instinct; she didn't know how she managed it, which probably explained why they were so erratic.

Yet now, when she saw that pendant, a yearning stirred within her. She didn't understand it, nor did she want to feel it. She just wanted to go home.

But still it stirred.

Lord Brant Firestoke walked the tiled corridors of Suncroft with King Daron. They were both of an age and had ridden together when Daron had been crown prince and Brant an ambitious young officer in the King's Army. The decades had matured them both, but neither had lost the honed edge to his personality.

"Muller is right on the verge," Brant said. "If we push any

harder, he is going to run." He frowned at his friend. "You must remarry. Sire an heir."

Daron quirked an eyebrow at him. "What makes you think any heir I sire would be better suited for the title than you consider Muller?"

"You would train him from birth, instead of starting when he was fourteen."

Daron's expression darkened. "I trained my son for thirty years. Look what that brought me. Heartbreak and sorrow. I will father no more children."

"His passing was a great sorrow." Brant had considered Prince Aron a fine man, one fit to become king.

"Yes." The tightness in Daron's voice said more than words. Even after so many years, he continued to mourn. "I lost a daughter that night, too. My son's wife, Sky. And my grandson. Jarid."

"They had so much promise."

Sadness shadowed the king's voice. "Even now, it bothers me that we never found Jarid's body. We buried my son and daughter. But how can I finish grieving for Jarid when I don't know how it ended for him?"

"I am sorry," Brant said. It galled him that they had never caught the highwaymen who forced the orb-carriage over a cliff and killed the family. The boy, Jarid, had been only six. Brant suspected he had been a mage. It was rare for the gifts to manifest in a male child, but Jarid's mother had been the greatest mage of her generation, perhaps for centuries. Neither King Daron nor Aronsdale had ever recovered from their deaths.

Brant couldn't imagine Muller leading the country. The young man was too busy polishing his boots and complaining about the bad manners of his friends. Thank the saints for Daron; Aronsdale needed his strong leadership now. Rumors were coming out of Harsdown, unsubstantiated but chilling: King Varqelle was planning the day he would conquer Aronsdale.

* * *

Muller's breath caught. "Saints above."

He stood in an arched doorway that opened out from the up-permost level of the Starlight Tower. The Star Walk stretched ahead of him, taking its name from star-shaped crenellations in its walls. It topped the fortified wall that surrounded Castle Sun-croft. During battle, archers crouched behind the walls of the walkway and shot through its star openings. The castle healer drew on the ten-sided stars for power when she tended injured archers.

Muller didn't come here often. Although he wielded a sword well, he had less proficiency with a bow and arrow. But what caught his attention today had nothing to do with arrows or stars. A short distance away, Chime stood gazing at the coun-tryside. The wild hoyden had transformed, draped now in a stunning dress, cream-colored with gold trim. It fit her grace-ful figure from neckline to hips, and fell more loosely to her feet. A gold belt rested on her hips, its tasseled ends hanging down the front of her skirt, the cord forming a V in front of her pelvis. A gold necklace gleamed against her creamy neck, and a circlet of diamonds sparkled on her head. Her glorious hair poured down her back like a waterfall.

Perhaps marriage wouldn't be so onerous after all.

He walked along the pathway, enjoying the sight as breezes wafted her hair around her shoulders. He would have to ask who designed her dress. The tailoring was superb.

"My greeting," he said, coming up to her.

Chime turned with a start, her face blushed from the wind. When she saw him, her tentative smile transformed into a frown. She turned back to observe the view.

Muller leaned against the wall. "Friendly today."

She didn't deign to look at him. "I have no wish of friendship with you."

"Pity, seeing as we're to be married."

She gave him a haughty look. "I would marry a bog-slug first." Belatedly she added, "Your Highness."

"Chime, let us make a truce, yes?" Now that Della had found a mage powerful enough to be his queen, they weren't going to let him delay his nuptials any longer—assuming the lady agreed, which seemed less likely every minute. For some reason, the idea of her leaving Suncroft flustered him. It made no sense; she was wild, rude, and uncouth. But he didn't want her to go.

"My uncle wants us to marry," he said. "Mistress No-Cozen wants it. Lord Firestoke wants it. Everyone does. We will exhaust ourselves fighting them." He grinned at her. "Besides, you didn't find me so offensive in the cottage."

She gave him a quelling look. "That is because I wanted to enjoy myself before I had to marry Prince Muller Dawnfield. I can't help it if I had the bad fortune to have my forbidden lover turn out to be my groom."

"You are the reluctant mage, eh? And I am the reluctant heir." He spoke wryly. "We make quite a pair."

"I'm not a mage."

"Why not?" He would have given anything to have her purity of gifts.

Chime averted her eyes. "I cannot handle it."

"I didn't take you for a coward."

She rounded on him, eyes flashing. "I fear nothing."

"You fear yourself."

"And you fear your title."

He had no argument with that. "At least I'm not afraid to admit it."

For a moment she simply looked at him. Then she said, "You need to help your uncle more. He is tired, that bone-deep weariness that comes when you have worn out your body and your health."

Panic sparked in Muller. "How dare you speak such of the king."

"It is true."

"How would you know this?"

"I'm not sure." She motioned at the castle around them. "Everything here is shapes, all the mosaics, lamps, walkways, windows—everything. Beautiful, perfect shapes. I feel...I don't know how to describe it. Too sensitized. On edge with everyone. People's moods, their pain, their need for light—I can't escape it here."

An ache for the beauty of her power filled him. "And you claim you are no mage?"

Her face paled. "I don't want this."

"You should." How could she throw away such a gift?

"As you should accept the truth about your uncle."

He wanted to deny it. He couldn't bear the thought. But he had seen Daron age this past season. The weaker his uncle's health became, the more Muller longed to assure him that Aronsdale would continue. It mattered to Muller, mattered a great deal, for he loved his uncle, who had been his guardian for half his life. This country was Daron's legacy; the king deserved a strong heir to carry on for him after his death.

Unfortunately he had only Muller.

The ramshackle cabin stood high in the Boxer-Mage Mountains, surrounded by stunted trees. Its thatched roof barely kept out the rain and the walls needed repair. The rocky earth couldn't support much in the way of crops, but the man who lived there coaxed a garden out of the infertile soil, enough to feed him and his ward.

The man's name was Unbent. Thirteen years ago, desperate and starving, he had made the worst mistake of his life, going on a midnight raid with Murk, a highwayman who robbed the gentry. They had intended only to stop the orb-carriage and take jewels and coins from its passengers. Unbent had never expected the carriage to go over the cliff and crash into a ravine. He never expected the man and woman inside to die.

Their six-year-old son had survived.

Murk had decreed they must kill the child, lest he reveal what happened. Unbent had fled then, taking the boy with him, determined to protect the orphan. He named the boy Dani and cared for him as best he could at the cabin. The accident left Dani blind, deaf, and mute. He had no lasting injuries Unbent could see, except for a scar on his neck, but his sight and hearing never returned, and he never spoke again after that night.

So they lived, mired in poverty, hidden from the world, never coming down from the mountain, cut off from humanity.

Unbent knew nothing about his ward's true identity.

The Broken Ring

"I can't do it!" Chime clenched the table, staring at the parchment inked in shimmering colors. "I can't remember what all these shapes and hues mean."

Della sighed. "We will try again."

Chime wanted to lash out in frustration, but she held back. It wasn't Della's fault she had trouble. In the three days Chime had been here, she had learned so little. It was another reason she had dreaded coming to Suncroft; no matter how hard she studied, she would never be quick.

They were sitting at a table in the parlor of Della's cottage at the castle. Sunshine slanted through the windows, casting colored light over well-worn tables and chairs. The windows were lovely, with stained glass in many shapes: diamonds, hexagons, squares, circles, and more. They made graceful patterns around larger round windows with clear panes. Vases of rosy box-blossoms brightened the room even more.

"Start with the colors," Della suggested. "What do they do for mages?"

Chime hesitated. "Color specifies the type of spell."

"Yes. Good. In what way?"

"Like a rainbow." Chime loved her mental image of a rainbow arching over sunlit towers of the castle. Thinking of it helped make this less intimidating. "Red spells create light."

Della nodded her encouragement. "And the others?"

"I don't know," Chime admitted.

"Think of spells as ways to bring light into people's lives." The mage mistress took an orange out of a bowl on the table. "What do orange spells soothe?"

The word "soothe" clicked for Chime. Relieved to recall something, she said, "Pain. They soothe physical pain. Yellow spells soothe emotional pain, like sorrow." She wondered if it worked on insecurity. If so, she could certainly use some yellow spells here at Suncroft.

"Very good." Della smiled. "How about green?"

"After soothing comes healing, yes?"

"Yes, that is a way to think about it."

"Green heals emotional wounds," Chime guessed.

Della shook her head. "To soothe pain, all you need to know is how to comfort someone. But before you can heal, you must understand what causes the pain."

"That isn't green?"

"Well, it is, in a sense." Della considered her. "Tell me—how did you know, in the cottage with Muller, that you weren't in danger from him?"

Chime snorted. "Heaven forbid, he might tackle me in the mud." She was still irked at him for that.

Della chuckled. "That must have been a sight." When Chime glared, the mage mistress tried to hide her smile. "But why weren't you worried? A strange man throws you down, then lures you to his cottage and makes improper advances. You weren't afraid?"

Chime crossed her arms. "Are you suggesting my behavior was inappropriate?"

"I think your behavior is fine. You haven't answered my question."

Ah, well. Why *hadn't* she been afraid of Muller? "I knew he wasn't going to hurt me."

"But how do you know?"

"I could tell."

"How?"

"I just knew. I felt it."

Della spoke quietly. "You made a green spell. Green is the ability to feel the emotions of others."

"Oh." Now that Della mentioned it, Chime did remember something about that on the scroll Della had given her to study last night.

"So if green is feeling emotions," Della prodded, "what about blue?"

"It heals emotions!" Chime *knew* that had been on the scroll, somewhere.

"Healing, yes," Della said, patient. "But blue tends to physical injuries. That is why the healer at Suncroft is a sapphire mage. Emotions are much harder to heal."

It was coming together for Chime. "In the rainbow, you have blue and then indigo. Blue heals injuries and indigo heals emotions."

"Yes." Della beamed at her. "A mage can make spells at her color and below. Most can do red and orange. It is more difficult to soothe emotions; it takes a strong mage to do yellow spells. Green mages are rare. Blue is almost unheard of; I know of only the healer at Suncroft. She is even a stronger mage than I."

"But you are mage mistress."

Della nodded. "The mage who serves as the King's Advisor needs ability, yes, but also political savvy."

It made sense to Chime. "What about indigo mages?"

"They probably don't exist."

Chime tried to read her expression. "Probably?"

"I think it must be impossible." Della paused, her face thoughtful. "How do you cure grief, anguish, misery? Time is the true indigo mage. Only it heals such wounds."

Chime hesitated, afraid of looking gullible. "I've heard it said that the royal line of Aronsdale, the House of Dawnfield, produced indigo mages in ancient times."

"So the legends say." Della smiled wryly. "It increases the mystique of the Dawnfields. But no historian has ever found a reliable record of such a mage."

Self-conscious now, Chime said, "What is my color?"

"I'm not sure, yet. Emerald, I think."

Chime brightened. "Like you!"

"I am a jade mage. It isn't as strong as emerald."

"It isn't?"

Della laughed. "Don't look so shocked."

A wave of unexpected jealousy swept over Chime. "If the castle healer is a sapphire, stronger than us both, doesn't that mean she must marry Muller?"

Della's mouth quirked upward. "I suspect her husband, children, and grandchildren wouldn't take kindly to the idea."

Relief washed through Chime. "She is elderly?"

"In her seventh decade."

"Ah." Chime would never admit it to Muller, but she had found herself unable to stop thinking about him. She touched the parchment in front of her, which was covered with shapes inked in a rainbow of colors. "I don't have much of a feeling for how the shapes work."

"Ask yourself this." Della rolled up the voluminous sleeves of her tunic. "How do mages use shapes?"

"To focus spells." Chime thought about the coins used throughout Aronsdale, so many different shapes, their value increasing with their number of sides. "The more sides a shape has, the better it concentrates your power."

"Yes, but only to a point. If you try to use a shape more powerful than your maximum ability, your spell dissipates."

Chime squinted at her. The few spells she had made had happened by accident rather than design. "I've never made a spell on purpose, so I doubt I need worry about it dissipating."

"It will come." Della touched her jade pendant. "Three-dimensional forms are stronger than two-dimensional. The more sides a shape has, the more power it can focus. You can use any shape up to the one of your maximum ability. If your highest shape is three-dimensional, you can also use any two-dimensional shape." She folded her hand around her pendant. "I can use three-dimensional shapes, but only with five sides or less."

"I could never use one with three dimensions."

"Certainly you can. At least eighteen sides. Maybe twenty."

"No! It is impossible." Chime made the denial out of habit. But then she hesitated. "You think so?"

Della smiled. "I think so." She tapped a glimmering silver circle on the parchment. "This is the highest two-dimensional shape—a polyhedron with an infinite number of sides."

Chime squinted at her. "A circle has no sides."

"But look." Della showed her the other shapes: square, pentagon, hexagon, each with more sides than the last. "The more sides, the rounder they look. If you had a polygon with two hundred sides, you could hardly tell it apart from a circle."

Chime traced a circle on the page. She enjoyed the drawings, finding satisfaction in them, especially those with three dimensions: pyramids, boxes, heptahedrons, and so on, the shapes becoming rounder as their sides increased, until they resembled faceted balls. Sudden insight came to her: a sphere had an infinite number of sides. It was the most perfect shape of all.

Concentrating on the sphere drawing, however, made her head hurt. She preferred faceted balls.

Della was watching her closely. "Only the most powerful mage can use a sphere."

"I like this one." Chime touched the drawing of a ball with twenty sides. "It feels right."

Della nodded with approval. "That may be your shape."

Excitement sparked in Chime. Perhaps she wouldn't fail here after all. "How would I find out?"

"Concentrate on it. See if you can make light."

Chime peered at the drawing. After a moment, she began to feel foolish. "Nothing is happening."

"Imagine light appearing," Della suggested.

She pictured a lamp on the table and focused hard.

Nothing.

"I feel silly," Chime said.

"It is all right," Della said. "Give yourself time."

Despite the kind words, Chime felt the mage mistress's disappointment. Della had hoped Chime would be a quicker study. Chime felt like a fraud. She had no idea how to be what these people wanted. She had felt accepted only that time when Muller came out to greet her on the Star Walk, and that had been because he liked her dress. It annoyed her. If she had to marry him, he could at least like her for herself rather than her clothes. He had been more fun in his cottage, before he knew her identity.

Muller was right about the two of them; the fop who dreaded the crown and the bumpkin who dreaded her mage power. If they were the best Aronsdale had to rely on, their country was in trouble.

* * *

Anvil took a tour of Castle Escar. He paced the blue marble halls, appreciating the high ceilings and polished columns, and the mosaics, silver, blue, violet, and white tiles with accents of red and gold. He stopped to view a series of interlocked geometric forms: triangles, quadrilaterals, pentagons, hexagons, heptagons, octagons, and so on, until the progression ended in circles.

Closing his eyes, Anvil pressed his hand against a circle and let it focus his power. He opened his eyes to find himself bathed in blue light. So easy.

Spells were simple to make—and to manipulate. All shapes bent to his will. *His* will. He had lived thirty-one years and spent most of them, since his eleventh birthday, on his own, searching out knowledge. He had traveled the width and breadth of first Aronsdale and then Harsdown, alone, ignored and silent. He researched every history on mages he could find. This he had learned: with the right incantation, spells turned inside out. Healing became injury and soothing became agony. Mages created light, but they could also burn.

A normal mage of his power would never twist his gifts, for what he did to others, he experienced himself. But Anvil had a difference, an imperfection some might say, though in truth it gave him superiority. He wielded every color except green. He knew nothing of emotions. He felt nothing of what he did to others.

So it was that no restraints existed on his power.

"What do you think of her?" Muller reclined on the sofa in his bedroom, holding a crystal goblet full of red wine, one of his booted legs up on the table and his other stretched across the sofa. The gold upholstery matched his fawn-colored breeches and golden tunic.

Sam Threadman continued arranging Muller's clothes in the wardrobe, an antique with a mirror bordered by frosted polygons. "She, Your Highness?"

"You know." Muller waved his goblet. "My bride."

"She is lovely." Sam paused. "And stylish."

"Not yet, much." Muller swung his boots to the floor and leaned forward, his elbows on his knees. "But just think what she could become!"

Sam answered dryly. "A mage, I would hope."

"Well, yes, that, too." Muller squinted at him. "I am trying to imagine being married."

Sam turned, the lines around his eyes crinkled with a kindly look. "Do you think of a family, milord?"

"A family?" *That* threw Muller off guard. Of course someday he would sire an heir. He had never thought about a family, though, beyond his duty to give Aronsdale its next king. He, a father? He didn't feel ready. He rather liked the idea of Chime as mother to his children, though. She would take no guff from them. He winced. Or from him.

In some ways, though, the idea of a family intrigued him. He was twenty-seven, certainly old enough. Both of his parents had long passed away, his father two decades ago and his mother several years after that. He had no siblings. King Daron was his only kin. The sparse nature of his family left him with a hollow space in his life.

"Yes," Muller said, surprised. "I am thinking of a family."

"Speaking of which—King Daron came here earlier."

Muller took a swallow of wine. "What did he say?"

Sam went back to arranging clothes. "Apparently you were expected at a meeting this morning with His Majesty and Cube-General Fieldson."

"Damnation!" Muller jumped to his feet, sloshing wine out of his goblet. "I forgot!"

Sam sighed. "I fear King Daron is unhappy with you."

"He always is." Muller thunked his goblet on a table. "I had better find out how much trouble I'm in this time."

"Good luck," Sam said.

"I'll need it," Muller muttered.

Chime ran into Muller just as he blew up Suncroft.

At least it seemed the entire castle could have gone up in that blast. She was running down a hallway, already late for her mage lesson. She had stayed too long in her bedroom, writing a letter to her family. She missed them so much, it ached within her. So she raced around the corner—and ran smack into Muller.

Light flared around them and the stained-glass window in a nearby alcove exploded inward.

"Saints almighty!" Muller grabbed her around the waist, shielding her with his body while broken glass showered the hallway.

"Goodness." When the tumult stopped, Chime peered around him, staring at the colored shards all over the tiled floor. "How did you do that?"

"I didn't do anything. Nothing!" He looked panicked. "What makes you think I did that?"

She blinked, aware of his arm around her waist and how good it felt. Embarrassed, she stepped back. His mood came to her vividly, here in a hall tiled with blue and gray polyhedrons in the floor, and with geometric wall mosaics of sky and countryside. Why would he deny the spell that burst the window? She knew without doubt the impetus had come from within him. She didn't ask herself how she knew; she wasn't ready to hear the answer.

"It takes a great mage to shatter windows," she said.

"The wind did it," he said quickly.

She put her hand on her hip. "The wind, pah."

"Are you challenging my word?"

He tried to look fierce, but Chime wasn't fooled. She had trouble reading his face, though; it was difficult to see past the beauty of his features to his expressions. She wondered if it had caused him problems in his youth. In her experience, boys as pretty as Muller took a lot of grief for it from other boys. If that were true, she would have thought he would welcome any power that gave him an advantage. Perhaps she was wrong about his gifts.

"Why do you stare at me like that?" he asked.

"You're a mage, aren't you?"

Muller laughed too loudly. "What an innovative idea."

"A mage." She had suspected it when he scorched her tunic in the cottage, but now she felt certain. "You've never told anyone and no one has figured it out, not even Della." That baffled her; given Della's ability to recognize mages, how could she have missed one as obvious as Muller?

"Ridiculous." He was losing his overly studied calm. "That is the most absurd accusation I have heard."

"Accusation?" The word hung between them. "Aren't you the one who called me a coward for evading my gifts?"

"You could help Aronsdale a great deal." He shook his head. "Doesn't that matter to you? If I could help that way, I surely would."

"Then why do you refuse to acknowledge your gifts?"

"I have no gifts." His voice actually shook.

This made no sense. "You deny you are a mage and no one else seems to realize it. But I see it clearly."

"Don't speak so loud." His panic flared. "You must never repeat what you just said."

"Why?" She crossed her arms. "You keep pestering me to use my mage gifts."

"Pester!" He glared. "I never pester."

"Pah."

"Chime, your gifts shine. You are light." The warmth in his voice faded. "I will tell you a truth, but you must swear never to reveal it to anyone."

That sounded intriguing. "I swear."

Muller lowered his voice. "I am a terrible mage. I can use only imperfect shapes. My spells are like the shapes that focus them. Imperfect. No matter how hard I try to achieve good, I cause damage instead." He spoke darkly. "I can never lead Aronsdale. I would do far more harm than good."

"Muller, no." She couldn't imagine such a thing.

"It is true. I am evil. My spells only destroy."

It puzzled her that he saw himself as in such a manner. He might be a scoundrel, but that didn't make him evil. He seemed oblivious to the purity of his emotions. She touched his arm. "You have much good in you."

He pulled away from her. "Don't be foolish. This isn't something that will go away with a few soft words."

Chime heard little beyond the word *foolish*. He thought her stupid, just like everyone else. "My apologies." Frost could have formed on her words. "Next time I won't be so foolish as to suggest you might be a better person than you allow yourself to believe."

His long lashes lowered. "You don't understand."

"Of course I don't." She thought of all the things he had said to her on the Star Walk. "I am a coward because I mislike being a mage, but I am foolish for thinking you are wrong to mislike being a mage."

He scowled at her. "Sarcasm doesn't become you, wife."

"I'm not your wife." Nor would she ever be, she decided. "Perhaps you ought to think less about what becomes people and more about what is inside of them."

"Very well." He motioned to a mosaic of yellow rings on the

wall that represented the sun. A few tiles were gone, leaving gaps in the circles. "You see those tiles?"

"Yes." She paused. "They are pretty. But broken."

"I was in a hurry, not thinking about shapes. I came around the corner and looked straight at the broken rings. My power focused through them before I realized it. When you startled me, I lost control." He motioned at the shards strewn across the floor. "This is the result."

She squinted at them. "Maybe you just need to learn how to make spells that work."

"What makes you think it didn't work?"

Chime looked up at him. "You wanted to break the window?"

"No. I was thinking about how much I disliked the cold drafts in here."

"What drafts?" It was completely still and warm.

He tilted his head toward the window. "You don't think it is odd to feel no breezes right now? The window is gone."

Chime stared at jagged frame with pieces of broken glass. It was all that remained of the window. She hadn't noticed the quiet air because she didn't expect wind inside the castle. But yes, it ought to be gusting in here. Outside, pennants on a nearby tower snapped in the wind.

She went to the window and stretched out her hand. No invisible barrier blocked it, nothing that would keep out wind. As soon as she reached past the frame, breezes rushed across her skin, yet not the slightest gust came inside.

She turned to Muller, impressed. "What did you do?"

"I'm not sure. I didn't plan the spell; it just happened—and exploded the window." His face paled. "That was a circle spell. What would happen if I went to higher shapes? Would I heal a person's arm by cutting it off? Cure unrequited love by making the desired person hideous? I don't even want to think of the harm I could cause people. My uncle. My friends." He swallowed. "The family I will someday have."

Chime wished she had a solution. "Can you learn to do better spells?"

He fisted his hand and banged it on his thigh. "I've tried. It doesn't work. I can only use flawed shapes to make flawed spells."

"Can Della help?"

"I asked her once if she thought I had mage ability. She said no. She was very apologetic." Wearily he added, "She can't see it because I am twisted inside. I can't tell her, because honor would require she tell my uncle. Then what? For the good of Aronsdale, they would have to remove me from the line of succession. Uncle Daron would have no heir. The crown would go to someone other than a Dawnfield." He rubbed his eyes. "I don't know. Maybe it should."

"But you aren't twisted." Chime had never been good with words. She spoke as if stepping through broken glass. "I will tell you a secret, as you trusted me with yours."

"A secret?" Now he looked intrigued.

"I have often felt emotions, but I wanted no one to know. And it is so erratic, how it happens."

"So you admit it."

"Only to you." She indicated the mosaics on the wall. "These focus my mood spells. I can tell this: the good inside you goes deep. You would never deliberately hurt anyone. If your spells twist, it must be because you don't know what to do with them." She hesitated. "Probably no one does. I've never heard of a mage like you before." Not that she knew anything about mages.

"That I have no wish to do harm changes nothing." He shook his head. "The harm still comes."

"Listen to us. We're so sure we aren't good enough to do what everyone says we must."

His face gentled. "You could almost make me believe otherwise." He took her hands slowly, giving her a chance to pull away. When she didn't, he drew her into an embrace. Chime laid her head against his shoulder, letting herself relax into his warmth. He bent his head, his cheek rubbing hers until she turned her head toward his. Then he kissed her. She knew she should stop, given that she intended to leave Suncroft in four weeks. But instead she savored his kiss, unable to remember why she wanted to go home.

"Mistress No-Cozen is gone?" Chime stood at the door of Della's cottage.

The circle-maid in the doorway had a scarf holding back her hair and she held a dusty mop. "I am sorry. She left this morning."

"But I had a lesson with her today." Now that Chime had seen how her ability to feel moods helped her understand Muller, she wanted to learn more. "We have so much work to do."

The maid smiled shyly. "I am sorry she isn't here, milady. I will tell her of your dedication."

Milady? Chime felt her cheeks redden. They treated her as a noblewoman, but she wasn't one. She needed to learn so much, not only magecraft, but protocols, customs, etiquette. She had to do it exactly right; otherwise, everyone would know Della had brought a fraud to Suncroft. The task seemed impossible.

King Daron had given her four weeks to decide about the marriage, but she had no doubt he was also deciding if he wanted her to marry his nephew. Unless they saw her make a good effort, she might lose Muller. Saints knew, he could be an exasperating man, and often she wanted to pack up and leave. But other times she felt confused and warm when she thought of him, unable to say what she wanted. He drew her, intruded on her thoughts, distracted her.

She finally registered what else the circle-maid had said. Dedication. No one had ever before used that word to describe Chime. In fact, when it came to her studies, they said the opposite. She stood straighter. "Do you know where I might find Mistress No-Cozen?"

The maid was apologetic. "She be in the Tallwalk Mountains, ma'am."

"Whatever for?" It was a ten-day ride from here.

"She heard rumors of another mage." The girl's face lit up. "Perhaps you will have a classmate, eh?"

"Oh. Maybe so." Dismay swept over Chime. Of course they were searching for another mage to marry the prince. Their present candidate had already run off once and might leave in a few weeks. What if Della came back with a better mage? Two weeks ago Chime would have been grateful to have another woman rescue her from marriage, but much had changed in the ten days since she had met Muller.

She tried to hide her anxiety. "Please let me know as soon as Mistress No-Cozen returns."

"I will, milady."

"Thank you."

Chime left then, miserable despite the bright day. If a better mage showed up, Chime would have to go home—and she wasn't sure she wanted to anymore.

Unbent straightened slowly and wished that his body, once so strong, matched his name. Years of toil had worn him down. He had spent the morning outside, under a leaden sky, cutting firewood for the winter and carrying stones to the cabin, to shore up its crumbling walls.

A rustle drew his attention. Dani had come outside and was standing near the door, staring with unseeing eyes toward the stunted woods beyond the cabin. His tangled locks blew around his face and shoulders. Unbent had washed Dani's hair this morning and shaved his beard. Now he could see the fine line of Dani's face, his regular features, the breadth of his shoulders and length of his legs. This was no rough youth. He had long suspected Dani belonged to the gentry, perhaps even the nobility. It was one reason Unbent had hidden here, high in the Boxer-Mage Mountains, avoiding all contact with people. The penalty for murdering a member of the gentry was life imprisonment; for a member of the nobility it was execution.

Several times Unbent had tried to take Dani down the mountain. But the youth refused to leave this cabin, protesting violently until Unbent gave in. So they remained isolated here, both of them safe, though whether from outer dangers or inner guilt, he never knew.

It grieved Unbent that he had so little to give his ward besides this rocky patch of hell. He had nothing else to his name. His one attempt to gain more had ended in catastrophe. What stupidity had possessed him to believe, even for one night, that highway robbery was the answer to his poverty? He and Dani would pay the price of that crime forever. He owed the boy the best life he could provide.

Over the years Unbent had come to love Dani as a son. He walked over now and stood with him, aware of Dani's greater height and strength. The youth had been exercising; sweat soaked his ragged gray shirt and rough trousers.

He laid his hand on Dani's arm, and the youth turned, his gaze directed above Unbent's head. Reaching out, Dani brushed Unbent's shoulder. He folded his large hand around Unbent's arm and tugged him toward the east side of the house.

Baffled, Unbent followed. This side looked much like the other, with cracked walls and thatching from the roof sagging down, but with no door or window. Dani pulled him to one corner and knelt on the ground, placing his hand on a stone there.

"I don't understand." Unbent knelt next to him. He talked to his son constantly. Dani never heard and never responded; for over a decade, Unbent had conversed with only himself or the rare visitors that happened by every few years. Dani had stopped speaking the night his parents died, when the boy had been six, if Unbent estimated his age correctly. That would make Dani nineteen now, a man, no longer a child, but unable to live on his own.

Dani set Unbent's hand on the stone. It was perfectly round. A sphere. Lifting it, Unbent realized someone had sculpted the rock, Dani certainly, since it hadn't been here a few days ago. He handed it to the youth, trying to understand. Dani settled cross-legged on the ground and bent his head over the orb.

Light brightened around them.

The radiance shifted through the colors of a rainbow: red, orange, yellow, green, blue, indigo. Then white light bathed them, beautiful light that defied the overcast sky. A sense of peace filled Unbent, one he didn't deserve. Did his son know he made light and joy? He didn't understand how Dani wove his spells, but he never doubted them.

Unbent would never forget that night when Murk, the other highwayman, had realized Dani had seen their faces and heard their voices. Murk tried to kill the boy then, intending to make sure Dani never saw, heard, or spoke again. Dani had survived the crash because his mother made a spell of protection. But just as she had only one life, so she could save only one life—that of her son.

Unable to talk with his foster son, Unbent would never fully understand what had driven Dani that night. He could only guess. In desperation, reeling from the loss of his parents, perhaps blaming himself because they died so he could live, Dani had done what should have been impossible. He had grasped his mother's spell and wrenched it, for some inexplicable reason completing what Murk threatened—Dani had taken his own sight, hearing, and voice.

No matter how Unbent tried to heal his son, nothing helped. Dani became a shadow mage, unseen and unknown. He cut himself off from his past life. Unbent had long suspected Dani feared that if he went among people, he would lose control of his power and hurt people as he had hurt himself.

Unbent had no mage gifts of light or healing, none at all, and it took an indigo mage to heal emotions. As far as he knew, no indigos existed, except perhaps Dani himself. He had heard legends of indigo mages in long ago times, but before Dani he had never believed those tales any more than he had believed a Saint of Waterfalls turned diamonds into liquid or a Saint of Buds made flowers open in the morning. This much he knew; he had in his keeping one of the most powerful mages alive.

And he could tell no one.

Iris

Chime paced through her suite in the castle. Blue and white sky mosaics tiled the domed ceiling, and the ivory walls had scenes of forests and lakes painted in their upper half. Gilt trim accented the moldings. But right now even the beauty of these peaceful rooms couldn't ease her agitation.

Today Della was bringing another mage to Suncroft.

A knock came at the door. Chime hurried to answer, stopped when she recalled her circle-maid was supposed to do it, and then remembered she had let the maid off for the day. It flustered her to have other people do her chores. Not that she had ever liked doing them herself, but she had never imagined people could make a living doing them for her. By rights, she should be the servant here, instead of the lady.

The knock came again. So Chime opened the door. Muller stood outside, his face creased with worry, his body resplendent in a brocaded blue vest and gold silk shirt, with blue leggings tucked into knee-boots, his gold hair glistening in the sunlight from a nearby window. He looked utterly gorgeous and thoroughly distressed.

Chime tugged him inside and closed the door. "Have you heard anything?"

"Nothing." He grabbed her around the waist and kissed her soundly. Every time he held her this way, she told herself to chastise him for taking liberties, but what she really wanted to do was take her own liberties with him.

After several moments, they parted. Muller smoothed a tendril of hair around her face. "My greetings."

She glared at him. "You are as much a rogue as ever."

He laughed and set her back so he could look over her dress, a gift his valet had brought this morning. It had a snug bodice, an ivory underskirt, and a brocaded overskirt that swept to the floor, all in colors and material that matched his clothes.

"You are a heavenly sight," he said. "I like the way the darker blue trim matches the embroidery on the hems."

Chime smiled. "You sound like a dressmaker."

He grinned. "I would make a great one, eh?" His smile faded. "Except I have to be a king instead and command the army."

Chime suspected he would have thoroughly enjoyed his life if he could have lived on a farm and designed clothes for the nobility. Unfortunately, not much demand existed for farmers with such skills.

"Della hasn't arrived yet," she said darkly.

"Run away with me," he urged. "Before she returns."

"You want me to run off with you?" She tried to look affronted, though in truth she wanted to flee, too. "You, sir, are incorrigible."

He put his arms around her waist. "You break my heart. Say yes."

She set her hands against his shoulders. "What is all this about going away?"

"If I have to marry, I want it to be you."

Her heart felt as if stuttered. She hadn't given him an answer about the marriage, yet he freely spoke of his feelings. The boys she had known in Jacob's Vale were sturdy, stoic types. They rarely mentioned to a girl how they felt, especially not without some reason to believe she returned their feelings. But then, perhaps she wasn't hiding hers from Muller as well as she thought. He was a mage, even if he didn't want to admit it any more than she did for herself.

Chime wasn't ready to say yes to the betrothal, though her heart bade her to do so. She wanted to scold him, to protect her emotions. But when she spoke, hope filtered into her voice. "Just because she is bringing a new mage, that doesn't mean you will have a new betrothed. Della says few have my ability." Chime didn't believe it; she struggled just to understand the word polyhedron, let alone use one for spells. But for the first time in her life, her studies interested her. She liked magecraft. "It would be unlikely this new mage is stronger."

"I hope so." Muller kept holding her. "I know you think I'm shallow and fickle, but I'm not. It's you I want. Not someone else."

"I never said you were shallow or fickle."

"You've thought it."

Puzzled, she said, "But I haven't."

"You say I should use my gifts. Well, I have. That is what they tell me."

"Then they're wrong."

"Of course they're wrong," he said matter-of-factly. "All my spells are wrong. But they always have a seed of truth."

She hesitated, unsure how to express herself. "What I have thought, Muller, is that you have a great more to you than you let people see, even yourself."

He shifted his weight. "I'm not suited for this king business. I don't like governing."

She couldn't help but smile. "You do seem to spend a lot of time avoiding your uncle."

His grin suddenly blazed. "Would you like to be king? I will abdicate in your favor."

She laughed. "I don't think it works that way. Besides, I wouldn't know how to be a king."

"Neither do I."

"You've trained for years."

"Yes, well, heredity and aptitude aren't the same."

Chime started to protest, but another knock at the door stopped her. She went to open it, aware of Muller standing behind her, an unchaperoned man in her suite. No betrothal had yet taken place.

When she opened the door, she forgot protocol and propriety. Della's circle-maid waited outside, her round cheeks flushed from running. "Milady!" She looked quickly from Chime to Muller, her face turning brighter red. "And Your Highness!"

Muller came forward. "Yes?"

"Mistress No-Cozen is back." The maid stopped to catch her breath. "She brought the new mage."

Muller resolutely took Chime's hand as they entered the Receiving Hall. Sunshine poured through the windows, slanting over Della.

A young woman stood at Della's side.

Chime felt as if bands were constricting around her chest, making it impossible to breathe. The girl looked about eighteen, with cheeks flushed a fetching pink, large brown eyes, and an incredible mane of chestnut curls that fell in waves to her hips. She was taller than Chime and had a much curvier figure, the voluptuous form men always seemed to notice. She glowed with health. Chime suddenly felt like a pale imitation. She glanced at Muller, certain he would have second thoughts about his hastily made oath to her a few moments ago.

Muller, though, didn't look intrigued by this new mage. In fact, he seemed bewildered. He hid it well, but Chime felt his puzzlement.

"Your Highness." Della bowed to Muller.

The new mage glanced from Muller to Chime to Della. When the girl bowed uncertainly, Chime realized that she, too, was new to court protocol. It helped a little with Chime's raging insecurity.

Della had made an extra effort to find a second mage. The mage mistress had apparently spent years recording all rumors, no matter how insubstantial, about mages; this year she had begun following up leads. After she located Chime, it hadn't been so urgent she keep looking—until Chime hesitated.

With dismay, Chime realized that even if she said yes now, the betrothal wasn't automatic. What if the King's Advisors decided she wasn't fit compared to this new mage? Chime wasn't ready to give her answer yet; agreeing to become queen was too overwhelming. But she didn't want the choice taken away, either. Given her behavior since Della had found her, though, the king and his advisors had reason to question her suitability.

Chime decided then and there that she would become a paragon, with no lock of hair or wisp of thread out of place. She couldn't make her intellect or experience any greater, but if no flaws showed in her appearance or conduct, maybe it would be enough. *She* would know the truth, that she was a fraud; nothing would change that. But perhaps her lacks wouldn't be so obvious to others—especially to this new mage.

Della brought the girl forward to Muller. "Your Highness, may I present Iris Larkspur of the Tallwalk Mountains. She will be studying with Chime."

"My honor at your presence, Your Highness." Iris's voice lilted with the lyrical accent of the Tallwalks.

Using mosaics on the walls, Chime fumbled to make a mood spell. To her unmitigated astonishment, she discovered that Iris felt no attraction to Muller, either. The other girl considered him too fashionable, too pretty, too everything. She preferred the strapping lads in her hamlet.

Chime blinked. Good graces, how had she known all that? Genuine green spells were welling up within her.

Muller inclined his head to Iris. "It pleases me to meet you, Mage Larkspur."

Iris murmured a response, her face red.

Chime spoke with awkward formality. "Welcome to Suncroft." To Della she said, "And welcome home, ma'am."

Iris managed a self-conscious smile. Then Muller spoke again, welcoming Iris with the verbal grace Chime had always admired in him.

So a new mage came to Suncroft. Chime walked with Muller through the castle. He spoke thoughtfully. "How odd."

"Iris?" Chime asked.

"She isn't what I expected."

"She is a mage. I felt it." Relief flowed through Chime. "But not as strong as me."

"No, I think not." He wouldn't look at her.

"Well. So." Chime suddenly felt magnanimous. "It will be nice to have someone to study with."

"If she can study." Muller rubbed his chin. "Her powers are shrouded. Something is wrong."

"Wrong?" Chime's unease stirred. "How?"

"I don't know." He gave her a forced smile. "Perhaps I imagined it."

"Perhaps." Chime earnestly hoped so.

* * *

Anvil paced with King Varqelle along a walkway atop the high wall of Castle Escar. The mountains dropped away in magnificent peaks to the south and rose ever higher to the north, cliffs in many shades of blue stone. In the slanting sunrays, they looked polished, as if a giant had sculpted them.

"Can you create moods spells to read the Aronsdale generals?" Varqelle asked.

Anvil walked slowly, his hands clasped behind his back as he endeavored to appear deep in thought. He couldn't reveal his inability to do mood spells; it would cast doubt on his claims to be a mage of great power. He had spent years living by his wits as he wandered Harsdown, never staying long in one place, doing odd jobs, his mind and body strengthened by his labors. He had told no one of his powers until he had come here, to Varqelle. But during all those years he had sought knowledge about magecraft from the histories and folktales of the villages he visited. He knew how to uncover secrets. He could learn what the king wanted to know just by going to Croft's Vale as a spy.

"Spells dissipate over distance," Anvil said, which was true. "If I focus through a sphere, I can reach across this castle, but at greater distances the spell becomes tenuous. Across the mountains is much too far." He paused as if pondering. "I need to go to Aronsdale."

Varqelle looked surprised. "You would do this?"

"If it pleases, Your Majesty." Anvil had never hidden his hatred of Aronsdale from Varqelle. He had left his home twenty years ago, as a lad of eleven. Mages were feared and reviled in those remote heights of the Boxer-Mage Mountains. He would never forget. The people of Stonce, the tiny hamlet where he lived, had called him pariah, monster, abomination, and in the end they would have killed him if he hadn't run away. Given the chance, they or others like them would finish that job—just as they had murdered his parents, sister, and brothers, who had done nothing more than reveal their mage power.

Except he could fight back. Unlike other mages, Anvil could reverse his powers without harm to himself. He felt nothing: no remorse, no regret, no dismay. Perhaps he had never possessed such powers of emotion; or perhaps those years of violence and cruelty in his childhood had scorched it out of his heart. Whatever the reason, he escaped his tormentors by using his spells against them.

The people of Aronsdale would never tolerate a mage who lacked the weakness they called remorse. If his ability to reverse spells without consequences became known, King Daron might order his execution. The sovereign wanted his mages powerless. But Anvil knew another truth: he was better than them all. They refused to acknowledge his superiority, but that would change. They would know better—and honor him as he deserved—after Harsdown conquered Aronsdale.

He spoke quietly. "If I return to Aronsdale, my life as Anvil the Forged could be forfeit without the protection of your army. But I can assume another identity."

Varqelle gave him an approving look. "A disguise."

"Yes." Although Anvil didn't relish the prospect, his great purpose required setting aside personal preferences. "I will need specifics on what you would like done."

"Get close to Daron's generals. Learn their plans." The king's eyes glinted. "Make them ill. Strike them with grief, sorrow, pain."

Anvil absorbed that suggestion. It had a certain appeal. He could certainly do spells to agitate rather than soothe, to hurt rather than heal. Aronsdale had caused him misery; now he would return the favor.

Yes, the idea had appeal.

* * *

Iris and Chime sat with Della at a table in the mage mistress's cottage. Colored sunlight slanted across them and lit the parchment they were studying.

Chime wished she could hide under the table.

"It is a simple spell," Della said, obviously trying for patience. "Concentrate on the drawing of the ring and use the techniques you studied last night to focus. Then make a spell of light. You can imagine the light, make a rhyme, think of heat, anything that helps."

Chime felt her face reddening. "I can't remember the techniques." She had studied hard, struggling to memorize the list so she would be prepared for her first class with Iris. But she was no better at these studies than any other schoolwork she had ever done.

"Surely you recall some." Della looked hopeful.

Chime spoke slowly. "Imagine light shining through the shape, yes?"

"Not through the shape, exactly," Iris said. "You imagine the ring focusing the light."

Della looked relieved. "Yes, good."

Chime stiffened. Iris couldn't have studied last night; the king's staff had kept her busy moving into a suite adjacent to the one where Chime lived. Chime had heard them while she plodded through her work.

"Now show me," Della told Iris. "Make a spell."

Iris caught her lower lip with her teeth and averted her gaze. "All right." She stared at the ring on the parchment, her forehead furrowed.

Nothing.

Iris lifted her head. "I can't."

That puzzled Chime. Quite frankly, she didn't see why Della wanted them to remember techniques for making spells. Either spells worked or they didn't. She stared at the drawing and it began to glow.

"Hai!" Iris gaped at Della. "How did you do that?"

"I didn't." The mage mistress glanced at Chime. "It was you, yes?"

"Yes." Chime shifted in her chair, aware that Iris had tensed. She hadn't meant to embarrass the other girl. As a peace offering she said, "Maybe if you had a real ring to focus your spells, you could make light."

When Iris stiffened, Chime didn't understand. Then she realized she had insulted Iris by suggesting she couldn't make a spell where Chime had succeeded, that Iris needed more concrete help.

Flustered, Chime ran her finger over the ring on the parchment. She hadn't intended to make a green spell, but it surged within her, revealing Iris's mood. The other girl reacted to Chime as she had to Muller; Iris thought Chime cold, too exacting in manner and dress. Arrogant. Seen through Iris's eyes, Chime didn't much like herself, either.

Chime felt heavy. No matter what she did, she offended people. If she behaved as she had at home, people here considered her common, crude, wild; if she did her best to copy court behavior and dress, they saw her as vain or proud. Chime knew she had faults, certainly more than her share, but surely she couldn't be as bad as people thought.

While Chime mentally floundered, Iris spoke to Della. "I memorized the images for focusing light through shapes last night. But when I *try* it, I canna make a spell." Her accent lilted more when she was upset.

It bewildered Chime that Iris could so easily learn Della's methods, yet she couldn't make a spell. Chime could barely remember the methods after studying all night, yet the spells came easily. She had no control, though. No technique. Maybe

Iris had the opposite problem; with too much emphasis on technique, she lost some natural quality.

"Maybe you think too hard," Chime suggested.

Both Della and Iris blinked at her. Then Della cleared her throat. "Well, yes, uh, I'm sure thinking too hard can cause problems."

"I'm sure," Iris said under her breath.

Hai! Now they thought she was stupid. Chime decided she would be better off if she kept her mouth shut.

After an awkward moment, Della said, "Maybe we should call it a day, eh? You two come back tomorrow morning."

Relief swept over Chime. "Yes, ma'am."

Iris practically jumped up from the table. "Aye."

After they bade Della good day, Chime and Iris walked back to the castle, across the slopes above the valley that sheltered Croft's Vale. Chime made another try at being friendly. "How do you like it here?"

Iris twisted a length of her hair. "It is so new."

"Are you glad to have come?"

"Yes, I think." Iris looked across the hills and meadows with longing. "It is so much prettier here. I don't miss the Tallwalks."

Chime couldn't imagine not being homesick. She never really stopped thinking about her family. She wrote them constantly and they replied often, but it wasn't the same. "Your parents must be sad that you left."

Iris gave her a sharp look. "My foster parents barely tolerated me."

"Oh." Chime heard the pain in her voice. Knowing her clumsiness with words, she suspected she would make matters worse if she pursued the subject. She tried to think of something more cheerful. "You have vigorous hair." It curled beautifully, so long and thick. "And quite the designs on your tunic."

Iris smoothed her hair, seeming unsure how to interpret the remarks. "Thank you."

Watching her, Chime admired the circles embroidered on Iris's sleeve. It reminded her of her crafts work at home, embroidering pillows and tunics, or painting designs on carts. She also enjoyed building the carts.

The shapes on Iris's sleeve sparked a mood spell in Chime; Iris wondered if Chime cared about anything besides hair and clothes. Disheartened, Chime turned away, looking up at the castle. She didn't know how to present herself to these people. Maybe she really was as shallow as they thought. Only Muller seemed to understand. And she could lose him. It startled her to realize how much she had come to look forward to seeing him each day. She hoped she was right about Iris, that the other girl had less mage talent than herself.

After they had walked for a while, Iris tried again. "Do you think we will have a war with Harsdown?"

"I can't really say." Chime had no idea. She had never paid much attention to events outside her village.

"I have heard rumors." Iris's forehead furrowed, a line between her finely etched brows. "Messengers came through town, merchants, minstrels, men looking for work, families seeking new land. They told of Harsdown building up its army." She gestured toward the northwest, where Harsdown lay beyond the mountains. "How can King Varqelle put so many resources into an army while his country starves? I donna know which would frighten me more, that it is true he takes so cruelly from his people or that he has more resources than we realize, enough to conquer us."

Chime felt denser by the moment. It had never occurred to her to consider such matters. "I've no idea."

Iris glanced at her. Although she tried to smile, she came across as sad more than anything else. "You and Muller seem well suited."

Chime didn't think she was being complimented. She spoke stiffly. "I'm sure His Highness agrees."

They continued on in silence.

Chime sat in the twilight, alone, on a bench curving around the window alcove at the top of the Starlight Tower. Tears rolled down her face.

"I'm not stupid," she whispered. "I'm not superficial or small-minded or vain." No matter how many times she said it, she couldn't forget the look on Iris's face, the same one she saw from Lord Firestoke or King Daron, even sometimes from Della. Only Muller didn't see her that way.

Even after only one day, Chime knew the truth: Iris would make a better queen. In one conversation she had shown Chime more about Harsdown than Chime had bothered to notice in the previous eighteen years of her life.

She leaned against the window, a rectangular pane that stretched from the cushioned bench to the ceiling, with glass circles inscribed within it, one on top the other. The twelve sides of the alcove each had a window panel, and every one glowed with Chime's green mage light, soft and fresh like leaves in the sun. Chime's lips trembled as her tears fell. She spread her palm over a glowing circle and a sense of well-being spread through her. But it wasn't real. No matter how many spells she made, nothing would change the truth. She wasn't good enough to become queen.

"Why do you cry?" Muller spoke from the shadowed entrance. He came and knelt on the bench, flattening the velvet cushions with his weight as he gathered her into his arms. Chime laid her head against his shoulder and put her arms around his waist. His mood came to her, focused by the windows, though they had stopped glowing, leaving her and Muller in the fading light of dusk.

"You are sad, too," she murmured.

He answered with pain. "She is a sapphire mage."

"Who?" Chime knew, but she couldn't bear to say.

"Della thinks Iris is a green mage, not as strong as you." He swallowed. "Della is wrong."

A tear ran down her face. "I will leave Suncroft."

"No!" He pulled her closer. "Not without me."

"It seems I cannot have you."

"Della doesn't know Iris is a sapphire," he said doggedly. "Nor does Iris. She cannot reach her gifts. I felt it the first time we met. She is stopped somehow, I don't know why. She may never find her potential."

"Did you tell Della?"

"I tried. Perhaps not as hard as I should, but I did try." He spoke with difficulty. "Della humors me. She doesn't believe I know anything."

"She is wrong."

He spoke bitterly. "I know how to cause harm."

"When you met Iris, you created a spell to sense her mind. It did no harm."

"No harm?" He made an incredulous sound. "You mean, except for almost destroying the life you and I might have together? Either that, or Iris goes without ever reaching her mage power."

"Almost destroying?" She knew so little about him, so few of his nuances and dreams, but the more she learned, the more he occupied her thoughts. "We have a chance?"

He answered slowly, as if unsure he should reveal his mind. "If I disappear with you and leave a message behind refusing the crown, what can they do? They must choose a new heir. Iris could marry him."

"King Daron will search for you."

"Perhaps. But I think not so hard." Muller sounded worn out.

Older. "Brant Firestoke, Cube-General Fieldson, Della, all of them, they know the truth. I am no king. I never will be."

"You will be a fine king. And Daron would search for you forever, Muller. He loves you." As much as Chime longed to run away, it was wrong. "We must accept our duties. I should never have said I would leave Suncroft. If Harsdown attacks Aronsdale, we must do what we can to help our people." Her voice caught. "Even if our very best is so very little."

"Ah, Chime." He pulled her closer, leaning his head against hers. "I feel a darkness coming. And I've no idea how to make it stop."

Pearls of Dawn

Summer passed in a haze of warmth, buzzing shimmer-flies, and blue skies. The farmers in the countryside around Croft's Vale tended their fields, nurturing corn, wheat, alfalfa, yellow and orange gourds, and other crops that would feed them through the colder seasons. They planted in geometric shapes, triangles here, squares there, circles elsewhere, filling in extra corners with flowers.

Festivals lightened the long summer nights in Croft's Vale, when country folk streamed into the village from miles around, families walking in together or riding painted carts pulled by oxen. Merchants came to the market from all across Aronsdale and other countries as well, filling the central square with stalls and people. At night, children ran through the cobbled streets waving sparklers. Dogs barked at them with enthusiasm and bounded onto barrels stored by the walls of taverns.

As the languid days cooled into autumn, a peddler rode into the village.

An unusual peddler.

Long and lean, with dark hair, he guided his wagon down one of the busiest streets. He stopped at the Clover Inn, where a wooden sign engraved with a clover swung by a sturdy chain. Bells hanging from the sign jingled in the breeze.

The man rented a room for himself, space for his wagon behind the inn, and a stall for his horse in the Clover Stables. Then he headed to the big common room of the inn, where patrons ate, drank, and gambled with marbles of many colors. After settling at a table and ordering a drink, he questioned the barmaid: Where might he find customers for his goods—goldware, crystal, china, many fine items for the discerning of taste, and coin, too, of course.

She had a ready answer: Castle Suncroft. Croft's Vale was prosperous, and some town folk might have interest in his wares, but the nobility were the ones who would buy large amounts.

So Anvil the Forged, disguised as an itinerant peddler, set up his cover for visiting Suncroft.

The knock came so early in the predawn hours that no hint of day yet lightened the sky. Muller groaned when Sam Threadman shook him awake.

"You've a visitor, Your Highness," his valet said.

"Go away," Muller mumbled. He pushed his pillow over his head. One of its tassels tickled his nose.

Sam pulled away the pillow. "You must come. It is important."

Muller grunted, tempted to order him away. But Sam wouldn't wake him without reason. He dragged himself out of bed and shuffled through his suite in his sleeping robe, his eyes bleared. Sam ushered him to the front parlor.

The instant Muller saw who waited for him, he came awake. "Lord Firestoke."

Brant looked as tired as Muller felt. He wasted no time. "You must come, Your Highness."

"What happened?"

"Your uncle." Brant's words fell like stones. "The king is dying."

As Muller entered into the dimly lit bedroom, a great weight seemed to press on him. He walked to the bed, torn with grief by the sight of the wasted man there, lost in voluminous covers of velvet and silk.

"Uncle Daron?" Moisture gathered in Muller's eyes. "Can you hear me?"

The king slowly turned his head. "Ah...I am glad you came."

"What happened?" Muller asked, bewildered. He knew his uncle tired easily these days, but Daron had seemed all right this morning.

"Too long... " The king's voice trailed off.

Muller looked around, desperate. Skylark, the castle healer, came to him, an older woman in a long flannel night dress and robe, with a braid of white hair hanging over her shoulder to her waist. She spoke in a low voice. "I have tried healing spells on him. From those, I know a vessel carrying blood in his brain has burst." Grief etched her face. "The damage was too much. I can ease his pain, but I cannot put back together what nature could never repair on her own. I tried—I—but I can't—"

Muller laid his hand on her arm. "I understand."

Tears glimmered in her eyes, what bards called the pearls of dawn, shed for those who passed away in the darkest hours of morning, before dawn gentled the sky with a new day's hope.

"Nephew..." Daron said. "Come closer."

Muller sat on the bed, taking care not to jostle his uncle. "I am here."

Daron watched him with faded eyes. "You will be a fine king. Believe that."

"Not yet. Please don't go." Muller couldn't imagine life without him. Daron was his only family. He knew his uncle far better than his birth father, who had drowned when Muller was seven.

Daron answered in a papery voice. "I have stayed too long. Must see your lovely aunt, eh?" His smile curved, a shadow of its former strength. "Respect Brant Firestoke. If you argue with him less and listen more, you might find he has better advice than you think."

Muller's voice caught. "Yes, sir."

"Remember...my love is always with you, son."

Muller's heart broke on hearing a word he had thought no one would ever use with him again. Son. His voice caught. "And mine is always with you, Father."

Daron smiled. Then the king of Aronsdale closed his eyes and passed from the world of men to that of spirits.

The slam of fists against wood shook Unbent out of a restless sleep. Barely awake, dressed in old trousers, he staggered out of bed and pulled on a tattered shirt. Then he stumbled into the only other room of the cottage. His foster son was crouched on the splintered floor, half dressed, beating the ground with his fists, his unfocused gaze wild, his face pale under the tangle of his waist length hair and the two day stubble on his chin.

"Dani!" Unbent ran to him. He knelt and laid his hand on Dani's shoulder. "What is it?"

Dani jerked away, his face contorted. A tear rolled down his face.

"Ai, Dani." It tormented Unbent to see him in pain. "Let me help."

But Dani could neither see nor hear his comfort, nor could he ask for what he needed. He rocked back and forth, his shoulders shaking with sobs, though he never made a sound.

Unbent stayed with him through the dark hours before dawn,

his hand on Dani's shoulder, offering comfort in the only way he could to his grieving son, though why Dani mourned, Unbent had no idea.

The people gathered on Mount Sky north of Suncroft, the only point in this region of Aronsdale higher than Castle Suncroft. They flowed around and up its slopes and filled the meadows, valleys, and hills all around, tens, hundreds, thousands of people, come from Croft's Vale and all the farms and towns within five days' travel of the castle. They stood in the pearly darkness before dawn. The wind fluttered their neck scarves and woolen capes, tunics, heavy leggings, and tasseled boots, all dark colors, brown, gray, black, somber violet and cobalt-blue.

The colors of mourning.

At the top of the hill, Muller stood with Chime. Brant and Della were with them, and Cube-General Fieldson, the head of the King's Army and the third King's Advisor. Chime's gray cape billowed around her like fog. The predawn light gave the world an unreal feeling. Five days had passed since King Daron's death, yet still she felt dazed. Muller had barely spoken since his uncle had passed away, silent as he went through the rituals and ceremonies that marked the death of a king, including the day Muller had spent in seclusion, as expected of the heir and future sovereign.

The Bishop of Orbs read the memorial in a clear, resonant voice that rolled throughout the hills, across the throng of citizens, all with their faces turned up toward him. When the Bishop finished, Muller spread the king's ashes on the wind, as Daron had requested in life, returning him to the land he had always loved.

Chime hadn't known Daron well and it saddened her that she would never have the chance now. Muller's grief overflowed into her heart. He mourned not only for his own loss, but for all Aronsdale.

* * *

Far down the hill, a peddler stood with a cluster of men from the Clover Inn. He listened to the memorial, his head bowed. People called him Wareman, for his gold and silver wares. Anyone seeing the glint in his eyes assumed it came from tears. Only he knew the truth. Anvil the Forged shed no tears for King Daron.

The glint was triumph.

Rebirth

Sphere of Rainbows

Winter had followed King Daron's death, but now spring gentled the land, offering new life to the countryside. Chime stood in the doorway of Della's cottage, savoring the golden morning. The sky arched above, as blue as the glass bowls she used for breakfast each morning. To the west, Croft's Vale and its farmlands basked in the sunshine.

Far down the hill, Iris was picking skybells and yellow box blossoms. She wore the tunic and leggings adopted by most young, unmarried women. Iris preferred earth colors, greens and browns, with accents of blue, whereas Chime preferred yellow, gold, and ivory. It was one of the many things they didn't have in common.

And yet, for all their differences, Chime had come to like Iris during their months together. She had trouble expressing it, though. Iris unsettled her. If the other girl cared what people thought of her, it never showed. She often came late to lessons or arrived in disarray, upsetting the order Chime struggled to create for herself. Chime had gone out of her way to change her behavior so she fit in, and Iris never seemed to try at all, yet Chime always felt as if she were the one who was lacking.

Chime knew she would never have Iris's quick mind, but she did her best to make up for it by applying herself. She didn't regret agreeing to stay at Suncroft and become a mage, though she sorely missed her family. Although she felt no more ready today to be queen than she had a year ago, when she had first come here, at least she stayed on an even keel now.

She was less certain about Muller now, though. He had never spoken of his uncle's death and he had found reason after reason to postpone his coronation. Their wedding would take place when the Bishop of Orbs crowned Muller king. The delays left her off balance, uncertain how much he truly wanted her, for all that he might swear his love.

"Iris!" The sharp call came from nearby. Chime glanced over to see Della standing at the top of the hill, her hands on her ample hips, glaring down at her pupil.

Iris turned with a jerk, the wind wrapping her hair around her body. Then she started up the hill. Seeing her wayward student on the way, Della headed back to the cottage. Chime had long thought Della's home was the wrong place for Iris to study; the hills and woods touched Iris more deeply than Iris herself seemed to realize. But Chime's attempts to say so always ended up muddled and awkward, until she gave up trying to explain what she didn't really understand herself.

"Pah," Della grouched as Chime moved aside to let her enter the cottage.

"Morning, ma'am," Chime said cheerfully.

Della waved her hand as she disappeared inside. Chime started to follow, then decided to wait for Iris, who was almost certainly in a better mood than their teacher. Chime stood in the doorway, nervously fiddling with her hair. She never felt as if she measured up to Iris, but she longed to bridge the gap that kept them from becoming friends.

As Iris reached her, Chime smiled. "You look lively today." Then she winced. She meant to say lovely. It was true, though; the wind had whipped Iris's beautiful hair into a wild, lively mane. She could be a forest goddess. It made Chime feel very boring.

Iris blinked. "Lively?"

"Windblown." Chime wished she could let her hair free that way. "Your hair is a mess."

Iris stiffened, and belatedly Chime realized she could have phrased her comment better. Mercifully Iris chose not to take offense. "I don't mind," she said.

Chime's spirits lifted as they went inside. She loved the cottage, with its windows in many shapes, some colored glass, some clear. Tinted sunlight suffused the room, warming the circular tables and the goldwood chairs with their carved backs. Throw rugs adorned the parquetry floor, woven from yarn in blue, rose, and goldenrod colors. Blue sphere-blossoms in yellow vases added accents.

Della bustled in from the kitchen and waved at them. "Sit yourselves down, you two. What is all this playing about, eh? We have lessons."

Chime and Iris moved to the table they often used by the windows. As the girls sat down, Della frowned at Iris. "Well then, don't you look healthy today."

Iris's cheeks reddened. Chime understood perfectly. Saints knew, she had squirmed often enough under Della's tutelage. And "saints" was right. They did know, for many of them took their essence from colors of the rainbow, which had special meaning for students of magecraft. The saints were actually spirits in ancient Aronsdale legends, including azure saints who glazed the sky blue and rose saints who added the blush to a young woman's face.

Iris said only, "Thank you, ma'am."

"Very healthy," Della grumbled. "What with all the fresh air you get, out who-knows-where instead of studying."

"Aye, ma'am." Iris looked ready to escape out to the fresh air again, either that, or hide under the table.

"Aye, ma'am?" Della crossed her arms. "I would rather hear, 'Aye, Mistress No-Cozen, I will be on time from now on.'"

"A-aye, ma'am," Iris stuttered. "I mean, I willna be late."

Chime sympathized with Iris, having often been on the spot with Della herself. She loved Iris's lilting Tallwalk accent. Chime spoke with a southern burr, which resembled the Suncroft accent. It was one of her few advantages here; she didn't sound provincial. But she would have given it up in a moment for the lyrical music of Iris's accent.

With a *humph,* Della went off to her office, probably to retrieve their class materials. Chime knew that beneath her prickly exterior, the mage mistress had a gentle heart. Not that Della would ever admit to such a secret.

Chime settled at the table, glad they were to start class. She tried to sound cheerful. "Yes, let us proceed, now that everyone is here."

"I didna come that late," Iris grumbled.

Chime could have hit herself upside the head with the heel of her hand. She never seemed to phrase her words well with Iris. She hid her fear with nonchalance, dreading the day when someone would discover Iris was the stronger mage. If only Muller would let them coronate him. After he and Chime married, it would make no difference how many other comely, powerful mages showed up at Suncroft. But as long as he kept putting off his ascension to the throne, she risked losing him to Iris.

Chime answered self-consciously. "Did I say that?"

"Well then, is'n that what you meant?" Iris asked.

"Perhaps we have a language difficulty."

"Nay, Chime, I donna have a language difficulty."

Chime stiffened, afraid she had sounded dim-witted. "I'm sure you can't help it."

Iris poked her finger into a green box-blossom in the vase on the table. "An' I'm sure you canna help but notice, aye?"

"Language, like appearance, is an art form." Chime thought of Muller's sensuous voice. She would rather listen to him than most anyone, especially Della in a grouchy mood. "Some people have the gift for its graceful expression. Others don't. It isn't their fault."

Iris stared at her. "I swear, I do truly think sometimes you clang."

"Clang?"

"You know the word?"

"Of course." Chime hesitated. "Don't bells clang?"

"Aye, they do certainly."

"But I'm not a bell." That was her mother's name.

Iris sighed. "It is'n important."

Even more defensive now, Chime spoke tartly. "Your speech is so quaint." She regretted the words immediately, but it was too late to take them back.

An image jumped into Iris's mind, one so vivid that Chime caught it without trying, her spell tuned by the many shapes in the room: the other girl imagined Chime with a vase of flowers dumped on her head. Iris's lips curved upward.

Chime knew she should be offended, but the image made her want to laugh. "Why are you smiling like that?" she asked Iris, all innocence. She knew why, but she wanted to see what the other girl would say.

"Smiling?" Iris flushed. "Uh...I was thinking you look radiant this morning."

The easing of Iris's tone so relieved Chime that she barely listened to the words, instead responding to their intent. "Oh, well, in that case. Of course."

Iris spoke in a low voice. Chime wasn't sure, but it sounded like, "And humble."

"What did you say?" Chime asked.

"Bumble." Iris floundered, obviously embarrassed that Chime had overheard her comments. "Bumble bees."

"Bees?"

"They are, uh, sunny and bright. Like you."

"Oh." Confused, Chime smiled. "Thank you."

Della returned then with scrolls, rescuing Chime and Iris from their excruciating conversation.

The lesson went well for a while, but then Della asked Chime to make light using a faceted sphere. Uncertain with her technique, Chime made an emotion spell instead. It focused through the powerful shape, revealing Della's mood. The success so delighted Chime that she spoke before she thought.

"You're frustrated with Iris," Chime said. "You worry she will never achieve her potential." The instant the words came out, Chime could have died. Saints almighty, couldn't she watch her tongue?

It was too late to undo the damage. Iris rose to her feet. "Well, then, and it be a pity for us all." Then she whirled around and strode away from the table. She grabbed her boots from the mat by the door and ran outside.

"Hai!" Chime stared at Della in dismay. "I am so very sorry."

"It isn't me who needs to hear the apology." Della shook her head wearily. "I know you mean well. But you must learn to be more careful."

Chime jumped to her feet. "I will go to her."

Della also stood up. "Seeing you will only hurt her right now, I think. Let me talk to her first. Give her time to cool off. Then you can talk to her."

Chime wanted to fix it now, to rush after Iris. But she knew Della was right. With reluctance, she said, "Yes. Of course."

After Della left, Chime walked dejectedly back to the castle. A man was coming down from Suncroft. He was dressed like a peddler, with russet pants and a green vest over a shirt with billowy sleeves. He carried a large russet sack, one of the special type that had folding shelves inside made from sheepskin. His dark hair and narrow face looked familiar, but she couldn't say why.

As they approached each other, he nodded, slowing to a stop. Chime spoke stiffly, afraid of saying the wrong thing again. "A fine morn, Goodman."

"My pleasure, ma'am." His smile didn't touch his eyes. "You grace the sunlight with your presence."

Chime felt terribly awkward with him. She wasn't sure why; he seemed very nice. But something about him felt...odd. "Thank you," she said.

He swung his sack off his shoulder and rested it on the ground. "Your betrothed drives a hard bargain, milady."

She hadn't known Muller was bargaining for anything. "What wares do you sell, kind sir?"

His voice took on a peddler's enthusiasm. "Gold plate like you've never seen. Here, let me show you." He opened his bag.

"I really can't—"

"Won't take but a moment." He pulled out a bundle and unwound the protective cloth. When he finished, he held a sparkling gold bowl inlaid with diamonds arranged in star patterns.

"Oh, it's lovely." Chime had never seen such a fine piece, even here at Suncroft where they had so many more beautiful things than she had ever imagined. "May I hold it?"

"Certainly." He handed her the bowl. "I have table settings, goldware, serving platters."

She beamed at him. "I will speak to Muller."

"Ah, ma'am, that would be kind of you. Kind indeed."

Chime gave him back the bowl. "Have a good day, sir."

"That I will." His eyes glinted. "I will indeed."

It wasn't until they parted that Chime realized why he made her feel odd. She had formed no mood spells with him. That itself wasn't unusual; under normal circumstances, she tried to avoid making them so she wouldn't intrude on the privacy of other people. But she didn't have enough control to stop it from happening if she found herself unexpectedly confronted with strong shapes. Although the stars on the goblet could have sparked her power, she had felt no hint of the peddler's mood.

Well, maybe she couldn't draw on stars. Or perhaps it was their color. She did best with green, though she could use any color of a lower rank. Or maybe her control was improving after all.

Still, the incident tugged at her.

Iris ran through the trees, uncaring of her path. She came out on a bluff above Croft's Vale. The village filled the valley below, pretty houses with thatched roofs, close enough for her to make out gardens and people, but too far to see the clutter and debris of so many inhabitants living together. Vines bloomed everywhere, spilling down trellises, winding up houses, and brightening flower boxes with rosy orb blossoms, star-flowers, green box-buds. The contrast with the rocky, sparse land of the Tallwalks where she had grown up made her heart ache.

She would miss this place.

Iris knew she wouldn't be at Suncroft much longer. Chime had only put in words what they all realized: the talent Della had thought she saw in Iris was a ghost, like drifting mist that seemed to take form and shape for a moment, but quickly faded.

She knelt in the grass and bowed her head. A tear ran down her face.

"What is this?" a voice said. "We've hardly started the lesson and already you are leaving."

With a start, Iris looked around. Della stood a few paces away, her hands on her hips and a scowl on her face.

"Hai, Della, admit the truth." Iris rose wearily. "I donna have it in me to be a mage."

Della came over to her. "Is that so?"

"Aye, that be so."

"So now you think you can take my place?"

Iris blinked. "Well, sure as the sun shines, I would never be thinking such a thing."

"No?"

"No, ma'am."

Della glowered. "I am the one who decides if you have what it takes to study with me, young woman."

"But I canna——"

"Pah." Della motioned around them, taking in the sky and the distant, hazy mountains. "You see all this?"

"Aye, ma'am."

"What is it?"

"Aronsdale."

"Aronsdale, Hairs-in-Dale, that isn't what I meant."

Iris gazed over the enchanting panorama and breathed in air scented by sweet grass. "It is a place of beauty and serenity."

"Serenity, pah. Aronsdale is a mess."

"It is?"

"It will be, after Prince Muller's coronation."

"Della!"

"Well, it's true."

"You shouldna speak of His Highness so."

Della spoke tiredly. "Then who will? He doesn't want the throne."

Knowing Della loved the prince as her own nephew, Iris understood what it took for her to make such an admission. Nor was it a surprise. Iris had long suspected Muller's reluctance to become king. But Aronsdale needed the royal family. The House of Dawnfield was the symbolic heart of the country; their loss would devastate the people.

"He is the heir," Iris said.

The older woman's voice quieted. "I speak to you privately, Iris, as one of the King's Advisors. We have delayed the coronation because if we push Muller, he may refuse the crown."

"But then who will be king?"

"We don't know. Probably one of his advisors, perhaps Brant Firestoke."

"Canna Chime reassure Muller? She is well an' sure a green mage." Iris spoke with difficulty. "I felt it this afternoon."

"She does have great gifts." Della sighed. "But one must also know how to use them."

Iris longed for Chime's gifts. Techniques were easy; Iris had no trouble learning those. But still she did no spells. Chime struggled to learn techniques, yet she made spells as easily as drinking water. If only they could combine their talents; together they might be the student Della deserved.

"It is only that the studies are new," Iris said. "She will learn."

Della sighed. "You are kind, Iris, especially given how she speaks to you."

Iris hadn't realized how well Della saw the tension between her young charges. The mage mistress seemed to know how to calm her. Della continued to talk, telling her of mages, and Iris inner turmoil began to settle. When they spoke of King Daron's death, she saw how it had devastated Della, who usually hid her softer emotions.

Finally Della spoke of what would happen after Muller became king. "He needs capable advisors, people with intelligence, compassion and foresight." Her gaze didn't waver.

"Someday you could be one of those advisors. You have both the strength of character and the mage power. Don't give up now."

Iris felt as if she were breaking inside. "I canna pretend to gifts I donna have."

"The power is there." Della made a frustrated noise. "I just don't know how to help you find it."

Iris indicated the woods around them. "This is the magic—trees, sky, flowers."

Della considered her. "The harder I push to make you study, the more you want to come out here."

"I donna mean disrespect, ma'am."

"I know, Iris." Della's expression turned thoughtful. "It's as if the studies *drive* you to seek the outdoors."

"It feels that way." Chime had several times tried to tell her the same.

"Do you have a special place here? One that makes you feel even closer to the land?"

Iris hesitated to reveal her secrets. But in her own gruff way, Della had mothered her this past year, easing Iris's loneliness. When Della had realized how ill-at-ease her charge felt in the castle, she had brought Iris to the cottage, giving her a home. Iris felt she had given back so little, no hint of the gifts Della strove to awaken.

"I have a place where I go to be alone," Iris offered.

"Will you take me there?"

Softly Iris said, "Aye."

Trees and ferns enclosed the glade, curving around and over-head, hiding this hollow in the woods. A stream flowed off a stone ledge and fell sparkling into a pool. Shape-vines hung everywhere in colorful loops.

Iris sunk into the grass by the water. "I come here whenever I can."

Della turned in a circle. "It is lovely."

Iris's tension trickled away. "It soothes."

"Don't you see what it is?"

"What do you mean?"

Della's face gentled. "Look at the shape."

Iris studied the hollow, paying attention to its form today. "I'll be a frog in a fig. It's a sphere!"

Della laughed. "In a fig, eh?" She settled herself on the grass next to Iris. "I have been through these woods many times and never did I see this place."

"It's always been here."

"I recognize the waterfall and some trees. But a sphere? It wasn't like this before. You have changed it."

"Nay, Della. How could I?"

"Perhaps the plants respond to your mage power."

Iris didn't see how such could happen. And yet...each time she visited this hollow, it soothed her more than the last, giving her a peace that eluded her elsewhere. Could she have molded the shape? "It seems impossible."

Della's eyes lit up. "Iris!"

"Aye?"

"Make a spell here."

Iris squinted at her. "That is an odd idea."

"Maybe an odd idea is what you need."

"I have no shape to focus my power."

"But you do." Della indicated the hollow.

Iris flushed. "Well then, sure, it be a sphere, too much for me."

"Try."

"I canna do it."

Kindly, Della said, "You won't know unless you try."

Iris feared to try, lest she fail yet again. But if she never took chances, she might as well live her life in a hole. She breathed deeply, centering herself. Then she concentrated. The waterfall shimmered with rainbows, and blossoms hung from vines, all colors, like mage spells —

Red.

Orange.

Yellow.

Green.

Blue.

Indigo—

With a great surge of power, her mind opened.

12

A Luminous Touch

Darkness and silence filled Jarid's life.

He sat in his favorite spot in a corner, on the floor where he couldn't fall. His foster father had stopped urging him to use furniture; after Jarid had grown large and muscular, he asserted himself simply by refusing to move when his guardian tried to put him in a chair. He didn't know his father's true name; he had never understood the signs the older man used to communicate it. Jarid had thought of him as Stone since that long ago night when the man saved his life, protecting Jarid like an unbreakable stone when Murk would have killed him.

Now Jarid imagined spheres, beautiful spheres, glimmering and vibrant in his mind. Over the years they had helped him focus on Stone, until he could sense his father's every mood. Lately Stone worried Jarid would become so immersed in meditations, he would forget to eat.

Jarid sighed without sound. Meditation was his only escape. Since that night his world had ended with the death of his parents, he had neither seen nor heard. On the rare occasions when visitors came, he knew only because their moods differed from Stone's. His father loved him; others found him strange, crippled, disturbing. Mercifully, in these remote mountains few people visited. He and Stone lived alone, cut off from the world, never communicating with it, neither for gossip nor great news. Stone didn't know his son was heir to Aronsdale. He and Jarid were simply two people in the mountains.

A vibration came through the floor, the tread of feet. The aroma of meat tickled Jarid's nose. He had distant memories of eating steaks from gold platters, but over the years he had begun to wonder if his recollections of loving parents and a grandfather who ruled as king were no more than a fantasy he created to fill the void of his life.

Jarid lifted his head, feeling changes in the air. Stone was in front of him, probably kneeling. He waited, and a moment later Stone carefully placed a dinner plate made from chipped stone in his hands. Jarid accepted it to calm Stone, but after his father left, he set the plate down on the floor. Then he sat, savoring the sunlight on his face. On these rare sunny days, Stone opened the frayed curtains and uneven shutters, knowing Jarid enjoyed the warmth.

Eventually the sun moved across the sky, no longer sending its rays through the window. Sorrow at its passing came to Jarid. He rose and did his exercises then, working his legs, arms, torso, any part of his body that he thought needed training. It meant a great deal to him that he could manage this on his own. He worked out constantly, having little else to do but make thatching for the roof or wander outside when the cold, foggy weather cleared.

Eventually he tired and settled into his corner again. After resting, he ate his meal. The meat had gone cold and the gravy congealed, but Jarid didn't mind. Little touched him now.

When he had first lost his sight, hearing, and voice, he had cried in silence for days, weeks, forever it seemed, unable even to feel vibrations in his throat that would have come had he been making sounds he couldn't hear. But over the years, he had become numb. He locked away his emotions, protecting himself. Now, full from his meal, he closed his eyes, more out of habit than for any need, and rested his head against the wall, content.

Shapes evolved in his mind.

He loved spheres. Even in that distant time he barely remembered, they had fascinated him. As a child, he had never understood why adults insisted he couldn't feel the moods of other people, or that a fully matured mage would have trouble doing what came so easily to him. They also claimed he couldn't heal, though he had made his kitten better when it had the wasting illness. So he had stopped telling people, except his mother, who believed him. She encouraged him to play shape-games that helped him focus.

Now he had nothing of her but those bittersweet games.

Jarid imagined cubes, rings, pyramids, bars, circles, polyhedrons, faceted orbs, and especially spheres, all in gem colors so lovely his heart ached. They were art to him. He knew, from Stone's mind, that he could light up a room. Jarid never saw the light—indeed, he had seen nothing since the night Murk had shattered his life.

Jarid had hated Stone that night, pounding the man with his small fists. As the years had passed, his hatred had faltered in the face of Stone's unexpected kindness. Jarid knew he soothed his foster father, that he helped heal emotional scars Stone had suffered, mired in the lonely destitution of these rocky hills where crops died and livestock starved. But nothing could ease Stone's crushing guilt.

Jarid knew that guilt.

Stone felt it every time he looked at the youth he had orphaned, every time he struggled to understand his ward's needs. If Stone had once been hard, the years had cracked his granite heart.

Jarid didn't know how he could both hate and love a person, yet he did. It didn't matter that Stone hadn't killed Jarid's parents; he had helped Murk attack the orb-carriage. But since that day, Stone had been a compassionate guardian, at first out of guilt, then later out of love, an emotion he couldn't hide from Jarid. In spite of Jarid's intent to remain cold, he came to return that love. He and Stone barely scratched out a living, but he didn't care; all that mattered had died that long ago night. Stone offered a refuge where he could withdraw from humanity.

Jarid had no idea how he appeared to other people, but he thought he must be hateful and hideous. He had felt that way since his parents died. Stone seemed to find him tolerable, but in the harsh reality of their lives, anything that wasn't actively lethal was tolerable. Jarid knew he should have prevented the crash that killed his parents, but *how,* he had no idea. He was a mage. He should have helped his parents. His mother had the power to save one life—and she had used it for her son.

She had died so he could live.

Moisture gathered in his eyes. Angry, he wiped it away. Struggling to banish his memories, he filled his mind with images. His thoughts expanded outward. And yet...today something was different. Tension built within him, a sense of straining, of *reaching.* His mental shapes blurred into a luminous rainbow fog.

Straining.

Reaching.

Seeking.

A tendril curled through the fog. Sweat broke out on Jarid's forehead. What invaded his solitude? He clenched the rough cloth of his trousers. Unaware and unknowing, the invader came closer, closer...

Leave me alone! The cry reverberated in his mind, and he suddenly felt foolish, reacting with such dismay to his own thoughts. For surely this "intruder" was no more than his own fevered imaginings.

But...he *did* feel it seeking, coming closer, so close. A green sphere vibrant with ferns wavered in his mind, a waterfall of light pouring through its brightness.

Beautiful sphere.

Sphere mage.

Rainbow.

And then he touched her mind.

Muller stood in the circular chamber atop the Mage Tower of Suncroft, across from the Starlight Tower in the southwest corner of the castle. This room was only a few paces across, with one window and walls made from polished silk-stone the color of pale violets. He hadn't come to look out, though. He had come for the shapes.

A thousand years ago a sculptor had carved these walls with a vine of shapes: a dot, a line; flat shapes from triangle to circle; three-dimensional shapes from pyramid to sphere. The engravings curled around the chamber at waist height, with vines of smaller forms rising and descending along the walls. The effect mesmerized Muller—and frustrated him painfully, for he could never focus with them. He had spent his life trying to achieve perfection in himself to counteract his mage flaws, but his every attempt failed.

Yet he never gave up. He kept hoping someday it would be different, that someday he would straighten the twists of his gift. Now he sat in the middle of the chamber and closed his eyes. Gradually his mind relaxed. When he had submerged into a trance, he opened his eyes and gazed at a hemisphere engraved on the wall in front of him. *Light,* he thought. He imagined the circular shape focusing it as a lens would focus sunlight.

Nothing.

After a while, Muller let his mind relax. He felt odd today, as if he stood on the edge of an abyss. He kept thinking of Iris, and it made him uneasy. Why did he feel as if she pushed him to the rim of that chasm?

The shapes on the curving walls intensified, until he saw them with a surreal clarity. Their power surged around his mind, a tangible force, but one denied to him. He reached for it, straining, and it eluded him.

Muller jumped to his feet, feeling as if he would burst. He heaved open the door and strode across the tower to another door. It opened into a room exactly like the one where he had just been—except imperfect shapes curled around the walls of this chamber, their forms either incomplete or distorted. Historians claimed the ancients had made the first chamber to help mages intensify their power and this one to imprison mages, trapping them with flawed shapes that diverted rather than focused their gifts.

Muller had his doubts. He had always wondered if other mages among his ancestors had also been born with this curse he suffered, an inability to use true shapes. His "talent" had to be in the Dawnfield line; mage traits were hereditary, another reason the queen had to be a powerful mage. This room could have been designed for them.

Again he sat cross-legged on the floor and centered himself. Power rose around him, erratic, dangerous, jagged. Opening his eyes, he focused on a shape, another hemisphere, this one with a chiseled gash in its upper arc. His power surged and he struggled for control, to focus the spells that wavered at the edges of his power.

Iris.

Why did he sense her? He searched with flawed spells, straining to understand. Incredibly, she was reaching with her mage gifts, not toward him, but across Aronsdale. Iris had finally harnessed her power. Dismayed, he fought the urge to lash out with his damaged spells and stop her before anyone realized her ability. He could never deliberately hurt anyone, especially Iris.

He felt the Other.

A power stirred unlike any Muller had known. It was impossibly far away; he should never have sensed it from here. But it was also impossibly huge. Unformed, untrained, and untamed, it filled the mountains like an immense bank of clouds. Iris reached across the valleys and mountains and rivers, beyond the forest and beneath the bowl of the sky, reaching, reaching, reaching—and touched that power.

Muller's world exploded in light.

Chime ran through the castle, her feet pounding on the stone floors. Muller's soundless scream reverberated in her mind, magnified by the uncontrolled burst of power that had torn through him. She took the spiraling stairs of the Mage Tower two at a time, never slowing as she passed landing after landing.

She came out at the top into an open area between two doors. Without hesitation, she heaved open the door on her right.

Muller lay sprawled inside the chamber.

Chime dropped down to kneel by him. He was lying on his side, his hair falling across his face. For one terrifying moment she thought he had died.

"Muller!" She shook his shoulder.

He rolled onto his back, opening his eyes, and she inhaled sharply, with relief. He stared up at the domed ceiling, his face dazed.

"Are you all right?" Chime struggled to form spell of sooth-ing, but the engravings in the room disrupted her focus. Her spells ripped on their jagged edges and fell apart.

"Iris?" Muller asked groggily.

Chime wondered if she should be offended. "I am not Iris."

His eyes focused. "No, you aren't." A smile curved his lips. "But you are truly a welcome sight."

"Hai, Muller! You scared me."

He sat up slowly. "Iris found him."

Chime looked him over for injuries. "Found who?"

"A mage."

"No! She discovered your secret?"

"Not me. Another mage."

"But where?"

"I'm not sure." He took a ragged breath. "We better find her. Everything just changed."

Muller paced in the Receiving Hall, his boots thudding on its tiled floor. He didn't see the sun-drenched room with its tes-sellated mosaics, didn't see anyone but Iris in the high-backed chair, her hands folded in her lap. He wished he felt even a frac-tion as calm as she looked.

"Are you certain?" he asked.

"Aye, Your Highness," Iris said.

"But Jarid is *dead!*" Muller stopped pacing. "My cousin, may he rest in peace, has been dead for fourteen years." He feared to believe her. When Daron had died, Muller had lost the last person he could call kin. To hope his cousin lived—no, he didn't dare.

Della was standing by Iris's chair, her hand resting on its high back. "His body was never found."

Muller resumed pacing, unable to stay still, his gait agitated. The floor was tiled in white hexagons, with blue hexagons nested within them, all the shapes too perfect to cause him trouble. "The rescue party thought he was thrown from the carriage when it went over the cliff. He could have fallen in any crevice. The caves and chasms in those mountains are a maze."

"It does seem impossible he survived," Della said.

Iris remained unperturbed. "Nevertheless, he did."

Muller stopped and frowned at her. "If that were true, he would have come home."

"How? He was a little boy."

"Not anymore. So where is he?" Muller demanded, probably louder than necessary. He so desperately needed to believe Jarid would have come back had he been able.

"I donna know," Iris said.

Her composure flustered him. He ought to quit bellowing; it wasn't helping. A good leader would encourage his people, win their confidence. But he didn't know how to be a good leader.

In a quieter voice, he said, "You say he exists, yet you don't know where."

"I can find him." Her face paled, making him suspect she had little desire to repeat her spell.

Muller wished Daron were here to advise him. He missed his uncle so intensely, he hurt inside. Although he could seek counsel from Brant, he had never been comfortable with the elder man, mainly because Brant had so many doubts about Muller's ability to rule. Knowing the saturnine lord was right didn't help Muller's confidence.

He came to a decision. "Very well," he told Iris. "Find him. Bring him here."

"Your Highness——" She hesitated.

Would she refuse? Worry made him stutter. "Yes, yes, speak up."

"Prince Jarid is the heir," she said.

"I know that."

"He can claim the crown."

"I doubt you will find him, but if by some incredible chance you do, he can have the title." The words came out before Muller had time to think them through.

Everyone froze, staring at him. He knew he shouldn't speak of his desire to give up the crown. It weakened his already shaky relations with the royal court, which would remain his court if Iris had made a mistake about this, which seemed likely.

"Your coronation is in ten days," Della said. "That hardly gives us time to look."

"Delay the coronation." It wouldn't be the first time. He had struggled these past months with an internal battle, dreading the crown but knowing he couldn't wed Chime until he accepted his title. If he had thought he was good enough for her, and for Aronsdale he would have set the coronation for tomorrow.

"It's been months," he said. "A few more days won't matter."

"It's been too long." Della pushed back the tendrils of silvery hair that had escaped the roll at her neck and were curling around her face. "Saints, Muller, you know the people are mourning King Daron. We've just come through a hard winter. They need the coronation as a symbol that life will continue. And Aronsdale needs a committed leader."

At the mention of his uncle, Muller felt bereft, missing a part of himself. He knew she was right, but he couldn't answer.

"The bishop canna coronate Lord Muller," Iris said calmly. "Prince Jarid is the heir."

Muller squinted at her. She had never called him "Lord" before. Unlike in the surrounding realms, in Aronsdale only the heir to the crown and his brothers used the title of prince. Muller had come into it only after Jarid died. Except Jarid wasn't dead, or so Iris claimed. How could this tale be true? No matter how long it took or how painful the truth, he had to know.

He took a deep breath. "If my cousin is alive, bring him to me."

13

The Lost Refuge

Unbent heard the strangers on the mountain before they came into view. Even if they were trying to hide their approach, their party was too large to keep secret. He waited at the edge of the clearing and listened to the clatter of hooves, of horses struggling for purchase on the steep ground. He didn't understand how they had found his cottage. No path led here through the stunted forest.

Maybe they hadn't found him. It could be coincidence they came up here. Perhaps a hunting party had gone astray in their search for game and had no idea anyone lived in this forsaken place. But that hope stretched even his credulity too far; these desolate woods had no game to entice a hunting party.

Unbent strode back to the cottage and opened the creaking door. He heard Dani inside working on thatching for the roof. The youth could do it by touch faster than Unbent had ever managed with sight.

A call came from behind him. "Ho! You there."

Unbent froze. Desperate, he reminded himself this wouldn't be the first time visitors had stumbled upon his cabin. He would do as always, introducing Dani as his son. Most people went out of their way to avoid the foreboding youth who could neither hear nor see. He turned slowly—

And knew he had trouble.

Eight soldiers were leading their horses across the clearing. The quality of their mounts and gear would have warned him this was a royal party even if they hadn't been wearing the king's colors, indigo, gold, and white. Their tunics and leggings, their chain mail and heavy boots, the insignia on their shields—it marked them as officers, seven hepta-lieutenants and a circle-captain. Three others came with them: a tall man with gray hair swept up from his forehead, surely a lord of importance; an older woman with a no-nonsense aura of authority; and a lovely young woman whose golden-brown curls framed her face and fell down her back.

Unbent stood in the doorway, his hands braced against the door frame. Icy wind blew his hair back from his face.

Within moments, people and horses were swirling before his cottage. The circle-captain came to him. "Good morn."

"My greetings." Unbent swallowed. "What brings the king's men here?"

The gray-haired lord walked forward with the older woman. The man stood taller than Unbent, indeed taller than anyone else there. He spoke with an aura of authority. "We come in friendship, Goodman—" He let the title hang like a question.

"Unbent." He could barely say his name.

The man nodded to him. "My greetings, Goodman Unbent. I am Brant Firestoke." Although he gave no title, Unbent could hear the "Lord" that should precede the name.

Firestoke indicated the woman with him. "Della No-Cozen, Shape-Mage Mistress of Suncroft."

Dizziness swept over Unbent. The mage mistress at the castle stood extraordinarily close to the king. And now that he thought about it, Firestoke sounded like the name of the king's highest advisor. Somehow he made his voice work. "King Daron honors me to send such notables to my home." He felt panicked rather than honored.

His guests regarded him oddly. Firestoke said, "King Daron passed away over three months ago."

Ai! Unbent thought he should quit now and curl up on the floor. "My—my apologies. I meant no offense."

"None given," the mage mistress said briskly. "We come to see your companion."

His companion? Dani, perhaps, though he didn't see how they could know he had a foster son. Perhaps they were guessing, trying to discover information. He spoke carefully. "I am pleased to help King—" He hesitated, unsure who to name. "King Muller. But I don't know who you mean by my companion. I have no wife."

Firestoke's voice crackled like parchment. "Prince Muller has not yet had his coronation."

Saints above. Unbent hadn't believed a person could blunder so often in so short a time. "I am sorry. Terribly sorry."

The young woman came over and inclined her head with respect, which flustered him even more. No one nodded that way to him. She dressed as a noble woman, in a fine velvety tunic and sky-blue leggings, with a gray riding cape and a billowy hood that covered about half her hair. But she spoke with the cadences of the Tallwalks, a mountainous region here in western Aronsdale.

"My name is Iris," she said. "May we see your ward?"

Unbent felt as if he were withering inside. How could they know about Dani? They couldn't take his son. It would kill him. "I'm sorry." His voice shook. "I don't know who you mean."

Firestoke glanced at the captain. The officer nodded in response and then approached Unbent. "We regret intruding on your privacy. However, we must see the youth who lives here."

Unbent wanted to refuse. "I have no——"

"Goodman Unbent." The captain spoke firmly. "We must see him."

Unbent knew then that if he denied them entrance, they would come inside anyway. With courtesy, perhaps, but without hesitation. Feeling bowed under a great weight, he walked into his house. Boots and mail clanked as they followed. He stopped at Dani's room, but he couldn't go inside. He couldn't do it.

A hepta-lieutenant stepped past him and pushed open the door, which had no knob. It swung inward, creaking on rusted hinges. Dani was sitting on the floor across the room, his back to the wall, his head lifted, his unfocused gaze turned in their direction.

"I'm sorry," Unbent whispered to him. Unfamiliar smells filled the cabin: dust and mud, wet wool, leather. Dani would know people had arrived.

The youth lurched to his feet, his fists clenched in front of him, alarm on his chiseled face. Unbent tried to go to him, but two lieutenants grasped his arms, one on each side, firmly holding him back.

Unbent strained in their grip. "Don't hurt him!"

Another lieutenant stepped into Dani's room, but then Iris spoke. "No. Let me go."

The officer glanced at Firestoke. When the lord nodded, the officer stepped back, letting Iris move by him. She walked toward Dani, slowly, her tread muted on the rough planked floor. The soldiers tensed, their hands on the hilts of their sheathed swords. Attuned to mages after so many years with Dani, Unbent felt Mistress No-Cozen's spells swirl in the room. Soothing spells. For his son.

Dani stretched out his arms, his palms outward as if to push back the invaders. Iris stopped a few paces away. She took an audible breath and then continued on, right up to him. The officers followed, ready to protect her.

Iris touched Dani's shoulder.

He swung around, his fist half open. The heel of his hand hit her shoulder and she jumped back, her face suffused with color. Then he jerked up his arms to defend himself. It dismayed Unbent to see his son so close to the edge, fighting his panic. He tried again to go to Dani, but the officers tightened their grip on his arms until it became painful. He had no mail, no armor, nothing but the flimsy, frayed cloth of his shirt.

"Let me go," Unbent said. "He's frightened."

"Give her time," Della murmured.

Iris went back to Dani. She brushed his arm, her touch so careful, her fingers only rustled the faded cloth of his shirt. He turned toward her, his shoulders hunched, his back pressed to the wall and his arms in front of his body. Unbent could only imagine how he must feel, faced with a room full of strangers he could neither see nor hear, people he had no reason to believe wouldn't harm him.

The soldiers had moved into the room and were only a few paces away from Dani and Iris now, except for the two who held Unbent. He fought his growing agitation, knowing it would do Dani no good if he struggled with these two and they knocked him out.

Then Dani reached toward Iris, his gesture curious rather than defensive. He wanted to touch her, it was how he greeted people. Unbent's hope leapt; the boy was going to let her stay. Her serene manner had calmed him. It would be all right, he wouldn't snap after all—

Then one of the lieutenants grasped Dani's arm.

"No!" Unbent cried. "Don't touch him!"

His warning came too late. In the same instant Dani touched Iris's cheek, the lieutenant pulled him away from the girl.

Dani panicked.

The boy whipped around, his fists swinging, his face contorted. Unbent went a little crazy himself then, wrestling with the men who held him back. As he struggled, he saw Dani grappling with three soldiers. They didn't strike out; instead, they tried to calm him. It did no good. Dani was a large man, well developed from work and exercise, and he fought with single-minded intensity. But as well as his physical prowess served him, it wasn't enough. Every time he freed himself from one tormentor, another caught him. No matter how great his strength or speed, he faced too many opponents—and they could see.

It took three soldiers to immobilize Dani. They pressed him against the wall and one of them laid a cloth against his face, covering his nose and mouth.

"Leave him alone!" Unbent shouted. One of his captors raised his fist to strike him, a blow that could break bones, judged by the man's muscled size. Unbent froze, his chest heaving. After watching him with narrowed eyes, the man lowered his fist.

Whatever soaked the cloth worked its evil on Dani. The boy sagged forward and would have fallen if the warriors hadn't held him up. His head dropped to his chest and his lashes lowered over his eyes.

"Why are you doing this?" Unbent cried. "He has hurt no one."

"But others have hurt him." Firestoke's voice came out like ice as he turned to Unbent, his face set in hard lines. "You will pay for what you have done, highwayman. You will pay."

Then they took Dani away, out of the cottage, without even letting Unbent tell his son farewell.

"The peddler troubles me."

Muller paced the tower chamber, stalking past Chime. She

Catherine Asaro

stood by the curving wall with its imperfect shapes, trying to forget the uncertainty that had rent their lives. Della and Iris had been gone for ten days. Their absence felt like a swinging blade. So for now, they tried to think of other matters.

"Why don't you like Wareman?" she asked. "He is courteous. And his goods are of high quality."

He stopped in front of her, his angel's face shadowed by the sweep of his hair. "Something in him is missing."

She laid her hands on his shoulders. "People say that about me, too. Sometimes a person doesn't come across well, even when they have good intentions."

Muller slid his arms around her waist. "Anyone who says such about you is utterly blind."

She dimpled. "Or else you are."

"Never." He kissed her, then let her go and indicated the room, with its walls of pale violet stone adorned by engravings. They reminded her of the strategy game Rocklace she had played with her parents and older brother, where a player earned points by making designs with small polished stones.

"Do you feel the power in this room?" he asked. "Does it make jagged lines in you?"

She shook her head. "I can't grasp it. I wish I could understand why the spells are so different for you."

He gave a self-deprecatory laugh. "So do I."

Chime hesitated. "You are different with me."

"What do you mean?"

She picked her words with care, trying to avoid the wrong ones. "You let me see your humility. Your vulnerability. To everyone else, you are this beautiful, glittering box with no flaw. But you let no one open the top and see inside."

"Because if they do, they will discover the truth. My defects. And then?" He averted his gaze. "I truly hope this man Iris found is Jarid. Aronsdale needs a king. Not me."

It made her ache to see him so convinced he would be less able to govern Aronsdale than someone who had grown up away from the court all these years. "You have spent half your life preparing to wear the crown. You shouldn't denigrate yourself."

Muller laughed softly. "I do believe, angel, that you are the only person alive who believes I am capable of denigrating myself."

Chime wanted to protest, but telling him other people thought he could denigrate himself would hardly be the most helpful statement. "I don't know about that. But you shouldn't do it."

He lifted his hand and lightly brushed her cheek. She felt an echo of power, as if a spell stirred. Suddenly light flashed at Muller's fingertip and a spark jumped from his hand to her face. She stumbled back, her palm over her cheek, her skin burning.

"No!" He raised his hands, palms out. "Chime, I'm sorry, I'm so sorry. I didn't mean—"

"It's all right." She lowered her hand from her face. "It doesn't hurt." And it was true; the burning had faded.

"I despise myself." He turned on his heel and strode out of the room.

She exhaled as the echoes of his power receded. At times like this, when it gathered within him, she sensed its currents, wild and chaotic. If only he could learn to harness that incredible power. But she knew of no spell that could heal his troubled gift.

Pyramid-Secretary Quill was part of the staff assigned to Chime. Today she and Quill sat at a polished table in Chime's ivory parlor. Quill was arranging her schedule. In the morning, Chime would study with Della, learning magecraft. At noon, she would lunch with emissaries from the Blacksmith's Guild who represented metal workers in Aronsdale, discussing how to keep prices for their work accessible to the majority of the population without undercutting the living of the blacksmiths. In the afternoon, she would see her history tutors, who were teaching her more detail than she had ever imagined wanting to know about the country she would serve as queen. For supper, she would dine with Muller.

Chime dreaded meeting with the guild representatives. Her grasp of economics barely extended to knowing how many coins it took to run an orchard. Discussing the finances of an entire country gave her a stomachache. It didn't help that Mistress Forge, the iron-haired women who led the Blacksmith's Guild, made Della No-Cozen seem cuddly in comparison. Mercifully, Brant Firestoke would do the negotiating at the meeting. But Chime feared her lack of experience would show, adding to her mortifying reputation of being slow in the mind.

Still, Chime was learning, despite herself. Her mother, Bell, would be proud to see her progress. Bell had tried for years to teach her these type of organizational skills, which Chime would have also needed as an orchard keeper. And Chime had to acknowledge she benefited from learning the history of Aronsdale; as queen, she would need to make wise decisions, not repeat past mistakes. When she wrote her mother, she spoke about her studies as positively as she could manage, but in truth she felt stifled. Knowing she would see Muller tonight, though, made the rest more palatable.

"You won't have many breaks." Quill showed her the schedule. "Perhaps a few minutes after lunch—"

"You might want to wait on that," a brisk voice said.

Chime looked up with a start. Della No-Cozen stood in the doorway of the parlor.

"Della!" Chime jumped to her feet. "When did you get back?" She felt as if she were teetering on a precipice. If Iris hadn't found Jarid Dawnfield, Muller would take the crown and Iris would become his queen.

Della had an odd quality. She seemed…subdued. She glanced at Quill.

The secretary stood up and bowed to Chime. "Shall we finish later, milady?"

"Yes. Of course." Chime nodded to her. "Thank you."

Della waited until Quill left and closed the door. Then she said, simply, "We found Prince Jarid."

Relief flooded over Chime. "That is wonderful!"

The mage mistress wasn't smiling. "Perhaps."

"What is wrong?"

"Chime—" Della paused.

"Tell me."

Della spoke tiredly. "He has lived all this time in the Boxer-Mage Mountains, barely scratching out a living with his guardian. He is like a wild man." Then she said, "And he is deaf, blind, and mute."

Chime stared at her. "Saints above. What happened?"

"We think he was hurt in the carriage accident."

"Who is his guardian?"

"A man called Unbent." Della spread her hands out, her palms upward. "He tells us nothing. And Jarid can't speak."

Chime's thoughts whirled. "What does it all mean?"

Della shook her head. "The youth we found is unfit to rule, but Iris swears he is the Dawnfield heir."

"What do you think?"

"Have you seen the portraits of King Daron as a youth?" When Chime nodded, Della said, "If you clean this man up, he would look almost exactly like Daron in those pictures."

Chime tried to make sense of it all. "Did you bring him here?"

"Yes. They had to keep him unconscious, though."

"But why?"

Della grimaced. "He otherwise attacked everyone who came near him."

"Surely his guardian can calm him down."

"Brant Firestoke left the man behind, in the custody of several officers from the King's Army."

It seemed harsh to separate Jarid from the person who took care of him. Chime could imagine how frightened Jarid must have been to leave the home he had known for years, unable to hear or see what was happening, or speak in protest.

And yet—as much as Brant often angered her, it always seemed to turn out that he had good reason for his actions. She was usually too busy resenting his lectures to admit that to him, but she acknowledged it to herself.

"Did Unbent mistreat Prince Jarid?" she asked.

"We don't know." Della rubbed her eyes, her fatigue showing through her usual stoicism. "I didn't have that impression, but we don't know enough yet. Brant separated them because he doesn't want Unbent to influence the person who may rule Aronsdale, even if in name only."

Chime didn't see how Jarid could be king. If they crowned him, they would also want him to marry Iris, for in unleashing her gifts, she had revealed her full power. Chime knew Iris felt a debt to the King's Advisors, who had made it possible for her to leave a life with no future and come to Suncroft. If they pushed for the marriage, she would probably agree. That meant a country girl with no experience would end up as the acting ruler of Aronsdale. Had Iris spent her life preparing for the title, Chime thought she would do well. But only Muller had that training. He couldn't take the crown unless the King's Advisors refused to accept Jarid as heir. They had serious doubts about Muller's suitability, yes, but those might pale compared to Jarid's difficulties.

A sinking feeling came over Chime. Together, Muller and Iris could do a far better job for Aronsdale than she and Muller. The idea tore at her. If Iris believed Jarid was the rightful heir, though, then even if the King's Advisors decreed otherwise, she might refuse to marry Muller. Her loyalty to the royal family would most likely outweigh her sense of debt to the King's Advisors. But if she refused their wishes, it would set her against them and cause a crisis for Aronsdale.

Chime grimaced as her thoughts circled around and around. "This is a mess."

"Yes." Della regarded her bleakly. "A mess."

14

Shadowed Mage

Two guards flanked the door of the chamber, large and imposing, in chain mail, the hilts of their sheathed swords gleaming at their sides. The auburn one spoke to Chime, apologetic. "I'm not sure you should enter, milady. Perhaps if you came back with Lord Firestoke—?"

Chime lifted her chin, striving not to let them know how much they flustered her. She was a mage; she outranked them in the royal court. She didn't want to ask Brant, who would almost certainly forbid her to visit this tower room. He was forever constraining their lives.

She gave the guards a haughty stare she hoped would hide how intimidated she felt. "I don't need the permission of Frant Birestoke."

The auburn man cleared his throat, though it sounded like he was trying to cover up a startled laugh. The other guard ducked his head, smiling. A flush spread on her cheeks. No wonder people thought her stupid, the way she garbled her words when she was nervous.

"Milady," the auburn guard began.

She spoke more carefully this time. "Shall I tell the mage mistress you refused me?"

He blanched, the color draining from his ruddy cheeks. "Nay, milady, please, you needn't bring Mistress No-Cozen."

Having been the source of Della's ire on more than one occasion, Chime sympathized with his alarm. "Very well. Please open the door."

He hesitated, then spoke firmly. "If he wakes up, you must call us in immediately."

Relief washed over her. "I will do so, Lieutenant."

He bowed to her. Then he opened the door and let her inside, giving her the chance to satisfy her raging curiosity.

The chamber was a tiled box, with eight walls, a domed ceiling and a tiled floor. On the octagonal table, a rose-glass lamp burned with a low flame, casting more shadows than light. A four-poster bed stood against the far wall. As Chime's eyes adjusted to the dimness, she made out a man asleep on the bed.

Jarid.

She went close enough to see him sleeping on his side, his wrists tied to a bed post. Her breath caught. They dared too much, binding him that way. Every one of them surely recognized this man. He had the same dark hair as the portraits of the young King Daron, the same handsome features and broad shoulders, the Dawnfield long legs. He resembled the late king, yes, but even stronger, taller, more fine of feature.

The resemblance ended there, however. King Daron had epitomized culture and elegance. This man was wild. He wore rags, all gray. A scar ran down his neck from his ear. His hair lay across his back in matted tangles and stubble covered his chin.

Chime didn't envy Iris marrying this stranger. Yet Iris continued to insist he was Jarid. Anyone could see his heredity, but if Iris expressed any doubt at all, no one would hold her to her initial judgment. Too much was at stake to make an error. Chime knew Iris had no wish for the crown; the Tallwalk mage stood by her assertion because she was honest. If Iris said this man was the grandson of the late king, she believed it to be true.

The man stirred, restless, and an odd sensation came to Chime. At first she didn't understand. Then she realized spells were swirling around her, diffuse, hard to define, unfocused. *He was a mage.* His power suffused the room even as he slept, pouring through her with a strength she had never experienced from Muller, Della, or Iris. He wove a type of mood spell she had never encountered before. It made her recall her youth in Jacob's Vale, the balmy summer nights when she and her friend Merry had snuck off to the barn and stayed up late, making squares of red light when no one else could see. They used to tell stories, especially those of legendary power within the Dawnfield line, whose ancient kings had reputedly wielded incredible mage gifts. But a limit existed. A mage might be strong enough to save a life, but no more, for the mage had only one life to give if the spell somehow turned around.

But those were only stories. It made Chime wonder if she overestimated the power of this stranger; whatever dreams haunted his sleep might create a misleading sense of his abilities, a sense, magnified by the high-level shape of this room. She hoped so, for she dreaded to think what it would mean if a mage of such incredible—and untamed—power were let loose in Aronsdale.

Chime found Muller at the top of the Mage Tower in the chamber with perfect shapes. He stood by the window staring out at Aronsdale. Going to stand behind him, she bowed her head and set her palm against his back.

"Chime." He whispered her name.

"You must do what you believe right." Her eyes felt hot with unshed tears. "Even if it means taking Iris as your bride."

"She deserves better. So do you." He spoke with difficulty. "Aronsdale deserves better."

"You misjudge yourself."

He turned then and pulled her into his arms. She held him close, her cheek against his shoulder.

"I know what I must do." His words sounded muffled against her hair.

She couldn't bear to hear any more, but she had to know. "What have you decided?"

He drew back to look into her face. "For so long I feared the day when I would have to wear the crown. Then you came, and I began to believe that maybe, just maybe, I could be a good king. You made me believe. I cannot tell you how much that meant to me. For the first time in my life, I've felt as if I were more than everyone's last choice." His voice caught. "Now I must do what is right for Aronsdale—regardless of what I want."

Chime touched the tears on his face. "I know."

Della paused in the doorway of the room in the Starlight Tower. Unaware of her, Iris sat in a chair by the bed, watching Jarid. The guards had bound the unconscious youth's wrists to a bed post, but Iris must have freed him. He lay on his back now, sleeping, one hand resting palm down on his stomach.

She wished Iris hadn't untied him. The girl believed she could have coaxed Jarid to come of his own free will, given more time. Perhaps she could have. But they had bungled their chance to earn his trust up at his cabin in the Boxer-Mage Mountains. The range seemed apt, somehow. The mountains took their name from a hermit who had retreated there centuries ago, embittered when he lost his family. Only the desperate lived in those cruel peaks, outcasts who had little to lose. Such as Jarid? No one knew what he might do when he awoke.

Iris reached out to the stranger asleep on the bed, then pulled back her hand and set it in her lap, as if embarrassed by her wish to touch him. Her impulse didn't surprise Della. For all his ragged appearance, he was a compelling man. How he and Iris had formed their remarkable bond or what would come of it, Della couldn't say, but she had no doubt it existed.

She spoke quietly. "Muller has made the announcement."

Iris turned with a start. Seeing Della, her shoulders hunched. She didn't ask what Della meant; she seemed to know instinctively. "He stepped aside for Jarid?"

Della nodded, suddenly tired. "Yes." She crossed the room and sunk down into a chair next to Iris. "It is official. Muller accepts this man as heir to the crown."

At first Iris said nothing, as if she were absorbing the news. Finally she spoke. "Will he help us with Prince Jarid?"

Prince. Iris had never doubted Jarid deserved that title. In her mind, Della could see Muller's haunted expression as he told her of his decision. "He plans to leave Suncroft. He thinks it best."

"But, nay! He canna just walk away."

"I'm afraid he can."

"He must realize Jarid canna rule."

Della understood Muller's decision; for him to stay at Suncroft after he gave up the crown could be seen as a deliberate provocation of Jarid. Aronsdale couldn't have two kings. But Jarid needed his cousin's help, but Muller didn't believe he could do more good by staying, and no argument Della had tried would convince him otherwise.

"He says the King's Advisors can help." Della thought of Brant's unconcealed disapproval of Muller. "What can they answer? Muller knew they expected to do exactly that with him. He says Brant is better suited to govern."

Iris regarded her steadily. "Muller is angry."

"Perhaps. But he believes what he says." Della glanced at Jarid. She envied his sound sleep. Regardless of how serene he looked now, however, he could be dangerous when he awoke. "You shouldn't have untied him."

"What will we do," Iris demanded. "Take him to his coronation in chains?"

"If we must."

"This is all wrong."

"Iris—"

"Yes?"

"I'm afraid there's more."

"More what?"

"From the King's Advisors."

"What do they say?"

Della spoke carefully. "We are all in agreement."

Iris regarded her warily. "About what?"

"Only a sphere mage could have reached across the great distance that separated this man from you."

Iris nodded, her face earnest. "Aye, Della, I think it is true. His talent is incredible."

"I didn't mean him."

Iris frowned. "Well and sure, it couldna been me."

"No one else."

"It was him who touched my mind."

"I was there. You initiated the contact."

"That canna be. Never have I even lit a room."

Della gentled her voice. "A room, no. But the trees and meadows, I think yes. The countryside stirs your power. That is why you have had so much trouble making spells. Inside the cottage, you didn't know how to reach the core within you."

Iris started to protest, then stopped. Della wondered how long she would avoid the truth. She kept at the girl, gently but without relenting. Finally Della said, simply, "Our greatest shape-mage must marry the king."

"Aye. Chime."

"No. Not Chime."

Comprehension swept across Iris's face. "Nay, Della. I canna be queen!"

"You must."

"Nay!"

"I am sorry. I know this is a shock." Della feared Iris would flee back to the Tallwalk Mountains, leaving Chime to marry Jarid. It would be a disaster. Muller would fight it. So would Chime. If they eloped, what then? Della had been lucky to find Chime and Iris, both unusually strong mages. She doubted she could find a third of child-bearing age. Aronsdale would have no mage queen.

Iris averted her gaze. "He is like a wild, injured creature. He doesn't even know my name."

Della laid a hand on her arm. "We need you. Please don't leave."

Iris gave her a startled look. "I can refuse?"

"We won't force you to marry." If they made Iris take the title and its responsibilities against her will, her anger could bring grief to Aronsdale. "But we need you. Desperately. Please don't turn away now."

Sorrow made Iris's voice bittersweet. "I canna be what you want."

"Then be yourself."

"It is not enough."

Della wished she could show Iris the potential that shone within her, untapped and new. "I believe it is."

Iris drew in a shaky breath. "When I agreed to come to Suncroft, I gave my word that I would do my best to fulfill what you saw in me. I had so little before. No family, no future, no one who wanted me. You have given me a home, though I give nothing back at all. If this marriage be so important—" Her voice cracked. "I can try, Della. But I canna promise I willna fail."

"Thank you." Della was breaking inside, seeing how much this hurt Iris. "None of us can make such a promise. We can only do our best."

"Aye." Moisture filled Iris's eyes. "None of us."

"It is a disaster." Brant stood at the window with Della gazing across to the Starlight Tower. He could see into a room there lit by orbs-bud candles. Iris sat next to the bed, her head bent as she kept vigil on their slumbering prisoner.

Della spoke wearily. "This matter of heredity reeks. We are asking children to do jobs people twice their age find crushing."

Brant could feel the weight of their youth. Jarid had just turned twenty and Iris was barely nineteen. For all that Muller frustrated him, Brant would have considered him best suited of these three to take the crown. Muller not only had the training, but of late he had shown a new maturity. With a good set of advisors, he might have managed. Jarid and Iris were ciphers—very confused ciphers.

"She has no idea what to do," Brant said. His fear for Aronsdale flared like mage-light. Nor was it only the country; he had grown fond of Iris, who reminded him of his daughter. Although he had come to respect her judgment these past months, she wasn't ready for so immense a responsibility.

"She is intelligent," Della said.

"That isn't enough." Brant turned to her. "We cannot crown that man tomorrow. What if he goes berserk during the ceremony? Our people are already demoralized. If they think we are giving them a lunatic for a king, saints only know what will happen. Aronsdale is weakened, easy prey. Without strong leadership, we may fall to Harsdown."

Della just looked at him. He knew his sharp words might fool most people, but not her. Jarid evoked so much of Daron, the king Brant had served with loyalty, respect, and the love of a brother. After Daron had passed away, Brant had fortified his emotional barricades, lest grief overwhelm him. Now came this boy, the image of his grandfather, wild and in such need of help, and Brant didn't know how to deal with him. He held up his distrust of Jarid like a shield, but the youth weakened his defenses.

"And if we cancel the coronation yet again?" Della asked. "What message does that send—that Aronsdale is such a mess, we cannot choose a leader?" She shook her head. "We put off crowning Muller too long."

"With good reason. The boy was ready to bolt."

"Well, now he has bolted," Della said flatly. "The situation isn't going to improve. I say this—clean up this man, bring him out tomorrow, put the crown on him and let Iris rule."

That sounded to Brant like a good formula for collapsing the government. "She has no training."

"She has aptitude."

"That isn't enough."

"We can guide her."

He gave her an incredulous look. "And just how do we explain her husband? He may not even make it through the ceremony without losing control."

"Bring his foster father here. He seems to calm the boy."

Brant weighed his answer. Almost no one knew he had already brought Unbent to Suncroft—and locked him in a cell. He wanted the highwayman where he could question him personally. But he hadn't told Della. If she decided to tell Jarid, nothing Brant could do would stop her. Unbent had already caused the boy great harm; the less time Jarid spent with the man who had crushed his life, the better.

He said only, "No."

"Why not?"

"I don't want him influencing our future king."

Della crossed her arms. "Just how long are your men going to hold him in custody?"

"It is better we separate Jarid from him. The boy needs a fresh start."

"And if Jarid wants him at the coronation?"

"We delay the ceremony."

"We can't. You know that. We have waited too long already." Della glanced toward the tower room where a frightened young woman sat with a lost young man. "Convincing Muller he wants the crown has become irrelevant. We must work with what we have. Waiting won't change that."

Brant knew what she feared. Harsdown grew stronger each day, as did King Varqelle's drive to conquer other lands. Aronsdale prevailed against them in border skirmishes because of its mages, who healed the wounded, buttressed morale, and predicted strategies based on the emotions of the enemies they fought. But Aronsdale was a fragile realm; if their will faltered, they could fall.

He spoke with reluctance. "Very well." He gave Della a dour look. "Just pray we all survive the ceremony."

A touch disturbed Jarid. He woke slowly, his mind hazed. The person stroking his forehead couldn't be Stone, his father; this hand was too small, with longer fingers and fewer calluses.

A woman.

As he caught her hand, images of octagonal boxes formed in his thoughts. It sometimes happened this way, his mental shapes mimicking his location. That implied he was imprisoned within an octagonal room. The images focused his mind, revealing her mood. She was…in pain?

Startled, he realized he was gripping her wrist too hard. He hadn't meant to hurt her. Chagrined, he released his hold. Although she pulled away, she didn't go far. Her scent came to him: woods, fresh grass, pine soap. This room smelled much cleaner the cottage where he lived with his foster father. The fragrance of orbs-bud candles filled the air. Memories flooded him: the dinner table alight with candles and rose-glass lamps; his father bidding him good night and blowing out candles in his room; his mother holding a candlestick, her wedding ring sparkling, inset with diamonds and amethysts.

What is this place? Jarid had no voice to ask. He felt his companion's mage gifts, but he couldn't tell what she wanted. He wasn't certain she knew herself.

Reaching above his head, he found a bedpost, its wood carved with shape-blossoms, their petals forming boxes and orbs. They felt familiar. Agitated, he struggled into a sitting position on the bed. Stone would never have let these people take him, and not because Jarid could implicate him in crimes. Stone protected him.

But…Stone wasn't here.

Jarid searched with his mind, spinning sphere images to focus. He found no hint of his father's emotions, only those of guards outside this room. The only reason they hadn't come in here was because the woman hadn't let them know he had awoken. Her mind glowed, ruddy flames lighting his isolation. Warm. Inviting.

Go away, he thought, afraid of that warmth.

He knew when she moved because air currents shifted. He wanted to strike out, as he had done with his attackers in the cottage. But her mood warmed him, like sunlight. She soothed.

Jarid gritted his teeth. He didn't want to be soothed. He preferred anger. These people had torn him away from his home and brought him to this place against his will.

A hand touched his forehead and he jerked away, wincing as pain stabbed his muscles, which ached from his fight with the strangers in the cabin. He slid back, away from the woman until he came up against a wall. Then he sat, one leg bent, his elbow resting on his knee, his hand curled in a fist.

The bed shifted, sagging with a new weight. Even as he tensed, someone brushed his arm. In instinct, he raised his fist. The intruder withdrew, which was what he told himself he wanted. No doubt he appeared gruesome to her. That thought bothered him more than he wanted to admit.

Then she returned and laid a tablet on his lap. The smell of wet earth tickled his nose. Baffled, he ran his fingers over the tablet. Its center was clay. He pressed the soft material, noting its cool, grainy texture.

Her long fingers brushed his hand, sending a shiver through him. It had to be from anger; her touch couldn't give him pleasure. He refused to allow it. He would retreat into the fortress of his mind and keep out pain.

She pressed her fingers into the clay, her hand moving against his so he felt her actions. Then she set his hand over the dents she made. It took him a moment to comprehend; many years had passed since he had touched such shapes. Words. Pictures. She was writing to him.

Jarid shifted his weight. Although by the age of six, he had learned some basics of reading, his education had ended then. He recognized only a few of her symbols. The disk shape sharpened his mind, though, stirring memories. He traced one picture she had made, a circle within a cluster of lines—no, an orb within crossed swords.

His family crest.

No! Jarid hurled the tablet away. He didn't hear it shatter, though surely it broke when it hit. He couldn't bear the truth she brought. But however much he fought it, deep in his mind he had known the moment he smelled the orbs-bud candles.

They had brought him home.

15

Hall of Kings

Muller opened the door to find Iris in the tower room, staring at Jarid—who was wide-awake and free, standing by the bed. His hair tangled around his shoulders and anger darkened his face. He lifted his head like a wild stag trying to catch an unexpected scent. Muller stepped into the room, concerned for Iris's safety. It disquieted him to know that he and this stranger were almost certainly cousins. Jarid seemed more animal to him than man.

Doubts tormented Muller, as they had since yesterday when he had relinquished the crown. Had he made the right choice? After months of knowing Iris, he believed that with help, she could become an inspired leader. He had grappled with his knowledge of her mage gifts ever since she came to Suncroft, knowing he should pursue the matter with Della but unable to bear losing Chime.

Della had no reason to take his judgment over her own. He could have convinced her by revealing his twisted mage power, but he would have lost everything: what little respect he had earned among his advisors, the safety of everyone's assumption that he hadn't inherited the Dawnfield talents—and Chime. Iris's discovery of Jarid had seemed like a gift, saving him from all that.

But like everything else Muller touched, this gift had twisted. Neither he nor Jarid were fit to rule.

So Muller had made the best decision he could. Aronsdale would be better off with Iris as leader, guided by the King's Advisors. He had done what he believed right, but uncertainty plagued him. He hadn't realized how much it had mattered to him that he would someday lead Aronsdale until he had relinquished that title.

Iris turned to him, her gaze questioning his presence here. He wanted to reassure her that he meant no harm, but Jarid riveted his attention. Muller crossed the chamber, never taking his gaze from his cousin. Jarid remained still, his forehead creased. Muller stopped in front of him and they faced each other, the same height, one light, the other dark. But Jarid wasn't looking at him; his gaze was directed to the left of Muller's shoulder.

Muller passed his hand in front of Jarid's eyes. His cousin didn't even blink; he just stood, his body tensed. Finally Muller found his voice. "Can you hear me, cousin?"

No reaction.

"Won't you speak?" Muller asked.

Jarid tilted his chin, but made no other response.

Muller glanced at Iris. "It is true, then. He has no sight. He hears nothing."

She nodded, her face pale.

"He has no voice."

"None," she said.

Muller struggled to contain his doubts. He couldn't withdraw his decision to give up the crown; it would throw Aronsdale into another turmoil. They couldn't hide the truth about Jarid much longer; too many people already knew. They had to deal with this carefully, lest it further damage a realm already grieving for its late king.

He could see fear in Jarid's unseeing gaze. Did he fool himself in thinking he also saw recognition? Perhaps. He might never know.

Muller spoke in a numb voice. "May your reign be long and full, my cousin."

Chime's breath caught as she entered the great Shape-Hall. Hundreds of candles glowed in candelabras, and lamps added their luster, filling the room with radiance. Gold and white mosaics gleamed on the high ceiling, and starlight flowed through floor-to-ceiling window panels.

Hundreds of guests mingled tonight, the royal court of Suncroft and gentlefolk of Aronsdale, glistening all. The men wore silk shirts, brocaded vests, and rich leggings, or uniforms with crisp tunics and trousers. The women dressed in lovely gowns that swept the floor, each a single hue; altogether they made a rainbow of color.

A stir came from across the hall. Hoping Muller had arrived, Chime turned toward the commotion. She didn't recognize the noblewoman who entered. Then, incredibly, she realized it was Iris. The other girl wore a luminous yellow gown that clung to her body, and topazes threaded the chestnut hair piled high on her head. Although Iris appeared calm and collected, Chime knew her well enough to recognize the truth; she was stunned, in a daze.

It surprised her to see Iris in yellow. On formal occasions, a mage dressed in the hue of her power. If Iris was a sapphire, as Della believed, she would wear blue. Knowing Iris, Chime suspected that Iris didn't believe she had reached Jarid with her magecraft. In truth, Chime didn't see how the two of them could have managed it even together. Either Iris could call on higher colors than sapphire, or Jarid had done it on his own, which would make him a mage with a power greater than any known in history.

Flanked by Brant and Della, Iris took her place at the head of a reception line to greet their guests. Even after accepting that Iris would assume such duties, Chime felt a pang of loss. She reminded herself that only a year ago she had wanted nothing to do with Suncroft. But since then she had come to accept her duties; now she felt adrift, unsure where she fit. As much as she missed her family, she was involved in life here now. She folded her hand around the pendant she wore, a faceted emerald ball on a gold chain. She could no longer imagine going home to tend the orchards.

"She looks different," a voice said, rich and light.

Chime turned with a start. Muller was leaning against the column, beautiful in ivory and gold, his hair gleaming, his blue eyes intent on her.

"My greetings," Chime said.

"You are lovely tonight."

She smiled. "So are you." Thoroughly.

He scowled at her, his face radiant even when he was angry. "Chime, that is not a compliment."

"Would you prefer some mud?" She grinned. "We could go slide around in it."

He laughed ruefully. "It would certainly give everyone here a good shake up."

"That it would." Her smile faded. "It feels so strange the way everything has suddenly changed."

Muller looked across the hall at Iris in the receiving line. "It is harder than I expected."

She took his hand. "Come walk outside with me."

He gave her a look of relief and nodded. They wandered out of the hall, past open double-doors with panes of beveled glass. Beyond them, the gardens waited, graced by what poets called the Azure Moon, full and blue in the sky, with the barest film of clouds veiling its disk. Its luminous rays silvered the sculpted bushes. One sculpture reared like a great dragon, the Saint of Chaos attacking a maze of trimmed bushes. Chime understood the moral of the Chaos story, that without tumult, serenity had no meaning. But the images still unsettled her. She drew closer to Muller, glad for his arm around her shoulders.

They strolled into the woods, where moss-draped trees overhung their way and thorny vines heavy with silvery blossoms curled on the tiled path. It was as if they were escaping the real world into a mystical realm free from the uncertainties of their lives.

Muller squeezed her shoulders. "You are so tense."

"It isn't over," she said in a low voice.

"Iris and Jarid have a difficult route." His strained tone hinted at his tension, but Chime respected his privacy and made no mood spell.

"It isn't only Iris and Jarid." She shivered, though the night was warm. "Sometimes I feel Harsdown glowering in the dark, crouched across the mountains like a beast waiting to spring."

His arm tightened around her. "Uncle Daron and I met with King Varqelle a few years ago. We hoped to arrange a treaty that would let our merchants cross his lands. It was hopeless. Varqelle has no interest in compromise. He sees Aronsdale the way a lion sees a deer."

"Do you think he will invade?"

"I don't know." Muller pushed aside a loop of vines hanging in their way. "He knows it would be a grueling war. Harsdown has a larger population than Aronsdale, including more trained warriors, which means he can put together a bigger army. But we are more robust. With our mages, we can do more. It evens up our sides."

"I don't really understand why mages give us an advantage. I know they heal and predict, but it is more, yes?" She asked in part to draw his attention away from his disheartened thoughts about tonight's ceremonies.

"It isn't one thing in particular," he said thoughtfully. "By itself, each mage talent wouldn't be enough to make such a big difference." As always, he talked naturally to her, treating her as the intellectual equal of his top advisors. If for nothing else, she would have loved him for that. "But taken altogether, the gifts can change the tide of a battle: to heal and save lives; to sense, judge, and interpret moods of your enemy; to build morale; to aid military strategies by reading the emotions of your foe's officers."

"But we give life," Chime said. "Not take it."

"Yes." His voice quieted. "Soldiers need the light mages give them: physical, emotional, healing. It eases their anguish."

"Hai, Muller." Chime paused at a bench where the path opened up enough to let moonlight bathe the area. "I grieve that war brings so much darkness."

"I too." He sat with her on the bench. "Chime—"

"Yes?"

He spoke with difficulty. "I don't know if I can bear to see you watch another man receive what I had thought would be my legacy to you and our children." He took an audible breath. "This is so much harder than I expected."

Chime held his hand. "I understand." She looked up at the sky, at the perfect disk of the moon. Her spell formed without her thinking about it, telling her of his pensive mood. She let it fade; she needed no spell to tell her about his need to save face.

"Why don't you go back now to the Hall?" she said. "I can come later."

He leaned his head against hers. "Thank you."

Chime closed her eyes, wishing she could ease the hurt inside of him.

He didn't immediately leave, though. Instead he spoke softly. "Will you visit me later tonight?"

That caught her off guard. In all the months they had known each other, he had never made such a request. He shouldn't, of course, until they were married, but the formal distance they were expected to maintain during the royal betrothal had grown more and more difficult.

Except they no longer had a royal betrothal. Uncertainty swept Chime. Was he asking her to be his lover instead of his wife? He had never actually said he wanted to marry; the King's Advisors had made the decision. Given the choice, surely he preferred a woman of the nobility.

After her silence grew long, Muller said, "I am sorry. That was presumptuous."

"I am on shifting sands," she said. "I do not know where it is safe to stand."

He brushed her cheek. "Stand with me."

"And if you walk away?"

"Why would I do that?"

"You no longer have to marry me."

Muller squinted at her. "I gave up the crown for you. I'm hardly going to walk away."

Her unease trickled away into the azure night. "I am glad." She kept it simple, not wanting to mar this moment by fumbling her words.

He waited. "Well?"

"Well?" She wondered what she had said wrong.

"I am glad you are glad." The hint of exasperation in his voice didn't hide his tension. "I would also appreciate being glad."

Ah. Now she understood. This time she hadn't said enough.

She curled her fingers around his. "Nor would I walk away from you."

He smiled, his lashes lowering, relief on his face. Chime had never fathomed why he disliked his eyes. They were gorgeous, especially in the moonlight. Perhaps she shouldn't tell him the effect he had on her; he might use it to entice her into forbidden diversions, such as sneaking into his room tonight.

Muller kissed her, first gently, then with more passion. As she gave herself to the pleasure, leaning into him, his hands roamed her dress, becoming bolder. She had to push them off her breasts.

He moved his lips to her ear. "Come see me tonight."

She answered huskily. "You are a terrible rogue."

"You make me crazy."

Her lips quirked. "You have always been crazy."

"Now you break my heart." He pulled her into another kiss, his most effective mode of persuasion. Chime began to forget why she couldn't go with him.

"Come on," he coaxed, his lips against hers.

She drew back. "Perhaps Sam Threadman should draw you a cold bath."

"You are maddening."

Chime touched his cheek. "Patience, love."

He frowned at her. "I have the patience of a saint."

"A handsome saint."

"Flattery won't help." His grin quirked. "Much." Then his smile faded. "I really should return to the Shape-Hall. If I am gone too long, it will look strange."

"All right. I will come in a bit."

He brushed her lips with his. "I will see you later."

This time he left his invitation vague; "later" could be in the Shape-Hall or afterward in his suite. She could answer without committing herself.

Taking his hand, she said, "All right."

He stood, his face silvered in the moonlight. Then he left, headed to the castle.

Brooding, Muller stalked through the garden. He shouldn't have asked Chime to come to his suite tonight. She might have a country girl's lack of concern about her sensuality, but here in the royal court, custom allowed him and his betrothed only the briefest touches, no more. That distance from her proved more difficult to keep each day.

He couldn't bear for her to watch him tonight during the ceremony. His loss of status as the Aronsdale heir shouldn't shame him, but it did. It made him want to hold Chime, lie with her, banish his doubts. She affected him at every level, more than the physical, but he didn't know how to express what he felt in any way except by making love to her.

Although in the country, people expected couples to wait until after marriage, they paid less attention to the behavior of a betrothed pair. He knew it well, having grown up on a country estate until his fourteenth year, when he came to Suncroft. Inheritance in rural areas went through the mother's line and her husband usually came to live with her. If confusion existed as to the father's identity, it might cause great pain to the people involved, but it had no effect on the legacy of the children.

Not so for noble or royal families, including his own. They followed customs over a thousand years old, from the era when southern potentates had overrun Aronsdale and established the House of Dawnfield. Southern countries such a Shazire and Jazid had more patriarchal customs, in contrast to the matriarchal ways of rural Aronsdale. So titles in Aronsdale went through the male line. As Jarid's closest male relative, Muller was next in line for the crown until Jarid had a son. No ambiguity would be allowed about who fathered Muller's heirs.

He knew why Chime worked so hard to refine herself. Her background as a rural commoner raised eyebrows. No one had openly questioned her conduct because she made such an effort to fit into the royal court. Nor did it hurt that with her golden beauty, she fit the part devastatingly well. But he knew she felt awkward with her role, causing an uncertainty on her part that led unperceptive people to assume she lacked intelligence. It angered him. They knew nothing. She had more common sense than the lot of them put together and her kindness was unsurpassed. She was everything special, desirable, and lovely, and well yes, maybe tact wasn't her strong point, but even so, she was an angel.

It had been wrong to invite her into his bed. Now that he would no longer be sovereign, the King's Advisors would have little wish to see him marry one of Aronsdale's most powerful mages. They would prefer she wed someone whose position and personality wouldn't distract her from her work, men similar to the husbands they had found for Della and Skylark, pleasant fellows, farmers, well respected citizens of Croft's Vale. Della was widowed now, but Skylark's husband still worked his land. They wouldn't openly force Chime to marry their choice any more than they had with Della or Skylark, but they could be persuasive.

Muller knew they would also love to find him a wife to compensate for his shortcomings. If his desire for Chime led him to act with dishonor, it would give Brant the perfect opportunity to stop the wedding. He could just hear the craggy lord: *Any unwed woman who lies with a man can't be trusted to carry a Dawnfield heir.* Muller would have laughed at the absurdity of it, except Brant really would use it to separate them. Given Muller's position in the line of succession, the King's Advisors had more authority to control his marriage than they did with Chime.

Muller pushed his hand through his hair. He had never wanted to marry. Then he had fallen in love with Chime and confused himself. If he wasn't careful, he could lose her even now, after he had given up a kingdom for her.

Chime sat in the moonlit garden, thinking. At home, she had been so unaware of life. Her biggest concern had been how to evade doing her sums. The queens of Aronsdale had always encouraged education for their people, but Chime had never appreciated her fortune. She had known so little about so much. In the market at Croft's Vale, it had stunned her to learn, from merchants who traveled, that most people in Harsdown were illiterate.

She could no longer blithely go about life, assuming days would stretch into years, never too demanding, always happy. And she *had* been happy, despite thinking she always had some annoyance to deal with. Compared to the concerns of the people here, her life had been simple. No longer could she turn from her duties as a mage, not now that she had begun to understand their importance.

Eventually she returned to the castle. She stood by a column near the door, content to watch the flow of people throughout the Shape-Hall, also called the Hall of Kings. Musicians were playing, a waterfall of bright melodies. People moved in graceful dances, forming and reforming patterns: stars, boxes, polygons, circles. The dais at the far end of the room was a great round disk, empty now. Flecks of gold in its white marble glimmered in the copious candlelight.

Everyone had passed through the reception line. Iris was talking with Brant, her hands folded in front of her dress the way she did when she was nervous. Chime suddenly realized she had forgotten to go through the line. She flushed, hoping Iris had been too occupied with all these changes to notice her absence, which would look like yet another insult from her fellow mage student.

Muller was standing across the room near the wall, his manner composed as he watched people dance. Chime held back her urge to go to him.

Across the room, a man entered, a disk-captain in a blue dress-uniform with silver trim. When Chime had first arrived at Suncroft, she had thought officers in the King's Army had shape-designations because they were mages. She soon realized her error. "Disk-captain" gave his status in the army. Each rank subdivided into shape-ranks, with triangle as lowest and sphere as highest. All captains outranked all lieutenants, so a sphere-lieutenant had lower rank than a triangle-captain, but he outranked all other types of lieutenant.

As the disk-captain conferred with Brant and Iris, the hairs on Chime's neck prickled. When Brant nodded to the captain, a chill went through Chime, though she had no idea why. The captain bowed to Iris, then to Brant, and then took his leave, striding through an archway behind them.

Brant offered his arm to Iris. They walked together down the hall, stopping here and there to chat with guests, seemingly relaxed. Only Iris's subtly tensed posture gave away her agitation. As she and Brant reached the dais, power stirred within the hall, pure and natural. With a start, Chime realized Iris was focusing her gifts through the dais. At first nothing happened, except that Chime had a sudden thought of forests, hills, and lakes.

A sense of peace spread in Chime. Iris's spell flowed throughout the hall, uneven and uncertain, but with great strength. Even having suspected Iris was the stronger mage, Chime had never realized she wielded such luminous power.

Iris and Brant went to the center of the dais, and Della joined them, along with a retinue of officers in blue and silver uniforms. Tall and stately, the Bishop of Orbs mounted the dais, his white hair swept under his miter, his gait regal. As the keeper of the Scrolls of the Saints, he was the highest spiritual authority in the land. Two pages accompanied him, one carrying a tas-seled cushion that held two gold circlets inset with diamonds and amethysts. Iris stared at the sparkling crowns as if they were ghosts.

All conversation stopped. The moment stretched out until Chime thought surely it would snap. Then guests began to turn, gazing down the glittering the hall. Puzzled, Chime looked to see what drew their attention. With stately progress, a retinue of officers from the King's Army was coming down the long hall, escorting a potentate, perhaps a prince from Shazire, Land of Silk and Silver, or Jazid where they grew exquisite teas, or even Taka Mal, a country of bulb towers and lace bridges. The dazzling prince walked in their midst, come to Aronsdale for tonight's ceremony.

Then Chime realized he wasn't a visiting king.

It was Jarid.

Night Glimmers

Jarid shone in the radiance of the candelabras, resplendent in a gold brocaded vest over a snowy-white shirt that accented his broad shoulders and well-built physique. Ivory-colored breeches clung to his long legs and tucked into gold knee-boots. Instead of a wild mane, now his luxuriant hair grazed his shoulders, neatly trimmed, glossy and night-black. It enhanced the classic lines of his face, his straight nose and high cheekbones. He had violet eyes, large and intense, framed by black lashes. A scar ran down his neck, giving his aristocratic features an edgy quality.

Two sphere-majors flanked him. Although they gave no overt sign they were guiding him, Chime could tell they were helping with a nudge at his elbow or simply their presence at his side. They managed well; had she not known he was blind, she would never have realized it now.

She concentrated on Jarid, focusing through the eighteen-sided ball she wore around her neck...and his mood leapt in her mind. Fear. Enemies surrounded him and he didn't know what they wanted. His anger and confusion sparked, ready to blaze. He controlled himself only with a phenomenal resolve. His inner strength was tangible, an iron will that must have carried him through fourteen years of a nightmare.

Incredibly, no outward sign of his turmoil showed. He continued with his retinue, approaching the dais, his head high. Iris's spell swirled in the hall, diffuse and unpolished, its warmth overflowing. With fledgling, uncertain attempts, she wove a spell to soothe Jarid.

Chime would have rejoiced at Iris's realization of her power if it hadn't hurt so much. How could Chime have ever believed herself the stronger mage? Iris's gifts had an unmatched purity and power. For one brief year, Chime had been the future queen, someone more than the wayward daughter of an orchard keeper. Now that was gone forever. She tried to feel gladdened that Iris was blooming with such grace, but she grieved over what she had lost.

Jarid's retinue ascended the dais and proceeded to its center. They didn't stop until he was standing with his bride, the two of them gazing at each other. Chime suspected she was one of the few people in the hall who realized Jarid wasn't looking directly at Iris.

Iris took his hand. Her gesture appeared charming, but Chime felt Jarid's mood roiling like a storm. He wanted to fight this inexplicable situation, but he held back—for he recognized his ancestral home. Memories jumped in his mind, so vivid that Chime caught them as part of his mood. In that instant, she knew his identity without doubt, for he remembered playing here as a boy, as the heir to the throne. Then anger and fear swamped his memories, threatening to explode.

Iris offered a spell of soothing, like rain misting over flames, calming Jarid. But when she tried a healing spell, it slid off him with no effect. Apparently whatever had hurt Jarid went too deep for even a sapphire mage to heal.

The Bishop of Orbs opened a book written in a gilded script Chime could see glimmering even from so far away. A gold tassel hung down from the tome. Iris and Jarid stood while he spoke ancient words in his resonant voice. When he finished, he asked Iris and Jarid to kneel. A sphere-major reached for Jarid, to guide him—and Chime froze. She felt Jarid's tension; he barely had control of his fear. He would snap if a stranger touched him.

Iris must have also sensed it. She shook her head at the major, and he hesitated, his hand above Jarid's shoulder. The others on the dais had gone still. Jarid tilted his head, the tendons in his neck as taut as cords.

Chime became painfully aware of everyone in the hall watching. She glimpsed Muller across the room, his gaze fixed on the dais as if he were mesmerized. The silence felt tangible. If someone didn't respond soon, the guests would realize something was amiss with Aronsdale's long-lost heir.

A new spell flowed out from Iris, its power untutored but radiant. She offered friendship to Jarid. He paused, his head tilted as if he were listening to a sound no one else could hear. Then he knelt with her, stiff and slow. Both he and Iris bowed their heads, though Chime thought Jarid did it more out of instinct than anything else.

The Bishop of Orbs turned to the boy who held the tasseled cushion. With care, the bishop lifted the larger of the two crowns and set it on Jarid's head. It sparkled, its amethysts and diamonds catching the candlelight. He repeated the procedure with the smaller circlet, placing it on Iris's head.

Jarid's bewilderment swirled through the hall, so tangible, Chime wondered that no one else seemed to feel it. He understood the weight of that crown. An immense grief for his grandfather's death came from him, but he didn't seem surprised.

Then the bishop read the marriage ceremony, his words rolling through the Hall of Kings while Jarid and Iris knelt before him. And finally it was done: Jarid and Iris were wed. Aronsdale once again had a king and queen.

Anvil stood in the gardens and watched the coronation through the open doorway. Jarid Dawnfield fascinated and repelled him. Anvil's spying had revealed much about this new king. They could clean his hair, wash his body, and dress him in brocades, but none of that would make him any less insane.

Far more interesting were the dignitaries and officers at the ceremony. Lord Brant Firestoke made a striking presence, imposing in his silver leggings and blue tunic, his silvered hair swept back, his gaze fiercely protective. Cube-General Fieldson was just as impressive in his dress uniform, a sharply pressed tunic and leggings in the king's colors, indigo and white, with plenty of gold on his shoulders and the cuffs of his tunic. His sword glinted at his side, sheathed but no less deadly for that.

Four other generals were in attendance and many lesser officers. They fascinated Anvil. He had been invited tonight because several nobles among the court had taken a liking to him, including Lady Chime. But he took care not to intrude too much, lest he could draw unwanted attention. Better to be inconspicuous.

He found it easier to blend in than he had expected. Although he had left Aronsdale nearly twenty years ago, it was disturbingly easy to fall back into the accent and customs. Being unobtrusive, fading into the background, he caught a wealth of snippets and rumors. Mood spells would have given him even more advantage, if he could have made them, but he did well enough without. He knew how to sort and store details, having spent a lifetime wandering by himself. He had learned to read situations of all kinds, including those that could mean his life or death.

Here in Suncroft, Anvil had learned a great deal that would interest King Varqelle. Many injuries weakened Aronsdale: a crippled king, a demoralized army with little confidence in their new sovereign, and a mage queen with neither the experience nor heart to rule. They put on a good show, but it didn't fool him. He understood what hid under their glitter and pomp. Aronsdale was in trouble.

The time was ripe for attack.

Lost in thought, Chime followed a corridor tiled in skybell patterns, carrying a candle in a silver holder. She longed to see how Muller fared, how he was handling Jarid's ascension tonight, but she held back, aware of how it would look if she visited him this late. Nor was she sure where she stood with him. He used many fine words to reassure her, but he also broke propriety by inviting her to his rooms. They both knew he no longer had to marry her. Despite his pretty words, he wouldn't be the first lord to take a common woman as mistress and wed a noblewoman. She had no intention of being part of such an arrangement.

But still. He hadn't suggested she be his mistress, any more than she had suggested what women sometimes did in rural Aronsdale, taking the male version of a mistress. She would never dishonor Muller that way.

Despite her uncertainty, she found herself headed to his suite. She went around the back, along a narrow hall to a recessed doorway, a discreet entrance used by Muller's servants. She disliked that her visit had to be hidden, but she knocked anyway, her heart beating hard. The candle flame wavered in the drafts, making her shadow flicker on the wall. It seemed forever she stood there, praying no one happened by to see her.

Then the door opened, framing Sam Threadman in the entrance. He must have been in bed; he had on sleep trousers under his robe and a white floppy cap with a fuzzy ball at the end of it. Chime expected him to frown or regard her with disdain. Instead he looked relieved. He held a candle much like hers, its light casting a glow on his face and shoulders.

"Lady Chime." He stepped aside. "Please. Come in."

Her face warmed with her blush. She entered a small room painted off-white, fresh and spotless. Three mops leaned against one wall by a pail. Sam murmured apologies as he hurried her across the chamber and into a nondescript hallway the same color. As they followed it to other halls, and yet others, she realized Muller's "suite" was an entire wing of the castle. Within moments they had reached wide corridors graced with mosaics in tessellated patterns of gold, blue, indigo, and white.

"How is Prince Muller feeling?" Chime asked.

Sam wouldn't meet her gaze. "Lord, milady."

She glowered at him. "Prince. He is Jarid's heir."

"Oh." Sam brightened. "Yes, you are right." He gave her a rueful look. "He's as well as can be imagined, under the circumstances."

"I saw him talking to Della at the ceremony." She recalled his stiff posture. "He didn't seem happy."

Sam sighed. "This is difficult for everyone." The lines around his eyes crinkled with a kindly look. "It was gracious of you to understand that he needed——" He paused as if he wasn't sure how to phrase what Muller had needed during the ceremony.

"To face it on his own," she said.

"He feels he failed you. And himself."

"But he hasn't! Iris will be a good queen." She didn't have to add, *Better than I.* Even if no one said it, everyone knew the truth. She wished it wasn't so hard to admit.

Sam stopped at an arched doorway bordered by gold and white mosaics. He knocked twice on the varnished wooden door, paused, and knocked again. Then they waited.

When the door opened, Chime expected another servant. But Muller stood there, holding a candle, still in his finery from the ceremony, his golden hair shining in the candlelight.

"Sam? Is something wrong?" He peered at his valet, then past him. When he saw Chime, his face warmed. Earlier tonight he had looked as if he had aged a decade, but now, as he smiled, the years dropped away.

"I am glad you came," he told her.

She tried to smile, but her lips trembled.

"Will you visit for a while?" he asked.

This time she managed an answer. "For a little."

His shoulders relaxed. He grinned at Sam and the valet beamed. Sam bowed to Muller, then to Chime, and then bustled off, his slippers whispering on the tiled floors.

Muller beckoned to Chime, and she walked into his room, wondering if he could see how nervous she felt. As he closed the door, she looked around, unable to meet his gaze. Her breath caught. His rooms were like him; ivory and gold, perfect, beautiful. Blue-glass vases with skybells added accents of color. The upholstery on the gilded chairs bore the seal of Aronsdale, an indigo silhouette of the castle superimposed on the sun. The room smelled of fresh flowers and orb-candles.

Finally she turned to the man at her side. He had gone still, like a nervous stag uncertain whether to run or stay. Unexpectedly it reassured her. Had he been smooth, confident, sure of himself, she would have wanted to escape, afraid he entertained women here often, making her only one of many. Instead, he seemed as unsure of himself as she felt.

"Do you like my suite?" he asked.

"It is lovely."

"Only because you are here." Then he reddened.

Her face relaxed into a smile. "Thank you."

Muller ushered her to a circular table with two round-backed chairs. A decanter of red wine sparkled there, with two goblets made from Rosedale crystal. He pulled out her chair, then sat across from her and poured wine for them. Raising his glass, he said, "To our new king and queen."

Chime lifted her goblet. "Iris and Jarid."

He wasn't smiling. "May they have productive lives."

"Hai, Muller." She set down her glass. "I know you wish them well. You needn't force out the words."

"Wish them well?" He took a gulp of wine. "I would have died if they had made you wed that madman."

She spoke with care. "To marry a king is an honor. I am glad for Iris." Glad that Iris had the honor instead of her.

His lips quirked. "You are becoming a diplomat."

She laughed ruefully. "I'm trying."

He reached across the table for her hand. "I haven't spoken properly. I am making a mood spell right now, and it tells me that what I haven't properly said agitates you. But my spells are fractured. I am unsure whether your disquiet comes from wanting me to speak or fearing that I will." He made a visible effort to fortify himself. "But speak I must."

Chime had no idea what he was about. "To say what?"

He inhaled deeply. "I would ask that you marry me."

His words caught her off guard. "You do?"

He looked like a man falling off a cliff. "I can no longer offer you a crown. But you will have a good life on my country estate."

Relief flooded Chime. She had thought she would have to make an unwelcome decision tonight, either give him up or consent to a liaison she would regret. Instead he made the honorable offer. Not that misbehaving with Muller would be disagreeable; she had begun to think it was high time she misplaced her virginity. His existence was exceedingly distracting. But it meant more than she knew how to say that he wanted to do this right.

His grip on her hand tightened. "You are so quiet."

Chime curled her fingers around his. "I would be honored to be your wife, here at Suncroft, in the country, or anywhere else. You need no crown to woo me." She dimpled at him. "With all these beautiful clothes you wear, who would notice a crown anyway?"

He grinned, his teeth flashing. "You make me a happy man."

She gave a mock frown. "I must say, I don't know how I will feel, knowing the groom is prettier than the bride."

He glared at her. "I am *not* pretty."

"All right," she said amiably. "You aren't."

Muller laughed with an ease she hadn't heard for days. "You don't have to agree so easily."

"You will always be handsome to me."

"Well, of course."

She smirked at him. "And humble, too."

"That, too." Then his grin faded. "I should like us to wed soon, before Brant and his cronies come up with some new and onerous duty that would preclude us from marrying."

"They want you to stay here and help Jarid and Iris." She took both his hands in hers. "It is the right thing, Muller. Iris has no background, and Jarid is furious and terrified. They need your help."

He pulled away his hands. "You are as bad as Della."

"Just think on it."

For a moment he didn't answer. Then he raked his hand through his hair, tousling the golden locks. Finally he set his hands on the table, clasping them carefully, as if he needed the security of their exact proper placement. With his hair disarrayed around his face, he looked vulnerable instead of exact, though. It made her want him even more.

He spoke in a subdued voice. "When Iris first said she had found Jarid, it seemed a boon from the heavens. Jarid would come, the unflawed king."

"You aren't flawed, no more than the rest of us."

"I cannot hide from the truth." His face paled. "But when they brought him home—he is wild. He could harm our country even more than me. Aronsdale is fortunate to have Iris."

She spoke quietly. "It is no flaw to see only darkness and hear only silence."

"It isn't that." Muller shook his head. "He is like an animal, Chime. It doesn't matter why; the result is the same. No fatally flawed king, or king's cousin, can be allowed to destroy Aronsdale. Our country is more important than either of us. We must protect our realm and our people."

"You aren't fatally flawed, Muller. You've never given yourself a chance."

His sudden tension seemed to snap in the room. "You are saying I should not have abdicated?"

"No. Jarid is the heir. It was right for you to do. And Iris is the queen he needs." She spoke firmly. "But you are a far better man than you let yourself believe."

He still had one hand on top of the other, and the fingers of his upper hand clenched the bottom hand so hard, his knuckles turned white. "Just as long as Jarid never rules."

Chime didn't know what to say. If she convinced Muller he was fit to rule, he would hate himself for giving up the crown; if she convinced him that Jarid was fit, he would despise himself for being less competent than his troubled cousin who had no preparation; if she said nothing, she felt disloyal to Jarid.

A knock came at the door.

Muller jumped like a startled cat. "That can't be Sam. He was going back to bed."

As Muller crossed to the door, Chime wondered if she should hide, so his visitor wouldn't see her here without a chaperone. Only Sam knew she had come. Even if it wasn't him, though, she didn't feel like scurrying away. Noblewomen here put up with too many constraints. They needed to live in the country for a while. They would be a lot better off if they just refused to accept all these onerous customs and traditions. So she stayed put.

Muller sought to protect her reputation, though, even if she couldn't muster alarm about being discovered. He opened the door only partway; as long as she remained at the table, she wasn't visible to whomever stood outside. She could see the edge of a man's blue and silver uniform. An unfamiliar voice spoke, low and urgent. Muller conferred with him, then bid him goodnight and closed the door. He came slowly back to Iris, his gaze distant.

"What is it?" she asked.

"Jarid. He and Iris have left the castle."

"Whatever for?"

His forehead furrowed. "Apparently our new king is agitated. Brant and several guards tried to go with them into the forest, but Iris sent them away."

Chime stood up. "What if Jarid hurts her?"

Muller met her gaze. "Pray he doesn't."

Dawn
of Rainbows

Spheres turned in Jarid's mind, spinning an endless dance. Never had they come with such clarity. They were even more beautiful than usual, but they gave him vertigo, which had never happened before. He shut them away, trying to clear his mind of everything but the woman.

Breezes cooled his face, a welcome change after his imprisonment in the castle. He would have sung his joy at such freedom, had he owned a voice. The woman had brought him here. Now she guided him through heavy foliage, though to where he had no idea.

His wife. These madmen had crowned him. And given him a queen. He had known the moment his grandfather died, three months ago, but he had never expected anyone to search for him. He felt surrounded now, caught, trapped. *Suffocated.*

Branches snagged his clothes and he stumbled. He was about to balk when the woman pulled him free of the foliage, into an open place.

Jarid froze.

Spheres jumped in his mind, spinning, spinning, spinning, throwing off sparks of light. He pressed the heels of his palms against his temples, dizzy with the beauty. He recognized this place; the woman had been here when she had reached across Aronsdale to find him.

Mist sprayed his face, hinting of a waterfall. The fresh scent of water and the fragrance of shape-vines tickled his nose. He drew pure air into his lungs.

His wife took his hands. He longed to know her, all of her, but he was lost in his darkness and silence and couldn't find his way. She put his fingers against her mouth, those lips he wanted to kiss until she moaned, though he would never hear her pleasure.

She spoke against his fingers. *Jarid. Husband.* Her full lips tantalized. The scent of soap and flowers hung about her like perfume.

He mouthed two words. *Your name?* When puzzlement came from her mind, he tried again. *Name?*

Iris.

Iris. It made her more real, a woman of colors he felt rather than saw: the ruddy flame of her touch; the gold of her emotions; the sunlight of her intellect; her serenity, like velvety leaves in spring; the open spaces she gave him tonight, as blue as the sky he never saw; and her indigo moods, her sadness when she came to him.

Unable to speak, frustrated in his attempts to fathom the disruptions in his life, he pulled her close, harder than he should, speaking with his body, his confusion mixed with desire until he couldn't separate the two. Anger and love, tenderness and rough edges: they jumbled within him. Alarm sparked in Iris, but he didn't want to stop. Not now. He needed her. He needed. He didn't know what to do with that need, how to satisfy it without hurting her, how to make her want him.

Then her hands moved, stroking his arms. Her spells flowed over him, calming, and he took an uneven breath, struggling for control. It bewildered him that she offered this trust, for he had known her so little these past days, only as an enigma he could neither see nor hear, only feel when she touched him.

Moving stiffly, he knelt on the ground, drawing her with him. The grass felt cool and prickly under them, its smell itching his nose. He had been a child when he lost contact with the world; he had no idea now what to do with a woman. He knew only that he wanted to clench her, press against her, fill her until he sated his driving hunger. He reached out and pulled her to his body, squeezing her in his arms, his muscles straining.

Iris stiffened and pushed against his shoulders. He was frightening her. But it was so hard to let go. He forced himself to ease his grip enough so she could jump to her feet and escape. To his unmitigated surprise, she stayed put. Instead she relaxed her hands on his shoulders and took a deep breath.

Let me, he thought to her. Even if he could have spoken, he knew none of the sweet whispers a woman would wish to hear. They were strangers; this fragile bond they were forging could fall apart if he let his true nature show. He was no king, no one to claim this woman. His guilt went too deep.

Iris moved her hands on his face and chest. He would have groaned if he could have; instead, he grabbed her wrists, his restraint crumbling. Pushing her backward, he unbalanced them both so she tumbled onto her back in the grass. Before she had time to react, he stretched out on top of her, grasping her small waist, the silk and brocade of her dress flimsy under his hands.

When she stiffened, Jarid knew he had pushed too hard, too fast. But no—she was caressing him, sweetly unskilled but with urgency. She wanted him. *Him.* He would have known if she acquiesced only because she was his wife; just as he felt the moods of others, so now he felt her excitement, her desire all the more arousing because he excited her. Him. No one else.

Jarid kissed her neck as he remembered seeing his father once do with his mother. No doubt he was too rough; surely a man came to his wife more gently. But he had no experience and so few memories. It astonished him that she accepted him despite everything. It made no difference that his world was dark; he saw her with his hands and felt her light-drenched moods. It mattered not that he lived in silence; he spoke with his touch, a language older than any verbal tongue, his callused hands scraping on her soft skin.

Her spell curled around him, released by the power in this place. Earlier tonight, in the castle, she had tried to reach him with a healing spell, but he had been stone. Her spell had skittered off the armored surface of his heart. Here in the forest, in this charmed sphere, he could be more open. After so many long years, he could let go. Her gift poured through him, into him, with tenderness.

Jarid stroked her and she responded with sweet passion. They explored each other, tentative at first, then with more urgency. So they joined together, protected within a sphere of life, misted with water. Her pleasure answered his, and their moods blended as they made love.

Some time later, he lifted his head. He was lying on his side, tangled in Iris's arms, flush with the afterglow of their joining. She slept beside him, her mind tranquil. He should have been content—

But he was *breaking* inside, the way ice on a creek in the high forest cracked after a long winter. His passion had flared like a catharsis, a great release of emotional energy he couldn't control. He didn't understand what was happening; he knew only that he was shattering. He thought of Iris and the pain grew worse. This pleasure came at too great a price; she weakened his defenses and left him vulnerable. He would have cried out, but he had no words.

Jarid lurched to his feet, pulling on his clothes. The strange forest sphere vibrated with energy, focusing his mind until he thought he would explode with the power coursing through him. A memory came from long ago, from the night his mother had woven her final spell to protect him: *the power of a life.*

No! He walked off, not even trying to lace his shirt. Dimly, he was aware of Iris coming awake, of confusion replacing her contentment. He stumbled into the pool and slipped, falling to his knees. Angered by his inability to see, he scrambled to his feet, splashing water. Then he strode away, swinging his hands in front of him as if he were fighting the air.

A branch jabbed his palm. Ripping the foliage out of his path, Jarid plunged forward, into the bushes that surrounded this place. He thrashed through the barrier, unheeding that it tore his clothes and gashed his skin.

Then he was free and running through the woods, his out-stretched hands scraping trees as he escaped the unbearable radiance of Iris's mind.

Iris sank down on a boulder by a stream. Jarid wasn't anywhere. She had searched for hours. The tears that had streaked her face were dry now, nothing could ease her heart. She had thought she reached him, but she had failed. Now he was gone, without food or warm clothes, unable even to ask for assistance. She had no choice but to return to Suncroft and request help in finding him. She doubted Jarid would forgive that betrayal of his trust.

Last night she and Jarid had found a haven together. Despite her many lacks, he had reached out to her in his own way. She had been foolish enough to believe she might help him recover from the nightmares that haunted his life. She had even dared

to hope their differences wouldn't matter, that he wouldn't care
if she came from a poverty-stricken hamlet of the Tallwalk
Mountains, fostered by a family that didn't want her, that she
had been born the illegitimate daughter to a mother who deserted her at birth. She and Jarid each lived in their own solitude, yet recognizing the loneliness of the other. Together they
might begin to heal.

But she had to face the truth. He was a king. No matter that
he had spent most of his life in an existence even harsher than
hers. No matter that she had given him a few moments of pleasure in the woods. He had been born to his title. He knew she
had nothing permanent to offer him.

The sky was lightening; soon dawn would come. Weary, she
rose to her feet and trudged toward the castle.

Jarid thought he had slept for several hours. In his perpetual
darkness, it could be hard to tell if he nodded off or slept
soundly, but he felt a difference in the air from when he had collapsed on the mossy ground. The scent of night-blooming flowers had faded. From force of habit, he opened his useless eyes.

Green.

For a long time he lay, absorbing it. His darkness had turned
green. For years he had seen colors only in his mind, and over
time those had faded. Yet now, everywhere, he saw green.

Green.

He became aware of details in that living tapestry: a twig,
gnarled and brown, poking through the moss; dark soil, rich
enough to buy a kingdom, under the ragged carpet of leaves; a
red pyramid-blossom opening in the pearly light that heralded
the dawn; iridescent dew clinging to leaves.

Jarid slowly rose to his feet. A pressure built in his chest until
he thought he would burst. He turned in a circle, unable to believe. If he could have made a sound, any sound, a sob would

have caught in his throat. His world remained silent, but he could *see* it.

He could see.

Forest surrounded him, trees draped in moss, with more shades of green, gray, and brown than he could count. Shape-blossoms added yellow here, violet there, a splash of orange. Tilting back his head, he saw slivers of gray sky between the overhang of high branches. He went to a tree and pressed his palms against its bumpy trunk. Insects scuttled away, a miraculous line of ants that wound along the bark.

Jarid didn't realize he was crying until a drop fell onto his arm. Pushing away from the tree, he wiped his face with the ripped sleeve of his brocaded shirt. He wanted to laugh, cry, shout his astonishment. Emotions welled within him and spilled down his cheeks as tears.

Walking through the woods was a miracle. Magic touched every sight, every leaf, bird, and twig. He had a hard time taking it all in, interpreting it all. He climbed a knoll, making his way through trees until he came out onto an open slope. At the top of the hill, he looked over the countryside. Woods and meadows rolled away everywhere, and in the north the castle stood on a higher peak, draped in shadows, waiting for the rising sun to turn it gold. Memories welled within him; he had often stood here as a child, cherishing this view.

Then he spotted a figure down in a meadow, a woman in a yellow gown hiking toward the castle.

Iris. His wife.

Apprehension and anticipation leapt within him. It had to be her. Iris had long, full hair and so did the woman below, her mane gloriously unbound. He remembered from his childhood that women at balls wore their hair swept up on their heads, but last night Iris had let her curls hang free down her back.

And last night he had run from her, afraid she would melt the ice around his heart. He had no defenses against her. He knew she could hurt him, but now he could think only of seeing her face. This morning, in the pure light of dawn, he fought his fear. He wanted to live again, not just exist.

Jarid started down the hill, tripping on rocks because he had so little experience taking himself anywhere.

Birds chirped, calling the onset of morning.

Grass crackled beneath his feet.

As he gained confidence, he increased his stride, until he was running down the hill.

Wind rustled the long grasses around Iris, enough so that she didn't know anyone had approached until a hand touched her shoulder. With a cry, she spun around.

"Jarid!" Before her fear of rejection could stop her, she threw her arms around him, so relieved to see him safe that she forgot everything else. He enfolded her in his arms and they held each other close. This wasn't like last night, when he had clenched her in desperation; now his mood seemed full of joy.

It wasn't until the light of dawn warmed Iris's arms through her torn sleeves that she came to herself. Pulling back, she looked up at her husband. He stared down at her, his gaze caressing her face.

His gaze.

Iris's breath caught. He was *looking* at her.

His lips curved upward. Then he mouthed: *You are beautiful, wife.*

The Power of a Life

No one saw Muller.

A great staircase swept down from the upper levels of the castle into the entrance foyer where servants milled around Iris and Jarid. The foyer had the shape of an imperfect hexagon, the wall with the doors to the outside longer than the other five. The curve of the stairs shadowed an interior door, another imperfect hexagon, its shape obvious but elongated. As Muller pushed open that door, his power surged. Desperate for control, he clamped it down.

Muller stopped when he saw the queen and king. Grass stained their fine wedding clothes, which had become ripped and tattered. Iris had a leaf in her hair. But despite it all, the newlyweds glowed. They stood in the dawn's light slanting through the open doors, staring at each other while servants bustled about them, clucking at their disheveled state.

Staring at each other.

Muller felt as if he were drowning. No man could look at a

woman that way unless he was really seeing her. None of the servants seemed fazed by their king's newfound sight, but then, none had known he was blind.

In another time and place, Muller would have rejoiced for his cousin. But all he could think now was that he had made a terrible, terrible mistake, one that would end with the fall of Aronsdale.

Jarid looked like a wild animal, his clothes wrinkled and torn, his hair disarrayed. What royal couple spent their wedding night in the woods? Muller stepped out of the shadows. "Jarid, what is this?"

The king turned with a start.

He could hear.

Muller struggled to breathe, to overcome his growing dismay. He walked forward and Jarid watched, his violet-eyed gaze never wavering. The servants melted away, taking their cue from the tension.

"It can't be," Muller said. "You can't see."

Iris answered with a smile, tears on her face. "It is a miracle."

Muller swung around to her. "How could this happen?"

Her smile dimmed. "What do you mean?"

"As long as he couldn't lead Aronsdale, it would have been all right. But *this*." Muller wrestled with his fear. "Now he can rule, but imperfectly." As if to mock him, his own power sparked, erratic and flawed, stoked by the imperfect foyer, making his anger hurt, adding unwanted vehemence to his voice. "It is wrong. Wrong! It will destroy Aronsdale."

Iris stared at him. "How can you say such a thing?"

Grief spread through Muller. In abdicating, he had made yet another flawed choice, this one possibly fatal for his people. "Fate must be laughing at us," he said bitterly. "No matter what decisions we make, no matter how lofty our intentions, we pay cruelly in the end."

"I donna understand——" Iris broke off when Jarid left her side and strode toward the staircase. He stared at Muller as he came forward, his gaze haunted, his joy gone. Then he started up the wide steps.

Iris caught up with Jarid midway up the stairs. She grasped his arm, pulling him to a halt—and in that heart-stopping instant, he spun around and raised his fist above her. Muller ran to the stairs, intending to sprint after them, but he stopped when he realized Jarid wasn't threatening her. Instead the king stretched out his arm, pointing at Muller.

"My cousin is right." His deep voice rasped with disuse. "Ask Stone."

They descended into the underground levels of the castle, their tread muted on pitted stone steps. Muller's thoughts whirled. *Ask Stone.* Why would those be Jarid's first words? Now the king refused to acknowledge anyone. He could hear and see, incredibly, but he had withdrawn into himself and spoken no more.

Jarid went first on the stairs with two guards, followed by Iris and Brant, then Muller and more guards. Muller needed no spells to know Iris was furious. Brant had let them believe Jarid's foster father had stayed in the mountains, in custody. Brant had lied. Muller knew he shouldn't be surprised they dealt with Unbent in secret. But Muller was the king's cousin, still heir to the crown. Brant should have told him.

Iris spoke to the lord in a low voice only he should have been able to hear. But the imperfect stairs magnified Muller's power, giving him bits and pieces of a discussion he had no wish to overhear.

"You had no right," Iris told Brant.

"I had every right." His voice was barely audible. "That man kidnapped the Dawnfield heir."

"He took care of Jarid like a son."

"He murdered Jarid's parents."

Iris jerked. "What?"

"You heard me."

"I thought highwaymen attacked the orb-carriage."

"That's right."

Her shoulders stiffened. "Including Stone?"

"Yes." Brant motioned toward the officers with Jarid. "Stone matches their description. They were the two guards knocked out during the attack on the carriage."

"You canna be sure Stone is the same man."

"He admitted it when my men questioned him."

"Why didna you tell me he was a prisoner here?" Iris folded her arms and rubbed her palms on them. "You let us believe he intended to follow us to Suncroft."

"I didn't want to upset the king." Brant exhaled. "You've had an empathic link with Jarid from the start. I couldn't risk your knowing, Iris. I'm sorry."

It tore at Muller that Jarid had thought of his foster father as "Stone." To a six-year-old boy who had lost his parents, their killers must truly have seemed like stone. That Unbent had cared for Jarid during the next fourteen years didn't change the immensity of his crime. Muller recalled Jarid as a small boy, laughing as he ran across the meadows outside Suncroft, his hands held out to his cousin. It was hard to reconcile that joyous child with this injured man. Jarid's face was set with lines of pain he should never have had at his young age.

At the bottom of the stairs, they followed a rough-hewn tunnel lit by torches on the stone walls. The head guardsman took a hexagon-shaped ring of keys off a peg and led them to a cell. The guard unlocked its heavy door and Jarid waited, stiff and distant. Muller felt his anger. How would the king react, seeing for the first time one of the men who had destroyed everything he valued? Unbent may have spent years atoning for his crime, but nothing could give Jarid back what he had lost, neither his parents nor his childhood.

With a grunt, the guardsman heaved open the door. Then he stepped aside, letting two soldiers enter the cell. Metal rang on metal as they drew their swords. Instead of following them, Jarid turned to the people in the hallway, his violet gaze startling in its intensity. The last time Muller had seen his eyes, at the ceremony last night, they had been unfocused.

The king held out his hand to his wife. It was the only time he had acknowledged any of them since that moment on the stairs when he had spoken for the first time in fourteen years. Less than an hour had passed, yet it seemed like ages to Muller.

Surprise flickered on Iris's face. She took his hand and they entered the cell together. Muller followed with Brant and the guards, going into a room with stone walls even rougher than in the hallway. Clean but bare, it had nothing but a chamber pot in one corner. The cell was in the outer wall of the castle, in the slope behind Suncroft, so it wasn't all underground. A barred window across the room let in sunlight.

A man was sitting on the cracked ledge cut from the wall. He watched them with weary eyes, his posture that of someone who awaited his execution. A ragged mane of hair the color of granite swept down his neck, and bushy gray eyebrows arched over his gray eyes. Stone. Except his true name was Unbent.

When Unbent saw Jarid, his face transformed into joy. Jarid was impossible to read as he went to stand before the highwayman, his profile to Muller now. Unbent looked up at his foster son, his expression dimming, his hands clenched on the bench. Muller waited for Jarid to condemn the monster who had helped murder his parents.

And then the king of Aronsdale went down on one knee and bowed his head before the prisoner in his dungeon.

At first Unbent seemed unable to respond. Finally he spoke, but in such a low voice, Muller barely heard. "What is this? You kneel to me? Surely not." He was talking to himself; he obviously expected no response.

Jarid lifted his head. "Surely yes."

Unbent froze. *"Dani?"*

"Dani?" Emotion roughened Jarid's voice. "Is that what you named me?"

"I—yes, yes, I did." Unbent started to reach for him, then shook his head. "What miracle is this, son?"

Brant Firestoke spoke harshly. "Do not presume to call His Majesty your 'son.'"

Unbent jerked up his head. "His *Majesty?*"

Muller froze. Surely Unbent knew Jarid was the Dawnfield heir?

And yet...Muller had seen the desolate range where Unbent and Jarid made their home. They had lived in one of the few places so remote that they could have been cut off even from news as big as the death of a king or his heir.

Muller spoke coldly to Unbent. "Yes. His Majesty. That night you murdered the heir to Aronsdale."

Turning to Muller, Jarid tried to speak, then stopped. Everyone remained silent, waiting while Jarid struggled to do what most people took for granted—talk. He finally answered in a rough voice. "Stone did not kill my parents. Murk was the one who drove us off the road."

"But I was there." Unbent rose to his feet, his knees creaking. "I, too, am responsible."

Jarid raised his hand to touch Unbent's face, the man who had been his guardian all these years, twice as long as his parents. "Any sin you committed, even that Murk committed, was far less than mine."

Unbent answered in a low voice. "No."

Muller felt currents of emotion swirling here, his awareness intensified by the imperfect shape of the cell. But he could barely read the spell. He sensed only that Jarid condemned himself and that it agonized Unbent.

"Stone—" Jarid's voice caught.

"Stone?" Unbent's voice caught. "Is that how you thought of me?"

"For strength." Jarid's voice turned bleak. "A contrast to Murk."

"I don't understand," Muller said. "Who is Murk?"

Unbent turned to him. "Murk planned the robbery. He was the other highwayman."

"And you only *now* reveal this?" The man's deceptions so angered Muller, he barely kept his voice even. "Better to protect your own, eh?"

Unbent's gaze never wavered. "Aye."

"Nay," Iris murmured to Unbent. "You did it for Jarid. You remained silent all these years to protect him."

Unbent hesitated. "Jarid?"

"My husband." Iris inclined her head to the king.

Stone's weathered face gentled as he turned to his former ward. "You have married this lovely young lady?" When the king nodded, Unbent smiled. "It is good." He hesitated, his smile fading. "Jarid—this is your name?"

"It is," Jarid said.

"I am sorry. I never knew."

Jarid touched his arm. "Do not be sorry."

Bewildered by Jarid's obvious love for this man who had ruined so many lives, Muller struggled to contain his emotions. "What does she mean, you remained silent about Murk to protect Jarid?" he asked Unbent. "What lies have you told my cousin?"

"Told?" Pain suffused Unbent's voice. "I have told him nothing and everything. I spoke to him for fourteen years, Gracious Lord, and he heard nothing. What did I tell him? That the boy punished himself for something not his fault? Yes, I told him. He never heard."

Jarid spoke in a rasp. "I am no boy."

"Enough of this, highwayman." That came from Brant. "Where is this Murk?"

"Gone," Jarid whispered.

"Gone?" Muller asked. "Where?"

Jarid didn't answer. Instead he walked to the window and gazed past its bars to the hills. His need for separation surrounded him like a shield, almost tangible.

"I cannot take you to Murk," Unbent said. "I am sorry."

Muller clenched his fist. "You will tell us where your partner has hidden."

"I cannot."

Brant's voice came like the wind that scoured the land in winter. "We have been patient with you, highwayman. That is done now. You will talk."

Unbent paled, but he said nothing.

Brant motioned to the soldiers. "Take him to the interrogation room."

"No!" Jarid turned from the window. "You will not."

"Why?" Muller asked. "Why, cousin?"

Jarid's voice had jagged edges. "You know the legend of indigo mages?"

"I have heard them," Muller said.

Brant spoke. "No indigo mage has ever been known."

"My mother," Jarid answered.

"That cannot be," Brant said. "We have no records."

A voice came from behind them. "No. But I recognized the signs in her."

Muller swung around. Della stood in the doorway, her silver

hair disarrayed around her face, her cheeks red as if she had run here through the wind. She wasn't breathing hard, though, which made him think she had been standing there for a while, listening.

"It is the legend of the indigos." Della came forward. "A mage's power is limited by the strength of her life. She can soothe, yes, but no more than she could soothe herself. She can heal only those injuries she could recover from herself and feel only emotions she can recognize and endure." Quietly she added, "An indigo mage would have the greatest power of all."

"The power of a life," Jarid said, his gaze hooded.

Iris spoke slowly, watching her husband. "To save a life—but only one, for she has only one life."

"Yes." Della's voice gentled as she spoke to Jarid. "Your mother saved your life in the crash, yes?"

His voice rasped. "She died so I could live."

Iris spoke with dismay. "Nay, Jarid, it is'n your fault."

"You must not punish yourself for their deaths," Della told him.

Muller struggled with his anger. To Unbent, he said, "You should have brought him home. How could you keep him in that hovel?"

"He didn't know who I was," Jarid said.

Brant narrowed his gaze at Unbent. "You could have made inquiries. You chose to protect yourself."

"Yes." Unbent met his gaze. "I did."

"Liar." Pain etched Jarid's face. *"Liar."*

"Son, don't," Unbent said. "Let it go."

"Why?" Jarid's voice grated as if it could tear his throat. "They should know the truth."

"What truth?" Muller asked.

"About Murk." Jarid's voice rasped. "About me."

"Dani, stop," Unbent whispered.

Brant considered the older man. "Whatever you're hiding, we will discover it."

"Stop." Jarid faced them, his body dark against the patch of light from the barred window at his back. He lifted his arms until his hands were at waist level, his palms cupped upward.

Then he began a spell.

Light filled his hands, as if he held a glowing red orb in each. He had a haunted expression, his face stark, lit from below. The rest of the cell darkened around him.

Della moved next to Iris. "A red mage?" she murmured.

Iris swallowed. "I think more. Much more."

Jarid continued to stare at Brant. The cell was growing hot, as if he held flames rather than light.

The spheres of light changed.

They turned gold—and Muller's exhaustion receded. As they shifted into yellow, his anguish over the flaws that scarred his life eased. The spheres turned green—and Muller knew, with devastating clarity, the self-loathing that filled Jarid. Why did the king hate himself? The orbs turned sky-blue, then sapphire. The ache of a sword wound Muller had taken many years ago vanished.

The spheres turned indigo.

Tears welled in Muller's eyes. Incredibly, impossibly, Jarid could heal even grief. Muller struggled not to respond; he had to deal with his doubts himself. But for the first time in his life, he believed hope existed, that he might someday control his mage gifts.

The spheres in Jarid's hands changed again.

Violet.

"Saints above," Della whispered.

"The power of a life," Jarid grated. "The power to give life—or take it away." He extended his arm toward Brant, his hand filled with violet light. "I took Murk."

Brant stared at him. "I don't understand."

Jarid's words dropped into the air like stones. "That night when he murdered my parents, I reached out with my mind—and I killed him."

19

The Imperfect Mage

Muller stood on a bluff and gazed at Croft's Vale, but instead of the picturesque cottages, he kept seeing Jarid's anguished face as he revealed what he had held in silence for so long. In his terror, six years old but with a blazing will to live, the grief-shocked boy had fought back and reversed the greatest spell any mage could make.

Mages brought light. They soothed pain. They healed. Ultimately, the most powerful could save a life. To reverse their spells, to injure others, violated the essence of their lives. No matter how justified their actions, no matter how the circumstances might warrant it, they couldn't endure using their spells for dark instead of light. Muller knew it well. He had spent his life struggling with his broken gifts.

Jarid's desperate act of self-defense had shattered him. It had broken the circle of his life. With an unrelenting remorse, the boy had finished what Murk tried to begin, taking his own sight, hearing, and speech.

Muller felt as if his heart were tearing apart. So much grief:

so many losses. He remembered the night King Daron had died; Muller mourned as much today as he had then. His uncle would have rejoiced at Jarid's return. Muller knew he should find comfort in knowing it would have gladdened Daron and perhaps helped to heal Jarid, but he felt only pain. Part of him would always believe his uncle loved him only because Daron had lost his son and grandson. Muller would never know otherwise; death had taken Daron before life could reveal the answers to Muller's unasked questions.

A rustle came from behind him, the wind playing with leaves on the ground. When it grew louder, he turned. Instead of leaves, Iris waited a few steps away.

Muller bowed. "Good morn, Your Majesty."

She flushed at the title. "Good morn, Your Highness." Breezes tossed her hair around her body. She indicated the rolling slopes and village below. "A lovely view."

"Like our royal family." The words were sour fruit in his mouth. "Beautiful on the outside, rotted from within."

Her voice gentled. "That is'n true, Muller."

"Isn't it? You heard Jarid—a shape-mage who can kill." He could hardly comprehend it. Had it been him instead of Jarid in that carriage, Muller dreaded to think what his mage "gifts" would have done. Destroyed his parents' bodies? Killed Unbent? Himself?

He feared Jarid because he feared himself.

"Jarid had provocation," Iris said.

"And if he feels he has provocation again?"

Lines of strain showed on her face. "Saints, Muller, look at what it did to him." She came forward so he could hear her better. "What if we hadna found him? Would he have spent the rest of his life atoning for being a terrified little boy who defended himself from the monster who murdered his parents and meant to kill him? He's suffered enough."

Muller answered in a low voice. "Before we knew anything about him, I had been so certain it would be best if I stepped aside. Then we discovered he was unfit to rule. Even that was all right for Aronsdale—you would do well in his place. And a child might come who had Jared's spirit. But he began to recover and suddenly we had a king who would rule, but imperfectly."

"Surely a flawed king is better than none at all."

His voice cracked. "Even then I didn't know the worst. He is an abomination. A mage who kills."

She spoke with that compassion of hers that seemed to have no limit. "We are all flawed, Muller. Just look at me."

He wondered if she had any idea how vital she appeared to others. "Iris, it may not seem so now, but you *will* come into your own as a mage, at least a sapphire, maybe an indigo, greater than Della, greater than Chime, perhaps even greater than Jarid's mother."

She started to speak, then stopped. He feared she would pursue this matter of kings and mages. What more could he say? In seeing Jarid, he saw himself. But no spell of healing could fix his soul-deep failings.

When she finally spoke, she said only, "In the past, Della said emerald was my limit."

"She was wrong. I told her so."

"You believed I had such power and you never told me?"

He pushed back his hair, moving with the grace he had never wanted rather than the warrior's power he longed to command. "Della didn't want me interfering. And she thinks I have no mage power." He tried to shrug, to show her estimation made no matter to him, but he doubted he fooled Iris. "She wouldn't listen."

"You should have told me." Iris could have condemned him. As queen she could have ordered him away, had him shunned, even imprisoned him. Instead she spoke with sympathy. "Except then you and I would have had to wed. And you want Chime."

He nodded awkwardly. "Yes."

"If I really am that strong of a mage, surely you knew it would come out."

"Once Chime and I were married, it wouldn't have mattered. We couldn't undo the union." He looked toward the castle, high on its bluff. "Then you found Jarid."

"That is why you sent me to get him."

"In part." He swept his arm out, indicating the countryside, castle and village. "What I said before is true. Aronsdale needs you. I would only bring sorrow to our people."

"How can you give up so easily?"

"You think I gave up?" She had no idea. Bending down, he dug up a rock and showed it to her. "What shape is this?"

She hesitated. "An oval."

"An imperfect shape."

"Very."

Muller offered it to her. "Can you use it for spells?"

She took the rock and concentrated on it, her forehead furrowed. Her power eddied around the edges of his mind. Instead of focusing her gift, the broken stone dispersed it like a jagged seashore breaking up waves.

"Nay, Muller." She gave him the rock. "It ruins the spell."

"As it would for any normal mage." Cupping his palm around the rock, he focused.

"Muller?"

He didn't answer, just continued to concentrate on the rock. His power swelled—and the rock suddenly turned red, glowing like a hot coal. Even knowing what to expect, he grunted and dropped it. When the stone hit the ground, the grass sizzled.

Iris gaped at him. "What did you do?"

"That," he said harshly, "is *my* mage power."

"But you have no—"

"No power?" He didn't know whether to laugh or weep. "Aye, so Della believes. Why? Because she can't feel a 'gift' as imperfect as mine. I can only use flawed shapes." He pushed the cooling rock with his boot. "You want me to create light? That was the best I could do. My spells always come out twisted. Wrong." He had to make her see; a realm that kept its freedom only because of its mages couldn't survive such a distortion of power from its highest authority. "But I have the Dawnfield mage strength, green at least, maybe blue. It would destroy Aronsdale to have me at its helm."

Iris's gaze turned luminous with moisture. "Hai, Muller."

He couldn't bear her pity. Looking down the hill, he saw an ethereally beautiful woman in a meadow below. She was walking toward their hill, her white dress drifting on the wind. "My betrothed," he murmured.

"Does Chime know?"

"Yes. She helps me. Soothes me." He rubbed the heel of his hand over his eye, hoping she hadn't seen the glimmer of tears there. "But we cannot deny the truth. She and I are flawed."

"Muller, nay."

He turned to her. "You think she doesn't realize she has far too much trouble understanding spells? She and I will never win acclaim for our gifts of the mind. But we complement each other."

"Acclaim means little." Her voice softened. "A love that makes each of you feel whole is priceless."

"A pretty thought." He tried to hide his pain. "But idealistic."

"Sometimes idealism is all we have." Iris watched Chime climbing the hill. "Jarid and I know so little about our duties.

All of us are flawed, Muller, but together, perhaps we can do what would be impossible for one of us alone." She turned to him. "Help us. Let me tell Jarid you will stay. He and I, we need you and Chime."

Muller knew he could never give her what she wanted. He couldn't measure up to the roles heredity and destiny had laid out for him. But neither could he give up, especially when she asked in such plain, earnest words.

"I will talk to Chime." He couldn't say more, lest he give her hopes where he had none.

"Thank you." Sadness showed on her face. But no, her expression hadn't changed; his spell with the rock had done more than he realized, sensitizing him to her moods. She was thinking of Jarid. After they had spoken with Unbent this morning, the king had withdrawn to his tower room, perhaps forever going back to the heartbreaking seclusion he had dared break for one day.

For the sake of Aronsdale, Muller knew he should hope Jarid remained isolated, leaving Iris to rule. But he couldn't help himself; he wished Jarid would return to them. He wanted his cousin back, his kin, his only remaining family. Neither Iris nor Jarid deserved the loneliness the future otherwise held for them.

But he feared for Aronsdale.

Iris felt Muller's grief. His golden hair blew about his beautiful face like the wings of an angel. She wished their conversation didn't hurt him.

"Look." She pointed down the hill, offering a distraction. Beyond Chime, a man was walking to Suncroft. "It is Wareman."

Muller watched the distant figure. "He unsettles me."

It didn't surprise her. "Why?"

"Something about him seems wrong."

She watched Wareman approach Chime. "I can't read him with green spells."

"You have only begun to learn your shape-gifts."

"It could be that." She spoke slowly, remembering her childhood. "But I have always had a knack for sensing people's moods, even before I knew any magecraft. With Wareman, I get nothing."

"I do." Muller grimaced. "When he is near, I can't breathe enough air."

Iris tensed as the peddler caught up with Chime. He must have called to her, because she turned around. Her posture relaxed when she saw him. They began to converse, their body language formal but not tense. "Chime seems to like him."

"She likes the beautiful things he sells." He sighed. "And Chime sees only light, never darkness."

Iris heard the affection in his words. For all that Chime scolded him and he glowered at her, they had a love few people found together. "You think this man brings darkness into Aronsdale?"

Muller hesitated. "He has a lack. He is missing a part of, well—I don't know how to describe it."

"Aye." Iris did know, but she held back, fearing to sound foolish—for to her, the peddler seemed to lack a part of his soul.

Jarid sat on the floor of the tower room with his back against the wall, as he had always done at home, in Stone's cottage. He pulled his knees to his chest and laid his forehead on them. Now everyone knew: he was an atrocity. He would return with Stone to the mountains and his isolation. As much as Jarid knew he had to go, he hated to leave Iris. But he would destroy her if he let her stay with him.

A knock came on the door.

Although he ignored it, silence no longer protected him. Nor could he shut out the compassion that flowed to him from outside. He shouldn't be able to sense Iris with a heavy door between them, but he did. She was becoming a part of him, one so close to his heart that he feared he would break into a thousand pieces when he left her.

The door opened. Jarid rose to his feet, his back to the wall as if he were facing an attacking army rather than his bride. Iris stood in the archway, guards looming behind her, their hands on the hilts of their swords, ready to defend their queen against their king. His view of the scene distorted at the edges of his vision; he hadn't yet fully relearned how to see.

Iris turned to the guards. "You may close the door."

"Your Majesty," one began. "You shouldn't risk—"

She lifted her chin. "I shall see my husband in private."

When the man hesitated, Jarid spoke in his gravelly voice. "You heard her."

The guard opened his mouth, then shut it again. With obvious reluctance, he closed the door, leaving Iris alone with Jarid. He knew he should insist she leave, but the words deserted him. He wanted her so very, very much. He put up his hands, palms out, to push her away.

"You donna fool me," she murmured.

"You must go," he said.

"Nay, my husband." Iris crossed the room, her hair swinging around her body. She stopped in front of him.

"You cannot love me," he said.

"You can say I will never be yours, but you canna tell me what I will feel." She spoke with tenderness. "Give us time to learn each other, Jarid. With you, I feel a closeness I've never known before. It is as if we have a place in the world. A home. Perhaps neither of us knows how to love the other, but the seed is there. Let us give it a chance to grow."

She besieged his defenses. His conflicted emotions bewildered him: he wanted her in his arms; he wanted to thrust her away; he longed to hope; he didn't deserve what she offered.

He drank in the sight of her hair, so full and curly, gleaming red, gold, and yellow. Her face glowed, her cheeks pink as if she had been running. He remembered their wedding night and his pulse quickened.

He spoke in a rasp. "I cannot promise you a life of the laughter and love you deserve."

"I couldna bear it if you left." She reached out to him with one hand, her arm outstretched.

It was too much. Jarid pulled her into his arms and laid his cheek on the crown of her head. "Iris——" His voice caught.

"Is it truly so horrible, to be with the likes of me?"

"It is a miracle. But you destroy my defenses."

She rested her head on his shoulder. "It is a good thing, to heal."

"It's killing me."

"Nay, Jarid. Living hurts, but that is'n death."

"I must never forget what I am."

"You are Jarid Dawnfield, King of Aronsdale."

"I am a monstrosity."

"Nay!" She drew back to look at him, her eyes flashing. "You are a marvel."

Jarid shook his head. "Muller is right. He is more worthy to be king."

"He didna say that."

"He doesn't want me to wear the crown."

"He wants it even less himself."

"He doesn't mean that."

"He means it." She set her palms against his chest. "Muller is also a mage, but his spells go awry. You fear you will kill because you have so much power within you. He fears he will kill because his spells twist out of shape."

He stared at her. "Muller is a *mage?*"

"Aye. He says I may tell only you."

Jarid leaned his forehead against hers. "He can learn to control his spells."

"He thinks not."

"I *cannot* accept the crown."

"You already have it."

"I will abdicate."

"Nay." Her melodious voice flowed over him. "What meaning would light have without darkness? Good is'n the absence of evil, it is our ability to rise above the shadows within. If you had no such goodness, you would have never punished yourself all these years." She touched his cheek. "That you have both light and shadows donna make you evil, it makes you human."

"I must go." He feared to accept this hope she offered. "You must stay."

Her voice caught. "I would miss you forever if you left me."

Jarid pulled her close again so he wouldn't have to look into her face. He couldn't speak his heart: *If I stay with you, I fear I will fall in love.* It hurt too much, for to love meant to risk the anguish of loss.

"We all leave this life someday," she murmured. "We canna let that stop us from giving our hearts. If we do, our lives have no meaning."

He knew leaving would protect Iris, but when he tried to imagine a life without her, isolated in his mountain refuge, it was unbearable. Great ice floes were breaking within him, as his defenses cracked and split.

"Let them crack," Iris murmured.

"I don't know how to love you." The words wrenched him.

She spoke softly. "Let us learn together."

It was a long moment before he spoke. Then he said "I will try. I will stay, my wife."

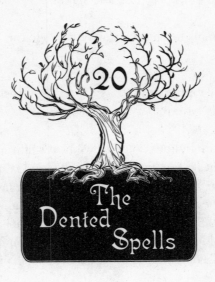

20

The Dented Spells

Chime sat alone, in a hexagonal alcove on a cushioned bench, surrounded by gilded walls and fine paintings. None of the beauty offered comfort. It rent her heart to think of Jarid as a boy, frantic to protect himself, unaware of his immense power. She had felt Unbent's unconditional love for him and Jarid's for his foster father. That they had found so great a gift in the midst of such tragedy made her tears fall.

She leaned her head against the wall, remembering how Wareman had spoken this afternoon, so solicitous, offering comfort. She couldn't tell the peddler why she grieved, but his kindness had eased her sadness. It made her wonder if he were a mage. She had warmed to him these past ten days, since they met.

A crinkling noise drew her attention. Raising her head, she saw Della in the entrance of the alcove. Dark circles showed under the mage mistress's eyes. "King Jarid wishes to see you."

Chime sat up straight. "Good graces, why?"

"I don't know." Della sounded exhausted.

"I thought he would speak with no one."

"Iris went to him. I don't know what she said." She let out a long breath. "Saints only know what he will do now. But he has asked to talk with you. It is a start."

Chime had her doubts about that, given her clumsy way with words. She thought of the Saint of Silence, a wind spirit that flowed across the land, sweeping away harsh words on currents of air. If only she had such a spirit to help her now. She would never forget the way Jarid's power had coursed through Unbent's cell, glorious and terrifying.

She spoke quietly. "He is an indigo mage."

Della didn't need to ask who she meant. But she said, "I don't think so."

"You must have felt his power." Chime raised her arms high. "It filled the room."

Della didn't answer directly. Instead she said, "In a rainbow, indigo comes between two colors."

Chime lowered her arms. "Blue and violet."

"Yes." Della continued in an odd voice, more subdued than usual. "We name mage powers according to the rainbow."

"You think he is blue?" Surely the mage mistress could see he had greater power.

Della's gaze remained steady. "No."

Suddenly Chime understood. "A violet mage? Nay! It is impossible."

"So we thought." Della gave her a wintry smile. "But impossible or not, it seems to be true."

"He is in such pain."

Della nodded. "We call our gifts light, but every power has its dark aspect. The mage who soothes can also upset. One who heals can also injure."

Chime couldn't bear such a thought. "No mage would willingly commit such evils."

"Mages rarely abuse their gifts. The price is too high." Della folded her arms as if she were cold. "In killing Murk, Jarid crippled himself, physically and emotionally. But he knows so little about his gifts. We've no idea how he will respond to us."

Chime thought of his wedding yesterday. "Last night he left the castle unable to see, hear, or speak. He came back this morning changed. I don't understand it."

"Perhaps you know better than you realize."

"I do?"

Della smiled. "Muller works his wonders with you, eh? Makes you see the world in a new way, hear new music, speak new joys."

Her lips curved upward. "He does, it is true."

"So Iris reaches Jarid."

Chime's mood softened. "By loving him, you mean."

"Well, by trying." Della squinted at her. "With Jarid, I expect it is not easy."

Chime could imagine. "Do you think Iris is indigo?"

"No...but I'm not sure. I had thought sapphire, but that isn't right." Della shook her head. "She uses her powers in ways I haven't yet untangled."

Chime tried to be happy for Iris. But it disheartened her. She had worked so hard, struggled to learn, to succeed. She might be less articulate than other people, slower, less adept, but incredibly, she had been the best mage. Now she had lost that. She had Muller and she rejoiced in his love. The rest of it shouldn't matter, but it did. For the first time in her life she had achieved something special and now it was gone.

Della was watching her. "Don't lose heart, Chime."

She straightened up. "Shall we attend the king?"

Chime unfolded her legs and stood up next to the bench. "I'm ready, ma'am." It wasn't true. But the time had come for her to face Aronsdale's enigmatic sovereign.

* * *

In the hierarchies of Aronsdale, mages ranked above all
others except the royal family, the King's Advisors, and the
Mistresses or Masters of the guilds: Blacksmith, Farmer, Husbandry, Crafter, Carpenter, Servers, and Merchant. Aronsdale
had only five full mages who were openly acknowledged:
Della, the Shape-Mage Mistress; Skylark, the healer for Suncroft, Croft's Vale, and as many villages as she could reach; Iris,
the Mage Queen; Jarid, who was an unknown; and Chime,
who had yet to establish a definite place but who ranked even
higher than Della by virtue of her emerald, faceted-sphere
gifts.

Chime told herself she had every reason to hold her head up
within the royal court. But her emotions refused to acknowledge what her intellect knew. She felt as unprepared to face the
king today as she had her first day at Suncroft, perhaps even
more so, given the differences between Jarid and Daron.

She entered the octagonal tower room with Della. The chamber reminded her of a treasure box capped by the domed ceiling, all tiled in blue and gold star mosaics. Iris and Jarid were
standing across the room, close together. Chime could tell they
had been embracing. They also looked as if they had been crying, their eyes swollen and red.

Power swirled in the chamber. The mosaics, the orb-lamp on
the round table by Jarid, the half sphere formed by the ceiling—
it focused their gifts, all of them, four of Aronsdale's mages.
When Della closed the door, completing the octagonal box, the
power surged, dizzying Chime. It was too much.

Then serenity flowed over her. She took an uneven breath,
regaining her mental balance. That sense of calm came from a
mage. She didn't think Della could make such a powerful spell,
and it didn't have Jarid's untamed quality. She looked at Iris and
the queen met her gaze, her face gentle.

Della bowed to Iris and Jarid. It startled Chime. She had yet to absorb the reality; Iris was no longer her fellow student, the girl who had moved to Della's cottage because it felt more like a home than the castle.

She was the queen.

Nor was Jarid a stranger isolated in his own private hell any longer. Yet even now that he could see, hear, and speak, he seemed locked within himself. Chime wondered if he would ever fully heal.

Steadying herself, Chime joined Della and bowed to the king and queen, more deeply than the mage mistress, taking longer, as a commoner would bow to royalty. "My honor at your presence."

"Please," Iris whispered. "Donna do that, Chime." She sounded dazed.

Straightening, Chime found herself looking at Jarid. This close, she reeled from impact of his eyes, so large and clear, a dramatic violet. Although the color wasn't unheard of in the east, where his mother had come from, Chime had never seen such before. She would have thought them unbearably beautiful if they hadn't been so haunted.

Iris spoke to him. "You willa be all right?"

The king nodded, his face strained. He touched her cheek, and she curled her hand around his fingers. Then Iris and Della withdrew from the chamber, leaving Chime alone with him.

Jarid leaned over the table, bracing his palms on its surface. With dismay, Chime saw his arms shaking.

"Your Majesty?" she asked. "Are you well?"

It was a moment before he said, "Well enough." His voice came like sand scraping on glass.

She wound the tasseled end of her belt around her hand, uncertain what to say.

Jarid closed his eyes, his head bent. After a moment he

opened them again. Finally he straightened up and indicated the chairs at the table. "Sit, please."

Chime sat. Folding her hands on the table, she strove for calm. Serenity. Maybe Iris could manage it, but she found it impossible. She wasn't sure where her gifts ended and Jarid's began; his power swamped everything else. Mage potential filled the room.

He sat across from her, his long legs stretched under the table. Then he leaned back as if to protect himself, his arms folded. His silence unnerved her. In all the protocol she had studied with Pyramid-Secretary Quill, they had never covered a situation like this one. She wanted to wind her hair around her fingers or pull at her belt, but she made herself sit still.

With so much power in the room, Chime formed a spell before she even thought about it. Beneath Jarid's impassive exterior, his moods surged: anger, hope, fear, confusion, wonder, a sense of loss. Too many impressions were flooding his senses. For fourteen years he had lived in the silent dark; now it all came too fast, too bright, too loud. She even caught brief images from his thoughts, sights distorted or wavered. Sounds echoed, became garbled, swelled, then faded.

Chime's fear receded. No wonder he sat there staring at her with such imposing silence. He was trying to find some coherence in that chaos of impressions.

"It is all right," she said. "Take your time." As soon as she spoke, she flushed, realizing she gave insult in suggesting the king needed to take his time.

Jarid, however, took no offense. He breathed out slowly, as if recovering from a long run. When he spoke, his voice had an unfinished quality. "I am unsure of protocols. If I offend, please forgive."

Chime took more care this time in her response. "You could never give offense, Your Majesty."

"No title..." He stopped as if it hurt to speak. Then he said, "Call me Jarid."

"Yes." She almost added, *Your Majesty,* but caught herself in time.

He uncrossed his arms, but he didn't seem to know where to put them. Finally he sat forward and rested his forearms on the table. "Mistress No-Cozen says you are her other mage student."

"Yes, I am."

"I need your help."

"What can I do, Your—I mean, Jarid."

"Something in Harsdown."

"Harsdown?"

"An Other."

"I'm not sure what you mean." She had trouble following his fragmented sentences.

He inclined his head, his hair rustling over his collar. It reminded her of Muller, who moved his head in exactly the same way. She saw the resemblance: both men had those high cheekbones, large eyes, and regular features. But where Muller was lithe, Jarid had a well-muscled physique; where Muller was gold, Jarid was dark; where Muller looked like grace and air to her, this man had stronger line to his jaw and a brooding demeanor.

"Harsdown," he repeated.

"Have you news about King Varqelle?"

"No." Resting his elbows on the table, he pressed his fingertips against his temples.

"Hai, Sire, I don't mean to push." Chime made a spell to soothe his headache, but it skittered around the edges of his mind, deflected by the sheer force of his own power.

"From Harsdown." He lowered his hands. "Its presence darkens the sun."

"But the day is bright." Belatedly it occurred to Chime that contradicting the king was a bad idea.

"Suncroft," he said.

She grasped at his choppy words. "Harsdown has threatened the castle?"

"Yes. Or no." He winced, rubbing his temples. "Something here. Nearby."

Chime glanced uneasily around the room. "With us?"

"No. Not in here." He stared at the table with a look so distant, she wondered if he had stopped seeing.

Then his spell formed.

It coalesced from the power around them and filled the chamber. Chime knew the truth then; Jarid had no match as a mage. Trapped within his dark, silent world, he must have fostered his gifts without ever knowing what he did, concentrating his power, undistracted by outside influences. He saw himself as darkness, but to Chime he was radiant.

He created a mood spell unlike any she had known. It saturated the room and spread outward, taking her with it like a mighty river carrying a leaf. Farther and farther it reached, throughout Suncroft and beyond. Jarid sat with his head bowed, no longer seeing, not blindness, but an immersion so deep into his trance that he lost touch with the world.

His spell was glorious.

Closing her eyes, Chime gave herself to the river of power. Her thoughts floated with his spell across the countryside, through the hills, into each succulent blade of grass, until she felt the burgeoning, fertile life. She submerged into nodding skybells, rosy box-blossoms, ancient trees draped with moss; she spanned the sky, as wide and as far as forever; she became part of Croft's Vale, cottages of sod and thatching, some with crumbling brick and mortar. She knew the blacksmith shop, the lumber mill, the inns and taverns, the market with fish carried in from Lake Mirror.

Then she hit a spike.

It disrupted the serenity of the spell the way a knife pierced a royal-bud. A darkness festered in Croft's Vale. The malevolence came from another mind, a sharp contrast to Jarid. Recoiling, Chime fell out of the spell.

She became aware of the room. Across the table, Jarid raised his head, meeting her gaze. With awe, she realized what he had done, creating a spell beyond any recorded in any of Della's histories. Green mages could sense moods only if they were near the other person, a few paces away. Jarid had reached across the land.

"That was incredible," Chime whispered.

He spoke in his rusty voice. "You felt the Other?"

She shuddered. "Yes."

"It came to Croft's Vale from Harsdown."

"How do you know?"

"I cannot...explain. But I know."

"What would you like me to do?"

"I cannot go into Croft's Vale."

Chime could imagine the tumult it would create if the long-lost prince, now king, showed up in the village. Nor did she think Jarid could handle such a commotion. He struggled to integrate the flood of impressions from his newly awakened senses. And he needed rest. His fatigue weighed on her mood spell like a great weight.

"You would like me to go?" she asked.

"You know the people," he said. "They accept you."

Chime had doubts about how much anyone here accepted her, but she let it go. His request puzzled her, though. "Wouldn't Iris understand what you need better?"

"She says she hasn't your experience with spells."

That surprised Chime. Iris had never said such to her. "Would you like me to search out more about the Other?"

"Yes. Bring a hexagon of army officers with you."

That seemed an overreaction. "I would draw too much notice if I went with guards." She smiled ruefully. "It would be obvious I'm not in the village to visit the market or a friend."

He paused, thinking. "Take Brant and Della."

It was a good idea. Even the most nefarious forces would quail before Lord Firestoke and Mistress Non-Cozen. Unfortunately it wouldn't work. "They are King's Advisors. They would draw just as much attention." She felt a blush spread through her cheeks. "People don't take me seriously, and I visit Croft's Vale often. They won't suspect anything if I turn up at the market."

He frowned. "You must take someone with you."

"My maids, of course." She brightened. "We can buy cloth for new gowns and tunics."

"You do this often?"

"All the time," she admitted. "No one will suspect us being there."

He nodded to her. "I thank you for your help."

Chime wasn't sure he should thank her for anything. Without his incredible spell flowing through her, she doubted she would find much in Croft's Vale. He seemed unaware of the full extent of his power.

Unease trickled over Chime. If Jarid ever chose to use his powers for other than good, nothing could stop him.

The market was a swirl of color, noise, and smells. Chime strolled with Aria and Reed, her circle-maids, two young women from the palace staff. They weren't mages; their circle rank signified their status, highest among the apprentices, but not yet full-fledged members of the Server's Guild with three-dimensional ranks.

Her maids chattered to each other, enjoying the market. Each carried a basket over one arm, and they had both let their hair down so it could blow in the wind. Chime longed to free hers as well, but propriety demanded she sweep it up on her head. She had asked Aria to braid gold and silver cords into it, though. If she had to present a restrained appearance, at least she could sparkle in the process.

They passed stalls where red-cheeked men sang out about their produce: oranges and tangerines from the south, apples and quinces from the west, fat carrots and lettuce, beans of every kind, and turban-shaped squash that resembled the exotic headpieces worn by merchants from the countries of Shazire and Taka Mal. Chime saw women in tunics embroidered with the geometric designs popular in western Aronsdale; men in the heavy boots and rough garb of the north; and children in flapping, colorful tunics who ran everywhere. The clang of metal hitting metal rang through the air as a blacksmith showed off his wares.

Aria, a slender girl with white-gold hair, smiled at Chime. "I do so love to come here on a sunny day." The maid indicated Suncroft on its distant hill, its yellow stone glowing in the sunshine. "Truly a home fit for the sun."

"A sun's croft." Although it comforted Chime that the castle had a humble name, she felt out of place in its elegance. She had wanted to accept Della's offer for her mage students to live in her cottage, but had feared that she would have had even more trouble then fitting in with the royal court at Suncroft. Yet Iris had stayed in the cottage until her marriage. Chime wished she had that confidence to ignore what people thought of her.

This morning, though, she enjoyed herself, exclaiming over glimmering bolts of cloth with Aria and Reed. As they sorted through the fabrics, she concentrated on those with patterns, using their shapes to focus her search for moods of the Harsdown presence. Cloth just provided flat shapes, though, limiting her spells. The only three-dimensional form near enough to help was the wooden ball that topped a nearby pole, a shape too powerful for her to use.

Chime hadn't risked wearing her faceted emerald ball. Given its great value, far beyond any other jewelry she had ever owned, she donned it only on formal occasions. It would have drawn attention here, besides which, it would be easy in this crowd for someone to steal it. She felt sure Della would have cautioned her about it, had Chime told her what she intended to do during her trip to market. But she hadn't revealed her plans to Della, knowing the mage mistress would also caution her against going. Chime wanted to do this, both for Jarid, who had asked for her help, and to prove to herself that she could be an asset here.

Eventually she bought two bolts of cloth and moved on through the market. She made a spell each time she passed an object she could use to focus, a pyramid box in a stall, a decorative faceted orb, a star hanging from a beam, but she found nothing unusual, no trace of menace. She only skimmed the moods of people around her; any more would have felt like an intrusion, a misuse of her gifts, making her nauseous.

The market filled a plaza, with buildings on four sides. Chime and her maids wandered among the stalls, stopping here and there until they reached the Clover Inn. Relieved to rest, Chime sank down onto a bench against a wall of the inn, under an awning. Aria and Reed settled next to her, talking companionably with each other.

To their right, the inn's door formed a rectangle, as did the sign hanging from a chain above it. A blue lamp swung by the door, a faceted orb hanging from a beam. Chime *felt* its shape. Twenty sides. It called to her. She hesitated to use such a powerful form without Della, who could help if her magecraft faltered or her spell backfired.

Chime sat listening to Aria and Reed until she firmed up her resolve. Then she focused through the faceted orb—and a surge of power hit her like a flood of cold water. With a sharply indrawn breath, she sat up straight.

"Lady Chime?" Aria turned. "Are you all right?"

"Yes, fine." It astonished Chime that she sounded so normal; inside she was humming with power. She smiled at her maids. "I'm just going to rest a few moments."

"Aye, ma'am." Aria made solicitous noises until Chime leaned back and closed her eyes. Then the maids began to chat again, their voices low.

Chime looked through her lashes at the faceted lamp. Seeing rather than touching it didn't let her build as much power, but with such a high level shape, her spell still formed with strength. The moods of her maids washed over her like sparkling water, Aria's amiability and Reed's curiosity. She reformed the spell to give them privacy. Then she let it hover around her like an invisible cloud. The pleasant day eased her thoughts, though she worried about Muller. He was struggling so hard to adjust to the changes in his life, so different from what he had expected these past fourteen years.

At first Chime thought her thoughts about Muller had stirred her disquiet. Gradually, though, she realized the disturbance came from outside of her mind. If the beautiful day, the voices of her maids, and the breezes were all part of a lovely melody, then what she picked up now were discordant notes. That bitter chord had the same threatening aspect she had sensed in Croft's Vale this morning. A presence lurked here, one she feared.

Then it noticed her.

Chime couldn't keep her voice from shaking. "I had to leave. He knew I was there." She was too agitated to sit, so she stayed on her feet, standing with Brant Firestoke in the Hexagon Room where he did his work. She felt slight and insubstantial compared to his tall, powerful figure.

Brant was half-sitting on the table where he spent many hours working on government documents, one of his legs braced against the ground. Jarid paced by the wall, his hair rustling about his shoulders like a dark curtain. Della and Iris stood at the other end of the table. Brant had also called in Cube-General Fieldson, commander of the army in the king's absence. Fieldson stood near the wall, intently watching and listening.

"You are sure he knew you were there?" Brant asked.

"I'm sure." Chime wished Muller were here, but he had gone out hunting for game earlier with a party from the castle.

Jarid stopped pacing and stood by a tall window, facing her, silhouetted against the light. "You said 'he.' Not it."

Chime made herself stop twisting her hands in the hem of her yellow tunic. "Yes, Your Majesty. The mind I touched was human." She shuddered. "Inhuman, too."

"How can he be both?" Della asked.

"How?" Fieldson's voice was as dry as a desert. "Ask any warrior in combat, Mistress No-Cozen."

"He felt so cold," Chime said. "Like ice."

"Do you know his identity?" Fieldson asked.

She shook her head. "I couldn't tell. But he might recognize me. His spell was stronger than mine."

In the same instant Della said, "His what?" Iris asked, "He is a mage?"

"Yes. His power was huge. But it had—holes." She didn't know how to put into words the lack she had felt. "It was missing something."

"No green," Jarid said.

They all turned to him.

"Green?" Fieldson asked. "You mean the mage color?"

"Yes." Jarid's voice rasped. "He doesn't have it."

The door to the office suddenly banged open. Chime jumped, her pulse ratcheting up, then exhaled when she saw Muller. He wore his heavy leggings, riding boots, and hunting jacket, and he hadn't even bothered to straighten his wind-blown appearance, which told her just how fast he must have come when he heard she had returned.

He strode over to her. "Are you all right?" Then he seemed to remember the others. Turning to Jarid, he bowed, his hair swinging forward. "My apology at my precipitous entry, Your Majesty." He sounded furious rather than apologetic.

Jarid nodded, his gaze hooded.

Chime felt Muller's emotions roiling. Obviously he had heard about her trip this afternoon, probably from his valet, Sam Threadman, who spent a great deal of time with Chime's maid Aria. To head him off before he blew up, she said, "Stop fuming, love. I am fine."

He took hold of her shoulders. "Then why did I hear such terrible rumors?"

Chime didn't try to hide what had happened. He needed to know about the danger. She outlined her trip to the village, using as neutral terms as possible, but by the time she finished, his face had turned red. He swung around to Jarid, his eyes smoldering. "You had no right to ask her to take such a risk."

"Take care, Lord Muller," Brant warned. "You are addressing His Majesty, the King of Aronsdale."

"He speaks truly," Jarid said tiredly.

Chime frowned at them all. "It was fine." It wasn't fine; she would never feel safe again, but that didn't change her responsibility. Nor would she stand for them treating her as if she were made of lilac-glass. "I am perfectly able to carry out such a mission."

"I don't want you going to the village again," Muller said. "Blazes, Chime, what if he comes after you?"

Jarid walked over to them. Chime had an eerie sense, as if he had shut out everyone but her and Muller.

"He is gone," Jarid said. "He was at the Clover Inn. After Chime found him, he left. He journeys to Harsdown."

Iris joined them. "Can you locate him now?"

Jarid glanced at his wife, including her in his sphere of concentration, shook his head. "I have lost him."

"How can you be sure it is him?" she asked.

"Through Chime. She linked to him and I followed his…" Jarid hesitated. "I don't know the right word. The echo of his mind?"

Chime wasn't sure what he meant, but if anyone had the power to sense another mage, it was Jarid.

Brant regarded him dubiously. "The echo of his mind?" He glanced at Della No-Cozen. "Perhaps I don't understand."

Chime suspected he was offering her a chance to make Jarid's comment look less strange. Della, however, remained true to her No-Cozen name. She spoke briskly. "I have never heard of a mage echo."

Inspiration struck Chime. "It is like a harmonic in music. Or the second arch of colors in a double rainbow. Jarid senses an echo of the power from other mages." She stopped as her sense of sanity caught up with her impetuous comments. She had never spoken up during a council among the King's Advisors. They would probably laugh now.

No one scorned her outburst, though. In fact, Della said, "With enough power, a mage might do such."

Fieldson had stayed back, saying little and hearing much, but now he came forward. "Do you fear a threat from Harsdown, Your Majesty?"

Jarid regarded him steadily. "Yes."

"Why now?" Muller asked.

Jarid spoke roughly. "A government changes hands. A country is vulnerable."

"Do you believe Harsdown poses an immediate threat," Fieldson asked. "Or a long-term one?"

"Immediate, I think," Jarid said. "The Other, this dark mage—he knows we have discovered him."

"We have no idea who he is," Iris said.

Chime recalled her sense of familiarity with the mage in the Clover Inn. She had assumed she recognized him because she had touched him before, through Jarid. But could it be more? Sometimes mood spells helped her recall a mood she had detected before. She tried to made a new spell using the room, but too many irregularities marred its form: windows, moldings along the ceiling, paintings on the walls. They were like a buzz that disrupted her concentration.

Jarid's power suffused the room, but remained latent. Muller had the opposite problem; he was struggling to hold back his power, which could easily surge in this imperfect hexagon. Chime no longer wondered that other mages couldn't feel his gifts; they were somehow at an angle to a normal mage. One had to be able to look around the corner to recognize him. She had from the start, but no one else seemed to see Muller as she did.

It suddenly came to Chime. "Plates!"

Everyone blinked at her with what she called The Look, which people took on when they thought she was making foolish comments.

"Lady Chime?" That came from Fieldson.

Her cheeks were burning, but she couldn't stop this time even if she did fear to make an idiot out of herself. This was too important. "The peddler. Wareman. We purchased some of his serving dishes."

"Wareman?" Della shrugged. "He is harmless."

"I am not so sure," Iris said. "He troubles me."

"Why?" Fieldson asked. He was taking her comments as seriously as he would input from any of the others.

Muller grimaced. "He has dark patches in his mage ability. No green."

"How would you know such a thing?" Brant asked.

Muller froze. Startled, Chime realized that with so many mages at Suncroft and so much tension driving them, he was having trouble guarding his secret. Too many people knew: Chime, Iris, Jarid.

The king answered. "Yes. Dark patches. Holes."

"I felt it, too," Iris said. "A lack of color."

Brant refused to be sidetracked. He considered Muller. "No green. How would you know this?"

"I told him," Chime said, speaking too fast.

Brant glanced at her. "I thought you liked Wareman."

"He has been gracious to me. But it is true, I cannot make green spells with him."

"Wareman is from Aronsdale," Iris said. "I donna believe he could have pretended his accent, gestures, and body language so well if he came from Harsdown."

Muller spoke tightly. "That doesn't mean he didn't betray Aronsdale."

"But why would he?" Chime could see no reason anyone would choose bleak Harsdown over lovely Aronsdale. Not that she had ever seen Harsdown.

Muller's face gentled. "Would that we all had your innocence."

She glowered at him. "I am not naïve."

"You are light," he murmured. Then realizing they had an audience, he cleared his throat. "So," he said to everyone. Then he seemed to run out of words.

Brant cocked an eyebrow. "Yes, Your Highness?"

Unlike in the past, today Muller didn't bristle at him. He said only, "If we face an immediate threat from Harsdown, we must prepare the army."

"Against what?" Fieldson asked. "We need more to plan for than an undefined threat."

"An invasion, perhaps." Jarid pushed his hand through his hair. "I cannot lead an army."

"Jarid, nay," Chime said. He stood there, muscled and fit, broad-shouldered, in every way the image of a warrior. "Do not say such a thing."

"It is true," Jarid said. "I can fight, but I know nothing of war strategies." He turned to Muller, his gaze steady. "You must lead in my place."

Muller started. "Your Majesty, I'm hardly—"

"You are my family," Jarid said roughly. "Call me by my name."

Chime wondered if Jarid knew how many protocols he had just broken. Muller was a member of the royal court; as such he was expected to use proper address with the king regardless of their kinship. Muller seemed stunned, but also... *relieved*. Perhaps Jarid had another reason for ignoring protocol, knowing how Muller wrestled with his change in status. For all that Jarid had spent years without his sight, Chime suspected he saw in other ways, into the heart.

Muller spoke stiffly. "I am gratified by your faith in my ability, Your—Jarid."

"Faith indeed." Brant looked as if he had bitten into a sour apple.

"Your Majesty," Fieldson began.

"I have made my choice. Lord Muller will lead my army." Jarid looked around at them all. "Do not underestimate my cousin."

In that moment, Chime decided she liked the king.

Jarid went to the window and beckoned to Muller. He joined

the king, his posture so tense, Chime wondered if he intended to refuse the command. But he stood with Jarid, gazing at Suncroft and beyond its walls to the hills of Aronsdale. Seeing them together, both the same height, one gold, the other dark, she felt a tightening in her chest.

They each fought their inner demons.

21

Forest of Dreams

Sweat dripped off Muller's face as he focused on his opponent, Arkandy Ravensford, a hexahedron-major and superb swordsman. The day's heat pressed down on them. Sunlight glinted off their swords, and those of the other warriors practicing in the Octagon Yard. In battle, Muller would wear leather armor and chain mail, but he eschewed it now, striving to harden himself. Although he and Arkandy wielded blunted swords, Muller's muscles ached from when Arkandy had pierced his defenses and whacked him in the torso.

Finally Arkandy stepped back and raised his sword, the signal to request a rest. Muller paused, acknowledging the break with relief.

Arkandy lowered his sword. "You fought well today."

Muller grinned at his friend. "You gave me a run."

Arkandy laughed. "Have to keep you working." He picked up a cloth in his pile of equipment and wiped sweat off his face. "Will you train with the men later?"

"After midday." Muller hadn't yet adjusted to the decree Jarid had made yesterday, naming him commander of the army. He felt no more qualified for the position than when he had expected to lead them as king, but he had never doubted his ability as a swordsman. During practice, he could forget his lack of confidence.

As he and Arkandy walked across the yard, Muller brooded. Watching the archers train this morning, he had been troubled by their poor aim. Could his mage power have contributed? He didn't want his presence to constrain the fighting ability of his men. A pulled bow formed a four-sided figure with uneven sides. A flawed shape. But it was *too* imperfect to stir his mage power, or so he had believed. Although he didn't think he had made spells that affected their aim, he could never be certain.

"You are quiet today," Arkandy said. He was a burly man about Muller's age, a country gentleman from a farm south of Suncroft. His wide face, brown eyes, and shock of golden-brown curls gave him a stoic appearance.

"What troubles you?" Muller asked.

Arkandy looked startled. "My apology. I've been thinking about Harsdown. But I didn't mean to sound querulous."

"You didn't." Belatedly Muller wondered how he had known Arkandy was worried. He hadn't consciously made a mood spell, but now that he thought about it, he felt his power simmering. He saw no shapes nearby that he might have inadvertently used to focus, however. Although he needed imperfect shapes, they had to be recognizable as geometric forms. The blade of his sword deviated enough from a triangle to cause only a trickle of power. It rarely threw off his ability to fight and it wasn't enough for a mood spell.

Muller glanced at the Mage Tower of the castle—and saw a tall figure in the window of the top chamber. A chill ran up his spine. Although the man was too far away to see clearly, he knew it was Jarid. An insight came to Muller, so unexpected that he stopped in the middle of a step, his foot raised.

Arkandy halted next to him. "Mull?" The nickname came from when they had been boys together, both sent to foster at the castle. With a grin, he added, "Are you doing a jig?"

"Pah." Muller set down his foot. "I could out dance you any day."

With an amiable laugh, Arkandy headed for the castle again. Muller went with him, unable to voice his confusion even to his closest friend. Although Muller felt certain he had made the spell that revealed Arkandy's concern, he also was convinced Jarid had helped shape it. He doubted his cousin had done it on purpose; Muller had picked up no sense of deliberate interference from Jarid. No, what he felt was far more surprising.

His spell hadn't twisted.

Muller hesitated to trust that impression. If Jarid had instinctively straightened the spell, it suggested Muller could learn to do the same. He feared to entertain that hope; it would make the disappointment that much harder if he failed. But he remembered Iris's words: *All of us are flawed, Muller, but together, perhaps we can do what would be impossible for one alone.*

"Are you all right?" Arkandy asked.

"Fine, yes. Just tired." Muller wondered, not for the first time, if Arkandy suspected his gifts. He glanced at his friend. "Tell me something."

"Yes?"

"Do I seem as accident prone now as I used to be?"

"I wouldn't say accident prone, exactly. You have bad luck."

"You could call it that," Muller grumbled.

"But yes, it does seem better, now that you mention it." Arkandy grinned at Muller. "Chime has a good effect, eh?"

"She does indeed." Chime didn't straighten his spells, but she did smooth his jagged edges. He had managed better since he met her.

They split up at the castle and Muller went on to his suite. His body ached, but even so, he felt better than he had in a long time. Perhaps he might conquer his mage gifts after all. He wanted to resist that hope, but it insisted on staying.

As Muller approached his suite, its gilt doors swung open. Sam Threadman, his valet, stood framed in the entrance, scowling mightily.

"How did you know I was coming?" Muller asked.

With dignity, the offended valet moved aside to let him enter. "I looked out." He indicated the round window by the door, which showed a stained-glass lark in a field of open royal-buds, those flowers that bloomed only a few days each year. Sam crossed his arms and regarded him with disapproval. "You are late."

"So I am," Muller said amiably. "Why were you looking for me?"

Sam shut the door. "The cube-general sent his pyramid-assistant to talk to your pyramid-assistant. Apparently you didn't tell your assistant you were training. So he sent his octagon-assistant to find someone who knew where you had gone." He glowered with great effect. "The octagon-assistant found your square-butler who found me."

Muller squinted at him. "That is a truly impressive chain of people."

His valet refused to be mollified. "I would ask that Your Most Esteemed Highness let us know where to find you so that we don't go running around the castle like callow young men in search of a purpose."

Muller held back his laugh. "No one would ever mistake you as such," he assured Sam. "Everyone knows you are the reason that the callow young man you serve manages to make his appointments on time when he does."

Sam finally relented. "Milord, you should not refer to yourself as callow. You have acquitted yourself admirably during these trying times."

That surprised Muller. "I'm glad someone thinks so."

"Certainly." Sam looked him over. "Though I must say, your apparel could use some help."

This time Muller did laugh, aware of his sweat-soaked shirt and leggings. "So it could."

While Sam set up a bath, Muller went into the hexagonal room he used as an office and stood at the rolltop desk, studying the scrolls he had taken from the library last night. They described strategies and weapons used in various battles in other countries. Aronsdale hadn't had a true war for so long, most of their military scrolls were outdated.

When Sam bade him return to his bedroom later, Muller discovered with gratitude that his valet had arranged for a tub of steaming water. Although the pumps at Suncroft made it possible to bring in water from an underground river, it wasn't easy to heat enough water for an entire bath.

An ivory screen surrounded the tub, a new one painted with colorful birds in exotic trees. Probably a member of Muller's staff had bought it in Croft's Vale from a merchant who came to Aronsdale from the south. Muller wished they could build a similar trade with Harsdown and countries to its west, but he doubted King Varqelle would ever let Aronsdale merchants travel freely through his country.

While Muller soaked in his bath, Sam stood on the other side of the screen and caught him up on the latest news. "Apparently the generals want to send me into Harsdown. They wish to discuss strategy with you."

"They always want to invade Harsdown," Muller said. "They never do. They know we probably can't win. Why the urgency today?"

"I can't say, sir. Their assistants didn't see fit to tell me." Now Sam sounded annoyed.

Muller smiled, glad his valet couldn't see him. Sam had never seemed to comprehend that a valet's duties didn't extend to the governance of Aronsdale. Personally Muller thought Sam had more sense than half the royal court.

"Tell me," Muller said. "What would you do about Harsdown if you thought they posed a threat?"

"What kind of threat?"

"Well, yes, that is the question, isn't it?" Perhaps that was why Fieldson wanted to see him. "Maybe they have new information." With reluctance, Muller stood up. "I should go find out what they want."

"I will see to your clothes." Sam sounded positively smug. "You will outshine those drab generals."

"That will impress them," Muller said dryly. "'Here is our commander, the best dressed soldier in Aronsdale.'"

Sam sniffed. "Clothes are no matter to take lightly."

Despite Sam's protests about sartorial flair, Muller donned only a simple tunic and leggings, light gold, nothing to draw attention. He doubted he would inspire confidence in his officers if they continued to think of him as a fop. He wasn't certain they were wrong, but he would endeavor to convince them otherwise anyway. In the past, Muller had bridled when his advisors lectured him, especially Brant, who always made him grit his teeth. But he had realized of late that if he spent more time listening, it allowed him to work through matters without becoming defensive.

He left his suite and headed to the Sunstone Hall, a long room Fieldson and Brant used for strategy meetings. He found them both there, seated halfway down the table that extended the length of the hall. Deep in discussion, they didn't notice Muller until he reached them.

Brant looked up with a start. Then he and Fieldson rose to their feet. "My greetings, Your Highness," Brant said.

Muller nodded to them both. "My staff said you wished to speak with me."

Cube-General Fieldson gestured to a chair. "Yes. We have news."

Muller sat with them. "Where is King Jarid?"

Brant pushed his hand through his silvery hair. "That is the problem. We don't know. He left the castle a few hours ago, with orders that neither Lord Firestoke nor I was to follow."

That gave Muller pause. It would be odd for any king to disappear; with Jarid, who knew what might happen. "Did he say why?"

"Not directly." Fieldson rubbed his chin. "He did mention Harsdown. I believe he intends to use his mage skills in searching for answers about the presence he and Lady Chime detected in Croft's Vale yesterday."

Brant spoke darkly. "Saints forbid he should just tell us what he is doing."

Muller almost smiled, but he held it back. It amused him to see Brant annoyed at someone else for once. He must have sought out Muller when the king disappeared, and the message became garbled along its convoluted path to him.

"Do you want me to search for him?" Muller asked. It sounded like Jarid had forbidden only Brant and Fieldson to follow. Muller had more leeway in his interactions with the king, given their kinship. Still, he didn't seem the best choice. "He would probably be more open to Iris."

Brant scowled. "It seems the young man also avoids his wife today. He told her not to follow him, either."

"Does she know where he went?" Muller asked.

"She has no idea," Brant said.

"He has been gone too long." Fieldson drummed his fingers on the arm of his chair. "Given the recent changes in his life, we have concern he is feeling—" He spoke carefully. "Perhaps overwhelmed."

Muller knew they feared the king was crazy. He didn't

think his cousin had lost his mind, but Jarid remained an enigma. "I will talk with Iris," he decided. "Then I will look for Jarid."

Brant raised his eyebrows. Muller immediately felt the familiar surge of insecurity that always came to him when he faced Brant's disapproval.

Then, incredibly, Brant said, "A good idea."

The rare compliment gratified Muller. He did wish, though, that Brant didn't look so surprised.

Iris walked with Muller along a blue gravel path in one of the castle gardens. "Jarid often withdraws. He needs to be alone." She brushed her hand along the slender trunk of a tree. "He feels inundated with people, sights, sounds. It is too much."

"What if he decides not to come back?" Muller had felt that way himself more than once, overwhelmed at the thought of ruling when he lacked so many qualities needed by a king. And he had less to deal with than Jarid.

"I've worried about that." Iris stopped by a cluster of royal-buds and cupped her hand around one. "The night we were married, he left me alone in the forest and went off by himself. I searched for hours. But he found me at dawn." She looked up at Muller. "And he could see."

Muller's thoughts gentled. Perhaps in loving Jarid, Iris used her mage powers to heal him. But that would mean she could heal grief, which only an indigo mage could do. Although he knew she had great strength, he didn't think it was indigo. She wasn't truly a sapphire, either, though. He had no idea how to describe her spells.

"Do you know when he started to hear again?" he asked.

She resumed her walk. "The morning after the coronation."

"You mean that morning we spoke with Unbent?" It was hard to believe only two days had passed since then.

"Yes." She considered him. "Why don't you take Unbent with you? Jarid trusts him."

As much as Muller disliked the idea, he knew it made sense. He also knew why no one else had suggested it; Unbent was the last person Brant and Fieldson wanted near the king. Jarid had ordered them to release his foster father and provide him a suite in the castle, but it was obvious they considered the decision foolhardy.

"I will ask him," he decided.

"My thanks, Muller."

Her use of his name startled him. In the past, he had barely noticed her deferential attitude toward him. Now their roles had reversed. Or no, that wasn't true. They were kin now. He bowed to her anyway, observing the protocols. He had made his decision to give up the crown; now he would accept the consequences.

A box-butler opened the door when Muller's pyramid-secretary knocked. Muller stood back while the butler and secretary arranged matters. Within moments, the butler was escorting them through Unbent's suite, with its scalloped moldings and sunbirch furniture. Circle mosaics worked into the chairs and tables had artful notches here and there, prodding Muller's power. To dampen his response, he focused on unbroken octagons that bordered the doorways.

The butler ushered him onto a balcony that curved out from the castle wall in a half circle. Then he withdrew with Muller's secretary, closing the beveled glass doors, leaving Muller alone—except for one other person. Unbent stood a few paces away, at the curved railing of the balcony, gazing out at the mountains. Muller was almost certain Unbent knew he was there, but the older man gave no sign. So Muller waited, giving him time.

Unbent looked far healthier today than when they had found

him in the dungeon. Color had replaced his pallor, he had shaved his beard, and his gray hair had a shine. He stood true to his name, unbent despite his advanced years. His haunted look remained the same, however.

Muller wanted to hate this man. Yet the king loved him, perhaps more than the father he recalled so little of now. It bewildered Muller. He would never forget Jarid's father. Prince Aron had been distant to most people, but never with his kin, including his young cousin. Muller had looked up to him, admiring his strength and steady nature.

Aron had died when Muller was fourteen. It happened so suddenly. It had been that way with everyone Muller loved: his grandfather a few months ago, his father when Muller had been seven, and his mother when he had been ten. Better to love no one than to weep so often. But Muller couldn't stop loving. He had never been able to wall away his emotions. He doubted his anger at Unbent would ever ease, but it was impossible to hate a man who had been such a devoted father to Jarid.

After awhile, he went to stand with the craggy farmer. "My greeting, Master Unbent."

Unbent didn't seem surprised by his appearance. "My greeting, Your Highness." His accent resembled Iris's, but with a rougher tone, lacking her melodic quality. Although their home provinces weren't far apart, he lived much higher in the mountains, in one of the most remote areas of Aronsdale.

Unbent looked at him. "No one ever gave me a title before."

"The king calls you father." Muller couldn't keep the tightness out of his voice.

"Aye. I don't deserve it."

Muller wanted to say, *No, you don't.* But only Jarid could decide whom he considered a father.

"King Jarid went into the forest earlier," Muller said. "No one has seen him since."

"He has always done so."

Always? Muller couldn't imagine letting a deaf and blind man wander alone in those desolate mountains where Unbent had lived with his foster son. "And you let him?"

"Yes. He needed to feel he could rely on himself."

"What if something happened to him?"

"He didn't go far." Unbent shook his head. "This power of his, I don't claim to understand it. I only know that Dani needs—" He stopped. "I mean, King Jarid."

It flustered Muller to hear Unbent use a nickname for the king. "Needs what?"

"Places outside. Trees, mountains, life. It renews him. But always, no matter where he went, I felt his power. I knew if he needed help. Then I would go get him."

Muller made himself ask for the help he resented needing from this man who had taken Jarid out of his life for so long. "Will you go with me to look for him?"

Unbent's brow furrowed. "Why? He is fine."

"How do you know?"

"We have a bond. I can feel his power."

Muller had thought only mages were sensitive to other mages. When he was near the king, he felt as if he were bathed in radiance, but they had to be in reasonably close proximity. Right now he felt nothing at all.

"Can you make spells?" Muller asked him.

"Nay. I'm no mage." Unbent hesitated. "I don't know how Jarid made that bond with me. But it became stronger over the years, until now I can always tell if he needs help."

"And you think he is all right?"

"He sleeps."

Muller wasn't sure what he expected, but that wasn't it. "You are sure?"

"Aye. His mind is quiet."

"Why would he go sleep in a forest?" It seemed truly strange to Muller.

"Maybe he didn't intend to." Concern shaded Unbent's voice. "He is exhausted."

"I should find him. He may not be safe."

Unbent hesitated.

"What is it?" Muller asked.

"And you would take me with you?"

"If you will come."

"A man you must surely distrust."

Yes, Muller thought. But he forced out the truth. "My cousin trusts you. He is what matters here."

"What will you do if you find him?"

"Ask him to come back to the castle."

"And if he says no?"

Muller held back his frustration. He knew Unbent wanted to protect Jarid. That his ward had turned out to be a king may have daunted him, but apparently nothing would stop him from treating Jarid like a son.

"I won't make him return," Muller said. "But I must at least try to convince him. I gave my word."

Unbent nodded, apparently willing to accept that answer. "Very well. I will go with you."

By the time Muller and Unbent had gone several miles, Muller was worn out. They hiked over hills and through woods scattered across the rolling countryside. Muller had considered himself fit, indeed, in good shape, but he needed all his energy to keep Unbent's pace. It gave him a new respect for the rigors of the life Unbent had lived.

Finally Muller slowed to a stop and bent over, bracing his hands against his knees as he gulped in air. When Unbent came back to him, Muller straightened up, still breathing hard. "Why are you in such a hurry?"

Unbent looked confused. "Hurry?"

"Never mind." Muller stretched one of his aching legs, then the other. "You are sure we're going to where Jarid sleeps?"

"Can't you feel him now?"

Muller almost said, *No, of course not.* But when he concentrated without the distraction of trying to keep up with Unbent, he did sense power around them. It seemed undefined, as if—well, as if it slumbered.

"Yes. I do." It daunted him to think Jarid claimed a mage potential so great, it encompassed the countryside. "How much farther?"

"Maybe a few miles."

Muller nodded tiredly and resumed walking, setting a slower pace. They went down a hill, through grasses waving at knee height. Wild flowers bloomed everywhere, sun-orbs and swaying fire-lilies. The terrain remained the same for the next half-hour, low hills with few trees. Eventually they approached another forest, this one more extensive than others they had passed through.

For the first time, Unbent hesitated. "He dreams."

Muller tilted his head. He felt it, too, an agitation in the slumbering aura of the woods. It didn't come from the wind or rustling grass. Muller didn't know which troubled him more, that Jarid had fallen asleep here, alone and undefended, or that his strength was so great, his nightmares inundated the land itself.

They continued on, more slowly now. After passing a few trees that straggled up the slope, they entered the forest. It was older than the woods around Croft's Vale and extended as far as Muller could see. Moss grew on the trees and shape-vines curled along branches, hanging down in great loops, vivid with rosy box-blossoms. Very little sunlight filtered past the dense canopy. Neither Muller nor Unbent spoke. Muller had an eerie sense that if the quiescent forest were disturbed, it would wake with an intelligence of its own.

Unbent never faltered. He made his way among the ancient woods as if he followed a well trod path. The forest had relatively little undergrowth, but fallen trees blocked their way, some so old that earth partially covered them and moss grew along their crumbling trunks.

The untamed beauty of the forest took Muller's breath. If he and Chime had time to themselves, he would bring her here. He didn't miss the irony, that this wilderness was the antithesis of the order they strove to keep in their lives. The forest called to the wildness he had suppressed within himself. His father had drowned when an unexpected thunderstorm hit while he was riding a horse through a narrow canyon. Three years later, Muller had lost his mother in a blizzard. The day the search party had found her frozen body, he had sworn he would never again let the wild control his life, either in spirit or reality.

Unbent stopped at a huge trunk that must have fallen decades ago, perhaps longer. Even lying on its side, it rose higher than Muller stood. Parts of it had caved in and new trees sprouted along its length. When Unbent grasped a handhold and begin to climb, the trunk crumbled under his feet. But he kept his purchase. He paused at the top, and for the first time his fatigue showed. His age seemed to press on him, his gray hair hanging about his weathered face and stubble darkening on his chin. Then he looked over the other side—and his demeanor lightened as if sunlight had broken through the forest.

Muller tackled the fallen mammoth. He almost lost his footing as he scaled the trunk, but he reached Unbent with no serious mishap. Leaning over, he saw Jarid sitting on the other side, sleeping against the trunk in a grassy area sprinkled with white star-flowers. The king's face clenched with whatever specters disturbed his dreams.

"By the spheres," Unbent murmured. "How can he be so fierce and so beautiful at the same time?"

For an instant Muller hated his cousin. Jarid was everything he longed to be—strong, fierce, powerful, a true warrior—and the king didn't even care. Then Muller pushed down his angry thoughts. Jarid had also lived in hell for fourteen years.

"What should we do?" Muller asked.

"Not surprise him," Unbent said. "When he is waking, he has less control over his spells."

"Do you think he might hurt us?"

"He has never harmed me." Unbent slanted a wary look at Muller. "Several times he set the woods on fire. He helped me put out the flames before it caused serious damage."

"And when he sleeps? His nightmares could bring to life whatever spirits live in these woods." Muller immediately wished he could take back the words. Any logical person would scoff at such an idea.

"You think spirits live here?" Mercifully Unbent didn't laugh. "Could be."

Although Muller hesitated to admit it, he felt as if the forest were aware of him. People would deride at the idea, he knew, though they found nothing odd in shape-mages. He supposed it was because mages were understood, whereas trees didn't have minds, except in myths and legends. Perhaps what he felt came from Jarid rather than the forest.

Unbent let himself down the trunk and jumped to the ground, landing far enough away that he didn't disturb the king. Jarid's head jerked and his hand curled into a fist, but he continued to sleep. When Muller glanced at Unbent, the other man shook his head. So Muller stayed put; Unbent knew better how to deal with Jarid.

Disturbances filled the forest. Vague shapes moved at the edges of his vision—

And a man screamed.

Trespass

The cry echoed through the forest. A man had shouted Jarid's name. Even more eerie, Muller recognized the voice: Prince Aron, Jarid's father.

Sweat dripped down Muller's neck. He forced himself to remain still, knowing the scream couldn't be real. Unbent showed no sign of having heard. He knelt by Jarid and laid his hand on the king's forearm. When the king jerked, Unbent froze, letting only the light pressure of his hand affect his son.

Jarid suddenly sat forward, his eyes opening fast. Heat rushed around Muller, like a flash fire. He saw no flames, but distortion rippled in the air.

As Jarid's gaze cleared, his rigid posture eased. He drew in an uneven breath. "Saints almighty."

Unbent spoke with a kindness he showed no one else. "It was bad this time?"

Jarid grimaced. "Yes."

Unbent spoke with difficulty. "For so many years I have

longed to offer comfort for your nightmares, to let you hear my voice. But now that you can, I don't know what to say."

Jarid touched his arm. "I knew you were there. It always helped."

Muller realized then that he had heard part of Jarid's dream. It troubled him to think that even now, Jarid continued to relive the death of his parents.

Unbent lifted his chin toward Muller, letting Jarid know they weren't alone. Looking up, Jarid climbed to his feet and spoke in his rusty voice. "My greeting, cousin."

Muller had no idea how to bow while crouched on a tree that could crumble beneath him. He half slid, half climbed down until he stood next to Jarid and Unbent. "My greeting, Your Majesty." Then he bowed properly.

Jarid acted neither surprised nor abashed that they had found him asleep. He had seemed desperate yesterday, overcome, but today he was calmer. Now that he had awoken, the sense of foreboding had receded from the forest.

Muller glanced around. The sunlight filtering through the foliage had an aged quality and shadows were gathering. "We should start back. Even if we leave right now, it will be dark by the time we reach Suncroft."

"You wish that I return." Jarid made it a statement rather than a question.

Muller wanted to say, *It is your home,* but he had no idea if Jarid felt that way anymore. He doubted it would do any good to say Brant and Fieldson wanted him at Suncroft. Nor did he think Unbent would help; if Jarid decided to stay here, Unbent would agree.

"Do you want to come back?" Muller asked.

"I like it here," Jarid said.

"You are sure?"

"No." The corners of Jarid's mouth lifted in a smile, and for a moment Muller saw in him the laughing boy who had run to him, cajoling his older cousin to swing him in the air. Regret for those days ached within Muller.

"I would like to see my wife," Jarid said.

"She will be worried," Muller said.

Jarid motioned at the forest around them. "This feels more like home. Suncroft is...alien."

"Is that why you came here?"

Jarid shook his head. "No. I wanted to search out Harsdown. Suncroft has too many people. They make noise in my mind."

"But why here?" Muller saw the appeal of the forest, with its untamed beauty, but he wouldn't have traveled so far to find such a place. Surely others existed closer to Suncroft.

"Iris goes to a hollow like this," Jarid said. "But I dislike intruding on her sanctuary." He motioned at the clearing around them. "So I found another."

Muller peered around. "Another what?"

"You do not see?" Jarid asked.

"Neither do I," Unbent said. "It is pleasin' wild, son, but so are other places."

"The shape," Jarid murmured.

Muller saw then. The branches arching above them, the depressed ground, the circular clearing—it formed a natural sphere. No wonder he felt such a gathering of power. Jarid was focusing through the forest itself. Its sheer size daunted Muller; it would take an extraordinary mage to harness its power.

"Incredible," Muller said.

"Impressive, eh?" Unbent beamed like a parent pleased with a child's cleverness. He didn't seem to understand the magnitude of what his son achieved. For that matter, neither did Jarid. They had no idea.

Muller regarded Jarid curiously. "Did you discover anything in your search?"

The king nodded. "The dark mage has returned home."

"To Harsdown?"

"Yes." Jarid pushed back a strand of hair that had fallen across his face. "We must go to Harsdown."

"Your army isn't ready," Muller said.

"I don't mean invasion. Just you and I."

Muller stared at him. "You are the ruler of this land. Until you have a son, I am your heir. We can't go alone into hostile territory." He could imagine what Brant would say to such an idea.

"We will go." Jarid's gaze remained firm. "Perhaps not this season or this year, but we will go."

"What makes you sure?" Muller asked.

"If we do not," Jarid said, "The twisted mage will help King Varqelle conquer Aronsdale."

Muller froze. Twisted mage? Did Jarid believe he, Muller, would harm Aronsdale? He tried to make a mood spell using the gnarled tree trunks, but they differed too much from a cylinder for him to use.

Suddenly Muller's spell snapped into focus. Jarid had meant the dark mage when he said twisted, not his cousin. Muller also felt Jarid's fatigue, the bone-deep exhaustion that a few hours sleep had barely touched. Jarid had no wish to return to the harsh existence of his life in the mountains; he wanted to stay at Suncroft, his ancestral home. But he was far more over-whelmed than he revealed.

The impressions faded; Muller lacked the skill to maintain such a powerful spell for long. But that interlude invigorated him—for during those precious few moments his spell hadn't twisted.

Jarid peered at him. "Muller? Are you all right?"

"Yes. Fine." With Unbent listening, Muller couldn't tell his cousin the miracle that had just taken place. He wasn't sure himself what had happened, but he knew this much; he had begun to see Jarid in a different light.

Della had known better days.

She, Brant, and Fieldson were in Brant's Hexagon Room on an upper level of the castle, the three King's Advisors facing off.

"Angry?" Brant looked ready to explode. "'Angry' barely touches it. I cannot believe you let him go with a *murderer.* Bad enough our king disappears. Now we have neither king nor heir. Perhaps this man Unbent fancies kidnapping both of them."

Della crossed her arms. "And of course poor, helpless Jarid and Muller, two strapping young men in the peak of health, are no match for an elderly man twice their ages combined."

Fieldson spoke tightly. "Muller said he was going with you and an octet of soldiers."

"That you let him go with only this man Unbent," Brant added, "verges on the criminal."

Della snorted. "Since when is it criminal to obey the commands of the royal family?" She had great respect for Brant and she knew his severity with Muller came from his affection for the young man, but she wished he would learn to show it in a more positive manner.

"It was bad enough when we only had Muller to deal with," Brant grumbled. "Now we have two of them. By withholding information from us, Della, you undermine our attempts to protect Aronsdale."

"And by refusing to listen to those two young men, you undermine their ability to learn." Della made a frustrated noise. "Muller is so at odds with himself, he barely knows where to begin with you. Stop pushing so hard." She glared at Brant. "Perhaps if you showed a modicum of trust in his judgment, he might develop enough confidence to trust himself."

He met her gaze. "Trust has to be earned. When has he done that? So far his major talent seems to be looking in the mirror."

"Oh, Brant." Della sighed. "So he likes to dress well. It is no crime."

Fieldson answered. "It hardly inspires confidence in his abilities as a military commander." He crossed his arms. "If Muller's behavior today is any example of how he will lead the army, I have grave reservations about the safety of Aronsdale. Quite frankly, I would feel more confident with Iris in charge."

"I donna think so." The lilting voice came from behind them. "I am the one who suggested he take Unbent."

Della swung around. Iris was standing in the arched doorway, tall and elegant in a simple tunic and leggings.

They all bowed to the queen. Brant said, "You honor us with your presence, Your Majesty," though he looked more irate than honored.

Iris's face was drawn. "Have they returned yet?"

"Not yet," Della said.

"I would know if Jarid were hurt." Iris spoke more as if to reassure herself than them. "I had thought, earlier, that he was afraid."

Brant stalked over to her. "Then why the blazes did you send Muller off with Unbent to find him?"

"Jarid's father knows how to find his son."

His fist clenched. "*Foster* father."

"Yes. Foster father." Iris made her words a rebuke. She went to a long window and gazed out over the walls of the castle to the hills beyond, which were shadowed in the gathering dusk. The sun had set half an hour ago.

Fieldson spoke. "Your Majesty, you say you knew he was afraid. Do you know more?"

Iris turned around. "It was vague. I wasn't even sure it was him. It seemed like Jarid, but also a child."

"In some ways he is a child," Della said. "So much in his life stopped after the death of his parents." Personally she thought both royal couples were painfully young, even Muller, who had ten years on the others.

"It is'n that." Iris's face took on an inward quality and Della felt the rise of her power, concentrated through Brant's office, a hexagonal prism, six walls capped by the flat ceiling and floor.

"I sense him," Iris said. "Like a fog. But I feel a man, not a boy. What I sensed before—it was him, but as a child."

"That makes no sense," Brant grumbled. When Della gave him a warning look, he added, "Your Majesty."

Amusement flickered in Iris's gaze. She inclined her head to Brant. "Thank you, Your Lordship."

Della held back her smile. Iris had changed a great deal in the past year.

A knock came at the open door. Turning, Della saw one of the triangle-pages, the ten-year-old son of a southern lord. His face was flushed as if he had been running. "Your Majesty!"

Iris smiled at the boy. "What is it, Randi?"

Excitement filled his face. "The king arrives!"

"About time," Brant muttered. He bowed to Iris, along with Fieldson. When she nodded, they left the office, Fieldson clapping Randi on the shoulder on their way out.

Iris spoke kindly to the boy. "Go on to the kitchens and see what sweets Cook has. Tell her I sent you."

Randi grinned. "Yes, ma'am!" Then he took off.

Iris went to Della, only now letting her relief show. "We had better go meet Jarid and Muller."

"That we should." With a sigh, Della added, "Before Brant takes them apart."

Chime stood on the Star Walk in the dusk. Light from torches and lamps shone through the open gate below, spilling down the hill and across the three men hiking to the castle. As soon as she had heard the gates grinding open, she had run up here to see if Muller had returned. The sight of him trudging up the hill flooded her with relief.

Two men strode out of the castle, headed down the hill. Chime needed no spell to tell her one of them was furious; his rigid posture said it all. It had to be Brant; she recognized his walk. The man in a general's uniform was probably Fieldson. Della and Iris appeared a moment later, moving at a calmer pace.

Everyone met halfway down the hill. Chime wanted to join them, but she hesitated to intrude. Although she and Muller planned to marry, she wasn't yet a member of the royal family nor was she a King's Advisor. She was simply a young woman learning to be a mage.

Using the star holes in the walkway, she made a mood spell. Brant's anger leapt up at her. He was using it to hide his concern for Muller and the tormented sovereign who so resembled the late King Daron. She sighed, thinking what a pair Della and Brant made, always growling and grumbling to hide the affection they felt for people. It had to be frustrating for them, having so many mages about who could see past their prickly exteriors to their gentle hearts.

After the group below entered the castle, Chime headed downstairs. Perhaps she would send Aria, her circle-maid, to see Muller's valet, Sam. If Sam told Muller that his betrothed had inquired after him, Muller might come to tell her what had happened. She hadn't seen him since he had proposed yesterday and she missed him terribly.

She was walking along a concourse on the ground floor, down an arcade of columns and arches, when a rustle came from behind her. Puzzled, she turned around. The arcade was empty. If someone had been there, they must have ducked behind a column or into an alcove. Or gone outside; doors to the gardens stood open farther down the concourse. She walked around the nearest columns, but saw no one. She was alone. The mosaics on the columns had stirred a spell within her, though, and she could have sworn she sensed someone's mood. It wasn't a mage, but someone cold and stealthy—

The hand clamped over her mouth and nose so fast, she had no chance to react. A sickly smell overwhelmed her and dark spots floated in her vision. She began to pass out.

Instinctively, Chime called on the mage skills Della had taught her. Only dimly aware now of the circle mosaics on the columns, she threw her power into them to make a ragged spell of light and heat. It barely worked. Her attacker didn't shout with alarm and collapse—but his hold did loosen.

Chime tore away and *ran*. On the verge of falling with each step, she raced down the arcade. She didn't dare pause, in case her attacker was behind her, his pursuit drowned out by the thud of her own feet. She sped out of the arcade, under an archway into a corridor. Desperate, she turned a corner—and slammed into an unyielding surface. A person. Arms grabbed her, holding on when she tried to jump back. She gave a strangled scream and hit his chest with her fists.

"Lady Chime!" The voice penetrated her panic. "What is it? What is wrong?"

She finally focused on the person she had barreled into: Sam Threadman, wearing the gold and russet livery of Muller's staff. Sturdy and firm, the valet stood holding her arms, his face creased with concern.

Chime spun around, whipping out of his hold, and stared down the corridor. It was empty.

"He's gone!" She turned back to Sam.

His face darkened. "Who hurt you?"

"I—I don't know." She tried to push a tendril of hair out of her face, but her hand shook so much, she couldn't even manage that small gesture. She could smell the cloying stench from the cloth her attacker had pressed over her face. She stumbled to the wall and slid down it until she was sitting on the floor.

Sam knelt next to her. "You need the healer."

Chime shook her head, but she couldn't speak. Bile rose in her throat. With great care, she lay down on the floor and closed her eyes. "Don't go," she whispered. "Please. He might come after me."

"I won't leave you, milady," Sam said. "But who might come after you?"

"Didn't see..."

Someone spoke to Sam, words too soft to overhear. Chime opened her eyes to see a rectangle-page, a young girl in the Dawnfield livery, a tunic and leggings, white, gold, and indigo. The page's face paled as she stared at Chime. "Hai, Sam, is she hurt?"

"I think so." He spoke urgently. "Go for Skylark. Tell her Lady Chime needs help. Then let Lord Firestoke know an intruder may be in the castle."

"I willa be right back." The girl took off, running around the corner, brown hair flying.

Chime's pulse began to slow. Sam continued to kneel at her side, a solid, reassuring presence. She closed her eyes and gave in to the effects of whatever had been on that cloth. For a time she floated, half conscious. Every few moments, she forced her eyes open to make sure Sam remained at her side. Then she drifted again.

"Lady Chime?" A soothing voice washed over her. "Can you hear me?"

"Ahhh..." Chime looked to see Skylark, the Mage-Healer of Suncroft, an older woman with blue eyes and two long white braids that hung over her shoulders.

Skylark was kneeling, holding a blue sphere in one hand. She laid her other palm on Chime's forehead and warmth flowed from her hand. "Does that help, child?"

"Not a child," Chime grumbled.

Skylark smiled at her glare. "I think you will be all right."

Chime slowly pushed herself up and sat against the wall. Sam was hovering behind Skylark, his face filled with worry. Chime wouldn't have expected them to be so concerned for her. She had believed people here viewed her with disdain, especially the servants, who knew her background as a country girl even though they had to treat her as a noble. She was a fraud. Yet Sam, the page, even Skylark, a powerful mage in her own right, genuinely seemed to care what happened to her.

The pound of boots came from the arcade. As Chime looked up, Muller ran around the corner. He skidded to a stop and dropped down next to her, his face flushed. Dirt covered his clothes, mud caked his boots, and his hair was tousled over his collar. She was dimly aware of more people coming around the corner, but she saw only Muller. With shaking arms, she cupped his face. He grabbed her into an embrace and hugged her hard, his cheek pressed against her head. Closing her eyes, she sunk into his arms.

It was several moments before they pulled apart. Then Muller turned to Skylark, who still knelt nearby, though she had scooted back to give them room. "Will she be all right?"

"I believe so. But she must rest." Skylark spoke to Chime. "You were drugged, milady. I think you inhaled a poison called blue-eye. In small doses it knocks you out." Quietly she added, "Larger doses kill."

Muller let out an explosive breath. "Chime, who did this? Tell me the name."

"I don't know." She was beginning to feel steadier now. "Someone came up behind me and put a soaked cloth over my face."

A rusty voice spoke. "He came from Varqelle."

Startled, Chime looked up. Jarid and Unbent stood in the hallway, both as disheveled as Muller, along with Iris, Della, Brant, and Fieldson.

"Do you mean King Varqelle?" Muller asked.

Jarid's voice rumbled. "From Harsdown, yes."

Fieldson spoke to Chime. "We have soldiers searching the castle. Can you tell us where to look for him?"

Chime did her best to speak calmly, describing as much of the incident as she remembered. When she finished, Fieldson sent one of his men to update the searchers.

"He probably escaped through the gardens," Jarid said. "He could be on his way back to Harsdown by now."

"Why do you think he came from Harsdown?" Brant asked.

"I felt it."

"How?"

Jarid seemed at a loss. "I just did."

"He links to them all," Chime said.

"Who links?" Fieldson asked.

She looked up at him. "Jarid."

"Links how?"

Everyone regarded her, expectant. Jarid seemed as puzzled as the others. Having lived all his life with his gifts, perhaps he didn't see how he affected others. She hardly knew how to explain it herself. "You cover all the valleys and dales," she told him. "Everywhere."

Jarid seemed bewildered. He glanced at Iris. "Do you feel this?"

She nodded. "I can tell if you are upset or happy," she said. "I don't even need my own spell."

Jarid touched his wife's cheek, the first time Chime had seen him show tenderness. Iris's face gentled, and for a moment it was as if she and Jarid were alone in the corridor.

Then Jarid spoke to Della. "What say you about this link? Do you feel it?"

"I sense your power," Della said. "But not a link."

He turned his violet-eyed gaze to Skylark. "Healer?"

"I'm sorry, Your Majesty. I don't feel it."

Fieldson considered them. "So it is just the three of you. Jarid, Iris, and Chime."

Jarid glanced at Muller, who met his gaze with an impassive expression. To Fieldson, Jarid said only, "Yes."

The general rubbed his chin. "I've never heard of mages communicating across such large distances before. Strategically it could be valuable."

Chime rose to her feet, leaning on the wall for support. The effects of the potion were fading, but her nausea surged when she moved. "The intruder—I don't think he was the Harsdown mage."

Jarid came over to her and spoke in a low voice. "You used a spell to escape the intruder." Only Muller was close enough to overhear.

"I made heat," Chime acknowledged.

"And it burned him."

"I think so."

"You gave pain with your gifts," Jarid said, intent.

Muller stiffened. "She was protecting herself."

"I mean no censure." Jarid regarded Chime. "I would be sure only that you do not censure yourself, either."

"Aye, Your Majesty." She wondered if the severity of her reaction came in part from causing harm with her spell.

Muller turned to the others and spoke to Fieldson. "We should increase the guard on the castle. We must have no more break-ins."

His assured tone startled Chime. She had never heard him address the King's Advisors with such confidence. In the past, he had avoided them and bristled when they cornered him.

"I can also put men on patrol outside," Fieldson said.

"Yes, that would be good," Muller said.

Usually Chime couldn't focus a spell on more than one person, but right now everyone's unease simmered in her awareness. The mosaics focused her power. They had given her the means to resist her attacker, perhaps saved her life. When she had first come to Suncroft, she hadn't appreciated their significance, but now she understood. The designs were two-dimensional, which limited the spells they supported, but they were everywhere.

It was no wonder Jarid's presence filled Suncroft.

Iris found Jarid in the octagonal tower chamber. He was sitting in the dark at the round table, his face silvered by starlight. His presence filled the room, blended with the light of an Azure Moon flowing through the window.

Iris sat with him. "What troubles you?"

His voice was low. "I cannot absorb it all."

She wanted to take his hand, but she feared he would withdraw. "That is why you left the castle today, yes?"

"Yes." His voice deepened. "Varqelle knows."

"Knows what, Jarid?"

"That our leadership is weak."

His intensity unsettled her. "You think Wareman spied for Varqelle?"

"I'm certain of it." He stood and walked to the window. Bathed in moonlight, he seemed more spirit than human. "But why attack Chime?"

"She is a powerful mage. Or she will be, someday."

"So are you, more so. And you are queen."

Iris went to him. "Chime is more vulnerable."

"Yes. But it is more than that. He needs her."

"Why?"

"I wish I knew. Somehow she is the key." His pain sparked, magnified by the patterns on the frame of the window. "We are so vulnerable—you, me, Chime, Muller. Varqelle seeks to demoralize us. To wear us down."

"Ask Brant and Fieldson for help." Iris wanted to reach out to him, but she held back, knowing he couldn't handle so much human interaction this soon, after so many years of isolation. "They have experience. Wisdom."

Jarid rested his forearm on the wall by the window and gazed at the starlit countryside. "That night, after our coronation, you helped me to unlock my prison. But I remain lost. I have sight now, but I cannot see what to do. I listen, but I do not understand what I hear."

"Let your advisors interpret for you."

"I have no trust in them." He glanced at her. "Muller is my cousin. I loved him when I was a small boy. I trust him now, even if he has no trust in himself."

She spoke softly. "And me?"

His voice roughened. "You terrify me." Taking her into his arms, he laid his head against hers. "You make me confront my nightmares. If you were to desert me, I would wither."

Her voice caught. "I won't desert you."

"I cannot see my path." He held her close. "But again and again, my spells turn me toward Harsdown."

"Hai, Jarid." Iris had no answers, for she feared he was right. Harsdown waited, dark beyond the mountains.

23

The Golden Halo

Anvil the Forged walked with Varqelle along the top of a fortified wall that wound through the cliffs above Castle Escar. The air was noticeably thinner up here and the sky a dark blue. Cold seared his lungs, exhilarating in a way he never experienced in the humid, overly fertile lands of Aronsdale.

Varqelle, however, looked less than pleased. "I fail to see how that slip of a girl escaped my agent. She has no use to me as a hostage if she runs away so easily."

"Chime Headwind is a mage," Anvil said. "She used a spell against him." It annoyed Anvil. Varqelle had sent one of his best men to catch the girl, a soldier with expertise in infiltrating even the most fortified refuges.

Varqelle tapped his long fingers on the hilt of the sword at his hip. "You assured me those incompetent children can create no worthwhile spells."

Anvil shrugged. "She instinctively defended herself. That is different from using her abilities in a military capacity. However, her spell was apparently rather crude. She was lucky. This time." Varqelle's man continued to hide in the countryside around Suncroft.

The king stopped at a crenellation in the wall. "They bedevil me, these people of Aronsdale." He motioned toward the distant countryside of Harsdown, far below the mountains, spread out like a game board, brown on brown. "My people starve. Aronsdale has more than we do. It troubles me, troubles me greatly."

It troubled Anvil, too, though for different reasons. He had wearied of his travels. At thirty-one, he was no longer a boy hungry for adventure. He desired a permanent home. Riches. Servants. A woman. It didn't decrease his need to strike at Aronsdale, but it changed the slant of his intentions. Aronsdale had robbed him of his home and family; it would give back to him now, make him rich.

He jerked his chin at the mountains in the opposite direction, toward Aronsdale. "The people beyond those peaks live in wealth while your people starve."

Varqelle snorted. "They may have more than we do, but I would hardly call it wealth."

"They are a boil on the face of the earth," Anvil growled.

Varqelle's laugh put an uncharacteristic smile on his face. "A colorful but perhaps apt description."

Anvil decided to probe for information. "I can see why you have such a history of problems with their kings."

"What history?" Varqelle asked curiously.

Anvil took a guess. "King Daron wronged you."

"Did he now?" Varqelle tilted his head. "How?"

Anvil could see this wouldn't work. Varqelle was too savvy to reveal anything unless he wanted it known. So he switched to a straightforward approach. "Isn't that why you have such difficult relations with Aronsdale?"

"Actually, Daron tried to improve them." Varqelle waved his hand. "He thought I would let his trade caravans go through Harsdown."

"It could be lucrative," Anvil admitted.

"I have no interest in enlarging Dawnfield coffers."

"Even if it enlarges yours?"

"Taking Aronsdale would enlarge them more." Varqelle scrutinized him as a strategist might study a map. "You are looking for a great passion in my wish to conquer them. A drive for vengeance or a burning hatred. What you seek isn't there. Aronsdale is a fertile land, one that would enhance my realms. If they gain strength through trade agreements, it makes it that much harder to overcome them."

"So power drives you."

"It has much to speak for it." Varqelle raised his chin. "I would see myself as king over more than Harsdown and Aronsdale."

That fit more with what Anvil had expected to hear. He intended to make himself so necessary to Varqelle, the king would believe his plans of conquest could never succeed without his mage. Anvil would rise among the elite of Harsdown until he was a power within his own right.

"They call you Varqelle the Cowled now," he said. "Someday it will be Emperor Varqelle."

Varqelle waved his hand. "To rule an empire is neither simple nor easily realized." His voice quieted. "Sometimes the way seems clear. Take Aronsdale and move on from there. Other times I have questioned the wisdom of this course. Profit exists in trade with Aronsdale. It is far less than I would gain by conquest, but it would be immediate." He drummed his fingers on the hilt of his sword. "Aronsdale has an army of a thousand men. I have more, but not much. I don't think I can overcome theirs unless I tax my people enough to hire mercenaries from the outlands. But these soldiers for hire are misfits, unreliable, criminals. And my people would suffer if I require more from them. They survive the taxes now, but they can little afford more."

Anvil tensed. He had no wish for peaceful resolution. Aronsdale was too full of mage power, too fecund. He felt ill there. He could never forget how his family had died, murdered by the people of Stonce, the hamlet where he had grown up. He wanted them to pay, all of them, every bigot and hate-filled native of that country. He had no doubt they loathed mages, despite the supposed respect accorded them by the royal court. If Varqelle sought peace, Anvil would lose his vengeance.

Varqelle fooled himself, though, if he didn't think his people already suffered under the current taxes. Anvil had seen it during his travels. He had thought to speak to the king on the subject, if an appropriate opening came up, but now he changed his mind. He had no wish for Varqelle to reconsider his plans to move against Aronsdale.

Besides, peace could never work. Jarid Dawnfield couldn't even make decisions for himself, let alone his country. "It might not take as much as you think to overcome Aronsdale," Anvil said. "This long-lost grandson who wears the crown isn't even sane."

Amusement flickered in Varqelle's eyes. "Perhaps he will simply give away his country, eh?"

"One can never tell." Anvil paused. "Sire, your people need more than any trade agreement can give."

Varqelle rubbed his chin. "It is a pretty country, Aronsdale."

"It should be yours. Without conditions."

"Yes, well, it isn't." The king leaned against the wall, his arms crossed. "How does your magecraft compare to that of this plethora of mages they have spawned out there at Suncroft? Four of them, isn't it?"

"Yes, four." That hardly constituted a plethora, but Anvil

didn't contradict the king. Other mages might exist in Aronsdale, minor ones, perhaps able to draw on low-level shapes in
two dimensions and warm colors, red, orange, more rarely
yellow. But mages of real strength were rare. The elderly castle healer at Suncroft and the wife of late King Daron were
the only full ones known in their generation; Della No-Cozen
and Jarid's mother were the only ones in the following generation; and Della had found only two in the current generation, despite scouring the country and chasing every rumor
she heard.

Had she followed rumors of him?

Anvil shuddered and pushed away the thought. "The Suncroft
mages are nothing. The girl Chime is a delectable piece, but she
has no brain. The healer is elderly and weak, and the mage mistress is a harridan. The queen is intelligent but untutored." Iris
Larkspur had a figure too full for his tastes, but he had seen the
voluptuous concubines Varqelle preferred. "She is well made,
though. You might enjoy her for yourself."

Although the king smiled, his expression had nothing of pleasure in it. "I have a wife. I sent her away."

Anvil had heard the rumors of Varqelle's bride. He married
a princess from the Misted Peaks, one of the western provinces,
to strengthen ties between their realms—and she had fled back
home less than a year later, taking his infant heir with her.

Tales abounded as to why the queen of Harsdown left her
husband, most rife with rumors of Varqelle's brutal appetites,
but one thing was clear: to bring her back, he would have to
fight the Misted Peaks, a more powerful realm than Harsdown.
Although Anvil believed in taking a firm hand with a woman,
he couldn't countenance brutality. However, Varqelle's
predilections were the king's business, not his. If Varqelle knew
a prize awaited him at Suncroft, it might add an extra entice-
ment to invade.

"You wouldn't marry Iris Larkspur," Anvil said. "Just enjoy her."

"Perhaps." Varqelle sounded bored, but Anvil knew him well enough to realize he was intrigued.

"As for the Suncroft mages," Anvil continued, "You have nothing to fear in terms of their ability to plan or defend against your forces."

"What about the king? I have heard he is a mage."

Irritation surged in Anvil. "The Dawnfields have long claimed male mages in their line. It is a legend, no more."

"You claim such power."

"I am unique."

"Perhaps not."

Anvil loathed acknowledging the possibility, but he couldn't deny it, not as long as other mages lived. "Very well. Let us assume this king is a mage. Unless he is stronger than myself, he couldn't hide his power from me. And I felt nothing significant from him."

"Perhaps he is stronger than you."

"Even if true, the point is moot. The fellow is mad. He can't rule." Anvil had no intention of allowing another mage to have superiority over him. The day Harsdown subjugated Aronsdale, Jarid Dawnfield would die.

Varqelle seemed unimpressed. "Right now the power in Aronsdale doesn't reside with the House of Dawnfield. They aren't the ones we need worry about."

Anvil knew he meant the King's Advisors. "His mentors may have wisdom, but it will do no good if the king ignores them." He laughed harshly. "Saints, Your Majesty, the idiot put Muller Dawnfield in charge of his army. I can't imagine what the prince will do. Dress the men in pretty clothes, perhaps."

Varqelle's gaze glinted. "Perhaps he could lead the knitting circle."

Anvil smiled. But then he said, "Muller Dawnfield does have skill with a sword."

"My concern is the Cube-General. If Prince Muller has sense, he will listen to Fieldson." Varqelle studied him closely. "You say your power can help bring me Aronsdale. Yet I have doubts about what you can do."

Anvil held back his anger. Varqelle didn't threaten or belittle him, which Anvil loathed. Instead the king questioned the extent of his ability. Anvil would have done the same in his position. It didn't offend him—much.

He placed his hand over a circular depression in the stone wall. Half closing his eyes, he focused, letting his power cycle through the colors, a trick he had learned over the years: red, orange, yellow, blue, indigo.

As Anvil's spell built, he sighted on the spire atop a jagged tower of Castle Escar to their west. Heat surged through him and he swayed.

Lightning cracked across the clear sky and hit the tower with an explosion of indigo light, shattering the spire. Debris rained over the castle and down the cliffs, echoes of its passage vibrating in the chill air.

Anvil raised an eyebrow at Varqelle.

"An impressive display." The king's voice hardened. "Do not damage my holdings again."

Then never question me again, Anvil thought. He had paid a high price for his gifts; he intended now to reap their benefits. "Think of it as a promise. I could reduce Suncroft to rubble if you so desire."

Varqelle surveyed the ruined tower. "It must take a great deal out of you to use such power."

It exhausted Anvil more than he would admit. A tower, a house, an outcropping; he could destroy such as those, but anything more taxed his limits. In his childhood, he had usually fallen asleep after such exertion. Even now, he couldn't sustain that level of power for more than a few seconds. He had no intention of telling Varqelle, however.

He said only, "I have plenty to spare."

"So you claim." The king nodded to him. "Help me gain Aronsdale and you will become its lord."

"A fitting bargain." It was no more than Anvil had expected, given their previous discussions. "However, I have one other condition."

Varqelle frowned. "You have too many conditions."

"But I have much excess energy."

The king waved his hand. "Go practice swordplay."

"This is a different sort of energy."

"And what might that be?"

"When we take Aronsdale, I want the woman Chime."

Varqelle gave a hearty laugh. "Ah. *That* energy." He clapped Anvil's shoulder. "Take her as you please."

He ran from the highwaymen, gasping, pain knifing his side. Someone screamed, his mother, his father...

Muller bolted upright, the velvet bed covers flying. His heart beat too fast and sweat plastered his hair to his head. Saints almighty, that nightmare had felt so *real*.

After a while his pulse slowed. He slid out of bed and grabbed the robe he had thrown over a chair, pulling it on over his sleep trousers and bare chest, belting it around the waist. He could barely see in the moonlight coming in a tall window. Restless and agitated, he padded out of his suite in bare feet.

With no interior windows in his suite, Muller could see nothing. Was this how Jarid had lived, in blackness? It disturbed Muller. Chime had used her gifts against her would-be kidnapper last night. As an emerald mage, she couldn't heal, which meant she couldn't injure, either, but she could make heat, and heat burned.

In the entrance foyer of his suite, faint light made the stained glass windows glow. Muller crept past a square-butler who had fallen asleep in a chair. He inched open one of the double doors—and made an unwelcome discovery. Two guards stood outside in the light of a torch on the wall, hepta-lieutenants it looked like.

Annoyed, he closed the door, quietly, so he wouldn't alert his dozing butler. After what had happened to Chime last night, it didn't surprise Muller that Brant assigned him bodyguards, too. Brant had probably ordered others to guard Iris and Jarid in the Royal Suite, too. Muller had sent guards to Chime's suite himself. But he loathed losing yet more of his privacy. It all weighed on him: his worry for Chime, his loneliness, the demands of his duties.

He should go back to bed, to rest for the morning when he would resume life, preparing to command the army. But when he thought of going on as usual, something inside of him snapped. Instead of returning to bed, he prowled through his suite, restless, until he reached the quarters for his servants. The rooms were freshly painted and spacious, with quality furnishings. He hadn't consciously planned to come here, but now that he had arrived, he knew what he wanted.

Loud snores came from Sam's bedroom. Sam had always claimed he slept silently, but his magnificent rumbles were vibrating throughout the hall. Muller snuck into a parlor outside Sam's bedroom, his footsteps drowned out by the noise. Floor-to-ceiling panels decorated the room, each about five hand-spans wide and framed by scalloped moldings. On one, he nudged aside a painting of a cottage surrounded by trees with red, gold, and yellow leaves. The picture hid a cluster of nail holes. Moving stealthily, Muller pressed the holes in a pattern his uncle had taught him twenty years ago, just as Daron's father had taught Daron.

The panel swung inward.

Hah! Muller grinned. It had been so long since he played in these tunnels, he hadn't been certain he would remember how to reach them. He readjusted the painting, then slipped out and closed the secret door behind him.

Chime opened her eyes into darkness. She wasn't sure what had awoken her, but she had a strange sense, as if the night had taken on a personality. Her songbird trilled, then fell silent in its gold cage, which hung from a hook on the wall by her wardrobe.

Her fear sparked. She wasn't alone. Someone was in her room. She tensed to strike out, but she made no sound, lest she alert the intruder. If she had to fight, she wanted the advantage of surprise. Reaching silently to the nightstand, she closed her hand around a glass vase. It would break well against a person's head.

"Chime?" a man whispered. "Are you awake?"

Saints almighty. A tickling sensation in her throat replaced her fear. "Muller?" She set down the vase and sat up, peering into the dark. A dark silhouette, tall and lithe, stood by her bed. "What are you doing here?"

"Is it all right?" he asked.

"Good graces, no." She whispered her response, so they wouldn't wake up her two maids in the adjoining room. Thank goodness she had closed the door between her room and theirs. Then again, she had also closed the door to the parlor and now it stood open, a lighter rectangle in the shadows of her room.

"How did you get in here?" she asked. "Brant put guards all around the suite."

"Secret passage." He sounded smug. "Only Dawnfields know about it."

"You are very misbehaved, skulking around that way."

"Just a few minutes. Then I will go."

She heard a catch in his voice. "Are you all right?"

"I keep having this damn nightmare." Then he added, "My apology for my language."

Chime had heard far worse in Jacob's Vale. "It is all right." She knew she should tell him to leave, but instead she said, "Stay for a few minutes."

"Thank you." The bed rustled as he sat on its edge.

She traced her finger over a polygon embroidered in the bedspread. A luminous gold circle formed above it and bathed Muller in light, making him look like an angel with his beautiful face, his tousled hair, and his robe clinging to his leanly muscled body.

"Ah, love," Chime murmured, appreciative.

"I've been worrying about you," he said.

"I was sleeping well." Her lips quirked upward. "Until a rogue snuck into my bedroom."

"Rogue!" He tried to glare at her, but his laugh ruined the effect. "You wound me, Chime."

She suddenly felt shy, having him in her bedroom. This was so improper it would give Brant Firestoke a heart attack. "You should go."

"I wanted to make sure you were here, that no one had run off with you."

She took his hand. Right now it was hard to care about protocols that had never felt natural to her in the first place. In the matrilineal culture where she had grown up, a girl from a landed family usually chose her own husband, who then moved into his wife's family home. Protocol there required the woman not compromise the man's honor by sneaking into *his* bedroom, but mention was rarely made of the reverse situation.

"You look tired," she said.

"It is my nightmares." He grimaced. "I dream an army from

Harsdown marches on Aronsdale, rank after rank of inhuman soldiers, mage creatures created by darkness." He sounded exhausted. "Or else I dream I'm Jarid and my parents are dying."

"I wish I could help." She tugged his hand. "Come sit with me."

Muller scooted over until they were sitting against the headboard, leaning together. "It helps just to be with you."

She laid her head on his shoulder. "I feel safer with you here. After last night——" She shivered, wanting to forget the attack.

"Hai, Chime." He put his arm around her shoulders, his long fingers rubbing the flimsy cloth of her nightgown. "You are so warm and I am so cold. Work your magic on me." He drew aside her hair and bent his head, pressing his lips against her neck.

"You stop that," Chime murmured. Her bird trilled at her voice. "You must leave before someone catches you and sends you to the dungeon."

He moved his lips to her ear. "I would risk any dungeon for you."

Chime ducked her head as his breath tickled her ear. He was rubbing her cheek with his, and when she turned her head, and he found her lips with his. As he kissed her, she slid her arms around his waist.

"Lovely Chime." He made the words a caress. Then he eased the two of them into the bed, under the covers.

Chime knew she should tell him to stop. But he felt so very fine. *Just a moment more. Then I will send him away.*

His hands moved on her body, tugging her nightgown, shaping her curves. She had admired his lithe beauty for so long now, wanting him, it really was impossible to stop. She rolled him onto his back, pinning him down. Laughing almost inaudibly, he lay still while she rained kisses on his face. Then he rolled her over and kissed her thoroughly, until her thoughts blended into a sensual fog.

Muller touched her with an alluring mix of strength and shyness. By instinct, Chime created pleasure spells, heightening their lovemaking. In the daze of sensuality, she felt the truth: he had kissed very few women, just as she had done no more than tease a few boys in the orchards. They had each chosen to wait, though their differing cultures allowed otherwise for both of them. Knowing they came together new and fresh, by their own choice, sweetened their passion.

They made love in the earliest morning hours, before dawn touched the sky. Both of them stopped caring whether they achieved the perfection they believed everyone wanted from them. In letting go, in letting themselves be their own flawed selves, they found a love more satisfying than any perfection could have given them.

Charmed Hearts

Winter settled its bleak mantle over the land. Blizzards covered Croft's Vale and heaped drifts around the walls of Suncroft. On some days a dull overcast pressed the countryside; on others the sky turned an icy blue and the air seared with its chill bite.

When they could make it through the snow, Chime and Iris went to the village with Della or Skylark. With their spells, they brought healing. When they could, they traveled to outlying farms. With their warmth and light, they helped hunters survive the harsh weather while finding game for their families or gathering firewood to replenish their stores.

Chime wore a pendant around her neck, an emerald ball with twenty sides, her highest shape. Iris carried a sapphire orb with sixteen facets, too few sides, or so Chime thought. Nor did the color seem right, not exactly. A mage could use any spells below her own level, but her strongest work came from the highest shape and color she could draw on. The queen had yet to define her gifts, making it harder for her to use them.

She struggled with spells, but those she did form had great power.

So the mages of Suncroft did their best to ease the long, cold winter for their people.

Sometimes Jarid came with them, against the wishes of his advisors. Other times he stayed at the castle, filling in the multitude of gaps in his education and dealing with his recovered senses. He spent hours each day practicing with a sword, learning a skill he had barely begun to practice as a boy of six. His strength and natural ability impressed Chime, but it was Muller, who had such great skill, she loved to watch, his muscles rippling as he parried with the king.

Sometimes at night, when the castle slept, Jarid's mood spells spread across the land, unfocused but resolute, seeking shapes in the hollows, dales and mountains, always searching, searching, for knowledge of King Varqelle and his dark mage.

Muller drowsed, shifting Chime in his arms. It had been several weeks since he had managed to slip into her room, making their time together now even more of a gift than usual. He sighed, content with his betrothed asleep in his arms, his thoughts drifting. Her songbird trilled in its cage.

The King's Advisors wanted him and Chime to wait until spring to marry, purportedly because it would be a better time for the people to celebrate, which would, as Brant put it, "heighten morale among the populace."

Heighten morale indeed. Muller knew why they delayed the wedding. Now that he was no longer destined for the crown, they balked at marrying him to one of the most powerful mages alive. As his wife, Chime would have many obligations that distracted her from magecraft. She might even end up assuming some of Iris's more mundane duties when the queen attended her responsibilities as the head mage in Aronsdale. The King's

Advisors would want a husband for Chime whose position and title didn't interfere with her work. But they didn't know. She had given him her promise.

Chime stirred in his arms, her head against his thigh, one arm thrown across his legs, her other folded under her head, her cheek resting on her hand. Muller smiled, stroking her hair back from her head.

"Lady Chime!" a woman called. With no warning, the door flew open. Light poured into the bedroom as Aria, Chime's circle-maid, hurried inside carrying a candelabra, followed by Della No-Cozen. Beyond Della, down the hall, Brant waited in Chime's parlor.

"Lady, come!" Aria cried. "We must—oh, dear." She stopped, her mouth open as she stared at Muller, his face and bare chest fully visible in the candlelight.

"Ah, hell," Muller said.

"I am *appalled*." Brant Firestoke paced in front of the two people seated on the brocaded sofa in Chime's parlor. "Utterly appalled."

Chime was too groggy to comprehend half of what Brant said. It made no difference; she didn't need comprehension to see that he was furious. Muller and her maid had helped her out of bed and thrown her into her nightgown and robe. Now she sat, blinking, her hair tousled all over the place. Della stood leaning against the wall, and Aria hovered in the doorway, looking anxious.

Muller sat stiffly at Chime's side, his robe covering him from shoulder to knees, though Aria and Della must have had quite an eyeful when they found him naked in her bed. He looked as bewildered as she felt. She couldn't imagine a worse disaster in their betrothal.

"Perhaps we should let them go back to their rooms," Della said tiredly. "We can continue this tomorrow."

"Yes." Muller pounced on the idea. "Let us do that."

Brant stopped in front of them. "We have nothing to continue. This betrothal of yours is ended." He glowered at Chime. "We have selected a groom for you, young lady."

"No!" Muller jumped to his feet. Although he was taller than Brant, he had neither the older man's broad-shouldered physique nor aura of power. Even so, he looked ready to take on Brant right then and there. "Chime and I have to marry now."

Brant crossed his arms. "You cannot marry her. She isn't a virgin."

"Oh for heaven sakes," Chime said. "Neither is Muller."

To her unmitigated surprise, Della laughed. When Brant glared, the mage mistress closed her mouth, though her eyes still danced. It wasn't what Chime expected from her no-nonsense mentor.

"You should be ashamed of yourself," Brant told Chime.

"Whatever for?" Chime asked. "I'm not the one who barged into my bedroom while I was peacefully asleep."

"I would hardly call the misbehavior we discovered 'sleeping.'"

"Of course we were sleeping," Chime said sweetly. "We were already done misbehaving."

Muller made a choked sound, and Della's face turned red, though Chime suspected it was because the mage mistress was struggling not to laugh.

"Very amusing, Chime," Brant said. "It changes nothing. You are no longer fit to marry a Dawnfield heir."

Chime stopped smiling. She stood up and faced him, aware of his greater height and presence, and how unsubstantial she probably looked in her robe. It didn't matter. She lifted her chin. "I am 'fit' to marry whomever I choose."

"You should have considered that before you lay with a man before marriage."

"This is ludicrous," Muller said. "I'm the one betrothed to her."

"Not anymore," Brant said.

Della came forward. "We shouldn't make any hasty decisions tonight. We have other concerns."

"What concerns?" Muller asked.

"Perhaps," Chime said tartly, "they refer to the concerns that prompted them to bring half of Aronsdale into my bedroom in the middle of the night."

"Chime." Della frowned at her.

Brant looked as if he were counting silently to himself. After a moment he spoke in a quieter voice. "Lady Chime, the king believes you are in danger. We thought we were rescuing you." He frowned at Muller. When the younger man raised his eyebrows, Brant turned back to Chime. "Perhaps we were."

"Very funny," Muller said.

"Why does Jarid think I am in danger?" Chime asked.

Brant paused. "I'm not sure."

"Well, so where is he?" Muller asked.

"With Iris," Della said. "He had a nightmare."

"Hai," Chime murmured, glancing at Muller. "Don't we all."

Brant spoke to Muller. "You are having nightmares?"

"Nothing unusual." He went on before Brant could probe further. "Perhaps Jarid overreacted."

"I don't think so," Della said. "He goes into a trace sometimes during his spells. His dream happened then."

"But I'm fine." Chime gave Brant a sour look. "Unless you count all this noise and tumult."

"Why didn't Jarid come himself?" Muller asked.

"He is still in the trance," Della said. "Iris fears to wake him." Chime squinted at her. "Why?"

It was Muller who answered. "If he is startled as he awakes, he can't always control his power. He starts fires."

"Ma'am?" a voice said behind them.

Chime turned to see Aria. "Yes?"

The maid came forward. "I am sorry to disturb you." She hesitated, glancing at Della and Brant.

"It is all right," Chime said.

"Your bird, ma'am," Aria said.

Chime blinked. "My songbird?"

Her face paled. "Perhaps you should come see."

Brant frowned. "What bird is this?"

"I keep it in my room." Chime headed for the hall. Over her shoulder, she said, "My betrothed gave it to me." Brant glowered at her.

Chime entered her bedroom with Aria and Della. When Muller tried to follow them into the forbidden bower, Brant grabbed his arm. Reddening, Muller stayed with him at the doorway.

Chime went to the gold cage hanging near the window—and gave a cry. The bird lay on the bottom of the cage.

"Everyone, out of the room!" Della's voice cut through Chime's dismay. "Now!" Before Chime could object, Della was propelling her toward the door. Aria had to run to keep up.

As Della pushed them out into the hall, Brant hauled Muller toward the parlor. "Keep going," Brant said. "Out of the suite."

Chime's pulse leapt, as much from confusion as their sudden exit. They ran into the hall outside, away from her suite.

"What happened?" Chime asked, out of breath.

Now that they had escaped the suite, Brant slowed down enough to answer her. "Your bird was a mine-dove. Miners used them to detect poisonous fumes back before mages figured out how to do it themselves."

"It didn't look sick," Chime said as they walked along the hall. "It looked dead."

"Yes." Della's quiet agreement struck Chime more than would have any exclamation. "Had you and Muller been in the room, you could also have been affected."

"Saints," Muller muttered.

"But it didn't bother us in the parlor," Chime said.

"The gas was probably released in your bedroom, too little to drift out to where we were," Della said. "At least not enough to cause us discomfort. The bird was also a lot smaller."

Brant frowned at Chime. "What about your maids?"

She glanced over her shoulder at Aria and Reed, who were a ways back, following them. "What about them?"

"How well do you know them?"

"They would never hurt me!"

"You wouldn't be the first noblewoman with such trust," Brant said dryly. "Nor the first to die for it."

"I used mood spells when we interviewed them," Della said. "They are loyal to Lady Chime."

"Yes." Chime glared at Brant.

Muller put her arm around Chime's shoulders. "We *must* protect her."

"And precisely how are we supposed to protect any of you," Della demanded, "if you traipse around in the middle of the night, sneaking away to your betrothed."

"She is no longer his betrothed," Brant said.

Muller glared at him. "Like hell."

"We need to ensure both of you are safe," Della said.

"If someone can poison us in our own beds," Chime asked, "how can we ever be safe?"

No one had an answer.

Iris paced the parlor of the royal suite, her hair tumbling down her back, her heavy robe and layered sleeping gown swirling around her legs. Chime stood with Muller, watching the queen and twisting her hands in the sash of her robe. Fieldson, Brant, and Della waited by the twelve-sided table where

Iris went over documents during the day. Skylark stood by the door, her lined face drawn with fatigue, her long white hair unbraided.

The queen stopped in front of Skylark. "How can you be sure this bird died of sleeping gas?"

The healer answered with composure, though unease showed on her face. "The gas left its mark on the bird, one strong enough that I felt ill when I focused my spell. It is the same sense I have when I check for gas in the mines."

Iris nodded, then turned to the maids, Aria and Reed, who sat huddled together on the brocaded sofa. "Neither of you felt anything?"

"No, Your Majesty!" Aria watched her with wide eyes. "Nothing, ma'am. I swear."

Chime spoke with care, hoping she didn't insult Iris as she had so often in the past. She didn't want the queen to hold those past exchanges against her maids. "I will vouch for Aria and Reed." In her side vision, she saw them watching her anxiously. "I have felt their moods. They are loyal."

"Very well." Iris said no more.

Relief swept over Chime, and surprise too, given her strained relations with the queen.

"So we have no suspects?" Iris asked.

"Not yet," Brant said.

Della looked around at them all. "We never found any leads on whoever tried to kidnap Chime last summer, either."

Brant frowned. "In both cases, they broke into the castle without our knowing and escaped without being caught."

Fieldson spoke. "It implies an expertise in covert operations that most people don't have."

"Who does?" Della asked.

He glanced at her. "Trained army officers."

"Could they come from Harsdown?" Iris said.

"Varqelle would certainly have such agents." Fieldson considered Chime. "But why you both times?"

"Because she's beautiful," Muller said. "Because she's a mage. Because she's sweet and lovely and vulnerable, and someone *wants* her, damn it."

"It could be." Della cocked her eyebrow at Muller. "But so are many women. Perhaps you are biased. The reason must be more than that."

"Fine," Muller said sourly. "When they kidnap her, we can discuss my bias more."

Brant spoke to Chime. "We will send you to a safe place. Somewhere in the country."

She knew what he was up to. "I would rather stay here."

Della spoke gently. "Perhaps it would be best if you and Muller separated for now."

Muller swore. "No, it would not be best."

Brant crossed his arms. "You should have thought of that before you went to her room."

The door to an inner room creaked open. As they all turned, Jarid entered, tall and dark, looming among the gilt-edged furniture. Chime recognized his distant expression; he had just surfaced from one of his trances.

The maids jumped to their feet and everyone bowed, except Iris. She went to her husband, even her tall figure seeming delicate next to his muscular form.

"My greeting," she said.

Jarid touched her hand, his face gentling. Then he looked around until he saw Chime. "You are all right?"

Chime nodded. "I'm fine, Your Majesty."

Jarid came to where she stood with Muller. "Apparently someone wishes to take you away."

Muller stiffened. "He won't get her."

"You would protect her?" Jarid asked.

"She is my betrothed," Muller said, sparing a glare for Brant.

"There is that," Jarid agreed.

"Your Majesty," Della began. "If I may speak?"

Jarid glanced at her. "Go ahead."

"Prince Muller was found this evening with Lady Chime."

"Found?"

Della cleared his throat. "In her suite."

Jarid frowned then and turned to Muller. "Is that true?"

"I can explain," Muller said quickly.

"Yes or no," Jarid grated. "Is it true?"

Muller flushed. "Yes."

Jarid scowled at him. "Patience is not one of your virtues, cousin."

"It changes nothing." Muller put his arm around Chime's shoulders. "We still wish to marry."

"As soon as possible," Chime added.

Jarid considered them, his eyes dark in the candlelight. Then he motioned to Chime.

Puzzled and uncertain, she went to him. He ushered her into the chamber he had just left. Shaped like a tiled box, it vibrated even now with echoes of his mage trance.

Jarid left the door open so both he and Chime remained in view of the others. But he spoke in a voice only she could hear. "Iris has told me about Muller's gifts, that he draws on imperfect shapes."

Chime felt as if she were adrift in choppy waters. How she replied could determine her future with Muller. If she steered badly, she could capsize in currents she didn't understand. She couldn't lie, but the less said, the better. So she answered only, "Yes, Your Majesty."

"You reach him. The rest of us cannot."

"Reach him?"

"He seems open with you."

"I think so."

"With others, he believes himself dangerous."

What to say? If she fumbled now, it could affect the dreams she and Muller shared. She wanted to insist he posed no danger, but it wasn't true. Muller had reason for his fears. If she lied to Jarid and that led to harm, she could never live with herself. Besides, Jarid made a mood spell, he would recognize any falsehood she gave him. If she told the truth, it could still cause grief, but at least Jarid would know she acted in the best interests of Aronsdale. It might help.

"Yes." Chime loathed the words she had to say. "Yes, he is dangerous."

"So." His face gave no hint of his thoughts. Lifting his hand, he indicated the doorway.

Miserable, she went with him back to the parlor, aware of everyone watching. She couldn't look at Muller.

Jarid went to Muller and crossed his muscled arms, frowning at his cousin. "It was appalling of you to compromise Lady Chime's honor."

"Your Majesty," Muller began.

Jarid held up his hand. After Muller closed his mouth, his face reddening, the king turned to Chime. "It was wrong of you to lie with him. It raises questions about your virtue."

Virtue, indeed. Chime fumed, but she held back her tart response.

Muller had no such reservations. "That is absurd," he growled. "She is an angel."

Unexpectedly Jarid smiled, his grin flashing, a startling contrast to his usual more somber moods. "I do not know if angel is the word I would use, cousin. I have seen her ire."

Mortified, Chime said, "Your Majesty, I do surely regret any—"

Jarid held up his hand. His expression had softened,

though. He turned to Brant Firestoke. "Please fetch the Bishop of Orbs."

Brant blinked. "You want me to wake him?"

"Yes."

"In the middle of the night?"

"It would seem the only way to get these two married before we have a scandal."

Chime barely held back her grin. Married? Yes!

Fieldson obviously had other ideas. "Your Majesty, surely a marriage now would be unwise."

"Well, probably." Jarid sighed as he regarded Chime and Muller. "You two will be my bane, eh?"

Brant spoke in a quiet voice. "I urge you to reconsider, Your Majesty."

"You're *always* urging," Muller said hotly. "Why don't you admit it, Brant? You don't think I'm good enough for her."

Brant started to answer, then seemed to think better of it.

Jarid turned to Della. "Two of my advisors urge against this marriage. What say you?"

She spoke with obvious reluctance. "I wish Muller and Chime could marry. They obviously love each other. But it would do more good if Muller wed a princess from Shazire or Taka Mal to bring us allies, and if Chime wed a man who wouldn't interfere with her work." Sadness touched her voice. "I am sorry. But I don't believe the marriage is in the best interest of Aronsdale."

Chime struggled with her disappointment. She had hoped Della would support them. As an advisor to the king, the mage mistress would speak for Aronsdale first, but Chime still felt betrayed.

Muller spoke bitterly. "Saints forbid it should matter what Chime and I want."

"Cousin, enough," Jarid murmured.

Muller's face reddened as he stared at the man who had taken his crown and now would take away the woman he loved. Chime needed no spell to know Muller's thoughts; he hated himself, first for abdicating and then for creating a situation that made him lose her as well. Well, it had taken two of them to manage that.

Jarid turned to Iris. "What say you, wife?"

Chime knew then that she and Muller had no chance of turning this around. Jarid placed Iris's opinion above all others. Remembering the many stupid, tactless things she had said to Iris when they were students, she wanted to curl up and vanish.

Iris regarded Jarid with an odd expression, as if she hurt inside. She said, simply, "Let them marry."

Chime was certain she had misheard. But everyone else was gaping at Iris as if they too had heard the words. Only Jarid remained unreadable. He held his emotions in check, isolating himself.

The king simply walked over to Brant. They conferred in low voices, their posture stiff, their faces tense. Then Brant bowed angrily. He stalked out of the parlor without a farewell to anyone.

Jarid turned to Chime and Muller. "He goes for the bishop."

It was the opposite of everything Chime had imagined for her wedding. She had planned a beautiful dress with diamonds; Muller would be resplendent in his best finery. They had intended to marry in the Hall of Kings with the royal court as their guests. Hundreds of candles would shed golden light over the festivities. Everyone would dance and dine all night, and people would talk of the grand event for years to come.

Instead she stood facing Muller, holding his hands, both of them in sleep clothes and bare feet, their hair a mess and dark circles under their eyes. The bishop had just pulled a robe over his sleep trousers and shirt. They had only a few witnesses: the king and queen, the King's Advisors, and Chime's maids. Everything she and Muller had planned, all their dreams for the great occasion had come to naught.

It was lovelier than anything she had imagined.

She looked up at Muller while the bishop read the ceremony, and her groom's eyes filled with an inner light more radiant than a thousand candles. Together, they made a spell of enchantment in the early hours before dawn.

And so they became man and wife.

III

The
Hollow Mage

25

The Sun's Bower

Spring came crisply that year. As meadows brightened with new life, the people of Croft's Vale and Suncroft ventured out to enjoy the warm days.

High on a hill, Iris sat in succulent grasses, surrounded by fire-lilies and white star flowers. Farther down the slope, Chime was running to Muller, her arms full of wild roses. In the three months since their wedding, they had been like sunshine on water. It hurt Iris to see them: they glowed, gold and beautiful, oblivious to the rest of the world. Iris had never doubted her advice to Jarid; Aronsdale needed the joy Chime and Muller shared far more than it needed foreign princesses or overworked mages. But she envied them their happiness, knowing she and Jarid would probably never find what they shared.

Her husband, the king, was standing on the edge of a bluff, gazing out at the vista of green hills. He wore rich garments now instead of rags, but he dressed simply, in dark trousers and a white shirt. She had no idea what he was thinking; even when she picked up his moods with her faltering spells, she had trouble interpreting them.

Still, Iris was coming to know her husband. He would never let go of the guilt that haunted him, but the mild days of spring eased his tormented moods. He had asked his foster father to stay, granting Unbent farmland to the south. The king rarely spoke, but fourteen years of honing his gifts to the exclusion of all else had turned him into a mage unlike any other described in the history texts. Few people knew about the extent of his power; his advisors cautioned discretion and Iris agreed. Too many unknowns remained; they had yet even to fully understand his abilities.

Muller also remained an enigma, his gifts simmering like embers, unpredictable. He and Chime were a haven for each other in a world that demanded more than they had to give. Iris longed to find such a refuge with Jarid, but they had no such fortune. They couldn't even settle into their roles. The queen served as the leading mage for the realm and the king as sovereign, but the more they learned, the more they reversed their duties. Jarid had little desire to govern but he could meditate on spells for hours. The process of governance suited Iris, to her surprise.

Her days felt unreal. For the first seventeen years of her life, she had believed her future held no more than scrabbling out an existence in the stony reaches of the Tallwalk Mountains. Her foster family had made no secret of their expectation that she would achieve nothing of significance. Even now, she had trouble believing she had talents to offer Aronsdale.

On the bluff, Jarid turned toward her, the wind rippling his laced shirt and its billowed sleeves. He had been distant and withdrawn earlier, but now he beckoned. Surprised, she rose and walked to him, breezes molding her silk tunic around her body, the gold top layer fluttering aside to reveal a rich blue layer underneath. Jarid watched, his gaze less fierce than usual. She savored the sight of him. It hurt, too, longing for closeness with him when they struggled just to know each other.

They sat together on the edge of the bluff. In the distance, Croft's Vale slumbered in the sunlight. Down the hill, Muller and Chime walked together, holding hands.

"They are happy," Jarid said, his voice rough even months after he had regained his ability to speak.

"Yes. They are." She wanted to ask, *And you?* But she held back. When he had agreed to stay at Suncroft, she had sworn to herself she would never push him. In the months since, she had done her best to keep that vow.

He took her hand. "Iris."

"Yes?"

He rubbed her knuckles. "A lovely day."

"Aye, it is." She wondered at his mood.

Softly he said, "It will never come easy for me."

"It?"

"Speaking."

She flushed. "Can you tell my moods that easily?"

"Not easily. But some." He touched her cheek. "My silences leave a woman lonely, I think."

"Nay, Jarid." Everything had changed when he came to Suncroft. The emptiness she had known all her life had begun to fill. It made her feel vulnerable; if you loved someone, it would hurt that much more to lose him. But it was better, far better, than loneliness.

"Silence donna mean absence," she said.

"It is hard for me to say what is inside."

Iris curled her hand around his. "It is you I want. Not words." She almost added, *Words can't love you,* but it was too much. They had wed as strangers. It was enough that he seemed content with their union.

He turned her palm up to the sky and cupped his hand under hers, as if they were holding an invisible orb. "Look." A sphere of light appeared in her hand, violet. His mage color.

Her pulse quickened. The power of that simple orb could vanquish any mage in the land. "It's beautiful." Terrifying and beautiful.

"Now yours."

"Mine?" No one yet knew her mage color.

"Watch."

The light changed into a rainbow. Every color swirled within the enchanted sphere.

Wonder spread through Iris. "It cannot be. A mage is one color, not all."

His voice gentled. "You are like none other. You have part of all of us in you." He lifted their hands together, offering the orb to the sky and land.

As she watched, marveling, the sphere rose from their hands, translucent in the streaming sunlight. Hills and meadows showed through its glimmering surfaces. It bobbed on the breezes like a giant bubble, rising higher, blown toward the village, its colors swirling. The orb drifted across the land, pulling out against the sky. Farther and farther it floated, stretching out...

And then it was done—and a rainbow arched in the blue sky. It was impossible in the clear weather, with nary a raindrop in sight. Yet there it was, a great bow of color over Croft's Vale.

"A gift to our people," Jarid murmured. "Light and the healing that comes after a storm."

Tears gathered in Iris's eyes. "It is lovely."

He cupped her cheek, his palm tingling with the power of the sphere. "It truly is."

He had given her a great weight. Now she understood; she had struggled with her spells because she confined them to one color. But in the woods and meadows, she had let go without realizing the truth. Her abilities flowed then, blue, yet blending a little of all colors.

Together, they sat in the sunlight, watching the colors in the sky, filled with warmth.

Anvil ran. He pounded up the hard path that wound into the mountains above Castle Escar. General Stonehammer ran with him, the beat of his feet keeping time with Anvil's pace.

They stopped at the top of the path, which surmounted a cliff. Stonehammer bent at the waist and braced his palms against his knees, heaving in deep breaths. Anvil waited, holding back his smile at the general's lesser physical prowess.

Lifting his head, Anvil looked over the mountains. The castle stood below them, and beyond it to the south and west, the Escar range extended as far as he could see, unusually sharp peaks alternating with knife-thin valleys. To the east, the folds of the Escar range rippled out toward the horizon: beyond them lay fertile Aronsdale.

Stonehammer straightened, breathing more normally now. "You set quite a pace." He rubbed the back of his neck, under the steel-gray hair he had pulled back from his face into a warrior's knot. He was an imposing man with a strong chin, a beak of a nose, and green eyes. His old leggings and light sweater hung on his frame, which may have lost some of the musculature of his youth, but which remained strong.

"I enjoy the air up here." Anvil inhaled with satisfaction. "It braces a man."

"Indeed." Stonehammer didn't sound braced. "Tell me something."

Anvil turned to him. "Yes?"

"Why do you wish to see Aronsdale conquered? Most men do not seek war against their own home."

He met Stonehammer's gaze. "I am not most men."

The older man scrutinized him. "Your people would call you traitor."

Anvil knew he had to answer with care. Stonehammer had spent a great deal of time with him lately, but Anvil didn't fool himself that the general enjoyed his company. As Varqelle's top officer, Stonehammer was studying the mage who had betrayed his own country, offering his services against Aronsdale. Varqelle meant to lead a campaign; Stonehammer's job was to ensure its success. Anvil had no doubt the general considered him suspect for his change of allegiance.

Bitterness welled in Anvil. "'My people' killed my family. They would have killed me if I hadn't escaped."

Stonehammer watched him with an unreadable expression. "King Varqelle tells me that you claim they did this because you were mages."

"They murdered my parents, then my brothers." Anvil's anger strengthened him. He had never hidden the truth. If he ever let his hatred go, he would shrivel into his grief. "They kept my sister and me for—for—" He shook his head, unable to continue.

The general studied him. "In a land where the king must marry a mage, where mages have higher status even than most dignitaries and military officers, you lived in a place where they killed mages?"

"Yes." Anvil made a conscious effort to stop gritting his teeth. "We are supposedly revered, but the truth comes out in wilder reaches of the country. We terrify people." He grimaced, his face flushed. "I lived that terror."

"But you survived."

His voice hardened. "They used my sister. When she died, it was my turn. But one of them had brought a sphere he looted from my parents' room. I focused through it." Anvil didn't flinch as he spoke. "And I killed them."

Stonehammer continued to watch him intently. "I have heard a mage cannot do such deeds."

Anvil wondered if he could ever explain the horror of that day. "I wanted to live."

"And to avenge your family."

"Yes."

The general stretched his arms, cracking the joints. "I regret, Anvil the Forged, that your life has given you such pain." He lowered his arms. "But if the misdeeds of your people have sent you to us, it is to our benefit and their downfall."

"A price must be paid."

"You demand a high one." The general jerked his chin in the direction of Aronsdale. "It is a small country, but a fine one. Govern it well for King Varqelle."

Anvil inclined his head. He doubted Stonehammer trusted him any more than before, but the general hadn't reached his high position by misjudging situations. Whatever he thought of Anvil personally, he would recognize his motivations. The language of vengeance crossed all borders, universal in its reach.

"This woman you want, though." Stonehammer shook his head. "Why is she worth so much trouble?"

"She is a valuable hostage."

"Not as much as the royal family."

Anvil smiled slightly, thinking of hair as yellow as corn and skybell eyes. "You have not seen her."

"I have heard rumors of her beauty." Stonehammer snorted. "Also of her stupidity."

Anvil's amusement flickered. "Her brain isn't what interests me."

"I hear she is a powerful mage."

"Indeed. As will be our children."

Stonehammer cocked his head. "I have been unable to place more agents in the castle. My last one left Croft's Vale months ago. Security there has become too tight for him to stay in that region."

"Then we will take her when we take Suncroft." Anvil could wait for his bride. He didn't like it, but he could be patient.

"Other hostages might be more valuable."

"No!" Even the suggestion of his losing Chime made Anvil sweat. "It must be her."

Stonehammer gave him an odd look. "Why?"

"It just must!"

"And if she has already wed this princeling of hers?"

Anvil had to make a conscious effort not to grit his teeth. "They will never waste her on Muller Dawnfield."

"Then she will marry someone else."

"And I will remove him." Anvil became aware he was clenching his fist. He opened his hand.

"So many deaths." Stonehammer wouldn't relent. "Where do you stop?"

Anvil understood what the general sought to learn. "I have no desire to kill." It wasn't true, but Stonehammer would trust him even less if he realized Anvil had no remorse in taking lives. "But if my talents can help King Varqelle bring Aronsdale under his guidance, I am at his service."

"Obsession has many forms. It can drive a man to great deeds. But it can also destroy him."

Anvil felt as if the general had punched him in the stomach. "I wouldn't know."

"Perhaps." Stonehammer's eyes glinted. "In any case, the rewards in taking Aronsdale are great."

"So they are," Anvil said. "So they are."

Muller circled Jarid in the Octagon Yard, his focus narrowed to his cousin. He lunged and Jarid evaded with unexpected skill. Then Jarid broke through his defenses and jabbed him in the side with his blunted sword.

"Hai!" Muller stumbled back, caught off guard by the parry from his usually less adept cousin.

Jarid looked undeniably pleased with himself. When they had begun working out, six months ago, Muller hadn't needed to defend himself at all. Although Jarid had natural aptitude and excellent physical fitness, he had little experience with a sword. However, Muller was discovering the hard way how fast Jarid learned. The king worked with single-minded intensity, training many hours a day. He had already surpassed many of the pages and even a few youths close to his own age. Muller knew he needed to pay more attention; his overconfidence could have ended his life if they had been using real blades.

Jarid lowered his sword. "Shall we try hand to hand?"

That gave Muller pause. They had never trained together without weapons. It was a good idea, though. If the army went into combat, Jarid could benefit from experience with hand to hand techniques.

"Yes, let's do." Muller motioned to a triangle-page, a boy of eleven. The fellow ran over and took their practice swords. Then Muller fell into a fighting pose, his fists up as he shifted his weight from foot to foot. He reminded himself to hold back so he didn't injure his cousin.

Jarid lunged.

The moment they grappled, Muller knew he was in trouble. Someone had taught Jarid to fight—and taught him well. He had greater strength and reach than Muller, and far more skill, though Muller had worked out all his life as a boy on his father's farm, a page here at Suncroft, and as a prince destined to be king.

Jarid evaded every move Muller tried, deflected his momentum, or otherwise stymied his efforts. He blocked Muller's swings but landed most of his own. Had the king not held back,

Muller knew he would be bruised and aching. Hell, he probably would be anyway. He was lucky Jarid hadn't broken any of his bones.

Then Jarid caught him in a hold that left Muller bent over, staring at the ground. He caught Jarid around the waist, but he couldn't exert enough force either to throw the king or break his hold. As Jarid drove him across the yard, pain lanced through his side where Jarid had struck him earlier. They staggered over a tiled circle, the royal seal, a silhouette of Suncroft against a yellow sun. The circle was imperfect, cut by the castle...

Like fire on oil, Muller's power flared. A spell burst out from him, but instead of helping his own injury, it slammed Jarid.

"Hai!" Jarid stumbled back as Muller let go of him. The king clamped his hand over his side in exactly the same place on his body where Muller ached from the blow from Jarid's sword.

"Saints, no!" Muller swore loudly. "Your Majesty, Jarid, I didn't mean——"

His cousin held up his other hand, stopping the words. He heaved in breaths, rapidly at first and then more slowly. Finally he lowered his arm. "I've never felt a healing spell turned inside out before."

Muller wished he could turn into a dust mote and blow away. Although Chime had told him Jarid knew about his warped powers, his cousin had never said anything. It had lulled Muller into believing his secret remained just that, a secret.

"You know about me," Muller said.

"Almost since the day I came here."

Muller had no idea what to say. He and Jarid regarded each other, the tiled circle with its imperfect sun between them.

"Do your spells often reverse that way?" Jarid sounded curious rather than critical. "You meant to heal yourself, yes? Instead you injured me."

"I never meant to hurt you——"

Jarid waved of his hand. "I know."

"My spells always go awry," Muller said. "They never work right." He was grateful he and Jarid had moved far enough away so the other men training in the yard couldn't overhear.

"Do you make the spells on purpose?"

"Sometimes."

"You should learn to do it properly."

Muller would have laughed if this hadn't all hurt so much. "If only it were that easy."

"Have you tried?"

He spoke tiredly. "My entire life."

Sympathy showed on Jarid's face, the last expression Muller had expected. "Several times, I felt you trying."

Muller tensed. "You knew when I was making them?"

"I haven't been sure before today. But yes."

"You never spoke of it."

Jarid exhaled. "Speaking…is hard."

Muller wondered if it would ever come easily to his cousin. This was certainly one of their longest conversations. "Do you remember the time Unbent and I found you asleep in the woods?"

"Yes."

"I tried a spell then." He thought back to that day, six months ago. "It didn't work at first, but then it snapped into focus. And it was right. No distortion."

"Good." Jarid didn't seem to realize the full significance of Muller's words.

"Never in my life have my spells worked." Muller wondered if he could even explain that incredible moment. "But twice since you've come, you've straightened them."

Jarid seemed bewildered. "I have?"

"That time, I think," Muller said. "And earlier that day. You were in the Starlight Tower, watching us train. I had made a mood spell, but it didn't work. But you—well, you touched it. Somehow. Then it worked."

"I remember you and Arkandy practicing, but nothing else." Jarid spoke awkwardly. "I felt overwhelmed then. I wanted to reach out to you, my cousin, but I didn't know how. Perhaps it came through to you as help with a spell."

Muller hadn't realized Jarid had wanted to connect with him then. "I am glad you did." It was an understatement, to be sure.

Jarid rubbed his side, a wry smile on his lips. "Would that today I could have made your healing spell work before it hit me."

Muller winced. "Sorry."

"Cousin."

"Yes?"

"If your spells go awry during battle—" Jarid left the sentence unfinished.

Muller had dreaded this question. For all his doubts, it meant a great deal to him that Jarid had given him command of the King's Army. He valued that show of confidence. He didn't want to lose it now.

"I've learned to suppress the spells," Muller said.

"You said you can't control them."

"Once they start. But I can usually hold them down if I'm prepared."

"What do your men think about it?"

Muller stared at him. "I never *tell* them."

"No one?"

"Saints no. Just Chime."

Jarid scratched his chin. "Why?"

Why? It seemed obvious to Muller. "Would you speak of killing Murk?"

Jarid's expression darkened. "No. But you have killed no one."

He answered quietly. "Not yet."

"Ah, Muller." He spoke roughly. "You and I have much to face, eh?"

"Aye." He smiled wanly. "Iris believes if we all work together, we can muddle our way through."

Jarid grinned, a rare expression. It lit up his face, calling to mind the joyful boy Muller had known so long ago. "Iris has good sense."

"She does indeed."

"Come, my cousin." Jarid indicated the castle. "Let us go back. Perhaps we can play a game of chess."

Muller blinked, surprised. "I would like that."

As they walked back, Muller thought of how close he and Jarid had been all those years ago. He would never forget the way six-year-old Jarid had looked up to him, seeing past his failings. Muller had mourned the loss of that kinship for many years.

Perhaps he and Jarid could find a way back to each other.

With a groan of relief, Chime lay down under the tree, glad to rest after hiking through the hills. She had spent the morning gathered herbs for Skylark, the castle healer. Aria and Reed had settled a few paces away and were chatting while they sorted the plants Chime had found into different baskets. It amazed Chime how little the staff at Suncroft knew about ordinary plants. She could find those herbs with her eyes closed, practically, but Aria and Reed had exclaimed with gusto over every one she pointed out. They seemed genuinely impressed.

They kept glancing at her now, concerned for some reason. When Chime waved her hand at them, they returned to their conversation, well aware she didn't want anyone hovering over her.

Beyond the maids, one of Chime's bodyguards paced under

the widely spaced trees. Her other guard came into view, and the two octahedron-lieutenants nodded to each other, then parted again, continuing their patrol.

"Never alone," Chime grumbled. Everywhere she went, maids and guards went, too. Maybe if she got them interested in each other, they would pay less attention to her. Brant would never let that happen, though; he had made it clear they must never leave her unattended.

As much as she chafed at having people about all the time, she appreciated their protection, for she dreaded even more the idea that whoever had come after her might try again. Even three months later, the death of her songbird left her chilled. Many people had been in her suite that night. Surely gas drifted from her bedroom into the parlor. That no one felt any effects suggested too little had gone into her bedroom to kill a person. It supported Muller's belief that whoever had done it wanted her alive. They had probably escaped while the King's Advisors were chastising her and Muller for their misbehavior.

Chime couldn't fathom why someone wanted to take her. Jarid and Iris were worth more as hostages, both as royals and as mages. Skylark also wielded more mage power. Della had less power, but she had decades more experience, which made her more valuable than Chime. Nor did Chime have political power. Brant or Fieldson would be more useful to King Varqelle, if he was the one behind the kidnap attempts.

With a sigh, Chime closed her eyes, too sleepy to think. She lay under the rustling tree, warmed by the late summer sun, inhaling the perfume of the white star flowers scattered about. Grass prickled her skin through her yellow leggings and her silk tunic, poking through both the gold layer on top and the emerald layer underneath. It all reminded her of how she had loved to flop down on her back in the meadows of Jacob's Vale. She missed her home so much. She wrote her family regularly, and they answered just as often, but it wasn't enough. She wanted to see them.

She thought often of the little things, the way her mother and father debated whether or not the Saint of Unfurled Leaves existed as a spirit that watched over orchards, as her father believed, or was a myth created long ago by monks who had drunk too much apple wine, as her mother claimed. She wanted to hear her brother, Hunter, singing as he filled buckets of water from the pump behind their house. He had such a beautiful voice. She longed to watch her youngest brother Drummer jumping down the stairs inside their house, seeing how many steps he could skip at once. She even missed the way Hunter and Drummer teased her.

As much as she longed to have her family here, though, she couldn't ask them to move from Jacob's Vale. The Headwind clan had tended those orchards for generations. Guilt tugged at Chime. Her parents needed help in the orchards. They had expected her to marry some strapping young fellow and bring him into the family. Probably she would have done exactly that if Della hadn't shown up. Now here she was, pretending to be a noblewoman and missing them so much, her heart ached.

"Ma'am?"

Chime opened her eyes. Aria was kneeling next to her, her expression concerned.

"Yes?" Chime asked.

"How are you feeling?"

Chime wondered what she was about. "It's a lovely day."

"Aye, it is." Aria hesitated. "Can we get you anything?"

"No, no. I'm fine. But thank you."

Aria motioned toward Reed. "We're here if you need us." The other girl waved to them.

"Thank you." Chime wished they wouldn't fuss so. She liked

being sleepy. For just a few minutes, she wanted to laze here in the grass, warmed by the sun.

After Aria left, Chime drowsed more. Some time later, she sensed someone else. Half opening her eyes, she looked through her lashes to see Skylark seated next to her, her white braids hanging over her shoulders.

"A fine morning," Skylark said.

"Hmmm." Chime thought it would be even finer if they would all leave her alone.

Skylark tried again. "You seem tired today."

"Hmmm." Chime closed her eyes.

"Are you sick?" Skylark asked.

"Just tired. Muller has a sore throat, though."

"I saw him this morning. He was quite irate with the world."

Chime's lips curved upward. "He gets that way."

"I helped his throat. Perhaps I can help yours."

Chime yawned. "My throat is fine."

"Shall I try a spell?"

Apparently they were going to pester her until she let them fuss. "Oh, all right."

Skylark laid her hand on her forehead. "Tell me about your favorite place."

Chime doubted "Muller's bed" would be an appropriate response. So she said, "My family's orchard."

"Imagine yourself there, relaxing."

Chime recalled the day King Daron's party had ridden into Jacob's Vale while she hid in the apple tree. Later, when she had come to know the king a little, she had discovered she liked him. She wished they could have spent more time together before he passed away.

Skylark sat with her for a while. Eventually she said, "Lady, are you awake?"

"I think so," Chime mumbled.

"I'm afraid I can do little to help."

Exasperated, Chime opened her eyes. "Well, I told you nothing was wrong."

Skylark smiled. "That depends."

"On what?"

"On how you feel about having a child."

"Hai!" Chime sat up fast. When her maids looked over, she reddened and waved them away. Then she lowered her voice. "Are you sure?"

"I think so. When was your cycle?"

"I don't remember. They come whenever they want."

"No regularity?"

"Not much."

Skylark chuckled. "It is fitting, yes, for you."

Chime regarded her warily. "Why do you say that?"

"You are a most impressive woman," the healer assured her. "You've a strong mind."

"Pah. You mean I'm wild." When Skylark laughed, Chime relented and smiled. The news pleased her. It would also overjoy her parents to know they would be grandparents.

If only she could visit to tell them the news.

"It wouldn't be for long." Chime lay with Muller on the bed, she wearing his tunic and nothing else, he in just his leggings. "Only a few weeks. You will love my family."

"Brant doesn't want us to travel," he said.

Chime glared. "Brant never wants us to do anything, may he suffer the pox."

Muller spoke wryly. "The worst of it is, he is usually right."

"Indeed. It is most annoying." Chime knew Brant's strictures made sense, but he had also wanted to separate her from Muller. They colored her responses to him. When it came to her child, though, she had to listen to good counsel even if she resented the person giving it. "Maybe Fieldson could send a polygon unit with us. Didn't you want to train them on that military thing?"

"'Thing'?" He smiled. "You mean field exercises?"

"Yes, that."

"I have been considering it."

"Well, then."

"Well, then, what?"

"You and they can go field exercise."

Muller grinned. "By accompanying your fierce and dangerous self on a visit to your family?"

"You make fun of me."

"Never, love."

She made a humph sound. "You know what I mean."

Muller set his hand on her abdomen. She had told him the news this morning, after Skylark told her. The mage predicted Chime would give birth in eight months.

"I would rather you didn't come with us," he said.

"Well, that would be useful," she said. "Have me visit my parents by not visiting them."

Although he laughed, he seemed pensive. "Ah, love, if I could, I would protect you from the entire world."

She gave him a frosty look. "I don't need to be sheltered."

"Even if you pulverized me for trying, still I would."

"I can travel."

He spoke firmly. "Brant will say no."

"He can't stop me!" She paused. "Can he?"

"The king can. And he listens to Brant."

"You must speak with Brant, then."

"But, Chime——" When she glared, he held up his hands. "All right. I will discuss it with him."

She kissed his cheek. "You are an angel."

Muller sighed. "I make no promises."

"Just see what he says."

"If I make Brant think the field exercises are his idea, he may believe they have value."

Chime took his hand. "You are the commander. You don't need his approval. Your ideas are worth as much as his."

His face gentled. "When you say it, I almost believe it."

"Believe it." Chime drew him closer, filling her arms with his warmth. She knew Muller would never shirk his responsibilities as commander of the King's Army. It gave her no satisfaction to know that, however. It only made her fear she would lose the father of her child to war.

Drummer

"No." Brant sat behind the table where he worked, scrolls scattered in front of him. "Absolutely not."

Muller was sitting across from him, ostensibly relaxed in a chair upholstered in wine-red brocade. "I need to train the men."

"Fine. Take them out in the field. But Chime stays home." Brant shook his head. "Muller, be reasonable. This is no trip for your pregnant wife."

In his heart, Muller agreed. He didn't want Chime traveling. She had suffered no more kidnap attempts, but that was probably due to increased security. Fieldson's men had investigated at Suncroft and in the village, and accounted for everyone's whereabouts on the night the songbird was poisoned. Either someone had contrived a false alibi or, more likely, the scoundrel had fled before they apprehended him.

Even so, he had promised Chime he would try. "She very much wants to see her family."

Brant raised his eyebrows. "And you agree?"

"Well, uh, no, actually."

He didn't look surprised. "Then it is settled."

"But I would like to meet her family. We never had a wedding for them to attend." He thought for a moment. "I could go train the men, visit her village, and bring her family back here for a visit." They couldn't stay long, with the orchard to look after, but a few weeks should be manageable this time of year.

Brant tilted his head. "It is a good idea."

"Well, then." Muller beamed. Then his good mood faded. "Now I must inform my wife."

To his amazement, Brant laughed. "You are a braver man than I."

"Ah, well." Muller could face armies, storms, even dragons, if those existed. Facing Chime, however, was another matter.

"Come on," Muller coaxed. "It is a good idea."

His wife crossed her arms and walked to the window of their bedroom. She proceeded to stare with absorption at the men training in the Octagon Yard below.

"Chime." Muller joined her. "The idea was to see your family, yes?"

She didn't deign to look at him. "The idea was to *visit* them."

"Too much danger."

She gave him a glare that could have incinerated the entire army. "I thought you were going to convince Brant."

"I tried."

"You did not."

Muller touched her cheek, his fingertip lingering in the way he knew she liked. "I did what I thought best."

"You are an impossible scalawag."

His lips quirked. "A scalawag in love with you."

"Pah." She put her hands on her hips. "Sweet talk will do you no good."

He drew her into his arms. "Will nothing melt your heart?"

"Nothing." But she put her arms around his waist and laid her head against his shoulder. "Absolutely nothing."

"You're smiling, Chime."

"I am not." She spoke against his shoulder.

"Yes, you are."

"How would you know?"

He grinned. "I just do."

"Pah."

Muller pressed his lips against her head. "You are my life. You and our child."

"And you, for me, you cad."

Muller held her close, glad she would be safe.

Varqelle the Cowled leaned back in his great chair and swirled the wine in his goblet, a fine piece of Wingham crystal. A fire blazed in the hearth, warming him and his guests, General Stonehammer and Anvil the Forged. Outside, hail whipped through the night and clattered against the beveled windows.

Stonehammer raised his glass. "A fine import, Your Majesty." He was relaxing in a chair by a table with an orb-lamp made from blue glass.

"So it is." Varqelle sipped his wine, watching Anvil. The mage was sprawled in his chair, his legs stretched out, his goblet on the table.

Anvil fascinated Varqelle. He seemed older than his thirty-one years, probably because he brooded constantly. Varqelle could count the times he had seen Anvil smile. The darkly handsome mage attracted the notice of many women, but he ignored them all. Except Chime Headwind. His interest in the girl seemed extreme. If Anvil had suffered such misery for his gifts, why did he want a wife who would bear him mage children? That game of kidnap had intrigued Varqelle, though, even excited him. He regretted his agent hadn't succeeded; Varqelle had looked forward to seeing Anvil's prey. He suspected more than lust drove the mage's thirst for the girl. It would be interesting to see what developed. First however they had a more important matter to attend—the subjugation of Aronsdale.

"Is the wine not to your liking?" he asked Anvil.

The younger man started. "My apologies. I am preoccupied with thoughts of tomorrow."

"So." Varqelle took another swallow of wine. "Are you ready to march, then?"

Anvil sat up straight. "More than ready."

Stonehammer considered him. "You have made many promises, Master Forged. I look forward to seeing them fulfilled."

"As do I." Anvil finally took his drink from the table. "It will realize a goal I have long held."

Stonehammer raised his goblet. "It is time Aronsdale came under Harsdown rule."

"Time indeed." Varqelle stood, and Stonehammer and Anvil rose as well.

The king lifted his goblet. "To tomorrow."

Stonehammer raised his glass, first to Varqelle, then to Anvil. "To tomorrow."

"Yes." Anvil spoke in a shadowed voice. "Tomorrow."

Muller enjoyed traveling cross-country with his men. He took the Hexagon Unit, six groups of six men, each headed by a hexahedron-major. The Pentagon Unit, led by Penta-Colonel Burg, had also gone on maneuvers, heading north while Muller went south. They hiked by day, scouting the land. Speed wasn't important, so they hunted game to augment their food supplies. It felt more like a vacation than a training mission. He gave up his elegant clothes for wool leggings and tunics that kept him warm. Summer was blending into fall, adding a nip to the air.

He conducted war games in the fields, valleys and woods, working the swordsmen and archers, either mounted or on foot. They also practiced hand to hand combat. The unit had brought more equipment than they would take into battle. Muller had them try assorted catapults, most small and easy to transport, others bulkier, harder to carry but more powerful. The men experimented with various types of boots and helmets. They wore chain mail over leather armor dyed in the king's colors, indigo and violet. When they traveled, flag bearers carried pennants that snapped in the breeze; when they rested, the men spent time making arrows, playing cards, and emblazoning their shields with Dawnfield the insignia of Suncroft. At night, they tried out ways of setting up camp, seeing what worked best.

Although the army had never stopped training, the country had lived in relative peace for long enough now that the military had lost its edge. Aronsdale had good relations with the lands to its south and east: Taka Mal, Jazid, Shazire, and tiny Blueshire. They fought skirmishes with Harsdown at their northwest borders, but nothing more. The two countries were evenly matched; Harsdown had a larger army but Aronsdale had mages. Beyond Harsdown, far to the west, the Misted Cliffs loomed, neither hostile nor friendly. The Cliffs seemed to have no interest in Aronsdale, but still, Muller could never be sure the peace would continue. So the King's Army practiced.

It took eleven days to reach Jacob's Vale. The town spread out among low hills in the southwest corner of Aronsdale a short ride from the border with Blueshire. Muller rode Windstrider, his restless black charger. The horse wanted to run and Muller longed to let him go, but he held him in check, keeping pace with his men. So the Hexagon Unit crested the last hill that separated them from the village where Chime had spent most of her life.

The Vale basked in late afternoon sunshine. People were working in the surrounding fields, and a cart pulled by two mules bumped down the hill ahead of the unit. The sleepy, peaceful quality of the scene appealed to Muller. He sent an emissary ahead to let the mayor know they were arriving and would like to camp outside of town. He hoped to purchase food stores and supplies here as well.

"Ho!" a young voice called.

Muller looked to see a boy running along with them. More boys joined him, waving at the soldiers and calling out excited greetings. By the time the unit reached the village, half the town had come out to meet them.

With guidance from the mayor, Muller directed his men to a clearing outside town where they could set up camp. As they swung off their horses, villagers wandered among them, cheerfully greeting soldiers, asking questions, and otherwise nosing in everywhere. Their lack of concern about the war party astonished Muller. Then again, people this far south had probably never experienced military conflict. From what Chime told him, most of them knew little about Harsdown. They might have heard about skirmishes between Aronsdale and Harsdown soldiers, but only as a vague threat in the far north that few took seriously.

A tall man with graying hair and a burly physique approached Muller, making his way through the controlled chaos of the camp. He looked familiar, though Muller felt certain they had never met. The fellow walked with the confidence of someone used to the respect and affection of his neighbors. As Muller straightened up from unpacking a tent, the man stopped in front of him and bowed.

"My greetings, Prince Muller. Welcome to Jacob's Vale." The resonance of his deep voice sounded familiar, too, though Muller couldn't figure out why.

"And mine, Goodsir." Muller nodded. "You have the advantage of me, I'm afraid. Do we know each other?"

The man paused, as if uncertain of his reception. "Not directly. But we have kin in common." He cleared his throat. "I am Appleton. You married my daughter."

Saints above. Muller had counted on having time to gather his wits before meeting his new family. Apparently news traveled fast here. He hoped he didn't look as nervous as he felt. "It is my pleasure to meet you, sir."

"My family would be honored if you would dine with us tonight." Appleton used formal phrases appropriate to the nobility, but it obviously wasn't natural to him. Judging from the casual way the people here ambled through the camp, Muller doubted they worried much about protocol.

"Thank you for your invitation," Muller said. "It would be my pleasure to join your family tonight."

Appleton's shoulders came down from a tensed position Muller hadn't realized they had taken until the big man relaxed. The man's face warmed in a more natural smile. "We look forward to making your acquaintance and hearing news of Chime."

Muller beamed. "There is much news." Tonight, he would tell them about the child.

His father-in-law paused. "Please forgive my lack of experience, Your Highness, but I have never invited a member of the royal family to supper before. Will you bring a retinue?"

Muller rarely went anywhere without one, especially now that Brant insisted he have protection at all times. He had no intention of hanging back if he had to go to war, but he had otherwise given Brant his word to accept a bodyguard. And of course he traveled with his aides and other attendants. If he showed up at Chime's home with a royal company, though, her family would feel obligated to feed them all. He had no wish to cause hardship.

"I have two in my retinue," he said. "My aide and my body-guard." He would take Arkandy and Archer.

Appleton looked taken aback. "Does Chime have body-guards, too?"

Muller inwardly winced. He had stumbled into a quagmire. He didn't want to start out with his wife's family by telling them someone had twice tried to abduct their daughter. Better to ease that gently to them, if at all.

"All members of the royal family have them," Muller said. It was true, though only since the kidnap attempts. But he needn't add that last.

"Ah. I see." Appleton relaxed. "I won't detain you any longer." His weathered face creased in a smile. "I did want to make sure you were welcomed. We look forward to your company tonight."

"Thank you, kind sir."

After his father-in-law left, Muller turned back to his work. As he set up his tent, Arkandy came over to him.

"Do you know him?" Arkandy asked.

"Not yet." Muller grinned. "I know his daughter."

"Hai! That was Chime's father?"

Muller chuckled. "Do not look so alarmed."

"You laugh," Arkandy said darkly. "Many a man has been brought down by overconfidence."

"I'm not facing Harsdown. Just my wife's family."

"I should think the former would be less fearsome."

Muller gave a rueful laugh. "Perhaps. Her father seems amiable."

"I hope so."

Muller slapped him on the back. "Tonight we will see."

Twilight settled over Jacob's Vale with the humid warmth of the southern provinces. Muller and Arkandy strolled along the streets together, but Archer insisted on ranging farther out, keeping surveillance. Muller was too nervous to complain. He kept reminding himself he had dined with royalty and nobles. It didn't help. The prospect of meeting Chime's family thoroughly intimidated him.

Courage, he thought. He wished Chime were here.

Even if she hadn't told him where to find her home, he would have known he had reached the right house by the two boys standing on the porch outside. They were younger, male versions of Chime, one fourteen and the other ten, both with tousled yellow curls spilling down their necks, large blue eyes, and angelic faces. Given what he knew of his wife, he suspected those innocent faces disguised a world of mischief.

"Ho!" the younger boy shouted, spotting Muller. The other boy shushed him.

As Muller came up to the door, the older boy bowed. "Good Eve, You Hi-highness."

"And to you," Muller said amiably.

"You don't look like a king," the younger boy said. "More like a minstrel."

"Drummer!" The older boy turned red. He spoke quickly to Muller, his words spilling out. "I'm really sorry, Your Lordship-ness. He didn't mean that. Really."

Muller couldn't help but smile at this new title. Nor had anyone ever mistaken him for a singer. He rather liked the daydream of wandering across the country singing love ballads. He would compose them all for this boy's sister.

"I'm actually not a king," he told them. "But I am the cousin of one. You can call me Muller."

"Oh." Drummer's eyes widened.

The door behind the boys swung open and a girl with yellow hair and blue eyes looked out. She looked too much like

Chime to be anyone except her sister, though Muller didn't remember Chime mentioning one. Perhaps a cousin.

"Hunter, Drummer, why—oh!" She stared at Muller. Then she shook herself and bowed. Warm light poured around her, silhouetting her body, though he could tell she had on a yellow dress, country style, with a flared skirt and fitted bodice. The lovely effect made him think of Chime.

"Please, come in, Your Highness," she said.

Muller bowed. "You honor me, Mistress Headwind. Are your parents in?"

The woman dimpled just like Chime. "Such flattery." She moved aside to let him enter. "My husband went to the cellar for some wine."

Her *husband?* Mortified, Muller realized his mistake. "My apologies, ma'am. I mistook you for Chime's sister."

Her laugh was as melodic as sparkling water. "Hardly an insult, I assure you. I am Bell Headwind."

"My honor at your acquaintance." He gave her a formal nod and entered the house with Arkandy and Archer. The two boys came close on their heels, making no secret of their fascination with Muller and his warriors.

Drummer looked up at him, wide-eyed. "Do you know how to use a sword?"

Muller smiled. "Yes, I do."

His eyes became very round. "Will you teach me?"

"Hush, Drummer," Bell murmured. She ushered them into the front parlor, her skirts swirling around her legs. In the candlelight, Muller could see lines around her eyes and a trace of grey in her hair, but it did nothing to mute her grace. No wonder his wife had turned out so lovely.

"Ho!" Appleton strode into the room with two bottles. "Here you are!" He greeted them heartily, including Arkandy and Archer in his hospitality.

Bell bustled off to check supper, taking Drummer with her for help. The rest of them settled in chairs around the hearth. It was a comfortable house with unexpected amenities, including a clock on the mantel and a round glass window. Most shapes in the room were either exact or else too far off from pure form to awaken Muller's gifts. The only problem was the fireplace, almost a rectangular box, close enough to tug his power. Fortunately the logs spilling out of it disrupted its shape enough to keep his spells quiescent. The absence of troublesome shapes relieved him; he would have hated to become "accident-prone" while he endeavored to impress his wife's family.

As Appleton poured out wine into blue-glass goblets, Hunter flopped down in a chair, a youth on the awkward edge between boyhood and manhood. Muller remembered well that gangly phase of his life, all long arms and legs. In fact, he sometimes felt as if he had never grown out of it. Hunter would clearly fill out into a more muscular physique, tall and brawny like his father.

They talked stiffly at first, Appleton formal and Muller nervous. Gradually, as they drank their wine, they relaxed. Then Bell returned with Drummer in tow and bade them all come to the polished table, clearly reserved for special occasions, with blue-glass place settings and silverware. It appealed to Muller. Even just a year ago he might have disdained the settings compared to the china, crystal, and gold they used at Suncroft. Now he wondered that he could have been so narrow as to miss the beauty of a home like this. Its harmony made him feel welcome.

Almost as soon as they were seated and the meal set out, Drummer began to fidget. He spoke eagerly to Muller. "When will you show me how to use a sword?"

"We might eat first," Muller suggested. The fragrant aromas distracted him.

Drummer lowered his voice. "You can learn me how to fight the night warriors."

"Night warriors?" Muller asked, curious.

"They prowl the mountains." The boy's voice was full of portent.

Arkandy smiled at him. "What do these night warriors do while they are prowling?"

"March." Drummer leaned toward him, his young face serious. "They march all day and night."

"Where do they march to?" Muller asked.

Drummer blinked solemnly. "They are coming to take over Aronsdale and steal Chime."

Steal Chime? The coincidence startled Muller.

"Oh, Drummer, don't be stupid." Hunter glared at him. "It's bad enough you make up stories, but do they have to have *Chime* in them?"

"Boys," their mother admonished. "Enough."

"It's not a story," Drummer said.

"Oh, really." Hunter leaned close to him. "And where did you see these terrible warriors who plan to take over the world?"

"Not the world, rockhead." Drummer poked him in the arm. "They just want Aronsdale."

Watching them, Muller felt a stab of loneliness. He wondered if they knew how lucky they were, having each other to fight with. He had longed all his life for a family. He would have given anything for a brother. It made him want his own children all the more. He thought of telling them all about the baby, but this didn't feel like the right time.

Appleton picked up the thread of a conversation from before dinner. "So Chime continues her studies with the mage mistress?"

Muller nodded. "She works with Della in the mornings. She used to spend afternoons in the village, visiting the elderly or

shopping at the market, but now she studies the government."
He thought it best not to mention why she no longer went to
the village.

"Chime, studying *government?*" Hunter smirked. "Aronsdale
is in real trouble now."

Appleton frowned at him. "Do not speak of your sister in
that tone."

"I wasn't making it up about the night warriors," Drummer
said.

"Boys!" Bell reddened, her gaze flicking to Muller.

"It is fine," Muller said. "Really."

Drummer fixed him with a firm gaze. "You will protect
Chime from them, won't you?"

The boy's insistence disquieted Muller. "Why do you believe
she is in danger?"

"Your Highness, please forgive the boy," Appleton said. "I
apologize for his tales."

"No need to apologize," Muller said. Drummer plucked a
chord within him. He recognized Chime in the boy, certainly,
but it went deeper than that resemblance.

"Does Chime do spells now?" Hunter asked.

"Beautiful spells," Muller said. It wasn't completely true;
Chime was still learning. But she had made plenty of progress.
"You should see her light a room." His voice softened. "Actually
she needs no spells to do that. Just herself."

Bell and Appleton beamed at him. His last statements seemed
to have put him in their good graces more than his other pleasantries. He wasn't sure why, but he was glad they were warming toward him.

"It's true about the night warriors," Drummer stated.

"Enough," Appleton said.

Bell gave Muller a wry look. "I hope this doesn't put you off
from having young ones of your own."

"Not at all." Muller wanted to know more about the night warriors, but he also couldn't let this opening pass. "Actually we—" He was suddenly self-conscious. "That is, I mean—as it happens, the contrary will soon be true." *There.* He had said it.

Bell blinked and Appleton squinted at him. Neither seemed to know how to respond, which made Muller suspect he hadn't "said it" as clearly as he thought.

"The contrary?" Bell gave a hesitant smile. "I'm glad you like the boys." Both Drummer and Hunter looked bewildered.

"Well, yes, I do." Muller was growing embarrassed. "What I meant to say, rather clumsily, I'm afraid, is that you will soon have more young ones in the family." His voice softened. "Chime is with child."

"A babe?" Bell's face lit up. "This is wonderful!"

"Ho!" Appleton grabbed the wine and poured out a glass for Muller, then for himself and Bell. "Well done, boy! Well done!" Realizing what he had said, he quickly added, "Your Highness, I mean."

Muller laughed. "Please call me Muller."

"A fine name." Appleton took a hearty swallow of wine. "So! When does the babe come?"

"About eight months," Muller said.

"Chime is going to have a baby?" Hunter seemed only now to absorb the concept. "That's strange. She won't know what to do."

His mother chuckled. "She will figure it out."

"Chime can't have a baby," Drummer stated.

"Why not?" Muller asked.

"Because she's my sister."

"What, our sister can't be a mother?" Hunter glared at him, though he seemed almost as disconcerted.

"You have to help her!" Drummer told Muller. "The night warriors will hurt her, just like they did her bird."

Muller's pulse surged. *Her songbird?*

"Drummer, you go too far," his father said. "You will go to your room now."

"No, wait, please." Muller turned to the boy. "What do you know about your sister's bird?"

"They killed it," Drummer said.

"The night warriors?"

"Yes."

A chill ran up Muller's back. "But who are they?"

"They're bad." Drummer made a face. "And they're coming to Aronsdale."

Appleton gave Muller a look of apology. "I've no idea why he is saying this. We've seen no one."

"Neither have we," Muller said. "My unit has been all over this area."

"They aren't *here,*" Drummer said. "They're north."

"Sure." Hunter snorted. "And you saw them just this morning, right? When you were up north."

Drummer ignored him. "I dreamed it," he told Muller.

Bell sighed. "Drummer, honey, you mustn't mix your dreams up with real life." To Muller, she said, "He doesn't usually go on this way."

"No need to apologize." Muller spoke kindly to Drummer. "Have you ever been tested for mage power?"

The boy blinked. "No."

"Mage power?" Hunter peered at his brother as if he might have odd protuberances sticking out of his head. "He doesn't have any. Chime did, even if she pretended she didn't. But not Drummer."

"How can you tell?" Muller asked. As far as he knew, only another mage could detect such powers.

Hunter faltered. "I'm not sure."

Muller glanced to Appleton and Bell. "Children often inherit the traits from their parents."

Appleton laughed uneasily. "I'm no sorcerer."

Bell started to speak, then stopped.

"Please," Muller said. "Go ahead."

She hesitated. "Sometimes it seems...perhaps I can make warmth. Or light. But nothing like Chime. Just a hint here and there."

"Like your sons," he said quietly.

"I'm no sorcerer," Drummer stated, copying his father's inflections perfectly.

Muller spoke with care. "Drummer, can you tell me what these night warriors look like?"

"Shadows."

"Shadows, how?"

"Their hearts are like shadows. They are like Chime, but shadowy instead of light. She is good. They are bad."

Everyone fell silent. Muller had little doubt what Drummer meant. Dark and light, the two sides of a mage's power. Chime embodied the best of those gifts, healing and empathy. If what Drummer described was real, rather than a child's nightmare, it chilled Muller. A year or two ago, he would have scoffed at the idea that a dark mage could bring an army. That was before Chime had touched the presence in Croft's Vale.

"Why do you think they are in the north?" he asked.

"The mountains are big." Drummer squirmed in his chair. "And black."

"How big are the trees?" Muller asked. The northern forests varied a great deal, with towering giants in the western foothills, smaller trees in the midranges, and stunted vegetation in the highest peaks.

"No trees," Drummer said.

Appleton looked from his son to Muller, comprehension in his expression. Only one mountain region had no trees: the pass from Harsdown to Aronsdale.

"Surely his dream is coincidence," Appleton said.

Muller spoke quietly. "When my cousin's parents died, I knew, though they were far from Suncroft. I dreamed it."

Bell put her hand to her cheek. "*You* are a mage?"

Muller took care with his response, acutely aware of Arkandy and Archer listening. "I come from a family of mages. Even those of us without true gifts may experience an echo of power from our kin."

Appleton leaned forward. "Could Harsdown actually be marching on Aronsdale?"

"Perhaps. We've seen nothing in the southwest. The Pentagons came west, too, but in the north." Unlike him, they had no link to Chime. By touching the mind of the dark mage, she might have inadvertently set up a bond with him, one Drummer caught traces of in his dreams. If so, the boy could be giving him information unknown to anyone else. It might be nothing, just a boy's dream. But the Tallwalk Pass was several days ride from the border; if Varqelle brought an army through there, it could be days before anyone in Aronsdale knew.

He nodded to Drummer. "I will think on what you have said. Thank you for letting me know."

Drummer straightened. "Thank you, Your Highness." He smirked at his brother. "Told you."

While the brothers glared at each other, conversation among the adults drifted away from Harsdown. Bell and Appleton chatted with Arkandy and Archer, who were clearly enjoying themselves. Muller sat in silence, preoccupied. If Drummer really had picked up an invasion, the situation was more serious than anyone realized. And Chime might be in danger. He couldn't make it back to Suncroft, though, before anyone coming over the Tallwalks reached Aronsdale. He ought to rendezvous with the Pentagons, who were about five days' ride from here. He had no time to waste; an invading army could reach Aronsdale in that time.

And if he was wrong? He would look like an idiot.

He considered the consequences. If they rode north and found nothing, Jarid would question his judgment, maybe relieve him of command. If he didn't go north and Harsdown had marched against Aronsdale, lives could be lost and villages destroyed, far more serious consequences than his looking stupid.

When viewed that way, the choice was obvious.

The Dark Dreaming

Muller strode though the camp, flanked by Arkandy and Archer. "We must go north as fast as possible. We'll need enough field rations so we don't have to hunt. And warm clothes. It's colder up in the Tallwalks. But leave everything here that isn't absolutely necessary."

"I will speak with the other hexahedron-majors," Arkandy said. "We should be ready to move within the hour."

Muller nodded, too tense to say more. Clouds had covered the sky and the only light came from torches his men carried. He wished they had a mage, more than just for light, but as a healer, too. However, all their mages were at Suncroft. He didn't bother to include himself.

He headed toward the edge of the camp—and was startled to see his father-in-law standing near the horses, with Drummer at his side.

Muller went to them, warming inside. "My greetings."

Appleton and Drummer bowed. Then the father indicated his son. "He would like to tell you something, if he may."

"Certainly." Muller smiled, charmed by the boy's earnest face and mop of wild curls. "It is good to see you, Drummer."

The boy watched him with a gaze that, if Muller hadn't known better, would have looked like hero worship. It made Muller ache inside; Jarid had looked at him that way when he had been six and Muller fourteen.

"I wanted to—to tell you." Drummer stumbled over his words, rushing them. "To wish you luck. I know we all said farewells and all tonight, but I wanted to 'specially wish you well."

A lump seemed to lodge in Muller's throat. Somehow he spoke around it. "That means a great deal to me."

The boy extended his hand. "This is for you." A cord with a metal ring lay in his palm. "It gives me good luck. It will for you, too."

"You honor me." Taking the cord, Muller peered at the flat ring. It was too well formed to stir his magic power. The fitting had probably come off an apple picking machine. He slid the cord over his head, letting the ring hang down his chest. "I will treasure it."

"You must bring it back," Drummer said earnestly. "Safe and sound."

Muller heard what he didn't say; it wasn't the charm he wanted to see returned safe and sound, but its wearer. He spoke gently. "I will. I promise."

"Good." Relief washed across Drummer's face. "And you can tell Chime that—well, really, she's not so bad."

Muller grinned. "That is high praise from a brother."

"I miss her a lot," Drummer admitted. Quickly he added, "But don't you *dare* tell her that."

"Nary a word," Muller promised.

Drummer gave him a shy smile. "Good night, Your Highness."

"Good night, Master Drummer."

Appleton spoke quietly. "Thank you."

Muller nodded, grateful to have met them. He watched as they headed back to the village. These people, his wife's kin, barely knew him, yet they welcomed him. During the past years, as he had assumed more responsibility and then met Chime, he had begun to feel more at ease with himself. He even looked forward to his life now. He just prayed it didn't all end soon in battle.

That night, the Hexagon Unit headed north. They didn't stop to rest until a few hours before dawn.

It was then that Muller had the first of the dark dreams.

"We must go!" Chime struck wildly at Aria, her mind fogged with sleep.

Her maid deflected the blows. "It will be all right," she murmured. "You were having a nightmare, that be all."

"No!" Chime came fully awake, sitting up in bed. "It was a message. Muller tried to reach me."

"He can't reach you across all the country, ma'am."

"I dreamed he is dying. He begs me to come." Chime clenched her fists in the covers. "I must go to the Tallwalk Mountains."

"The Tallwalks are north, milady. Lord Muller is south." Aria spoke calmly, as if it were a perfectly natural for a noblewoman to wake up suddenly and insist on riding off across the countryside in the middle of the night.

Chime slid out of bed, her bare feet hitting the stone floor, her nightgown swirling around her calves. "He went north."

"Now why would he do such a thing?"

"I don't know." Chime couldn't calm her agitation. "How did you know I was dreaming?"

Aria helped her into her robe. "You were acting muchly strange, Lady Chime. Your voice sounded wrong."

"My voice?" Chime stopped with one arm in her sleeve. "What do you mean?"

"It didn't sound like you." Aria hesitated. "It was deeper. And you spoke a language I didn't recognize."

Chime put her arm in the sleeve. "I don't remember."

"It was eerie."

"All the more reason I need to reach Muller."

Aria regarded her sternly. "You can't run off into the night by yourself."

"I have to warn him."

"About what?"

"He could die."

"How?"

Chime made a frustrated noise. "I don't know."

"I think the dark mage haunts your dreams."

That gave Chime pause. The nightmares did have an odd sense, one that felt...oily. It reminded her of the presence she had touched in Croft's Vale. She shivered. It was a desecration of spells to give nightmares instead of comfort. If a mage could invade her dreams, she would fear ever to sleep again.

She regarded Aria uneasily. "To enter someone else's dreams, especially from so far away, seems impossible."

"How do you know he is far away?"

"King Jarid says he is in Harsdown."

Aria handed her the sash for her robe. "It be a bad time, milady. A bad time indeed."

Chime exhaled. "Aye."

"You cannot ride off with no plan or protection."

Chime knew Aria was right, much as she hated to admit it, but she had to do something. "Perhaps Jarid will send a messenger to Muller."

"To Jacob's Vale?"

"No. The Tallwalks."

Aria regarded her dubiously, but she made no further protest. Chime told herself that her fears were misplaced, that she was having wretched dreams because of the changes in her body due to her pregnancy. But she didn't believe it for a moment.

Despite the cold night, sweat soaked Muller's shirt and hair. He tossed on his pallet, unable to sleep. Vague dreams always troubled him now. He recalled nothing specific, only a sense of threat that remained after he awoke.

Night warriors, Drummer had said.

For a while he lay on his back listening to the rustles, coughs and rattles of his sleeping men. Finally he clambered out of bed, fully dressed, and pulled on his jacket. Then he paced through the camp, past snoring warriors in bed rolls.

At the perimeter, he nodded to Archer, who was on sentry duty. The lieutenant lifted his hand. Muller continued on—

And jerked as a nightmare hit him, the same undefined sense of menace that plagued his dreams, but coming now while he was awake. With a gasp, he dropped to his knees and bent forward, his arms crossed over his stomach while he vomited behind a tree. Every rock, plant and tree seemed to loom over him, threatening and harsh.

After Muller finished, he simply knelt, gulping in air while tremors shook his body. He had no idea what had spurred the waking nightmare, but the sensation was mercifully fading now.

"Commander?"

Muller raised his head to see Archer approaching. "Is everything all right?" the lieutenant asked.

"Yes." Muller climbed slowly to his feet. "Fine."

Archer's expression clouded. "The feel of mage power be around here. It isn't right."

"An eerie night." Muller stayed noncommittal, afraid Archer felt his power. It would hurt morale if his men thought he had mage gifts that disrupted their ability to fight. He felt certain he could control his spells, but he wouldn't know how to convince them. With rumors of a dark mage, he could even be in danger if the truth became known.

He spoke awkwardly. "Seems I drank too much this evening, eh?"

Amusement flickered in Archer's face. "We all do now and then. Have a good evening, Commander."

Muller lifted his hand in farewell as Archer continued his rounds. Then Muller returned to his pallet and lay down. It was bad enough nightmares haunted his sleep, leaving him worn-out in the mornings. He didn't know what he would do if they invaded his waking hours as well. How did he fight this formless threat that stalked his life? At least Chime was safe at Suncroft, untouched by the evil here in the north.

He had to discover who—or what—was coming through the Tallwalk Pass.

Chime stood on the balcony of her suite, bathed in the light of a Jade Moon, the gold and green layers of her nightdress swirling around her body, catching on her ankles. Her hair drifted in the wind. It wrapped her body and pulled toward the rail of the balcony where her hands rested, then blew back from her face. She raised her head to the night sky with its cold stars. The moon had turned the color of jade, perhaps from dust in the air or the filmy clouds, or maybe from the Saint of Halos, a spirit that surrounded the moon with a glowing nimbus.

Chime raised her arm and opened her hand to the sky. An emerald orb lay in her palm, faceted with twenty sides, sparkling. She focused on it, pouring her power into the jewel. A sphere of light formed around her, blended with the moonlight, but a richer green, like leaves that unfurled from an apple tree in the spring, soft grass on the hills, or the water in a mountain lake shaded by ferns. She stood within the radiant sphere, gazing across the land that rolled away from the castle, the velvety slopes and curves of Aronsdale.

Then she reached.

She had neither Iris's colors nor Jarid's strength. She could teach like Della or rely on decades of experience, as did Skylark. But Chime knew now her gift; she could create spells of mood and empathy in a way no one else seemed to touch.

The sphere of light rose into the air, leaving her on the balcony in the endless breezes. It floated above her, luminous, rippling in the air. It was only a mood spell, only encouragement, hope, nothing substantial. It might dissipate before it reached its goal.

But still she would send this charmed sphere.

Go, she thought. *Go to them. To the warriors of Aronsdale deep within the hills and woods, uncertain what they face. To the women and men who stand on the borders and look toward the unknown. To my love, wherever he strides the land. Go to them. Give them succor.*

"Go," she whispered. "Go to Muller."

The orb drifted over the land, spreading thinner and thinner, until only a faint emerald glimmer remained in the air that blended into the moonlight and the forever reaches of the starry sky.

Jarid opened his eyes, aware of light, nothing more. Even now, months after he had regained his vision, he was still learning to see.

Gradually his mind interpreted the scene. He had fallen asleep in Iris's forest haven, the hollow where they spent their wedding night last spring. He felt gifted by the trust she had shown when she revealed this sanctuary to a man who, though her husband, was a stranger. Perhaps it had started that day she reached across Aronsdale and found him in the mountains.

Jarid stretched and sat up, enjoying the hollow. The waterfall splashed like music. Some leaves on the trees had turned red and gold; others remained green. Summer's warmth was fading into autumn, but he cared little about the cold. He and Unbent had endured far worse in the winters when they ran out of firewood.

His unease came from another source. Foreboding had troubled him for days, invading his sleep and now intruding on his days as well. It exhausted him. He had come here to meditate, probing for the source of his disquiet. He hadn't learned its cause, but at least he had slept well.

Closing his eyes, Jarid wove power through the sphere. His spell made no outward light; it turned inward, within him, like red embers. He went through orange, then yellow. A sense of well-being spread over him.

For green, he deepened his concentration. As he had often done these past months, he sought Harsdown. Della claimed it was impossible to feel emotions over so great a distance. She believed such spells could extend no more than a few paces around the mage who created it. Yet he had always reached much farther with Unbent and now with Iris.

So much else of what Della said made sense, it was odd she would be so wrong on this. Everyone seemed to share her conviction that what he achieved in his trances should be impossible. He had too few referents to interpret their response. Rather than endure their skepticism, he kept the full extent of his powers to himself.

He had no idea if precedents existed for his gifts. None of the tales sung by bards answered his questions. Nor did the history scrolls in the Suncroft library help; he couldn't read well. He had just begun to learn before he lost his sight. Now he had tutors, but the slow process frustrated him. So he searched as he had done these past fourteen years: with spells.

Shapes filled his mind: bars, polyhedrons, circles, and

spheres, always glimmering spheres, glistening, spinning, spinning. It puzzled him that other mages used objects or mosaics to focus; he preferred mental images.

His spell flowed across the country and over Suncroft. He sensed its people as a pale wash of moods. Then he found Iris, visiting an outlying town, meeting the citizens who now called her queen. Her presence filled him with emotions he barely understood. It had taken him months to comprehend that he loved his wife; he had no idea how to tell her.

He found Della next, who warmed Suncroft like a banked fire. Chime shed golden light over the castle, as did the girl-child she carried, another mage. Fatigue wore on Chime from her pregnancy and sleepless nights. He made a healing spell and offered it to her. She didn't sense what he was doing and distance weakened his spell, but her mood did brighten.

Jarid lay down in the grass, his hands behind his head as he increased his concentration. He thought of Unbent and his spell reached past Suncroft to the outlying farms. His father was plowing a field, content with hard work under a warm sun. He suffered none of the nightmares that tormented Jarid's nights and apparently Chime's also.

It puzzled Jarid that he and Chime had such troubled dreams. He continued his search, reaching toward Harsdown. The more area he covered, the more diffuse his spell became, until he could barely identify individuals. Far to the north, he thought he touched Muller, but that made no sense. His cousin had gone south to visit Chime's family.

Jarid ranged farther, to the northern Aronsdale border, a fifteen-day ride northwest. His head throbbed with the strain...time to withdraw—

Then he hit the true nightmares.

28

Decision

"They are coming through the mountains." Jarid strode down the hall of the castle, so fast that Brant, Fieldson, and Della had trouble keeping pace with his long-legged stride. He had run the entire way here from the forest.

"Both armies are from Harsdown," Jarid said. "One comes through the Tallwalk Pass and the other is in the Boxer-Mage Mountains."

"How can you be certain?" Della asked, out of breath. "It is too far."

Jarid stopped, and the others halted around him like water churning past a boulder in the river. He regarded them all; if one chose leaders according to wisdom and experience, they would rule Aronsdale. Heredity had chosen otherwise, but he had no illusions about his lack of preparation. He needed them. If he wanted their help, he had to convince them of his claims.

"Iris and I reached each other," he told Della.

"You weren't as far away," she said.

"We were a ride of ten days apart. What I sense now is about fifteen days away. Why should I manage one and not the other?"

"Iris is also a mage," Brant said. "A powerful one."

"You did it together with her," Della said. "This time it is only you."

Jarid shuddered. "He was also there."

"He?" Fieldson asked.

"The dark mage." Jarid began walking, more slowly this time. "He comes with King Varqelle's army."

"This isn't much to go on," Fieldson said.

"Muller is on his way north," Jarid added.

Brant frowned. "He went south."

"Nevertheless," Jarid said. "He now goes north."

Fieldson shook his head. "We need solid information. Evidence. Proof."

"Here." Jarid had brought them to a tall set of doors with circular stained-glass windows on either side. Protocol dictated he should go to his own suite instead of this one and then send for the person he wanted to see, but he was tired of formalities. Had he grown up at Suncroft, perhaps he would have more patience with "proper" procedures, but as far as he could tell, it only made everything take too long. He didn't have time.

Today Brant didn't argue; he just rapped on the doors. The circle-maid Aria answered. When she saw them, her mouth opened in an O. Then she remembered herself and bowed. "You honor us with your presence, Your Majesty."

Jarid didn't feel like he honored anyone, but he kept that to himself. "I would like to see Lady Chime, if she is here."

"She is, Sire." Aria moved aside so they could enter. "We will bring her immediately."

As Aria ushered them into the gold and ivory parlor, the maid Reed appeared. After a flustered greeting, she bustled off to find Chime. Jarid's advisors settled into the upholstered chairs, but he felt too restless to sit. He paced by a tall window, through sunlight that pooled on hexagonal patterns in the parquetry floor.

Jarid sensed Chime's power as she entered the parlor. He turned to greet her, then froze, dismayed. She was trying to present a bright appearance, golden in her silk tunic and leggings, her hair shining, but nothing could hide her pallor or the dark cycles under her eyes.

"Lady Chime." He strode over to her. "Are you well?"

"My greetings, Your Majesty." She bowed. "I had a restless night, that is all."

"The nightmares."

Her voice trembled. "It is nothing."

"Tell me."

She twisted the long sleeve of her tunic. "I am sorry if I have troubled you."

"Chime." Jarid put his hand on her shoulder.

For a moment she seemed ready to insist she was fine. Then her smile crumpled. "I dream Muller is dying."

"No wonder you are tired." Jarid led her to one of the small sofas. "I have nightmares, too, but I remember so little. Only malice." He sat with her, aware of his advisors around them in high-backed chairs.

Della leaned forward. "But you remember this last vision, yes, Your Majesty?"

"A vision?" Chime's eyes looked larger than usual compared to her pale, drawn face.

"I had one about Harsdown." Jarid shifted his weight, restless. "I saw two armies. Varqelle has sent them."

Chime spoke slowly, her words guarded. "In my dream, I see Muller going north, to the Tallwalk Pass. Baleful spells stalk him. Meanwhile, the Harsdown army sneaks around Aronsdale, going through the Barrens to our north. They plan to attack Suncroft from our eastern border."

"Ah, saints," Della said. Fieldson exhaled and Brant shook his head. When Chime gave them questioning looks, Jarid spoke. "In my vision, one army comes over the Tallwalks and the other comes through the Boxer-Mage Mountains even farther north."

Chime stared at him. "We cannot both be right."

Jarid grimaced. "We dare not be wrong."

"Could it be a trick?" she asked.

That gave him pause. He knew he could be mistaking what he saw, but it had never occurred to him it might be a deliberate attempt to mislead him.

"Why do you say that?" he asked.

"My nightmares feel strange." Chime glanced at Fieldson and Brant, then away.

"You may speak in front of my advisors," Jarid said.

She reddened. "I've no wish to waste anyone's time."

Jarid understood that hesitation all too well, having felt it himself on more than a few occasions. He spoke wryly. "If you worry they will find your comments strange, have no fear. I've already overcome them with the strangeness of mine."

Della laughed, then stopped when Brant scowled at her.

Chime answered with care. "Aria said I spoke during one of my dreams. She said I sounded like another person. And that dream—it seemed rotted from within."

"Malignant." Jarid spoke without doubt.

Surprise flickered in her gaze. "Yes."

"I feel that when I awake."

Chime shuddered. "It is the Harsdown mage."

Fieldson was watching her closely. "You believe this mage seeks to trick you with dreams?"

"I have wondered." Chime twisted the cuff of her sleeve. "It could just be bad dreams, a wife missing her husband."

"I am not missing your husband," Jarid said, smiling. "At least not that way. But I have the dreams, too."

Brant blinked. "He told another joke. That's two in one night." When Della glared at him, he raised his hands, palms out.

Jarid took no offense. It was true, he hardly knew how to laugh. But since Iris had come into his life, his spirit had lightened.

"We have one unit in the north," Fieldson said. "Two, if Lord Muller took the Hexagons there. They will need support if Harsdown forces come through the mountains." He shook his head. "But sending more of our forces into the north would leave this area undefended."

Brant rubbed his chin. "If it is a trick, it is effective. Make us believe invasion comes from the logical place, our northern border with Harsdown. So we send help. Meanwhile, they attack from another direction."

"What direction?" Jarid asked.

"Suppose they have sent an army through the Barrens that lie to the north." Fieldson thought for a moment. "If they cross the River of Stars and go south around our eastern border, they could enter Aronsdale through the Pyramid Foothills. From there, they could reach Suncroft."

Jarid tensed. "And if we meanwhile sent our forces north?"

"It would take at least fifteen days to reach our northwestern border with Harsdown and that long to return, if we found no threat." Fieldson shook his head. "An army coming through the Barrens could arrive here at Suncroft before we returned."

Fieldson slapped his knee. "We need more information. We must send riders. Our fastest."

"*If* both of these armies exist." Brant shook his head. "Where would he get enough men for two?"

"Mercenaries," Della said.

"He cannot afford them," Brant said.

Fieldson's voice hardened, revealing the honed edge he rarely showed, the iron that had made him a general above his other contemporaries. "If he thought he could finally take Aronsdale, he would tax his people to starvation and empty his coffers. He could replenish them from Aronsdale if he conquers us."

"Who would he hire?" Jarid asked.

"Rebels from the Outlands beyond the Misted Cliffs," Fieldson said. "Escaped criminals, loners, madmen."

"Not the most motivated or loyal material for an army." Brant grimaced. "I wouldn't trust them fighting for Aronsdale."

Chime watched them, her gaze hollowed by exhaustion. "But Varqelle cannot win. Even if he has one mage now, we have more. Our mages are our advantage, the reason he never tried this before." She looked around at them. "Aren't they?"

"Yes." Della spoke heavily. "But we were so closely matched. This dark mage may be enough to tip the balance."

Brant raked his hand through his silver mane. "Or maybe Harsdown has sent no armies and we create nightmares for ourselves." He glanced at Jarid. "My apologies, Your Majesty. But we must consider the possibility."

As much as Jarid wished it was only bad dream, he knew otherwise. He turned to Aria, who stood with Reed in the entrance arch of the parlor. "You said Lady Chime spoke oddly during her nightmare."

"Aye, Your Majesty." Aria came forward, hesitant, and stood behind Chime at the sofa. "With a man's voice."

"Chime, like a man?" It was hard for Jarid to imagine such, given her dulcet voice.

"I know it be sounding odd. But her words were all strange and wrong." Aria looked apologetic. "I didn't know the language."

"She repeated the words to me," Chime said. "I recognized none of them." She sat as straight as a rod, her hands folded in her lap, but it only made her look more vulnerable.

Jarid wished he could reassure Chime. "How many languages do you know?"

She swallowed. "Just ours."

"Are you certain?" Brant asked. "Jacob's Vale isn't far from our southwestern border. Surely travelers came through there, especially from Blueshire and Shazire. Perhaps you have heard their languages?"

"A little," Chime said. "The words I spoke sounded nothing like those."

It frustrated Jarid to know so little about Aronsdale. Had he been raised as expected, he would have traveled widely with his parents, seeing this country and others, learning their ways. Instead, he could barely speak or read his own language, let alone others.

"Can you repeat the words?" Brant asked.

Chime looked up at Aria. "Do you recall?"

She hesitated. "Something like 'All-air nell-air.'"

"*Allar nellari,*" Della murmured.

"Aye, ma'am!" Aria shot her a look of relief.

The words chilled Jarid, though he couldn't have said why. "What is it?"

"Part of an incantation," Della said. "It is ancient. Thousands of years old. Supposedly it helped mages focus through shapes imagined rather than seen or touched."

Jarid frowned. Here it was again, their insistence that one needed real shapes to focus. He couldn't let it go this time, not given what was at stake. "It isn't necessary to see or touch the shapes. That strengthens spells, certainly, but you can make them without it."

A long silence greeted his words. Finally Della said, "Is that how you do it?"

"I had no choice." He paused, uncomfortable. "I couldn't see."

"Hai," Chime said. "Of course."

"Perhaps you are what the ancients sought to create," Della said.

Thinking of the ancient words Chime had spoken, he shuddered. "I need no incantations, either. Especially that one."

Brant was watching him with that intense concentration that unsettled Jarid, as if his advisor could see through any shield or defense he raised.

"Why not that one?" Brant asked.

"The words have malice in them," Jarid said.

Brant glanced at Della. "Was that the full incantation?"

"Not quite," she said. "*Allar nellari remalla.* It means 'Sphere inside-out.'"

Chime recovered enough of her spirit to look affronted. "You never taught it to Iris and me."

"It doesn't work," Della said. "It does nothing."

"Then how would Chime know it?" Brant asked.

Della exhaled. "I don't know."

"Those words feel ill." Jarid had to make a conscious effort not to clench his fists. "And why would Chime speak in someone else's voice?"

"Maybe I was hoarse," Chime said.

Concern creased Brant's face. "Have you been ill?"

"Actually, no," she said.

"This connects to those armies Harsdown has sent." Jarid's frustration roiled. "Somehow."

Della considered him. "As our strongest mage, you may pick up what we miss. And you are uninfluenced by any styles of teaching magecraft. That could let you see in ways we have lost. But it also means you are the most untutored. You could make more mistakes." She spread her arms out, palms up, then dropped them. "I just don't know."

"We can't base strategy on dreams," Fieldson said.

"Mages have always helped the army," Della replied.

"But never with something this uncertain," Brant said.

"Muller has already made his decision." Chime wound the belt of her tunic around her hand. "He went north."

Fieldson studied her face as if he sought to read the essence of her spells there. "You can't be certain."

Jarid leaned forward. "He is near the Tallwalk Pass."

"Why would he do such a thing?" Brant demanded. "Muller never takes the initiative." When Chime stiffened, he relented slightly. "I apologize, Lady. But what you describe would be out of character for him."

"In the past, yes," she admitted. "Nevertheless, it is true."

"The Hexagons have only thirty-six men and no mages," Fieldson said. "They couldn't take on two Harsdown armies. They would be slaughtered."

Chime's gaze flicked to Jarid, her face strained. He could imagine what she felt, fearing for Muller, for his life, for the twists of his off-kilter powers. Jarid would always remember Muller as the hero of his boyhood; now he saw depths in his cousin that Muller had only begun to plumb. He didn't doubt Muller would carry out his duties no matter what the cost. No matter how much Jarid wanted to offer words of comfort to Chime, but nothing would change the truth. Her husband could die if Harsdown attacked.

"The Pentagon Unit is in the north," Fieldson said. "The Hexagons could rendezvous with them." He rested his elbow on the arm of his chair, his pose an unconscious study in regal posture.

A pang of grief stabbed Jarid; his birth father had often sat that way. Fieldson was nothing like Prince Aron; the general had a calm nature that contrasted with Aron's intense style. Jarid remembered his grandfather telling his father to trust Fieldson, that their strengths would complement each other. Jarid hadn't thought of that in more than fourteen years, but now the memory tumbled back.

Unable to sit any longer, Jarid rose and paced to the window. It calmed him to see the countryside, tranquil now as the sun dipped below the hills and shadows filled the land. Too many memories were coming back, prodded by this place, these people, this life. And his dreams. Could the dreams be a trick meant to draw his army to the wrong place while Varqelle attacked elsewhere? Or had they inadvertently stumbled on his plans? But who was right—him or Chime? The survival of Aronsdale depended on their decision.

Jarid turned from the window and spoke to Brant. "Your recommendation?"

He answered immediately. "Send your fastest riders north to investigate. Have them report back to us."

Jarid nodded and looked at Fieldson. "Yours?"

"Send the Heptagon and Octagon Units north, with half the infantry and archers."

Brant frowned. "It would leave Suncroft undefended. The infantry would also slow down the polygon units."

"The Nonagons and Quadrons will be here, as well as half our infantry and archers." Fieldson said. "One messenger cannot provide reinforcements to our northern forces."

Jarid spoke to Chime. "What think you?"

"The invaders are coming to Suncroft." She fisted her hand on the arm of her chair. "They are coming through the Barrens. I'm sure of it. We must defend this area."

It troubled Jarid that he and Chime had such different impressions. Perhaps Della was right, that he knew too little about his gifts to interpret his vision. He glanced at the mage mistress. "And your recommendation?"

Della answered quietly. "You must go north yourself. You have the best chance of challenging this dark mage."

Jarid shifted his weight uneasily. "And if he isn't north? If these dreams of mine are a trick?"

"You must use your judgment," she said. "No one else has as much power to see as you."

To see. Had fourteen years of blindness given him another sort of sight? Jarid rubbed the back of his neck, working at the muscle kinks that never seemed to relax anymore. His choices loomed with disaster. He didn't want Suncroft inadequately defended, but neither could he strand Muller with only one or two units to face an invasion.

He had to decide. But what. *What?*

Jarid looked around at the others. "I will take the Heptagons and a party of mounted archers north. We will rendezvous with our forces there. If we find nothing, we will return as soon as possible."

"And if you encounter Harsdown?" Fieldson demanded. "If Varqelle has hired mercenaries, you won't have enough men, especially if you leave the infantry here. He could have hundreds of men."

Jarid wished he could be more certain of his vision. "I dream they come on fast, flying over the land. They cannot manage such with foot soldiers and carrying supplies for a large company. If we are to meet up with them before they slaughter our people in the north, we must also travel fast." He spoke with foreboding. "If we are too late to help, all the infantry in Aronsdale will do no good."

"And if you are outnumbered?" Fieldson asked.

"I will send a rider for reinforcements."

The general spoke grimly. "Even your fastest rider would take twenty-five days to bring back reinforcements."

Jarid pushed back his hair, tangling it around his shoulders. "We will have to manage with what we have."

He feared that no matter what choice he made, it wouldn't be enough.

29

Dawn Ride

Aria stared at Chime, aghast. "Lady, you *cannot*."

"I must." Chime hurried through her bedroom, her slippers flapping on the floor.

Supper with Iris, Jarid, and the King's Advisors had taken forever. Iris would rule Aronsdale while Jarid was gone, and they had wanted to discuss a great deal. Iris obviously had doubts: was she needed more as sovereign at Suncroft or as mage queen with the army? While the others debated, Chime had listened, keeping quiet, lest she make a verbal slip and give herself away. But supper finished with no mishap. In the hours since, she had stayed in her suite, waiting for the castle and her guards to sleep.

Waiting to escape.

Once before she had run away. It seemed ages ago now, though it had only been about a year and a half. Then she had been escaping Muller. Now she would go to him.

They wouldn't take her with the Heptagons. Skylark and Jarid were their mages. Pah. Skylark was too elderly for the journey and Jarid had too little training, besides which, he was supposed to lead the Heptagons. They needed a young, active mage. Her. They just didn't appreciate that. So she would take care of matters herself.

"You will be expected to bid the king farewell in the morning," Aria said. "You must appear."

"I told Reed I was sick." Chime rummaged through the wardrobe against the wall, shoving aside silk garments, looking for the sturdy tunics and leggings she had brought from Jacob's Vale. "I asked her to say farewell for me." She gave Aria her most earnest look. "I've had so much trouble with morning sickness, he won't be surprised."

"You haven't had one day of sickness." Aria crossed her arms. "King Jarid is a powerful mage. He will know you have gone off somewhere."

"Yes, if he decides to search me out with a spell. But why would he? He knows how tired I've been." She pulled out her old clothes. "Hah! I knew they were here."

"Lady, you cannot do this." Aria tried to take the garments away from her. "It is crazy."

Chime pulled back her clothes. "I'm going. I'll join the Heptagons after they've gone too far to send me back."

"Why should it be too far?" Aria demanded. "The king can send you here anytime."

"He won't." Chime pulled on her leggings under her nightgown. "Not if they are well out from the castle."

"And why is that?"

"The army has always taken the strongest mages in the land. It is a duty of the mage queen. Why else choose the most powerful mage in the land to marry the king?"

"That isn't what I asked. And you are not the queen."

"Well, I'm close."

"Queen *Iris* isn't going."

Chime glared at her. "That is another problem. She should go. Pah. Men." She waved her hand. "If they listened to us more, the world would be much better off."

Aria chuckled. "Aye." Then she remembered she was angry. "Stop changing the subject!"

Chime yanked off her nightgown and pulled on her tunic. Twisting her hand around her back, she struggled to button it up. "I have duties, too."

Aria started to fasten the tunic for her, but then she jumped back. "What am I doing? I won't help you do this."

Chime contorted herself until she managed the buttons. "But you are coming with me."

Her maid's mouth dropped open. "What? No!"

Chime untwisted herself. "I need you. Please. You're the only person I can trust."

Aria glared at her. "You canna trust me, ma'am. I will tell Lord Firestoke of your crazy plan."

"You would never do that." Chime went back to the wardrobe and poked around until she found her old boots. "Please come with me."

"Never. Noblewomen do not dash across the country with only their maid, chasing the king and his army."

"I won't be chasing him." Chime sat on the floor and pulled on one boot. "I'm leaving first. He will be chasing me."

"He can't chase someone he doesn't know is there." Aria knelt next to her. "He will be furious."

Chime fastened up her boot. "He'll survive."

"Lady." Aria put her hand on Chime's arm, stopping her movements. "What about the baby?"

"Harsdown is going to attack Suncroft." It was one of Chime's reasons for leaving. If Jarid wouldn't listen to her, she would act on her own counsel. "I don't intend for myself or my child to be here when Varqelle arrives."

"You cannot ride with an army while you are pregnant."

"Why the blazes not?" Chime yanked on her other boot. "It doesn't make me helpless. And read your history. Many pregnant mages have ridden with the army."

"That was hundreds of years ago."

Chime finished strapping her boot. "Harsdown comes here. I will not let them take me and my child. What if they attack in both the north and here?" The thought felt like a dagger in her heart. "Muller could die without my ever seeing him again. I want to be with him."

Her maid spoke in a quieter voice. "Lady Chime, if you leave here with only me, you could be kidnapped by whomever tried before. They almost caught you inside Suncroft. It would be easy to grab you out there."

Pulling up her legs, Chime rested her arms on her knees. She knew Aria was right, but she couldn't sit here in the castle. "I have to go."

"You cannot."

Chime stood up, pulling Aria with her. "Come on."

"Where?"

"To see Jarid."

"Ma'am!" Alarm suffused Aria's face. "It is the middle of the night."

"All the better. He will be too sleepy to protest."

Aria gulped. "If you plan on taking on the king, I would like to be in another country, if you don't mind."

Chime smiled. "You will be fine. Come on."

"Hai," Aria muttered as Chime pulled her out the door. "I must be crazy, too."

Unable to sleep, Jarid sat against the headboard of the bed. Iris stirred, her hair brushing his leg. He shifted her head into his lap, wishing he could sleep, too. Her body was warm, her skin bare. He had never understood how she could feel so much softer than himself and yet be so much stronger inside. She was the cane that kept him standing.

Jarid smiled. She was also the siren that called to him. Her chestnut hair tumbled everywhere on the pillow. During the day, she tended to be reserved, but at night—ah, the night.

Sliding under the covers, Jarid filled his arms with his voluptuous woman. It puzzled him that she considered herself fat. The women of the royal court that she considered beauties were much too skinny.

He caressed her breast. "Are you awake?"

"Hmmmm?"

"Was that a yes or a no?"

"A no," she mumbled.

"Ah." He tickled her side. "Now are you awake?"

Iris sighed. "Jarid, you must rest for your trip."

"I'm not sleepy." He moved his lips to her ear and let his breath do the tickling. "And you are very warm."

Iris laughed sleepily and slid her arms around him. "You, sir, are terribly misbehaved."

"You're my wife." He rolled her onto her back. "We can misbehave all we want."

A tap came at the door.

Jarid paused, frowning. Then he turned back to Iris. Her lips felt warm against his, her body ready for him.

Another tap.

Jarid swore under his breath. "I don't believe it."

"Let's pretend we're asleep," Iris said.

"I'm the king. It could be a crisis."

She made a noise of protest low in her throat. "It would behoove our crises to wait until morning."

He laughed, a rare sound, one that only happened with Iris. "That it would." Then he dragged himself out of bed and pulled on his indigo robe, belting it at the waist. Silver geometric designs bordered its hems, stirring his power. It filled the room, which had six walls in a hexagon, with a domed ceiling.

Instinctively he imagined the room divided into two parts, the dome and the hexagonal box. A mood spell grew around him, but he held it in check. With Unbent, alone in the cabin, they had desperately needed his gifts; it had been one of their few ways to communicate. Here it became less vital. Nor did he have a connection to the people here. They had no reason to want him sensing their moods. So he respected their privacy. Right now, though, he did catch enough to identify the person beyond the door; Standson, his sphere-butler, always patient. Someone waited with him——

Chime?

Jarid didn't know whether to fume or worry. He liked Chime. She had a great deal of common sense. He enjoyed the bold spirit she hid under a veneer of impeccable conduct. Right now, though, he could have done with less of the bold and more of the impeccable.

He opened the door to find Standson, stoic in sleep clothes and a robe. "Yes?" Jarid asked.

"My apologies, Your Majesty," Standson said. "I am terribly sorry to disturb your rest." He looked terribly sorry to have had his own disturbed. "We have a problem."

Jarid looked past him to where Chime waited with Aria, her circle-maid. "So we do." He glowered at his cousin's wife. "I thought you felt ill, Lady Chime."

She came forward and bowed more deeply to him than protocol dictated. But then, protocol didn't encourage waking the king in the middle of the night, either.

"I apologize, Your Majesty," she said, contrite.

Jarid tried to glare at her. It was difficult because she looked angelic.

"Jarid?" Iris's sleepy voice came from behind him. She joined him at the door and leaned on its frame. "Chime? What are you doing up?"

"I must talk to the king," Chime said, the picture of sincere urgency.

"Well, here I am," Jarid grumbled. "So speak."

Iris gave him an exasperated look. Then she gestured to Chime, inviting her inside. "Come sit with us."

As Chime and Aria entered the suite, Jarid crossed his arms. Standson gave him a look of apology. Aria's face was so red, Jarid wondered her cheeks didn't catch fire. For good measure, he glared at her, too.

Iris set up candles on a table, and they sat around it in wing chairs with gold upholstery emblazoned by the Dawnfield crest. The octagonal table concentrated Jarid's spell. He hadn't intended to read Chime's mood, but it jumped out at him. She meant to ride with his war party in the morning.

"Absolutely not!" he exploded. *"Out of the question."*

They all blinked at him. Warriors, criminals, rogues, kings— those he could handle. What to do with three women watching him in polite bewilderment was another story altogether. He felt outnumbered.

"Never," Jarid added for good measure, giving Chime the full force of his irate stare. She smiled sweetly, her face aglow in the candlelight.

"Jarid, dear." Iris spoke carefully, as if he were perhaps dangerous. "What are you talking about?"

He frowned at his wife. "She thinks I am going to take her and Aria with me tomorrow."

Iris seemed nonplussed. "With the Heptagons?"

"I absolutely will not," Jarid told them.

Aria spoke quickly. "Well, I'm glad that's settled." She stood up. "We are sorry to have——"

"Aria, sit down." Chime yanked her back into the chair. The maid sat with a thump, a tendril of hair flying around her face.

Chime folded her hands in her lap. "Your Majesty—"

"Using my title won't help," he growled. "I will *not* take you with me. That is final. You may go now."

"But I must go with you," Chime said in her most sensible voice.

"You are worried about Muller," Iris said.

"Where I come from," Chime said, "a wife looks after her husband. If he is in danger, she rescues him."

"What, now you're a lady warrior?" Jarid tried to ignore the quelling look Iris gave him. At least she had the sense to speak no rebuke. He was the king, even he was only twenty. He was in control here. He couldn't believe they were discussing this absurd proposition at such an hour of the night. Brant would have apoplexy. Maybe that was why Chime had come now; his advisors were in bed. She knew they would never countenance such an outrageous scheme. Well, neither would he.

"I must do something," Chime said. "I need to help."

"The answer is no," Jarid said. "N. O."

"What if Iris was in danger?" Chime turned to the queen. "Or if you knew Jarid needed you. You would go to him."

"Well, yes, I would," Iris said.

Jarid almost groaned. If Iris decided to insist that she go after all, it would encourage Chime in this madness. He turned his darkest scowl on his wife. "You would stay here at Suncroft."

Her smile curved. "I would rescue you, my love."

"You would do no such thing." The conversation was getting away from Jarid and he didn't know how to pull it back. Blustering probably wasn't the answer. He spoke more calmly to Chime. "I understand why you would like to come and I appreciate your offer. But you cannot. The danger is too great. I'm sorry."

"It is more dangerous to stay here." Fear shadowed her face. "When Varqelle's army arrives, what will they do to the pregnant wife of your current heir? Better I go with you."

The idea that Varqelle would attack his home made Jarid ill. She was right; she would be in danger either way. But Suncroft had walls and warriors. "We are leaving many soldiers here."

"You will have many in the north, too," Iris said. "The Heptagons and the two units already there."

"You can't be sure Muller has brought the Hexagons," Jarid said, though he too had sensed their movements.

Chime sat up straighter. "I am certain."

"Such a journey poses dangers to your child," Iris told her.

"Less than staying here," Chime said. "I am not afraid to go."

Jarid answered sternly. "But I am, for you."

"You need mages," she said. "I am a mage."

"I also," Iris said. "I should go."

Saints almighty. Jarid leaned toward her. "I have a mage. Myself. I need you here."

"You need me with the army more." Iris rubbed her eyes. "I have worried about this all night. Brant and Della are better suited to govern in your absence than me. I can do far more to help the army than I can do here."

"And suppose we are attacked?" Jarid demanded, both of her and of Chime. "You could be hurt. Even killed."

"So could you," Chime said.

Jarid was about to retort when he saw Iris pale. Damn. He didn't want her reminded of the danger to himself.

Aria spoke to Chime in a low voice. "Ma'am, His Majesty has made his intent clear. We should leave the king and queen to their sleep now."

"I am glad one of you has sense." Jarid rose to his feet. "A good eve to—"

"Jarid, love," Iris said. "Please wait."

Ah, hell. He sat down. "Yes?"

"I was chosen as queen for my mage power. I've read the histories: even as recently as five generations ago, the queen rode with the army. You will need as many mages as possible when you face the Harsdown mage. By every precedent, I should ride with you."

Jarid leaned toward his wife and spoke in a firm voice. "You are not going with me." Sitting up straight, he faced Chime. "Neither are you."

Chime smiled sweetly. "Will you lock us in our rooms? Tie us to a chair, perhaps?"

"Of course not. I am the king. You will do as I say." He folded his arms, letting them see his resolve. "You can argue all night. It will do no good. I have made my decision."

"It is an outrage!" Brant strode with Jarid across the Yard of Circles. All around them, the Heptagon Unit was preparing to ride, men and horses filling the predawn hour with quiet commotion.

"*Both* of them?" Brant demanded. Remembering himself, he added, "My apology, Sire. But to take Chime and Iris strikes me as unwise." To put it mildly.

"Don't tell me," Jarid muttered. "Tell them."

"You are the king."

"Have you ever faced Iris and Chime together, without backup? No reinforcements? No battle plan?"

Brant smiled. "I hardly think talking to our two lovely mages is like going into battle."

Jarid snorted. "Little do you know."

"Simply tell them no."

He slanted a weary look at his advisor. "I tried."

"You can't let two slips of women wear you down."

He knew the real reason Brant was upset, even if the curmudgeon refused to say it. Jarid pulled him to a stop. "They mean a great deal to me, too. I don't want them in danger. But they are right, we must have strong mages on this trip. Skylark is too old for such travel and Della isn't much younger. We also need mages at Suncroft, if Harsdown comes. Skylark and Della may lack in endurance, but they have decades of experience in magecraft. They would be more effective here, where they can do their best work without fatigue."

"*If* Harsdown comes."

"Chime is convinced."

"And you?"

"No. But she has a link to Wareman." Jarid gazed across the yard to where Iris and Chime stood by their horses, deep in conversation. More to himself, he added, "How do you argue with such a love as that driving Chime? In her position, I would insist on the same." He wished he knew how to tell Iris what she meant to him.

"Yes, well, they're just women."

Turning back to him, Jarid spoke dryly. "Would you like to tell Chime Headwind she is 'just' a woman?"

Brant blanched. "I see your point." He motioned at Cube-General Fieldson, who was conferring with several officers near the stables. "What does he say?"

"A surprise, actually. He didn't object."

"Why not?"

"He felt as they did about Skylark. He also thinks we need two mages with the army, in addition to myself."

Brant wearily rubbed the small of his back. "I don't like it."

Jarid watched his wife, her glorious hair covered by a shawl. "Nor I."

"I hope you're wrong about the armies in the north."

"What I sense is tenuous," Jarid admitted, more and more uneasy with that truth as the time neared for them to leave.

Brant's breath came out in puffs of condensation. "The Dawn-field line has such odd mage powers."

Jarid tensed, thinking of Muller. "What do you mean?"

"Your ability to sense people over so much distance." He paused. "But perhaps your strength is no surprise, given the way your ancestors married such strong mages."

Jarid didn't speak his thought, that the Dawnfield gifts had become too concentrated. No one should hold such power. In his darker moments, when he thought Varqelle might take all that mattered to him—his realms, his regained senses, his home, his wife—darkness moved within him. No mage could ever be free of that temptation, to use such power against others.

Yet Muller seemed to long only for the light. Jarid thought of the Mage Tower. The chamber with flawed shapes unsettled him, but he could see why Muller preferred it. In that place, alone, Muller could practice spells without doing harm. That wing of the castle was ancient, over a thousand years old. In the distant past, had other mages wielded powers such as Muller grappled with now? Although no histories mentioned such gifts, few records survived from ancient times. The traits could lie dormant for many generations, yet still become enhanced as the Dawnfields bred ever stronger mages.

Fieldson came over to them and bowed to Jarid. "We're about ready to leave."

"Thank you, Cube-General." Jarid smiled slightly at Brant. "Take care of Suncroft for me."

Brant laid his hand on Jarid's shoulder. "May blessings of the saints go with you."

Jarid inclined his head. He suspected they would need all the blessings they could find.

30

Magescape

Chime sat astride Silvermist, her gray mare. They knew each other well now, she and this horse, and she loved riding her through these hills. They had left Croft's Vale and its farmlands far behind. Every now and then she saw a thatched cottage in the distance, but they otherwise rode through unsettled lands. Scattered trees dotted the hills and meadows, but few wild flowers remained, only snap-lions that grew in wild red and gold profusion in the shade in groves of trees. The early morning light had the aged feel of late summer, when the sun crossed lower in the sky. Tomorrow would be autumn's first day, beginning the long, cold slide into winter.

All around her, the Heptagon Unit and King's Archers rode in lines of warriors, the powerful muscles of their horses rippling, their leather armor and chain mail creaking. Up ahead, Jarid cantered with Fieldson. Iris rode next to Chime on a large mount, a dappled mare. The wind pulled at the raised hood of the queen's riding cape.

"Jarid seems quiet," Chime said. She felt awkward with Iris, unsure what to say, but she tried anyway.

"Aye." Iris sighed. "Talking is'n his strong suit."

"It has never been mine, either. I seem to do it a lot anyway." Belatedly it occurred to Chime that she had just left herself open for a well-deserved retort.

Iris only smiled, though. "You've a lovely voice."

That startled Chime. "Thank you." She remembered her stupid comments last year about Iris's accent. If only she could take them back. It had been so long, though. She hesitated to speak, lest she remind the queen of a forgotten slight.

They rode for a time, protected against the chill by heavy wool cloaks with hoods. They wore leather armor most of the time, acclimating themselves to it, learning to move and function. Both had daggers sheathed on their belts.

After a while, Iris said, "I had wondered..."

"Yes?" Chime asked.

"About your nightmares. If you donna mind my asking?"

"Go ahead."

"Is anyone else in them besides Muller?"

Chime understood: Iris wondered if the dreams foretold anything for Jarid. "Only Muller. The rest is vague."

"Vague." Iris exhaled, her breath making plumes in the air. "Jarid says this also." Her hair blew across her face and she pulled it off. "I havna had any nightmares that I remember, but I have trouble sleeping. My mind is a pincushion." She reddened. "It is foolishness, I know."

"If it is," Chime said, "then I am foolish, too."

Iris hesitated. "I have had an idea."

"An idea?"

"Aye. Suppose you, Jarid, and I pool our gifts? We might be able to sense more that way."

It was an anomalous thought. Then again, this was an anomalous situation. Apparently even Jarid couldn't reach as far as Harsdown.

"I wouldn't know how," Chime said.

"Nor I," Iris admitted. "I suggested it to Della before we left and she said it couldna be done."

Chime disliked giving up. Besides, supposedly neither violet nor rainbow mages existed, either. "She has never worked with anyone like you or Jarid."

Iris grinned. "She also said that."

"Have you asked Jarid?"

"Aye. He is willing to try."

"What would we try, exactly?"

Iris pondered for a moment. "Maybe if we all make mood spells at the same time, for one another, we can combine them."

"You think that would give us more reach?"

"I hope so." Iris's hood was slipping off her head, and she pulled it back up. "We need to understand this Harsdown mage better."

Chime remembered his *wrongness* and her dismay when he had recognized her. "If we look for him, it could alert him to our presence."

"It be a problem," Iris said. "But he has the hole. He canna feel moods."

"He can't use green," Chime said. "But he can sense it. He felt my spell." She had no doubt about that.

Iris twisted the reins she held. "An indigo mage can heal emotional injuries. If he reversed his spell, he could cause such injuries. In that sense, he would reach other minds even if he hadna empathy for them."

"You think he is an indigo?" The idea discouraged Chime, but it didn't surprise her.

"I would like it to be untrue." Iris watched her husband riding ahead. "But if these dreams you and Jarid suffer come from spells, their creator must be powerful indeed, able to draw on high level shapes, even spheres."

Chime shuddered. "A gloomy thought."

"Aye." Iris's gaze turned bleak. "That it be."

The three of them gathered together that evening.

Jarid sat against a tree, one leg stretched in front of him, the other bent so he could rest his elbow on his knee. He held a ball of purple marble, one almost too large to fit into his palm. Iris sat on his right and Chime next to her. Chime had her emerald ball with twenty sides, and Iris held a similar diamond orb that sparkled with rainbows. Guards patrolled the area, warriors armed with sword and bow, far enough away so they didn't intrude, but close enough to reach the mages immediately if needed.

Iris looked at Chime and Jarid. "Ready?"

Jarid squinted at his wife. "What do we do?"

"Make mood spells," Iris said.

"I've never deliberately made one for more than one person," Chime said. "Though sometimes I pick up more."

"It is the same for me," Iris admitted.

"I may have made such spells," Jarid said. "I've never analyzed it."

An idea came to Chime. "We could imagine links to one another while we make the spell. Some quality to remind us of the other two people in the link."

Excitement flushed Iris's cheeks. "Let's try."

Holding her ball in both hands, Chime bent her head and closed her eyes. The orb focused her power well, with the right number of sides for her greatest reach but not too many to cause strain. She thought of the forests, hills, and meadows that had awakened Iris's latent gifts. So, too, did nature rather than human constructs seem to reach Jarid. Chime imagined the queen and king in a forest lush with foliage, leaves fluttering and grass rustling.

As her spell built, she became aware of Iris, an arch of color over the land. Beyond the queen, Jarid loomed, a force at the edge of Chime's mind. But when Chime reached for them, her spell faltered. She tried to focus and the spell skittered away.

Dismay touched Chime. She couldn't do this. She would let them down. Taking a deep breath, she made a simpler spell, one as yellow as the sun, this time soothing herself. As her agitation calmed, her previous spell recovered. Chime became the countryside; the queen became sky and sun. They existed in a charmed landscape.

A magescape.

Her sense of Iris deepened. Chime had never known that before coming to Suncroft, Iris had felt as if she belonged nowhere. Emptiness had frozen her life; no one offered her affection. It saddened Chime, whose childhood had been filled with the love of a close-knit family. Instinctively she offered Iris a spell of warmth.

Power swept the magescape, bracing and wild. *Jarid.* Chime felt him holding back, for fear his spell would disrupt the tenuous balance Iris and Chime had managed. Even with that caution, he came in like a huge wind, or a flood that filled an ocean, or an uncounted number of stars pouring silver light everywhere.

Hai, Chime thought, impressed.

Aye. Iris's answer was sunlight.

North, Jarid thought.

Chime imagined mountains rising against a blue sky. She had never been north, though, so she had no idea how the range should appear.

Here. Iris sharpened the peaks, making them harsh and magnificent, rearing up into a darker sky. *The Tallwalks.*

They flew through the peaks, heading for a pass that cut sharp lines in the range.

There. That came from Jarid.

Chime's focus dipped into the pass. Yes! She saw it. Jarid had been right; an army was coming through the pass.

They will soon arrive. Jarid's thought resonated. He went farther north, rising in the mountains. The forests dwindled to nothing, leaving bare peaks streaked with snow. *The Boxer-Mages,* he thought.

Chime suddenly realized Jarid could only guess at the appearance of the mountains he had called home. Although he had never seen them, he had caught images from Unbent's mind. Incredibly, he longed for that harsh, unrelenting beauty. He missed the simplicity of his life there, so different from the complications he lived now.

Again they rushed toward a pass, but when they plunged into this one, they found nothing but snow and barren rock. Chime had been right; no army was coming through that pass.

Her head began to ache. The magescape wavered, but when she tried to refocus, pain stabbed her temples.

Succor washed out from Iris. *Let it go.*

With an exhale, Chime released her spell. As it faded, the pain in her head receded. She opened her eyes to see Iris watching her. Jarid still seemed in a trance, his eyelashes dark against his cheeks.

"Are you all right?" Iris asked.

"Yes." Her spirits lifted. "That was incredible."

"Aye." Iris glanced at Jarid, who hadn't stirred.

"Both Jarid and I were right," Chime said. "An army comes through the Tallwalks, but not the Boxer-Mage Pass."

Jarid opened his eyes and looked straight at her, his pupils so large, his eyes were black with only a ring of violet. "I saw no second army, either."

"Perhaps he sent only one," Iris said.

It was then that comprehension came to Chime, making her feel ill. "Varqelle does have two armies, but only one comes through the mountains. The other goes to Suncroft. That way, no matter *what* we decide, we will be wrong."

Jarid swore. "It cannot be."

"He tricked you!" Chime said. "The Harsdown mage knew he couldn't hide the armies, so he made you think both were *here*. What if you had brought your entire army north?" Belatedly, Chime realized she had just insulted the king. Hastily she added, "You are a most potent mage, Your Majesty. Of course the trick didn't work."

Jarid spoke wryly. "It worked well enough." He rubbed his eyes. "I did have a sense, at the edges of our spell, of movement in the Barrens."

"We could try another spell." Chime tried to ignore the ache in her temples.

"I don't think tonight," Jarid said. "We must rest."

Chime agreed; they would solve nothing if they injured themselves.

But later, in her tent, she couldn't sleep. She lay on her back listening to the sentries pace outside, their chain mail clinking. What if Muller and his men met the Harsdown army before they could rendezvous with reinforcements? From what she sensed, the Harsdown forces greatly outnumbered Muller's Hexagons.

It could be a slaughter—and Muller would die.

The Covetous Spell

The nightmare never ended.

Muller trudged along a bar of land in the swamp he and his men had reached late this morning. Mist hung above the stagnant water, giving the bog an otherworldly quality. Its stench had worsened as the day passed. But none of it mattered. Compared to the walking nightmare he had lived these past days, the swamp was nothing. The foreboding that had plagued his dreams never left him now, waking or sleeping. He felt lightheaded, unfocused, nauseous.

Arkandy trudged next to him, stabbing his staff into the ground to make sure they didn't step into mud. "Vile place," he muttered.

"Aye." Muller drew himself up straighter and set his chin. He refused to give in to whom—or to what—plagued him with these waking dark dreams.

Up ahead, a murky figure formed out of the mist. It was Archer, waiting.

"Do you recognize the path?" Muller asked. He had taken the

short cut through the swamp only because Archer knew this area, having grown up in a nearby village.

"Aye." Archer indicated a branch of the land-bar they were following. "We go through there. It gets slippery, though. We should pass the word on to the others that they should take extra care."

Muller nodded wearily. He sent Arkandy back to warn the men, then plodded on, following Archer's indistinct form.

Gradually Muller became aware of an oddity. Silence. He had stopped hearing the murmurs, coughs, and squelching tread of his men. Puzzled, he stopped and called out to the figure he was following. "Archer?"

The figure dimmed, vaguer, almost gone.

"Archer, stop!" Muller started after him, but his foot slipped on the wet hexagrass, and he barely stopped himself from falling into the water.

No one was in front of him now.

Muller swung around, his fear surging. "Arkandy!"

No answer.

Saints almighty. How had he lost his men? They had been together. He had followed Archer and the men behind him should have followed him. If he had taken a wrong turn, so would have everyone else.

He headed back, peering at the ground. His footprints showed here and there in the mud, but he couldn't find tracks in the slick hexagrass. As he continued, the tracks faded until they vanished completely.

Muller stopped, his heart beating hard. He was lost. He couldn't see more than a few feet in any direction. The swamp was alive and malignant. Alarmed now, he looked around, searching for broken shapes. The hexagrass might do, with its elongated, six-sided blades, but it provided only small, two-dimensional forms. He had disks on his sword belt, but he had chosen the ornamentation carefully, every form perfect. Nor would the hardened metal be easy to bend.

Then he remembered Drummer's gift. The ring hung on a leather cord around his neck. He pulled it out, closing his hand around the talisman. *Forgive me, Drummer,* he thought. Then he squeezed the ring, pushing in on its soft metal until it dented, creating a flaw.

His gift sparked.

Power gathered around Muller. With his eyes closed, he strained, using a green spell to search for his men. He didn't know if their moods would lead him to them, but it was better than nothing.

Reaching.

Contact.

No! Muller recoiled. He had no idea what he had found, but it sure as blazes wasn't his men. His twisted spell had thrown him into a darkness so complete, it remained even when he opened his eyes. Frantic now, blind and lost, he struggled to wrench free of the contact. The link held him like a vise, using his own spell to trap him.

The dark dreams touched him.

They descended like ice, a night without stars, the wings of a giant crow. The ring dropped from his suddenly cold hand. The chill pierced his inner self, the place where he drew on his power. Dimly he heard someone scream.

Himself.

Terrified, he grappled with the dark dreams, straining to free his mind, but he couldn't break the spell, his *own* spell. It should have dissolved when he lost the ring, but whatever had caught him refused to let go. Another mage was adding fuel to this spell. It came from far away, too far, a spell of emotional soothing, but reversed, turned inside out, corrupted, made hideous. Instead of comfort, waves of revulsion surged over Muller.

"Saints, no." The words tore out of him. He dropped to his knees and groped in the mud, unable to see anything in the crushing darkness.

Then his hand closed around the ring. He clenched it so hard, its edges cut his skin. As pain lanced through his palm, the dark spell weakened. He concentrated, trying to regain control. His mind echoed with pain. But he kept on, his teeth clenched, his jaw aching.

The darkness lightened. But rather than the light of day filtering through mist, an emerald sphere surrounded him, glistening, drawn by his spell, his mind, his dented ring from Drummer. Leaning forward, Muller braced his fists on the ground, his head hanging down, surrounded by the beautiful emerald light. He thought of Chime.

"Commander!" The shout came out of the mist.

Muller gulped in a breath and nearly choked on the foul air. "Here!"

They called back and forth until he heard the tramp of boots. Then, suddenly, Arkandy was there, putting a strong hand under his forearm, helping him to his feet. "Good graces, Mull, you're as pale as the fog."

He took a shaky breath. "Where did you all go?"

"I thought you were ahead of me." He shook his head. "I could have sworn I never lost sight of you. But it was so foggy. When I tried to catch up to you, the man I was following—" He stopped, his face reddening.

Muller was aware of his men gathering around them in the mist. Quietly he said, "The figure dissipated."

"Yes." Arkandy cleared his throat. "I know it sounds strange."

"It happened to me, also." Muller pushed at his hair, which hung in lank, wet strands around his face. He couldn't speak of how the Harsdown mage had used his own spell to strike at him, but he needed to warn his men.

"This dark mage attacks with spells." He lifted his hand and uncurled his fist. The bent ring lay in his palm, which was bleeding where it had cut him. "Any shape can draw his power, even the thought of one. I lost this and I couldn't see, but still he attacked."

Arkandy spoke harshly. "What mage would do such?"

"One with too much strength and too few morals." Muller clapped him on the shoulder. "But nothing we can't handle, eh?"

Arkandy didn't smile. But he did say, "Aye."

Muller glanced at Archer, who had come up behind Arkandy. "How much farther?"

"Not much, Your Highness." Archer wiped the back of his hand across his forehead, which was beaded with moisture, either from his exertion or the dank fog. "About another half hour."

"Well, let's go, then."

As they set off, trudging in single file along the bar of land, they passed Muller's warning back along the line, that they shouldn't even think of perfect shapes. He listened to their voices, muted in the heavy air, and wondered what was happening to Aronsdale, that even their thoughts were no longer safe.

The overcast sky matched Chime's mood. They had ridden for hours in a drizzle. She had used oil to waterproof her cloak, but the rain eventually soaked through even the heavy, treated cloth.

She thought of Muller, trapped in darkness, fighting for his life. The image disturbed her. Nowhere felt safe. In the two days since she had blended spells with Iris and Jarid, they had managed it twice more, always searching. They hadn't located Muller's unit, the Hexagons, but they had no trouble sensing the

Harsdown army in the Tallwalk Mountains. Jarid had also located the second army heading through the Barrens. That both he and Chime had been right gratified neither of them.

Chime also sensed the Pentagon Unit, only days away now. Jarid sent scouts ahead to contact them, while the rest of the Heptagons trudged in the rain. The dread that had pressed Chime since before they left Suncroft never left her now, as if her nightmares invaded her waking hours. She touched the sphere that hung around her neck. In some ways, it worked better than the larger ball of green marble she had packed in her saddlebags. Although this smaller orb couldn't focus as much of her power, its size helped her fine-tune the spells.

Chime formed a yellow spell, imagining light to push away her melancholy. An answering spell stirred...*outside* of her.

The spell swept down like a hawk that had spotted prey and plunged straight for her. Someone settled behind Chime on the horse. Her body suddenly felt leaden. Before she could react, the presence behind her reached around her waist, grasping. She tried to push him away, but her limbs had become too heavy. She couldn't move, couldn't cry out, couldn't even open her eyes. He groped her sides, then moved higher and fondled her breasts. Chime tried to shout, but she could neither speak nor hear.

He moved his hands to her legs and slid them under her thighs. Furious and terrified, Chime strained to break their connection. His spell formed a blanket of power, smothering the light. No, not his spell; he had used *her* spell, turning around the yellow one meant to soothe her agitation. To escape this nightmare she had to regain control of her spell.

A memory came to her, the incantation she had spoken in her sleep: *Allar nellari remalla.* Sphere-inside-out. Della claimed it didn't work. Perhaps it only worked for a sphere mage. But it was a reversal. Could it work against a sphere mage?

Allar nellari remalla. Chime thought.

The sensation of hands fondling her faded. Then it came back again, redoubled, accompanied by a surge of anger. In desperation, she bit hard on the inside of her cheek. Pain flared, disrupting her focus, and an echo of pain came from the dark mage who invaded her spell.

Allar nellari remalla. Sphere-inside-out.

Her attacker's fury surged—

And he was gone.

Chime gasped, her sight returning, leaving her in painful brightness. She could see the Heptagons again, hear the clank of mail, the snorts of horses, the rustle of leaves on the trees.

"No!" Chime shook from the aftershocks of the twisted spell.

"What is it?" Iris drew her horse closer.

"Iris—no." Chime felt clammy, cold, icy.

Jarid was making his way back among the warriors, headed straight for Chime. The wind whipped his dark hair around his face, uncovering the scar on his neck. Chime sat up straighter on her horse, trying to regain her composure, but she couldn't stop shaking.

Iris drew Chime's horse to a stop. The queen jumped off her mare and handed the reins to one of the men. After Chime slid down to the ground, Iris led her to a tree at one side of trail. The entire unit was stopping, seven sets of seven men, forty-nine total, and fifty archers, plus Jarid and Cube-General Fieldson. It mortified Chime to think she had caused this disruption.

"What is it?" Iris said her. "What happened?"

"A spell." Chime choked on the words. "But reversed. Instead of healing, it injured."

Concern creased Isis's face "Are you hurt?"

Her anger sparked. "He touched me. I bit him." It served him right, but nausea surged within her anyway. She had done harm with her spell. No wonder Jarid loathed the incantation. She felt the cold more than before, inside herself as well as without.

"Who is 'him'?" Iris asked.

"The dark mage, I think." Chime shivered and pulled her cloak tighter. "He touched me places. If I hadn't broken his spell, I think he could have done whatever he wanted."

Iris's forehead furrowed. "But no one was there."

"He was there." The rough voice came from behind them.

Chime turned with a start. Jarid stood a few paces away, stiff in his posture. Iris glanced at Chime, a question in her gaze. When Chime nodded, Iris beckoned to her husband. Jarid came forward, walking slowly, as if Chime were a wild doe he feared might bolt.

The army stretched out along the trail, the horses stamping and shifting, the men talking to one another. No one disturbed Chime, Iris, and Jarid, though the men glanced their way every now and then. She wondered if they felt the oppressive aura, or if they just thought her flighty, unable to endure the rigors of the ride.

Jarid spoke to Chime in a low voice. "I saw a darkness descend on you."

She just shook her head. She wasn't ready to speak of it yet.

Iris was watching her. "Take your time. It will be all right."

Chime couldn't fathom her kindness. "Why don't you hate me?"

"Hate you?" Iris looked bewildered. "Why?"

"I've said such awful things." Chime wound her fingers in the tassels of her shawl, under her cloak. "When you first came, I was so afraid you would take Muller. I didn't know how to act..." She trailed off, feeling like an idiot.

It was a moment before Iris answered. "It is past now." Her face gentled. "You've a kind heart, even if you donna see it yourself."

Jarid snorted at Chime. "Never could fathom what you see in that skinny cousin of mine."

Chime warmed at the thought of Muller. "He does surely shine like the sun, Your Majesty."

He made an exasperated noise. "If you don't stop calling me 'Your Majesty,' I shall banish you to——" He paused. "Well, to someplace."

Chime managed a smile. "Aye, Jarid."

He paused, then spoke with care. "I would like to ask about the attack."

Chime dreaded speaking of it, but their banter had eased her fear. She no longer felt gripped in ice. And he needed to know what happened, even if she wished to forget.

"It is all right," she said.

"Do you know where it came from?" he asked.

She motioned toward the mountains, looming a few days' ride away, dark in the rain. "North."

"What happened?"

"I made a spell to lighten the heaviness."

"Heaviness?"

"It hangs over us," Chime said. "But the Harsdown mage caught my spell and twisted it around."

Jarid stiffened. "Are you saying that by using our mage abilities, we give him a way to attack us?"

"Yes, I think so."

"We must stop him," Iris said.

"How can he do deliberate harm with his spells?" It shook Chime to remember the incantation she had used against him. "I would die before I turned my gifts against people that way."

Jarid's expression darkened. He abruptly turned on his heel and strode away from them.

Chime stared after him, confused. Then, realizing what she had done, she swore. "I am an idiot!" She might as well have stabbed him over Murk's death.

Iris watched her husband walking among his men. "I think he knows you didn't mean him."

Chime started forward. "I should apologize."

Iris caught her arm. "It is best to let him be."

"I am so sorry."

Iris spoke quietly. "Are *you* all right?"

"I will be." Chime hoped that was true.

Iris shook her head. "This dark mage is obsessed with you. Canna you call for help when he attacks?"

"He made it so I couldn't see, hear, or speak."

"How did you stop his spell?"

"I used that incantation, the one I spoke in my sleep." She ran her tongue over the inside of her mouth. "And I bit my cheek until it bled. It disrupted the spell. His influence comes from a great distance, so it must strain him to extend it so far."

"That he does it at all is chilling." Iris watched the king, who was speaking with Fieldson now. "I fear what it would do to Jarid if this mage stole his senses. He has struggled so to adapt. To lose it all, again, would destroy him."

Chime lifted her chin. "We won't let it happen."

As they headed back to the others, Chime brooded. If the dark mage could turn their own spells against them, she dreaded to think what he might do with Muller's injured gifts.

32

Gathering Winds

Anvil rode astride Snowhawk, a white charger that glowed in the misty day. General Stonehammer rode with him, his gaze sharp as he scanned the steep trail their company followed down through the Tallwalks.

"Lot of fog," Anvil commented.

"It makes good cover." Stonehammer glanced at him. "Though by now they must know we are coming."

"They have an idea." Although Anvil tried to hide his fatigue, he suspected Stonehammer knew how much his mage efforts exhausted him. As they neared the Aronsdale forces, though, he didn't have to extend himself as far, and the strain eased. "Some of their forces are here. Others are at Suncroft."

Stonehammer's eyes glinted like splinters of green glass. "They weren't supposed to know we divided the army."

Anvil wanted to say it meant nothing, but downplaying the situation would only hurt their still considerable chances of success. With Varqelle leading the greater part of his army to

Suncroft, he could take the castle even with a substantial portion of the Aronsdale army there. Anvil could aid this smaller force with his magecraft. They would face a contingent of archers and two Aronsdale units, perhaps three if Muller Dawnfield showed up with the Hexagons. Anvil had misled them, pushing their party too far north. It troubled him that they had ridden north at all, though. Muller shouldn't have known to come. But come he had.

"They have more mage power than I expected," Anvil said. He recalled his interaction with Muller in the swamp, when he had spelled the princeling into losing his way. If Dawnfield's men hadn't found him, Muller could have died in that bog, ridding Anvil of an irritant that interfered in his intentions toward Lady Chime. Muller had caught him by surprise by fighting back with that bizarre spell of his. Even stranger, a green spell had also protected him. Anvil didn't understand how a spell of compassion and empathy could be *strong*. In his experience, empathy weakened a person, leaving him open to attack.

"It isn't only the king," he added. "His cousin, it seems, is also a mage."

Stonehammer cocked an eyebrow at him. "Surely you do not mean Muller Dawnfield."

"It would seem so."

The general laughed. "Impossible."

"Apparently not."

Stonehammer's smile faded. "Then unacceptable."

"Well, yes. But unfortunately true."

"That gives them advantage."

"I think not." Anvil recalled how easily he had turned Muller's faltering gift against the prince. "He uses shape-magic the way a child with crippled legs moves. He will never run, never walk, only crawl."

"You make odd predictions." Stonehammer guided his horse

around a hillock covered with hardy stone-hedge, its small blossoms wet in the fog, their violet color so vivid they seemed to glow.

Malice stirred in Anvil for this prince who blocked his approach to Lady Chime. Anvil had earned his high status among the elite of Harsdown; no one had given him any title or advantages due to his heredity. Muller Dawnfield deserved his failings. "He must have an unpleasant life, always fighting his own spells."

"Hard to believe men would follow such a commander."

It surprised Anvil, too, especially after the past few days. He had developed respect for Stonehammer during this ride. The general could be hard, yes, demanding, never relenting, but he was also fair. He had none of the weaknesses Anvil had seen in Suncroft, where officers listened too much to their men, undermining their own commands. He had even heard that Cube-General Fieldson had once granted a soldier leave to be with his wife the day she gave birth. Appalling. Stonehammer would never have tolerated such a dereliction of duty.

"I don't think Dawnfield's men know he is a mage," Anvil said.

The general slanted him a glance. "How would you know?"

Anvil shrugged. "People in Croft's Vale love to gossip about the Suncroft mages. It's one of their favorite pastimes. I never heard a word about Muller."

"So." Stonehammer thought for a while, the planes of his face thrown into a contrast of shadows and light by the slanting rays of the sun. "If he is a faulty mage, perhaps his spells could be manipulated."

Anvil nodded his agreement. His thoughts precisely.

The line of riders coiled down the trail like a dragon shrouded in fog. They had seven units of forty men each, a total of two hundred and eighty, plus Stonehammer and a mage. Anvil had touched many minds as he haunted the Aronsdale warriors, spreading unrest and sadness. He predicted Harsdown would face the Pentagons, with twenty-five men and a commander; the Heptagons, with forty-nine, their commander, and Chime; about fifty archers; and maybe the Hexagons, with thirty-six and Prince Muller. That made about one hundred and sixty men plus a mage. Although the numbers favored Harsdown, Anvil didn't fool himself that they offered an easy win. Aronsdale had claimed a good army even before Muller stepped up their training. They lacked experience, but so did Harsdown.

That he detected only Chime as a mage suggested Jarid had stayed at Suncroft with his queen. Anvil couldn't be sure, though; he had trouble sensing Iris, who for some reason had no signature color. Even if she was green, like Chime, he would know; although he couldn't create such spells, he could sense when others used them. Jarid remained an enigma. Anvil had believed no mage wielded a power greater than his own, but now he wondered. If the king surpassed him, Jarid might hide within a shield of his greater strength.

Anvil gritted his teeth. He could never tolerate such a mage. If the king and queen had ridden north, he would kill Jarid and capture Iris. If Jarid had left his lovely bride at Suncroft, she would be a fitting prize for Varqelle. Either way, Chime Head-wind was here.

It gratified him to know he would be the one to take her.

Muller sat by the campfire on a log, his elbows on his knees, holding his head in his hands. He was aware of his men making camp, fixing dinner and tending horses, but he couldn't move. His headache pounded. Lifting his head, he looked at the twilit sky. Silhouetted against it, towering over the camp, the Tallwalk Mountains raised their harsh peaks to the heavens. *I won't let you defeat me,* he thought.

"Commander?" Arkandy approached, holding two metal pans. The aroma of stew wafted over Muller, making his mouth water. He made himself straighten up. "Have a seat."

Arkandy settled down and handed him a plate. "Head still hurt?"

"A bit."

Arkandy stabbed a chunk of meat with his knife. "Blasted spells." He stuck the meat in his mouth and chewed with gusto.

"An understatement," Muller muttered.

"It gets worse, eh?"

Muller poked at his dinner. "Yes."

"I've felt pressure now and then. Like a ghost."

"You have?" Muller had hoped his men wouldn't be affected. "How bad is it?"

"Nothing I can't handle." Arkandy took another bite of stew. "How does he know to target you? What tells him that he has the commander?"

His phrasing relieved Muller. Arkandy could have asked *why* the mage targeted him, but apparently he assumed it was because Muller led the unit. "Probably he recognizes my mind. If this mage is Wareman, he knew me at Suncroft."

Archer came over to them, a skein of wine in his hand. "We've secured the camp, Commander."

"Good work." Muller motioned at the log. "Rest awhile."

Archer sat on his other side and offered him the wine. "This might help your head."

"My thanks." Muller took a long drought. It had helped last night and perhaps it would tonight. Tomorrow they would reach the foothills of the Tallwalk Mountains. Then, saints willing, he would engage the reprobate who was making his life hell.

The Heptagons and the King's Archers poured down the slope into the camp of the Pentagons. Chime rode in the middle of the unit, accompanied only by two sphere-lieutenants, since Iris had gone up ahead. Mist drifted around the warriors of both units as they mingled and prepared to ride out together.

By the time Chime reached the camp, Jarid and Iris were conferring with Penta-Colonel Burg, commander of the Pentagons. He stood almost as tall as Jarid, a burly man with a blocky face and sandy hair in a thick braid with an iron clasp at his neck. He carried a great deal more weight than most men, all of it muscle.

Restless and unsettled, Chime rode slowly around the edges of the camp. She had only gone a short distance when an odd sensation came over her, as if the mist were burning her skin. She brushed her face and the feeling vanished.

She glanced at the lieutenant closest to her, a gangly fellow a year or two older than herself, riding to her left. "Did you feel anything hot?"

He tilted his head, curiosity in his blue eyes. "Nay, Lady. It be beastly wet and cold this morning."

"That it is." The prickle of heat disquieted her. These past two days, since the Harsdown mage had attacked, Chime had taken care to hide her gifts, making no spells. Iris and Jarid had done the same. She felt the dark mage searching, but as long as she suppressed her gifts, his spells slid over her like hot oil. But she couldn't hide forever. It did the army no good to bring mages who couldn't make spells.

Chime rode up a ridge shaded with straggling trees. Here in the foothills of the northwest mountains, the soil was rocky and the plants hardier than the lush foliage of southeast Aronsdale. She guided Silvermist to the top of the ridge and pulled the mare to a stop. Then she sat on her horse, looking over the controlled tumult below as the two army contingents combined.

She touched the gold chain around her neck, then slid her hand down to the emerald ball at the end. She held it in her palm, turning her hand up to the sky. Silvermist stepped restlessly beneath her and she murmured to the horse until it calmed.

Focusing through her sphere, Chime slowly built a mood spell. Emotions washed over her from the soldiers below: tension, conviction, relief at seeing one another, and determination. At the edges of her spell, darkness hovered. She immediately let the spell fade, before the dark mage became aware of her. He already knew she rode through these lands, but she had no intention of giving him any handle to grasp.

The combined forces soon moved out together. Their superb organization and ability to cooperate with such ease spoke well of Fieldson, who had commanded this army for over two decades. It gave Chime new insights into the general. He could have balked when Jarid put Muller in charge, but instead Fieldson had worked tirelessly to prepare the new commander. Remorse tugged at Chime; she had been so busy resenting Fieldson, she had glossed over the many fine qualities that made him a strong leader and inspired such loyalty in his men.

They rode steadily, though their progress was slowed as the land became steeper and uneven. As the sun rose, the fog thinned, until by the late morning she could see the Tallwalks through a haze. Foreboding continued to plague her thoughts.

Scouts ranged ahead, searching for signs of Harsdown. Iris came back to ride with Chime, and Jarid increased their guard from four sphere-lieutenants in the traditional quadrilateral formation to six in a hexagonal formation. The trees thinned out and had a stunted look now. They had left the meadows far behind; only bristly patches of grass grew in cracks in the stone. The horses picked their way with care.

Riding with Iris, Chime spoke in a subdued voice. "We must use our spells to search for Harsdown."

"Aye." The shadows under Iris's eyes were darker today and lines of strain creased her face.

Chime hesitated, leery of appearing a coward. "I fear if I make a spell, the Harsdown mage will find me."

Mercifully Iris didn't disparage her statement. She said only, "I may be able to help. Mood spells are your forte more than mine, so you should search. But I can offer a shield as you work."

That gave Chime hope. A year ago, she probably would have made some foolish comment trying to cover her insecurity, but that no longer seemed important. She said only, "Yes, let's try."

With a deep breath, Chime closed her eyes. It made her more aware of her exhaustion; right now she thought she could fall asleep while sitting in the saddle. But she couldn't let her focus weaken. Grasping the orb on the chain around her neck, she did her best to concentrate. Instead of seeking one person, she imagined her spell as a twenty-sided sphere, emerald. Then she let it grow. Iris shielded it with a rainbow sheen that expanded in a layer of protection, gossamer in appearance yet stronger than any spell Chime could have summoned.

A blurred sense of the warriors came to Chime, their moods blended together. Although they felt far less of the oppressive foreboding that bothered her, many were discouraged, their morale low. She formed a yellow spell of soothing and released it to flow across them. Although no one consciously seemed to realize what happened, their moods lifted.

Meanwhile, her green spell continued to grow. Less then two years ago, she hadn't believed she could make even one spell properly; now she juggled two of them, green and yellow, shaping and building both. The rainbow film stayed with here, its colors swirling. Not only did Iris protect her spells, she also added support, helping Chime cover more distance. Yet for all that Chime reached across the land, she touched no more minds. Few people lived in these unfertile lands.

Chime's head began to throb. She was overextending herself. She started to release the spell—but then she sensed a distant cluster of minds. A cold determination came from them, like iron manacles. She eased under their notice—and found a mage.

Wareman.

Her heart beating hard, Chime withdrew, hidden by Iris. As her spell dissolved, she became aware of soldiers on horses around her, and the fog that hung about the stunted vegetation in the still air.

She spoke to Iris in a low voice. "Varqelle's forces have passed through the Tallwalk Pass and are descending the mountains. If we keep this pace, we should meet up with them tomorrow afternoon."

Iris tensed. "We must tell Jarid."

"Yes. Immediately. They have many men, a much larger force than ours." Chime looked toward the spare, majestic peaks of the Tallwalk Mountains. "So it comes."

That evening, Jarid doubled the sentries on guard. Chime couldn't sleep. She turned over and over, futilely seeking a comfortable position. Finally she gave up and lay on her back staring at the tent overhead.

A tap came at her tent. "Lady Chime?" Jarid's voice rumbled.

She sat up, startled. A man shouldn't visit her tent at night, but she couldn't forbid the king, particularly not after the way she had insulted him a few days ago. Their interactions had been strained since then.

Chime yanked on her robe, clutching the collar around her neck. Then she raised her voice. "Come in, Your Majesty."

Jarid pushed aside the entrance flap. "I'm sorry to disturb you." Ducking his head, he came inside and fastened up the flap so he and Chime were in view of the sentry on patrol outside. He sat by the opening, giving her plenty of space. He gave her a look of apology. "I would have brought Iris, but she finally fell asleep. And she hasn't slept in so long."

"I understand," Chime said. As mages, they had to rest. They could do little for the army if they were too exhausted to perform their craft.

"I would ask your help," Jarid began.

"Anything I can do."

He rubbed his eyes, his motions slowed with fatigue. "Are you certain you cannot estimate the size of the Harsdown force? Anything you can tell us might help."

"My spell was stretched too thin to distinguish individual minds." Chime thought back to this afternoon. "Would a comparison to help?"

He smiled dryly. "At this point, any mote of information would be more than we have."

"You have about eighty men here now, yes?"

He nodded. "Seventy-six, plus you and Iris."

Chime considered for a moment. "I think Varqelle's force has more than twice our numbers."

He tensed. "That many?"

She spoke with reluctance. "Yes, I think at least."

"Can we take them?"

"Your Majesty, I couldn't say. I'm no strategist."

"I would just like your opinion."

Chime forced out her answer. "No. I don't think so."

His gaze darkened. "What about our spells?"

"Iris and I discussed an idea." She suspected Iris had already told Jarid, but he would want to hear it from Chime, to verify she consented. "We can probably affect Varqelle's men in a manner similar to how the dark mage discourages us."

"Hurt their morale."

"Yes. Or make them feel sick."

"Won't these spells hurt you?"

Her hands felt clammy. "Yes, I think so."

"Chime, you don't have to do this."

"Yes. I do."

His face contorted. "I hate this."

Softly she said, "I also."

"I will help you and Iris in your spells."

"You are king. You must lead the army."

He snorted. "Fieldson is better fit for that job."

"Your Majesty, you are a great—"

"No, I'm not." He spoke tiredly. "I'm a good fighter with my fists and a fast learner with a sword, but I can't spend most of my life with no experience and expect to command after a few months. Fieldson trained this army. Muller has spent the past fourteen years learning to take command. I hid in the mountains."

"You mustn't condemn yourself."

He shook his head as if banishing the subject. "Were you able to contact Muller at all?"

Chime let it go. "Not yet. I should have sensed him by now." It had troubled her all day. His moods always came to her with buttery warmth, even when he was grumpy or upset. "I would know if he was near."

Jarid rubbed the back of his neck, massaging the muscles. "We need the Hexagons."

"Yes." Chime didn't know what else to say.

"I cannot ask this of you or Iris."

Chime understood what he meant; without the Hexagons, they would need other methods to prevail over Harsdown. Spells. She dreaded using her gifts that way, but if Aronsdale needed it to survive, she would do what she could to help.

"I pray it doesn't come to that," she said. "We need to defeat this dark mage. If he falls, his warriors will lose heart."

"We can hope." Jarid stood slowly, bending so his head didn't push the top of the tent. "I will see you in the morning. Sleep well."

"And you, Your Majesty."

He departed them, leaving the flap swinging behind him. Chime lay back down and closed her eyes, knowing that somehow, someway, she had to sleep, to build her strength.

Tomorrow they would engage their enemy.

The Tallwalk Cliffs sheered into the sky. A trail switch-backed up them, narrow enough to make the Hexagon Unit ride single file. Muller sat on Windstrider, the reins limp in his hands, his head falling forward, his back bent. He kept going by sheer force of will, drained by lack of sleep and his headaches.

Muller avoided looking down. He didn't want to know how high they had climbed. Thoughts of Chime supported him; she was sunlight and warmth, safe at Suncroft. He had known he loved her, but he hadn't realized how much until he became mired in this gruesome trek and feared he would never see her again.

He straightened his back, battling the fatigue that dragged at him. His unit finally reached the top of the cliffs, coming out onto a level area. Gigantic crystal formations jutted up, towering over them—and offering many places for enemies to hide. The crystals drew Muller, all those imperfect six-sided spears. He spontaneously created a spell, frayed and unsteady. The moods of his men came to him in jagged spikes, nothing clear except their tension, which was obvious anyway. But he sensed only his men; the outcroppings hid no other warriors.

So they crossed the plain, making their way among the eerie formations under an overcast sky. Muller focused his spell forward, toward the Boxer-Mage Mountains. He should stop using his gifts, lest the dark mage find him, but he feared walking into peril even more.

Muller knew when he touched Wareman. The dark mage tried to warp Muller's spell, but it had started out twisted. So when Wareman reversed it, he *fixed* the twist and the spell worked as it should have in the first place, revealing Wareman's mood to Muller. So it was that Muller learned a hard truth: Wareman had tricked him. The Harsdown army had gone through the Tallwalk Pass, not the Boxer-Mage Mountains. They were halfway down the mountains now, into Aronsdale, well to the east.

Muller swore at this new knowledge. But it didn't end there. Slowly, inexorably, the dark mage focused on him. Sweat ran down Muller's neck and he wanted to rub his palms on the leather that protected his legs. He kept his focus on his nemesis. Pain stabbed his temples, but he held his mental ground, gritting his teeth. He had spent a lifetime learning to subdue his warped spells. Now he turned that knowledge outward to the mage attacking him.

Wareman's rage flared, blazing, firing Muller's head with pain. Muller responded as he did when his spells of warmth backfired; he imagined water cascading over the blaze. It receded, then leapt again, fighting him. Muller envisioned an indigo sphere enclosing the fire, smothering it the way a bell smothered a candle flame. The fury dimmed, faltered—and withdrew.

Muller gulped in a breath, opening his eyes. *Saints almighty.* He had to go east and find the Pentagons fast.

He just hoped they weren't too late.

"The Harsdown forces are north of us," Chime said. She rode with Fieldson through the foothills of the Tallwalks. "Our scouts should sight them soon."

"And their numbers?" Fieldson asked.

"Almost three hundred, I would guess."

He nodded, rubbing his chin. "Now that we have a better idea of their route, we must think on where we will engage them. Do you detect anything about the territory around their company?"

She thought back to her last mage search. "A little. I can develop a sense of the surrounding land based on how they feel about their travels. It's difficult now from this far away, but I can do more as we get closer."

"Excellent." He looked up the mountains rearing before them, no longer distant. "They're already through the pass, so they will be descending toward us."

"Does that make a difference?"

He turned to her with a grimace. "If we fight them on an ascending slope, they have advantage. Our best scenario would be to split up, sneak around from either side, and ambush them from above."

Chime had her doubts. "I don't think their path takes them through land where that would work. Travelers in valleys or sheltered areas have different moods than those who ride exposed. They are on cliffs or open slopes, I think. We might have no place to hide."

His expression darkened. "If they went east after coming through the pass, instead of straight down the Tallwalks, it would put them in that kind of terrain. It's all cliffs and wide, rocky slopes, no low or protected areas. An ambush wouldn't work there."

"We could wait for them down here." Chime indicated the foothills. "An ambush might work better."

"People live here." Fieldson motioned to the west. A cottage showed in the distance, smoke curling out of its chimney, with a barn and stables beyond it. "If we let Harsdown down this far, they could easily sack the farms and kill the families that tend them."

Chime hated the thought. A chill went through her; if the invaders made it as far as southern Aronsdale, her family could lose their orchards, home, and lives.

"If we can't get around them in the mountains," she said, "what else would work up there?"

"Engage them in a flat region." He pulled his hair back from his widow's peak. "Can you affect their decisions about their route? Nudge them a bit more eastward? We could aim for the Tallwalk Plateau."

Chime held back her shudder. "If I try to influence them, their mage might take notice of me."

He motioned to where Iris rode with Jarid up ahead. "Can they shield your efforts?"

Although normally Chime would never speak in less than positive terms of the king, she had to give Fieldson the truth if they were to survive. "His Majesty doesn't have the training or subtlety to do it. But Queen Iris might."

"Very well. If they agree, let us try that plan."

"General Fieldson—?"

"Yes?"

"The men are tired. I feel their moods. We've come so fast and pushed so hard."

"Yes. I know. It isn't the way to approach battle." He lifted his hand, then let it drop onto his saddle. "But we have no choice."

Fatigue weighed on her as well. "If it makes any difference to know, the Harsdown warriors are also tired. They have come fast, too, I think hoping for the advantage of surprise."

His face gentled. "Aye, Lady, it makes a difference."

As the general went on ahead to speak with Jarid and Iris Chime continued on with the company, the Pentagons, Heptagons, and archers riding onward, lines of horses wreathed in fog.

Iris soon came back to join her. With the queen shielding her mage work, Chime sent bad-mood spells to the Harsdown army. If she thought they were veering eastward, she eased up her spells; if they veered west, she redoubled her efforts. Being an irritant to them made her head hurt, but she kept at it, refusing to quit even as it drained her resources.

Suddenly energy flooded her, light, support. Jarid.

Thank you, she thought.

A sense of welcome came from him.

Chime detected three groups: the Aronsdale company; the Harsdown army descending from the pass; and a group in the west. The third company felt like Aronsdale warriors, possibly the Hexagons, but even now she caught no trace of Muller. Surely if he rode with them, she would know.

A band seemed to constrict her chest, making it hard to breathe. She picked up *nothing* of Muller. Distance would make it difficult, true, but she touched other minds. Surely she should be even better able to sense her husband, a mage.

Unless someone had injured him. Or worse.

"The groups come from different directions." Crouched next to Anvil, Stonehammer drew a map in the pebbly dirt. He tapped the arcs he had made for the mountains. "The Hexagons are here." Then he set several rocks to the east. "Two units here, possibly Pentagon and Heptagon, plus the archers."

Anvil studied the diagram. "I have felt no mages for the past two days. It makes me suspicious."

Stonehammer glanced at him. "Perhaps they disguise themselves."

"Neither Muller nor Chime has the experience to do such. I studied Chime while I was in Croft's Vale."

"And Muller Dawnfield?"

Anvil thought of the prince. "No one knew he was a mage. I didn't until these last few days. I doubt he has tutoring in the use of his gifts."

Stonehammer rose to his feet, lifting his head, his hard face thoughtful. He and Anvil had paused in an open area while the army rode on down a wide, rocky trial, led by officers under Stonehammer's command. "Why else wouldn't you feel the Aronsdale mages?"

Anvil stood up next to him. "Fieldson may have left Lady Chime in a village. With Muller, I'm less certain. He is unlike any other mage I've encountered."

Stonehammer smiled slightly. "It is hard to take the idea seriously, given his reputation."

"Ah, well." Anvil spoke with reluctance. "He may have more to him than we realized."

The general walked with him to their horses. "Could he be hiding Lady Chime somehow?"

"I doubt it."

They mounted their horses and set off, soon catching up with the army. In this rocky territory, they had to go slow, enough to let the mounted warriors talk among themselves. Arguments sparked and sputtered.

Stonehammer's gaze darkened. "This irritability seems unnatural."

"It may be." Anvil knew all too well how spells could be turned to such purposes, given the way he had haunted the Aronsdale army. He found it hard to imagine their mages would try a similar ploy, though; they were adamant about never using spells for harm, crippled by their ingrained tendency to remorse. Only he had the superiority to rise above such weakness.

They might try, though, if Aronsdale became desperate. It made him suspect Chime; the dim-witted beauty liked mood spells. But that would mean she still rode with Aronsdale and had somehow hidden from him. His anger sparked; she would pay for trying to evade him.

He should have felt it, though, if the pall hanging over the men came from mage-meddling. Although he couldn't make such spells, he could sense their presence. The puzzle intrigued as much as annoyed him. He had spent his life using his spells for his own survival. Anvil liked having a bigger purpose. He was part of a great undertaking, the making of an empire. This year Varqelle would take Aronsdale; in the future, who knew. Shazire, Jazid, Taka Mal, maybe someday the land of his wife, the Misted Peaks.

Anvil closed his hand around his mage ball, a heavy metal sphere with an indigo sheen that hung by a chain from his leather belt. He sent out a spell, seeking the Aronsdale forces. It didn't tax him at all now, with the groups so close. He searched for Chime, but again he found no trace of her. When he turned his attention to the Aronsdale warriors, he easily distinguished individual minds. It gratified him to verify they had less than half the number of men that rode with Stonehammer.

Gradually Anvil became aware of another spell. It covered the land like the iridescent sheen of a bubble. He had trouble gaining purchase on it and couldn't associate it with a color. Odd.

Tiring, he let his spell fade. Although he had continued to ride, he hadn't been aware of the countryside. Now he saw they had descended below the tree line, into hills with stunted woods and stubby grasses. Stonehammer had drawn ahead and was speaking with a major as their horses picked their way across the uneven terrain, which had many shelves of rock and loose stones.

Anvil nudged the general with a spell, and Stonehammer glanced back. He beckoned to Anvil, then returned to his conference, probably thinking it had been his idea to summon his mage. Hiding his smile, Anvil rode closer until he could overhear the general and major. He already knew the plans they were discussing. However, the major had an alarming suggestion; he wanted to offer the outnumbered Aronsdale forces a chance to surrender in return for their lives.

Anvil gritted his teeth. He loathed the idea. No one in Aronsdale had ever shown him mercy. Why should he do so for them?

Eventually the discussion finished. After the major rode on ahead, Anvil spurred his horse forward and caught up with Stonehammer. When the general glanced at him, Anvil frowned.

"You disapprove of something?" Stonehammer asked.

"Yes. Negotiation."

"If we can avoid bloodshed, we should." Stonehammer seemed more at ease now that they knew how much they outnumbered their opponents. "War is a last resort, Anvil. It destroys the lands we seek to annex and builds resentment in the population. We must consider every alternative."

It was all Anvil could do to keep his voice calm. "As the people of Stonce gave alternatives to my family?"

The general scrutinized him. "I doubt these people were involved in those deaths."

"'These people' rule the country." It didn't matter that they weren't the ones who had tortured or murdered his family. They were all part of the same breed.

"Perhaps," Stonehammer said. "But nevertheless, we will offer them the chance to surrender."

Anvil knew the general well enough to recognize the finality of his decision. He schooled himself to calm until he had control of his rage. "Very well." If they didn't engage the Aronsdale army here, he would find other ways to destroy the figures of power in that country. For now, perhaps it was time to broach a related concern. "The Aronsdale mages may be playing with unusual spells."

Stonehammer cocked his head. "You have detected this?"

"I detect a *lack*. A sphere of blankness. I suspect one mage shields the other."

"Muller and his wife?"

"I don't think it is Dawnfield."

"Then who?"

"I can't say."

"They know about you, then."

"I suspect so." As much as Anvil disliked making that admission, it served no useful purpose to deny the possibility when it could affect the outcome of their engagement. "It fits their style. A shielding spell would protect them from my powers without causing me injury." He flexed his hand as if preparing for work. "But I may be able to mimic the effect. Use it to my own advantage."

"Good." Stonehammer spoke thoughtfully. "These mages intrigue me. I hope we take them alive."

Anvil thought of Chime, gold and green. "I, too."

"My eldest son has always wished to meet a mage. Perhaps you will bring Lady Chime to visit."

That startled Anvil; it was the first time the general had indicated any interest in him outside of the military. It suggested Stonehammer had begun to see him as someone worth cultivating, a positive sign.

"It would be my honor," Anvil said.

The general inclined his head.

A call came back from the front. Stonehammer urged his mount to a faster pace, and Anvil accompanied him up a long ridge that crossed their path. They reined in their horses at the top, looking out. On the other side, the ridge fell steeply away to a plateau; beyond the plateau, the mountains resumed their downward march. Far in the distance, well below the mountains, the gentler hills of Aronsdale hid in fog, visible only in glimpses of green and the fiery colors of autumn in the trees.

On the plateau, the Aronsdale army waited.

33

The Tallwalk Plateau

Bile rose in Chime's throat as she stared up at the ridge where the Harsdown army appeared. Wave after wave of mounted warriors crested the long roll of land until they made a jagged line against the cold blue sky. Tendrils of fog curled around the legs of their mounts.

Chime and Iris sat stride their horses, surrounded by a traditional formation that protected mages during battle, seven mounted warriors in a heptagon. Both mages wore leather armor, with long daggers sheathed on their belts. They waited in the southwest corner of the plateau, across from the northern ridge where the Harsdown army loomed. To their left, rocks jutted out of a sheer cliff face, forming a partial, jagged cover. The plateau stretched for as long as a horse could run for several minutes, until it reached its eastern edge, which dropped down into the mountains. A shelf jutted up behind the mages, and beyond it the plateau also plunged down in a cliff.

Even half-hidden over the overhang of rocks, Chime felt exposed. Ideally mages stayed off the battlefield; however, they also had to be close enough for their spells to work. Up here, this was the best they could do.

All across the plateau, Aronsdale warriors had taken polygon formations, the Pentagons in five-sided figures and the Heptagons in seven-sided, according to how they had trained to fight. Archers waited behind them, quivers on their backs, bows ready. The Aronsdale men stood firm, staring at the Harsdown army on the ridge.

Chime shivered despite her heavy cloak and armor. She couldn't sense Wareman, but she had no doubt he waited above. Did he know about Jarid? Although some histories described kings who were mages, little record existed of how they drew on their power during battle, or even if they did at all. Given the way Jarid condemned himself for his act of self-defense against Murk, she feared that if he used his gifts in combat, it would destroy him.

For interminable moments, the two armies considered each other. Just when Chime thought she would snap with tension, a rider separated from the Harsdown forces and came down the rugged slope, his mount stepping across the shelves of rock and through the tough grasses.

Jarid and Fieldson rode out to meet the envoy where the plateau met the slope. Iris watched her husband with a bleak gaze. The queen clenched the diamond orb she wore on a chain around her neck and a spell rose about her, one Chime saw as a translucent shimmer of rainbows. Chime focused through the emerald sphere she wore, extending a mood spell toward the Harsdown envoy. She couldn't tell much, but she sensed no intent to deceive on his part.

After conferring with Jarid and Fieldson, the envoy wheeled his mount around and rode back up to his army. His horse climbed the stony ridge with an assurance that spoke bluntly of its superior training. Harsdown was known for rugged country; Aronsdale had only gentle hills, except here on its border. Fighting in this region gave Harsdown an advantage, but Aronsdale had to stop the invaders before they reached populated areas, which meant confronting them here.

Chime spoke to Iris. "That messenger was nervous."

The queen answered in a leaden voice. "They offer us our lives in return for our surrender."

"Surrender?" Chime wanted to say *No!* But she knew how few options they had. "Would Jarid consider such?"

Iris watched her husband return with Fieldson to the Aronsdale army. "He refused."

Although Chime was glad, she didn't fool herself that it changed the desperation of their situation. "Harsdown fears a long battle."

"With good reason." Iris turned to Chime, her gaze stark. "We must help."

Chime's pulse surged. They had made their plans; the time had come to put them into action. As the stronger mage, Iris could better endure spells of harm, whereas Chime's talent lay in strengthening moods. So Iris would fight Harsdown while Chime helped Aronsdale.

Holding her faceted sphere, Chime focused, striving to submerge into her concentration until she lost awareness of the soldiers above them. Power rose within her, funneled through the emerald in her hand.

Then the Harsdown army charged.

With many shouts, they thundered down the ridge on horses that seemed to fly across the rocky ground. The Aronsdale cavalry surged forward, maintaining their polygon shapes, their war cries echoing in the mountains. Chime's spell rolled out to the closest polygon formation, a heptagon, filling it like a cup. She poured confidence into the spell, encouraging the fighters, helping to firm their wills, sharpening their sight and hearing. As a green mage, she could neither heal injuries nor improve a person's physical condition, but she could make them *feel* stronger, and for many, that made all the difference.

When the first Harsdown warriors reached the plateau, their lines met the Aronsdale polygon formations like waves smashing against rocks. Swords clanged, vibrating in Chime's ears as she deepened her magecraft. One by one, she filled the polygons of warriors with her spell. Harsdown made every effort to scatter the polygons, but each time they disrupted one, another formed, the new shapes holding together with uncanny accuracy as Chime strengthened them.

The Aronsdale archers strode past the polygons and fired a volley of arrows, their shots whirring through the air. They stepped back, drawing new arrows from quivers on their backs while the swordsmen in the polygons engaged the Harsdown warriors. Only Aronsdale fought in geometric patterns; the Harsdown men came on in wave after furious wave of humanity and horses.

Every time an Aronsdale warrior affected by her spells took an injury, Chime gasped, feeling a phantom sword slash her side, a blow strike to her leg, a ghost arrow bite into her arm. Each time, she sent a spell to ease the pain. She was dimly aware of Iris bedeviling Harsdown, disrupting their morale even as the queen shielded the Aronsdale combatants from similar spells sent by the dark mage.

To Chime, the battle was a chaos of fighters and horses surging across the plateau, many of the men silent with grim determination, others shouting with fury, some grunting with exertion, a few cries of pain. Men behind the Aronsdale polygons used catapults to rain rocks and small boulders over the advancing Harsdown forces while other Aronsdale soldiers engaged the Harsdown infantry.

A horse reared and threw its rider as an arrow stabbed its flank. The men protecting Iris and Chime moved closer, swords and shields ready. Chime could see Jarid nowhere. If Iris knew how her husband fared, she gave no sign. The queen's gaze had become distant, as if she fought in a place even darker than the bedlam around them.

Gradually Chime made sense out of the battle. She could distinguish the Suncroft insignia burned into the leather armor of Jarid's men. The Harsdown warriors had the cliffs of Escar emblazoned in white and black on their shields and they dyed their armor blue. Slowly but inexorably, Aronsdale was losing both ground and numbers to the blue. She clamped her hand tighter around her sphere and continued her spells.

Pain suddenly erupted in her side, not her own, but from an injury to someone else. She groaned as a pentagon-lieutenant went down, toppling off his horse, a youth who had brought her meals during the ride here and helped set up her tent. She flooded him with a spell of succor—and felt his life seeping away.

"Iris!" Chime's cry rang out.

"Aye." The queen sent a spell to the youth, helping clot the blood that pumped from his wounds, healing torn organs, easing shock. The boy dragged himself off the field and collapsed behind a boulder. His wound incapacitated him, but his life force strengthened. He would live.

In that instant, when Iris dropped her guard, the dark mage attacked. His power hit Chime like ice and she reeled under the blow. Her spells wavered, losing focus.

I protect! Chime called on her power, raising a spell into a blaze around her. She threw heat at the dark mage and his attack faltered. She reeled with the backlash of her own heat spell, a fever burning her cheeks, but she never retreated.

Then she saw him. Protected by warriors, Wareman sat

astride a white charger on the ridge. His power slid over her, oily and possessive. Hardening her resolve, she hurled a spell of loathing at him. His power receded—and came back with more force, angry. With deliberate intent, he let her feel him attack Aronsdale. She clenched her teeth as the suffering of the warriors hit her like a blow. She flooded them with spells of support, struggling to maintain her strength in the face of so much violence. Bone-tired but resolute, she continued, wrestling down her dismay. She refused to let the dark mage cow her.

Then she saw Jarid.

Tall on his horse, surrounded on all sides, he fought like a man possessed. For all that he had less ability with a sword than many other warriors, they fell on every side beneath his blade. He fought with spells, yes, not to harm but to *know*. With split-second speed, he gauged the moves of his opponents, responding to their intent almost before they knew what they planned themselves. Light blazed around him, terrifying, as if he were a celestial avenger descended to earth.

But even the king's incredible power couldn't turn the battle. Relentless and implacable, Harsdown eroded their forces.

Then the dark mage rode down the ridge.

Fear slammed through Chime. She picked up nothing from him, no response to her spells. He plunged deep into the fighting on the plateau, yet no one touched him. A sphere of protection surrounded him, as if he had mimicked Iris's shield, but twisting the spell to his own purposes, causing pain to anyone who penetrated its borders.

Then Chime realized where he was headed. She drew her dagger from her belt and spoke in a low, hard voice. "Keep away from me."

One of her guards turned. "Lady, what is it?"

She jerked her hand at Wareman. "He comes here."

Iris paled. "Then we will stop him."

Chime wasn't so certain. The battle was taking a toll greater than she could have imagined, draining her until she could barely summon her gifts. Iris had more strength, but she was flagging now as well. All the time, Wareman forged toward them. Their guards readied their swords and shields, forming a bulwark, while Chime and Iris backed up their horses. They could only go toward the open plateau on their right; behind them, the plateau plunged down in a cliff, and to their left another cliff rose up into the mountains.

An Aronsdale man broke through to Wareman, brandishing his sword. The dark mage fought him, parrying his blows with cold efficiency until he forced the man back out of his protective sphere. Chime poured her remaining strength into anger spells against Wareman. He made no attempt to counter her; instead he turned on her protectors, hitting them with infirmity and pain. He was so close, she could see a large ball hanging from his belt by a chain, its indigo metal reflecting sunlight. The saints had truly deserted them if this monster was an indigo sphere-mage.

Wareman suddenly surged forward, reaching the guards who shielded Iris and Chime. He engaged them with determination, barely seeming winded, let alone worn out by combat. Chime wouldn't have believed one man could take on seven, but even as that thought came to her, one of the Heptagons went down. Other Harsdown warriors closed in, and soon Wareman was no longer fighting alone.

Chime edged Silvermist onto the battlefield, one hand on the reins and the other clenching her dagger. Swords rang all around her. Somehow she and Iris had become separated. Leaning over her horse, she set off along the edge of the plateau, her heart beating hard.

A Harsdown man swerved toward Chime, his sword raised above her head. Her spells were ragged now, but she had become hyper-sensitized to the battle. His emotional reaction to her was so strong that for one instant she caught an image of herself in his mind. Her long yellow hair was flying about her body, disarrayed, wild, glowing in the fog. Her eyes were huge and fierce and her cloak billowed out behind her, its hood loose in the wind. She raised her dagger, its blade glittering in the misty sunlight. The warrior froze in midswing, staring at her, his mouth open—and Chime shouted at her horse, spurring it past him.

Someone grabbed at her arm, then lost his hold. She twisted around—and found herself staring into the gray eyes of the dark mage. His horse was running alongside hers, too close, kept from bolting only by a calming spell from Wareman. He grabbed at Chime, catching her around the waist. Shouting the Aronsdale battle cry, she thrust at him with her dagger. She aimed for the crack where his chain mail and armor met his helmet at his neck. He jerked to the side and her knife sliced his skin in a shallow cut.

Then he yanked her off Silvermist. Striking at him with both her fist and her dagger, she almost fell between her mount and his. Their horses kept running as he threw her stomach down onto his mount. Chime rammed her elbow at his crotch and he swore violently, though his armor protected him. The battle wheeled past while she stabbed, kicked, and struck with her fist.

He had lost the mage ball chained to his belt. She grabbed at the heavy chain that now swung free, but then she started to slide off the horse, which had outdistanced Silvermist and was pounding along the edge of the plateau. She lost her grip on the dagger and it fell to the ground, vanishing in the melee around them.

In an instant of clarity, Chime knew she would be crushed beneath the hooves of the horses if she fell. Wareman hauled her back up. He spurred his horse into an even faster pace and fled with his captured mage.

Bell Chase

Muller led his men up the Slate Incline, holding back his impatience. He forced himself to hold in Windstrider, his horse, so the charger didn't stumble on the sheets of rock that formed the long, shallow slope they were climbing. Arkandy rode at his side, his face drawn with lines that hadn't been there a few days ago.

Shouts beat against Muller's ears, coming from up ahead. He motioned at a ridge that rose to their left, then curved around and crossed their path. "They must be beyond there."

"Damn Tallwalks," Arkandy muttered. He urged his horse faster over the broken ground, surging ahead of Muller.

"Hai, slow down!" Muller called. "We will do them no good if we cripple our horses."

"Hell, Mull." But Arkandy reined in his mount.

Muller turned to his unit, which was spread out now along the incline. "Ho!" He pointed toward the ridge. "Up there."

A shout went back among the men. The terrain began to smooth out, letting them increase their pace, more and more, until they were pounding up the long incline. Muller and Arkandy reined in to a halt at the top, their horses stepping restlessly, the Hexagons gathering around them. On the other side, the ridge plunged down in a rocky slope, navigable for a steady horse, but dangerous.

Aronsdale and Harsdown had arrived before them.

A battle roiled across the plateau below the ridge where Muller gathered with his men. Swords flashed in the mist. Surrounded by men and bodies, Jarid fought like a wild spirit, a saint of chaos, his body glowing with light. On the far edge of the plateau, Iris was edging her mare around the battle, guarded by Aronsdale warriors.

With a shout, Muller sent Windstrider down the hill. Battle cries rose around him as his men surged to aid their countrymen. They came on hard, hurtling into combat, full of vigor and anger.

So the Hexagon Unit fought their first battle, the first of their lives for most of the men—and so they turned the tide of combat for Aronsdale, from desperation to survival.

Muller found Jarid standing by his horse near the cliff that rose up from the westward edge of the plateau. The king held the reins of his mount, his chest heaving as he gulped in air. Muller jumped down next to him, the two of them surrounded by men tending to horses. Far in the middle of the plateau, Fieldson was directing the clean up of a battle Aronsdale had just barely won, with the aid of the Hexagons. Muller had expected Varqelle's army to be much larger than what he had found here. It disquieted him to see so few Harsdown warriors. Where were the rest, the infantry, the archers, the rest of the cavalry?

Jarid exhaled. "You are a welcome sight, cousin."

Muller tried to grin, but it felt forced. "It looked like you might appreciate some help."

"Aye." Jarid glanced across the plateau. Following his gaze,

Muller saw Iris kneeling by a prone man. When Jarid saw her, safe and well, his brow smoothed.

Even knowing a mage queen might ride with the army, it shook Muller to discover she had fought in battle. He thanked the saints Chime was safe at Suncroft. In using his twisted spells to shield himself from the dark mage, he had cut himself off from her, too. Although he didn't expect to sense her from this far away, he couldn't help but feel a sense of loss. He wouldn't relax until he held her again.

Jarid was scanning the plateau. "Where is Chime?"

Three words. It was only three words.

They stopped Muller's world.

"Chime?" Muller stared at him. "She is at Suncroft." He suddenly, urgently needed that assurance.

Jarid turned to him, his posture growing very still. "She came with us."

"With the army?" Muller froze. "You let my wife, my *pregnant* wife, ride in an army?"

Jarid offered no excuses. He said, simply, "Yes."

"Saints almighty, *why?*"

"For the same reason you and I came." When Muller began to protest, Jarid held up his hand. "Cousin, listen. Harsdown has sent an even larger force to Suncroft. She knew that better than any of us." He motioned at the battlefield out on the plateau, littered now with shields, broken swords, arrows, and rocks from the catapults. Iris was treating the injured in a sheltered area near the western cliff.

Jarid's men had laid out the bodies of those who had lost their lives either for Aronsdale or Harsdown. They chose the northern edge of the plateau, where the Saint of the North would know to find them for their journey to the Northern Lights, the gateway to the ocean that would carry their souls to the land of the spirits.

Jarid spoke quietly. "We needed every bit of help. Had any of us not been here—Chime, Iris, you, myself, any of our soldiers—we probably would have lost this battle."

Muller couldn't hear. Wouldn't hear. "Where is she?" Unable to contain himself, he strode away, knowing his abrupt departure was an insult to the king, but afraid he would offend Jarid far more if he stayed. He couldn't bear to think of Chime in battle.

He stalked across the plateau, and soldiers stepped rapidly out of his way. They were cleaning up, tending the injured, and mourning the dead. He felt as if he were breaking inside, seeing the men he had trained, ridden with, dined with, and fought with lying broken. Or worse.

Jarid caught up to him and walked at his side, keeping his long-legged pace. At first Muller ignored him. But finally he slowed down. "I don't see her." He struggled to keep his voice calm. It didn't matter how formidable Chime could be when she set her mind to something, he still wanted to sock Jarid for bringing her with the army.

"She was with Iris," Jarid said.

Muller didn't trust himself to answer. He could see Iris kneeling by another man, a lieutenant laid out on his back. The queen had her hand around a diamond sphere that hung from a chain around her neck. As Muller came up to them, her patient looked at him with eyes surprisingly free of pain, given the wound in his side, which had soaked the bandage around his torso with blood. The fellow was hardly more than a boy, with a cowlick of hair.

Muller didn't want to interfere with her work, but he couldn't hold back his concern. "Have you seen Chime?"

Iris glanced at him. "She was with me a few minutes ago." She spoke kindly to her patient. "You must go easy for the next few days."

The youth gave a shaky nod. "I will, Your Majesty."

She smiled at him, then stood up and spoke to Muller. "Chime and I were separated in the fighting."

"Do you know what happened?" Muller asked.

"She isn't here?"

Alarm flared in Muller. "Nowhere!"

Her voice gentled. "You and she have a link. Perhaps with my help, you can reach her."

Muller was suddenly aware of the injured man listening to them. "How?"

Iris motioned a lieutenant helping her, a man with a healer's patch on his shoulder. She left her patient in his care and took Muller's arm, leading him away. Jarid followed but kept his distance.

When they were off by themselves, Iris spoke to Muller in a low voice. "Make a spell with me. Your link to Chime is stronger than mine."

He was willing to try anything. "I need a shape."

She showed him her diamond pendant. "Try this."

He tried to focus through the pendant, but it did no good; the faceted diamond had too much symmetry. Dropping his hand to the hilt of his sword, he focused on the long, stretched shape. It stirred a spell within him, but one too weak to be of any use. Then he remembered Drummer's ring, lying under his shirt. He pulled out the cord and folded his hand around the bent circle of metal.

Muller formed a green spell, striving to rebuild his link with Chime. Iris's power washed around him like a river of rainbows, enhancing his efforts. His breath caught; she had such a tremendous gift. His spell spread across the land, searching, searching...

Pain. It stabbed his temples. Instead of Chime, he had found the dark mage, running up against the mage's mind as if he had

hit wall. He tensed for the counter attack. When he felt nothing, he realized Iris had surrounded his spell with a glimmering emerald sphere that hid him from Wareman—

Emerald?

That protective sphere didn't come from Iris. Green wasn't
her color...

Muller let his spell fade, becoming aware of the army around
them. Iris was holding her diamond ball, her gaze clearing. No
one had disturbed them, probably because Jarid stood a few
steps away, his arms crossed. Several of the king's men paced
nearby, guarding the king.

"I didn't find her." Muller wondered about the green sphere,
but it had given him no sense of her location, if it did come from
her. "Only the dark mage."

Iris's gaze darkened. "He took her."

No. Muller wanted to shout his protest; it took all of his control to answer quietly. "Do you know where?"

"I only caught impressions of his mood." She looked out toward misty Aronsdale. "I think they are riding to Suncroft, to
rendezvous with Varqelle."

Muller swung around to Jarid, speaking loud enough for the
king to hear. "I must go after them."

Jarid came forward. "How will you find them?"

"I need a scout. Arkandy Ravensford."

"Take who you need. The rest of us will follow." Jarid's face
had turned grim. "We must reach Suncroft before Varqelle."

Muller knew it was impossible. But they had to try.

He couldn't bear to think of Wareman inflicting his vile person on Chime, such a sweet-natured, dulcet angel.

"You bog-warted slug!" Chime swore with gusto, using language no noblewoman would ever have known, much less spoken. "If you don't let me go, I will change you into a slime toad."

"Not likely." Wareman sounded as if he were gritting his teeth. He spurred his mount, the charger he called Snowhawk, into a pace too fast for them to talk.

With her wrists bound behind her back, Chime had trouble keeping her balance. Wareman sat behind her, his arms around her waist, the reins in his hands. Wind streamed past her face as Snowhawk raced across the valley. She didn't know whether to shake from fear or punch the cretin who had run off with her. Both would be satisfying, but she had no intention of letting him see her fear and she couldn't hit him over the head with her arms bound.

At the end of the valley, the ground sloped up into a rocky hill carpeted by wild grass. The plants were greener here than in the mountains, with star-flowers scattered everywhere. As they climbed the hill, Wareman let his horse slow down. Chime hadn't wanted to risk falling from the horse before, but at this more sedate pace, she immediately began trying to work her wrists free.

"Hold still," Wareman told her.

"You are unpardonably rude," she said. "Untie me."

"Stop twisting around, or I will——" He paused as if he hadn't thought of a suitable threat.

"Will what?" Chime redoubled her efforts.

He grabbed her upper arms, holding her in place. "I will tie your legs, too."

"How? The horse is in the way." She yanked at her bonds. "I guess I'm so terrifying, you must tie me up to protect your helpless self."

"Blustering saints, woman!"

"What do you want with me?"

"You will be my wife."

Foolish mage. "I'm already married."

"Enough," Wareman growled. "You are married only as long as Prince Muller lives."

"No! You mustn't hurt him."

"It appears I must, if I am to wed you."

"Coward. I would marry a slug first."

"Woman, silence!"

"No." She was too furious to care how he threatened her. "Untie me."

"If I untie you, will you be quiet?"

That caught her off guard. She had expected more threats. After a startled pause, she said, "All right." In truth, she was growing too tired to fight anymore. The battle had exhausted her.

Anvil worked at her bonds with one hand while he held the reins in the other. When he loosened the ropes, her arms fell free. She held back her groan of relief as she brought them in front of her body. Burn marks showed on her wrists, but the ropes hadn't cut her skin. She rubbed her arms, trying to regain the feeling in them.

They crested the top of the long slope and started down its other side, entering a forest of hardy trees, taller than those in the Tallwalks, with bristly leaves. Mist drifted around them.

After a while her captor said, "I am called Anvil the Forged."

Chime snorted.

"You should show more respect," Anvil said. "You are riding with an indigo sphere-mage."

Although Chime knew he had great power, she had nursed a hope she might have overestimated its extent. "Why do you hate everyone in Aronsdale?"

"I don't hate you." Then he added, "Though I must say, your manner of speech leaves much to desire."

"You ride with our enemies and kill our people."

He answered flatly. "Aronsdale killed my family."

"Aronsdale?"

"The people of Stonce. I was eleven years old."

Chime blanched. She couldn't imagine losing her loved ones. "I am sorry about your family."

After a moment he said, "So was I."

She hesitated. "Do you mind if I ask what happened?"

He told her then, his voice low as he related the violence that had culminated in the vicious murder of his family and the brutal use he had endured. By the time he finished, she felt tears on her face.

"I am so terribly sorry," she whispered.

He spoke numbly. "Since then, I have had no green."

It no longer surprised her. What he had experienced could have burned it out of anyone.

After that they rode in silence. Chime needed to absorb what he had told her. Although he pushed Snowhawk hard, the powerful charger easily kept the pace, moving as if it were part of the fog hanging about the trees. Red birds chittered in the branches and blue ones flitted from perch to perch. As the dusk gathered, the coos of echo-doves drifted eerily through the trees.

Chime spoke uneasily. "When do we stop?" She doubted his horse knew the way in daylight, let alone at night.

"Can't stop."

"King Jarid will catch you even if you keep going."

"Jarid." Anvil spoke as if pondering a puzzle. "The Mage King."

Chime tensed. "That's absurd." The less he knew about Jarid's mage abilities, the better.

"Oh, come now. Everyone saw him ablaze. He is a mage, Lady. A powerful one."

She doubted it would do any good to deny it. So she said nothing.

Despite his initial refusal, Anvil did eventually rein Snowhawk to a stop under a cluster of trees. "We will camp here for a few hours." He jumped down from the horse, then reached up to help her. Ignoring his offered hand, Chime slid down and landed with a thump. "And then?"

He tilted his head, considering her with a half smile. "We go to Suncroft."

"You will never take the castle." She thanked the saints he couldn't make a mood spell and know she feared otherwise. "It is impregnable."

"Is it now?" Anvil nudged her toward one of the trees. "We must eat. And rest."

Rest. She would never admit it to him, but she felt so drained, she could hardly move. However desperately she needed sleep, though, she couldn't lower her guard now.

Anvil indicated the ground by the tree. "A seat for the lady." He smirked. "Not what you're used to, eh?"

Chime thought of the orchards she loved. "It will do." She settled in the damp grass around the trunk.

He tended to Snowhawk, but he didn't shed his mail or armor, though it surely had to be uncomfortable. He kept his sword at his side as well. After they ate a supper of dried fruit and beef jerky, he gave her a blanket from his saddle bags. Chime glowered at him, unwilling to admit she was cold. She wrapped the blanket around her shoulders, but held back her shivers, determined to hide her vulnerability.

Leaning against the tree, she closed her eyes. Despite her intent to stay awake and escape from Anvil, she dropped into a fitful doze. Every few moments she stirred, then drifted off again. Then Anvil was shaking her awake. It seemed no time passed, yet pearly light filtered through the mist, which had thickened until it turned the world white and formless.

Groggy, Chime peered up at Anvil. He had never tried to touch her during the night, but now he gripped her shoulders and watched her with a frightening intensity.

"Don't look at me like that," he said.

She lifted her chin. "Like what?"

He propelled her toward Snowhawk, which he had already prepared for the ride. "I suggest you don't try my patience." He heaved her up on the horse and swung up behind her.

Chime held back her retort; better to bide her time than to goad him into taking action against her that might make it harder to escape later, if a more auspicious opportunity arose.

They set off through the fog, chewing on hard cakes. She strained to hear in the indistinct morning, but the fog muffled everything. However, she didn't sense Anvil using spells to throw off pursuit. It took green to affect perceptions, but even if he could have managed with another color, he seemed to have exhausted his power yesterday. So had she. Right now, she doubted she could do even a simple red spell.

Anvil held her around the waist as they rode. He remained as taciturn as yesterday, his mail bumpy against her back. Chime soon dozed off, her head hanging down, slowly regaining her strength...

Chime awoke with a start. The fog had lightened with daylight. She also felt lighter. Stronger. Her spells simmered, ready for use. Moving stealthily, she curled her hand around her sphere pendant. If she could reach a mood spell back along the way they had come—

"None of that." Anvil clamped his hand around hers and yanked, breaking the slender chain. It fell away from her neck, hanging down over his fingers.

"Don't." Chime clenched her hand around the sphere, her fist caught within his. "You cannot."

"I can." He pried open her fingers and wrested the sphere away from her. "A powerful shape, lady. Less than my best, but good enough."

She answered through gritted teeth. "Go to hell."

"I think not." He sounded less than amused.

Pah. Chime wished on him curses of the Saint of Foul Water, who made stagnant puddles smell bad. She studied the horse, the reins, even his boots, but saw no shapes she could use. Had the sky been clear she would have tried using the sun, but clouds covered the world.

Anvil focused with her sphere, which she could neither see nor touch now that he had stolen it. Despair settled over her. His power was too strong. She would never escape. The melancholy annoyed Chime. She fought it, knowing Anvil was using reversed yellow spells to weaken her will. His mage strength baffled her. She understood why the gifts showed up in Dawnfield males, given how they bred for the traits. But why would an entire family in a remote mountain village manifest such strength? It was unusual enough to find just one mage. The traits might run in families, but they rarely manifested with power in more than one person, and then only every few generations.

As the fog burned off, Anvil pushed Snowhawk harder. Chime needed no spell to recognize his tension; he had few defenses here. He had fled the battle yesterday, but she doubted King Varqelle would consider it desertion. He needed Anvil at Suncroft. He had probably ordered his mage to avoid capture at all costs.

A bird called through the trees, a waterfall of notes. It reminder her of the songbird that had died from sleep gas. That gave Chime pause. Dignitaries from Jazid, a country far to the southeast of Aronsdale, had presented it to Muller. No birds native to these hills could make such trills. So where had it come from?

The bird warbled, closer now.

Chime stiffened, then tried to relax, lest she give away her interest in the bird. Could someone be trying to let her know they were following? It could be men from the King's Army, come to capture Anvil. Or it could be nothing. The chirps of many birds and insects leavened the day, though she hadn't noticed before. Perhaps she had imagined the other—

There! The trill was closer, a unique call.

"Why do you keep tensing up?" Anvil demanded.

"Why do you think?" She didn't need to put on an act to communicate her loathing; it came naturally.

"You don't like me, eh?" He pulled a length of her hair. "You had better get used to me, gold girl."

"My name is Chime."

"Aye. Chime Headwind." He spoke dryly. "Or was that Headstrong?"

She ignored him.

The trill came again—and this time Chime caught a flash of purple among the trees.

Anvil swore and kicked his horse. "Go!"

Snowhawk took off like a streamer through the fog, his white coat glowing in the pearly light.

"You're done for!" Chime said.

"Quiet!" He urged the horse faster.

Chime suspected then that their pursuers had just notified each other that they had found her and Anvil, using a trill that only they would recognize—which meant they probably came from Suncroft.

"You're finished," she said, twisting in his hold.

Anvil grabbed her roughly. "Hold still!"

They were going too fast now for her to answer. Snowhawk broke out of the woods onto a long, lush slope that stretched down to a rolling meadow. Anvil gave the horse full rein and its stride ate up distance. Shouts came from the trees. Craning her head around, Chime saw a rider burst out of the woods, a man on a black charger, his hair streaming behind him, gold in the luminous morning.

"Muller!" The wind grabbed her words and threw them away, but she didn't care. Saints, she relished seeing him!

Anvil yanked her around. Clenching her fist, she rammed her elbow into his torso. It hit his armor and he grunted with surprise. Turning, she struck him against the side of the head, though it made her shift precariously on Snowhawk. He raised his arm, warding off the blow, his face furious, then shoved her to the front again.

Snowhawk kept running, undaunted by the pursuit. With dismay, Chime realized they were outdistancing Muller. She grabbed the reins, yanking, trying to slow them down. She would rather risk falling than have Anvil escape. The horse stumbled, then regained its stride.

"Are you crazy!" Anvil struck her across the back. "You will kill us both."

Chime gritted her teeth, but she kept struggling with him, trying to slow down Snowhawk. At the bottom of the slope, the ground became muddy, interfering more with the horse's pace. Twisting around, she saw Muller gaining on them and another rider farther back. Relief swept over her: Anvil wouldn't make it. Muller would catch them.

Suddenly Anvil reined in his horse, pulling so hard that Snowhawk reared and trumpeted his protest. Chime held on, clinging to the horse's neck. He came down with pounding hooves, agitated and ready to bolt. Anvil maneuvered him around to face the way they had come, right in line with Muller's approach.

Muller rode forward, slowing down. Chime recognized the second rider behind him, Arkandy, his approach wary and careful.

A short distance away, Muller reined Windstrider to a halt. "Are you all right?" he asked Chime.

"Don't speak," Anvil told her. He drew his sword, letting it slide close to her leg. She froze, aware of its honed edge. In her side vision, she saw him raise the weapon, the blade glinting.

"Coward," Chime muttered. "You haven't the skill to best him."

"Be quiet," Anvil said in a voice only she could hear.

Muller's face hardened. "Don't hurt her."

"You want her back, eh?" Anvil snorted. "I can't imagine why."

Arkandy walked his horse to Muller and reined in next to the prince. Chime didn't fool herself that Anvil had no chance against three of them. She had felt the power of his spells.

Muller drew his weapon, a beautifully crafted blade with round gems in the pummel. Arkandy put his hand on the hilt of his sword but went no further.

"Interesting," Anvil commented. "How do you plan on fighting me while your wife sits here?"

Muller's jaw worked. "You would hide behind a defenseless woman?"

"Defenseless?" Anvil made an incredulous noise. "That tongue of hers could level the Tallwalk Mountains."

Muller looked ready to explode, but he held his temper. Chime concentrated on the gems in Muller's sword. She was too far away to focus her full strength through them, but a spell stirred within her.

Dizzy, she thought, fanning the scrap of power. Then she threw the spell at Anvil. When it hit him, she reeled as well, her head spinning as if she had been twirling in circles.

"Ah—" Anvil swayed behind her, his sword dipping. Then he clenched Chime's tunic. "So," he said to Muller. "You do have shape-power."

"You speak nonsense," Muller said.

"So it was Lady Chime." Anvil shifted behind her, his sword poised near her shoulder. Then she realized he was coaxing Snowhawk to back up.

Muller's forehead creased. He nudged Windstrider forward, following step by step. Arkandy came with him, slowly, everyone careful not to startle anyone else. As Anvil retreated, he lowered his sword until the flat of the blade rested on Chime's leg.

Muller's face paled. "You have nothing to gain by injuring my wife."

"True," Anvil said. "She has more value as a hostage."

"What do you want?" Muller asked. They all continued to move across the plain in their odd, cautious procession.

"Free passage away from here," Anvil told him. "When I reach Suncroft, I will release her."

A muscle jerked in Muller's cheek. "We know Varqelle is riding to Suncroft. You will take her to him."

Anvil didn't answer. As they continued their strange walk, Chime felt him concentrating on the sphere he had stolen from her. His spell gathered. Alarmed, she focused again on the gems in Muller's sword, but he was too distant now. She knew then why Anvil backed up; it moved her away from shapes she could use to make spells. She tried to draw on the sphere Anvil had taken from her, but she could do nothing without seeing or touching the orb.

Anvil's spell continued to grow. The air became hot and indigo light brightened around them. His sword blade felt heavy against her leg.

Muller's face blurred in the light. "If you hurt her, I will see you die."

"I doubt it," Anvil said. The heat worsened; within moments, it could be hot enough to ignite grass.

Angry, knowing Anvil intended yet again to dishonor his gifts, Chime concentrated harder on the gems in Muller's sword, straining until her head throbbed. A faint spell awoke within her. Instead of attempting to counter Anvil, who had far more power, she latched on to his spell—and *shoved*.

The heat suddenly diminished, shifting instead into brighter light, hard on the eyes but far more benign.

Anvil swore. "What the blazes?"

Chime smirked. "Actually, no blazes." She couldn't overcome his power, but she could funnel it into a positive spell.

Then she moved.

Chime jerked hard, twisting in his hold, catching him off guard while he struggled with his faltering spell. The edge of his sword sliced her leg, cutting through the tunic and her skin. Losing her balance, she toppled off the horse. Snowhawk's body went by in a white blur. She hit the ground with a jarring impact, her arms crumpled under her body as she tried to break the shock. Her leg twisted, wrenching the sword gash, and she gasped.

Chime scrambled to her feet, but she seemed to move in molasses, especially her leg. The world slowed down. Anvil jumped off his horse, reaching toward her with one hand while he raised his sword with the other. Muller lunged forward, parrying with him, and their swords rang together.

Stunned, unable to react fast enough, Chime stumbled backward until she hit the trunk of a tree. It jolted her time awareness back to normal. She stared in dismay as Muller and Anvil battled on the meadow, trampling grass, their swords slicing the air. Before today, she had loved to watch Muller practice, admiring his grace, but she saw nothing beautiful in his movements now, knowing he could die if he missed a blow.

Although Snowhawk stepped away from the commotion, he didn't run. Arkandy slid off his mount, grasping its reins. He moved toward Muller's horse, but Windstrider shied away. True to the code of shape-warriors, Arkandy made no attempt to interfere with Muller and Anvil; it would have been dishonorable. Right now, Chime couldn't care less about codes; she wanted her husband to survive. Period. Nothing else mattered.

Muller and Anvil seemed evenly matched, but as they lunged back and forth, their feet dancing in intricate patterns, Chime realized Muller had the advantage of his longer arms. His slender build also hid a physique far more muscled than people realized. Now he used his strength and flexibility to drive Anvil back. Sweat dripped off their faces and ran down their armor and mail, which gave some protection, but interfered with mobility.

Suddenly Anvil lunged, not at Muller, but toward Snowhawk, making a break for freedom. Muller blocked his way—so Anvil whirled and ran for Windstrider instead.

Caught off guard, Muller hesitated for one moment; in that instant, Anvil reached the charger and vaulted onto its back. Windstrider reared in protest, trying to throw him off, but Anvil held on. He shouted at the horse and hit it hard with his heels. The startled animal bolted then, racing across the meadow.

"No!" Muller slammed his sword back into its sheath and ran after them, his long legs pumping hard, eating up the distance.

"Mull, you can't catch him!" Arkandy yelled. He shook his head as Muller kept running. He watched for a moment, then looked around the meadow. When he saw Chime flattened against the tree, he came over to her.

"Are you all right?" Arkandy asked, his gentle voice a startling contrast to his implacable appearance.

Chime nodded, though she was shaking for some reason. She couldn't feel the wound in her leg. "I'm fine."

Anvil had ridden so far ahead now, he was barely visible in the hills. Muller gave up trying to catch him and headed back, covering ground in his long, loping run. It finally hit Chime that nothing was keeping them apart. She took off, limping as fast as her injured leg allowed. Neither of them slowed much as they drew nearer, so they ran right into each other. Laughing and crying, they embraced, and she hugged him hard, so grateful to have him alive and whole that she couldn't speak.

For a long time they held each other. With her head against his shoulder, she could see his pulse in the veins of his neck. Gradually, as their hearts slowed, they pulled apart.

"I knew you had come north," she said. "Everyone thought I was wrong. But I knew."

He managed to smile. Then he kissed her, his lips eager. Chime melted against him, closing her eyes, aware of nothing but how it felt to touch him again.

Someone cleared his throat.

They turned with self-conscious laughs. Arkandy stood a few paces away, holding the reins of his horse and those of Snowhawk, the charger Anvil had left behind. It was a beautiful animal, with fine breeding and clear eyes.

Arkandy offered Snowhawk's reins to Muller. "It seems you have a new horse."

Muller scowled. "Windstrider will never tolerate that dark mage."

"He is a good rider," Chime said, wishing otherwise. "And he treats his animal well." She disliked having to admit Anvil had any good qualities. Windstrider had always been loyal to Muller, and he had a charger's fiery personality, but unfortunately he also tended to respond to riders who knew how to treat a horse.

Muller let Snowhawk snuffle around him. "She is well cared for," he admitted. He regarded Chime and Arkandy uneasily. "We must get to Suncroft as soon as possible."

Chime heard what he left unsaid: they had to arrive before King Varqelle could take the castle.

The Relentless Waves

The Pentagons, Hexagons, and Heptagons poured over the hills above Croft's Vale, interspersed with the King's Archers, rank after rank of warriors. Chime stood with Muller and Jarid at the top of a ridge while men streamed past them and down into the fields. Pages had taken their horses to tend and feed. On a higher hill, across the village, Suncroft reached its spires into the sky.

King Varqelle's army had arrived first.

The Harsdown army surrounded the castle. They had already overrun and looted the village, though they had let its people flee to the hills. With Croft's Vale subdued, they moved on, filling the slopes and meadows, settling in for what would have been a siege had Stonehammer's forces prevailed in the north. Instead the Aronsdale army spilled across the land, ready to challenge them for Suncroft, the crown jewel of the realm.

Muller stared at the massed army. "Saints."

"Hardly." Jarid sounded as if he were gritting his teeth. "Devils, more like."

Just men following their king, Chime thought, weary. She felt only dismay that her premonition about Varqelle bringing a substantial army to Suncroft had been accurate. A pall hung over her, the exhaustion of spending the last eleven days tending to wounded men, helping Iris and Jarid. She couldn't heal, but she could ease the pain of the soldiers, giving comfort. The royals worked alongside the army medics, using magecraft to aid the mundane treatments of splinting broken bones, cleaning wounds, and the like.

Jarid turned as Iris came up to them. He held out his arm to her. "How are our patients?"

She took his arm. "Impatient to heal."

"A good sign."

"Aye."

Fieldson approached them, accompanied by Arkandy and several other men. When Jarid nodded, the general said, "We've fifty-eight men able to fight in the polygons, about thirty archers, and another forty or so with injuries. Maybe twenty of the injured could fight if necessary."

Moisture gathered in Chime's eyes, as it had other times since the battle. Iris had told her of the memorial service they held on the plateau that day, for the warriors who lost their lives, both those of Aronsdale and Harsdown.

Fieldson looked out at the distant army camped around the castle, his gaze bleak. Hundreds, even thousands, of warriors had converged on Suncroft. After a moment, he said, "We have General Stonehammer as a hostage."

Jarid pulled back his blowing hair, catching it into a warrior's knot on his neck, redoing the ragged leather tie. "Perhaps Varqelle will negotiate for him."

"Perhaps."

Iris indicated the distant castle. "The Quadron, Octagon, and Nonagon Units are within Suncroft's walls."

"They should be," Muller said.

"That would give us another one hundred and sixty-four polygon warriors, counting their three commanders," Chime said. "Add to that the six hundred we have in archers and other infantry, and we've almost nine hundred."

Fieldson let out a tired breath. "But the polygons are the key of our offense, the way they work with the mages and coordinate the army. Three of our prime units are diminished." He indicated where Penta-Colonel Burg walked with one of his pentahedron-majors, deep in discussion. "He no longer has a pentagon of pentagons. Right now they are one square and a rectangle of triangles. Either that, or a quadrilateral of four-sided figures. They have trained to cope with such losses, but it isn't how they were optimized to fight. The same is true for the Heptagons and Hexagons. You may not be able to work with them at all. Their formations are imperfect."

His last sentence caught Chime off guard. Nor was it only her. Muller stared at him, his mouth open. "Saints all-blowing-mighty!"

Fieldson blinked at him. "I beg your pardon?"

Muller turned red, the flush bright on his pale skin. "My apologies. I had never thought of a reduced polygon unit in exactly those terms."

Fieldson scowled. "Well, you should have."

Chime could tell Muller didn't mean what Fieldson thought. Of course Muller knew polygons would be less effective in a second battle if the first had eroded their numbers. But he hadn't realized he could work with such polygons—as a mage. He had spent his life suppressing his gifts, in a country that had known no major conflict for generations. Even in the days when they had gone to war, mages had contributed as she and Iris had done in the Tallwalks. He worried his flawed spells might hurt his men's ability to fight. And that could happen.

But he might also have abilities that would be invaluable to the army, if he could learn to use them. Had the ancients who created the chamber of flawed shapes in the Mage Tower intended to create a war mage?

Jarid and Iris were watching Muller, comprehension in their gazes. They couldn't reveal him as a mage now; the shock could disrupt morale, particularly if the army feared their commander would make spells that could go awry. They had no time to prepare either Muller or his men. But this gave an entirely new slant on his gifts.

When Fieldson began to look puzzled by the silence, Iris spoke up. "General, do we have a count yet of Varqelle's men?"

He motioned to Arkandy. The hexahedron-major stepped forward and spoke. "My scouts estimate one thousand five hundred, Your Majesty."

Jarid grimaced. "And they are rested. We are not."

"Our men are eager to fight." Arkandy's voice sparked with anger. "This is our home."

"We also know this land," Iris said. "They don't."

"And we have five mages," Chime said. "Three here, two in Suncroft. Varqelle has only one."

Jarid laid his hand on the hilt of his sword. "Pray that will be enough."

Varqelle the Cowled sat in the darkwood throne in his tent, his long legs stretched out, his elbow resting on the arm of the chair, a mug of hot, spiced wine in his hand. He wore his leather armor and sword belt, though he had removed his chain mail. Diamond studs glinted in his ears.

King Varqelle considered the Aronsdale messenger who stood before him, his forehead sheened with sweat. The man was a hexahedron-major, a solid fellow with tangled curls that might be brown when they were clean. He had come without weapon, shield, mail, or armor, wearing only dark trousers, a wrinkled shirt that looked as if he had slept in it, and dusty boots. Varqelle had no doubt the man had ridden with Jarid's army from the Tallwalks; anyone stationed here wouldn't appear so travel weary.

"Arkandy Ravensford." Varqelle let him stand while he sat comfortably, scrutinizing the tired man. "I have never heard the name."

"It is not a common one, Your Majesty." The stiff quality of Ravensford's voice matched his posture.

"Oh, I don't know," Varqelle murmured. "It sounds common to me."

Ravensford's ruddy cheeks flushed, but he made no response. Varqelle noted the man's self-control. This one would conduct himself well in battle. He had lived through the Tallwalk engagement, which suggested he had skill with a sword. The Harsdown warriors who had survived and made it to Suncroft described it as a brutal combat.

Varqelle thought of the men he had lost in that battle and his anger sparked. Yes, warriors died in war, but that changed nothing of his disquiet or sorrow at losing such good men. Some of the fighters had been mercenaries, however, including those who deserted his forces after they lost the engagement. He would attend to them later. About thirty of his men had made it here to Suncroft. He doubted many others would arrive; those who had escaped, had stayed together. Jarid had managed to take no prisoners.

Except one.

"So." Varqelle took a long swallow of wine from his mug. The spices burned his throat. "King Jarid wants to bargain, eh?"

"General Stonehammer is unharmed," Ravensford said. "He would return to you as he left."

"So you say." Although Varqelle maintained an outward nonchalance, Stonehammer's capture disturbed him. Jarid's forces had let the other Harsdown warriors escape as they concentrated on catching the one of greatest value. Varqelle depended on the general, a brilliant strategist who knew how to shape and train an army. The king intended to conquer other lands after he took Aronsdale, including the Misted Cliffs west of Harsdown. Especially the Misted Cliffs. He would reclaim his pale, lovely wife and his son. To ensure the success of those conquests, he needed Stonehammer. But Stonehammer would be the first to advise against compromising his chances of success here.

Varqelle sipped his wine while Ravensford stood before him, his boots denting the Shazire carpet. Finally the king lowered his mug. "What does Jarid want in return for my general?"

The major met his gaze. "Anvil the Forged."

Varqelle didn't even bother to laugh. "Try again."

"Stonehammer for Anvil."

"The mage is of greater value than the general." It was true. Varqelle had more confidence in Stonehammer; he trusted Stonehammer more, though he trusted no one fully; and he considered the general a friend, as much as he was capable of friendship with anyone. But regardless of all that, Anvil had more value.

"I will guarantee safe passage to the mage queen out of Aronsdale after the war," Varqelle offered. In truth, whether or not he let Iris Larkspur go would depend on whether or not she pleased him. The bargain meant nothing; after Varqelle defeated Aronsdale, Jarid would be in no position to demand compliance with any agreements.

The major crossed his arms. "That is no reason for King Jarid to return Stonehammer now."

"True. But it is the only trade you will get."

Ravensford's jaw tightened.

"You may tell your young king this." Varqelle sat back in

his chair. "After I have taken Suncroft, I will negotiate the terms of Jarid's surrender. At that time, we will discuss Stonehammer."

Ravensford never lost his composure. "His Majesty is willing to bargain with you now for the general. The same may not be true after his army has defeated yours."

Varqelle set his mug on a table next to his chair and rose to his feet. He stood a head taller than the major. "Understand me. General Stonehammer is a good man. He doesn't deserve whatever your king plans for him. But the general would no more expect me to compromise this campaign for him than your Cube-General Fieldson would expect such of King Jarid."

Ravensford's gaze never wavered. "You won't take Aronsdale."

"Oh, I think I will." He gestured in the direction of the castle, his long fingers lazy in the air. "My agents tell me how many soldiers hide within Suncroft. And I've seen what remains of your other units. You have no chance. You will lose." When Ravensford started to answer, his face flushed, Varqelle turned his hand palm out toward the man. "You are alone, here, Hexahedron-Major. You came without weapons. I respect that. I will let you leave in the same manner." His voice deepened. "But do not try my good will. It may not hold."

Ravensford took a deep breath. Then he bowed, his movements stiff. "At your leave, Your Majesty."

"You may go."

So Ravensford went back out into the chill night. Varqelle picked up his wine and sipped it slowly, considering the tent flap that swung from the major's departure. Varqelle felt tired, though he had hidden it from his visitor. He had no liking for the battle they would fight with Jarid Dawnfield and his army tomorrow. But fight he would, for his desire to expand his territories was greater than his reluctance to kill. One day his name would be remembered in all the history scrolls, the visionary who made Harsdown an empire. Varqelle the Mighty.

Yes, they would remember his name.

On a blustery morning in autumn, when brittle leaves blew across the land and a chill turned the wind sharp, the armies of Aronsdale and Harsdown met in the trampled meadows below Suncroft. They turned the formerly idyllic countryside into a battlefield.

The polygon units within the castle swept out into the combat, a human wave pouring down the hill. The armies surged back and forth, attacking, retreating, surging forward again. Harsdown always pressed toward the castle, climbing its hill and being beaten back, only to force its way forward again.

So it was that under the watery light of a sun veiled by thin clouds, war came to Aronsdale.

Vale of the Sun

For Chime, the day blurred. The Mage Guard of the King's Army hid her and Iris in the woods on a hill well above the fighting, a walk of ten minutes from the battle. Chime could see the combat, but with several thousand men fighting, she could locate no one in particular. Beyond the battlefields and their roiling armies, Castle Suncroft raised its spires into the sky.

Chime focused through the large faceted ball she had brought with her, imagining golden hues, the color of confidence, until a shimmering haze surrounded her. She sent the spell to the Aronsdale warriors, flowing it across the land. *Success*, she willed. *You shall triumph. You are strong and alive.*

She couldn't see Jarid, but she sensed him in her magescape. He flared like lightning. Surely a king should stay back, protected, but he refused, driven to battle with single-minded intensity. Never did she feel him use spells to injure, but that changed nothing. With his sword, he killed again and again, and it exacted a price on his conscience he would never forgive.

She couldn't find Muller in her magescape, but she felt his presence. Several times, when her spells broke on the jagged edges of polygon units, he reached out, trying to help—and her spells surged in power. Then his presence would vanish again, his concentration turned to battle and survival.

It had agonized Chime to see him ride to war this morning. She prayed for his return tonight. When soldiers began carrying wounded men to her, she submerged her fears in work. She bandaged and soothed, easing pain while Iris staunched gashes, set broken bones, and wove her spells. Then she would turn back to the battle, pouring her spells into the polygons as best she could manage.

The combat raged until Chime lost all sense of time. Always when the injured came in, she looked for Muller. Always she asked after him. Her heart sang when someone reported seeing him alive; her mood plunged when no one could say if he lived. Day faded into evening and still the injured came. The battle raged and the polygons fragmented. She and Iris alternated between helping the injured and using their spells in the battle. She worked in a daze, calling on her deepest resources.

Finally, in exhaustion, she fell asleep sitting up, her head falling forward, blood-soaked bandages in her hands.

A trill awoke Chime. She stirred, reassured by the melodies of her songbird. Then she remembered; her bird had died. She heard only the familiar warble of redwing night-canaries so common throughout Aronsdale.

She opened her eyes to see a drowsing camp, warriors sleeping fitfully around her like a bulwark, lit by the ghostly light of an Azure Moon. Iris slept nearby, leaning against a tree, her arms limp at her sides, a blanket across her lap. Warriors paced through the trees, sentries on patrol. Some of the injured moaned in their dreams. In instinct, Chime formed a spell to counter their pain.

Silence had otherwise fallen over the countryside. The armies had apparently withdrawn to recover and recoup. She hadn't realized they would do such; subconsciously she had expected them to keep fighting. The exhaustion of the hundreds of men spread across the hills pressed down on her; both armies were drained. Death had parched their ranks. Many of the soldiers wanted to return home. She felt the same.

Moving stiffly, Chime stood up, her joints aching. A sentry came over, a tall man in battered armor. "How do you feel, milady?" He indicated her leg, which was newly healed from the wound Anvil had given her. "Does it cause you trouble?"

"Nay. It is fine." Hope filled her. "Have you news of my husband? Commander Dawnfield?"

"My apology, ma'am. I don't know."

She tried to hide her disappointment. "No need to apologize, kind sir."

"Would you be liking something to eat?" He indicated a slope that rolled down slightly from where they stood in the direction of the battlefield. "We've stew down by the campfire."

"I would like a little, yes." She nodded her thanks and limped toward the slope. When he tried to help her, she waved him away, not wanting to appear weak.

The campfire had died to embers. A few men sat around it on logs, and others patrolled the area. Chime intended to stop for food, but she felt too restless to sit. So she walked on past the fire. Sentries watched as she paced, but none stopped her.

Finally she reached the edge of the woods. She stood under a tree and stared across the battlefield below to the hill where Suncroft stood in the distance. Torches burned on its walls and in many windows, turning it gold even in the night. She couldn't bear to think of that beauty falling into Varqelle's hands.

A sentry approached. As he drew near, she spoke in a relieved whisper. "Arkandy!"

He grinned, coming to stand with her under the tree. He had taken off his upper armor and wore only a plain shirt. "A good eve, Lady Chime."

"And to you." She swallowed. "I can't find Muller."

He motioned to the castle. "He and the king retreated with Cube-General Fieldson within its walls."

Relief poured through her. "It is secure then?"

"Nay, Lady, not at all. It isn't safe for you to go."

Chime winced. Arkandy knew her too well. "I had the impression earlier today that the battle had turned in our favor."

"For a while." He lifted his hands and let them drop again. "But then it changed. It is this mage, Anvil the Forged. He has such power. He destroys our will."

She thought of Anvil, trapped in the horrors of his past until he turned the lives of everyone around him into similar misery. "I heard Varqelle refused to trade him for Stonehammer."

Arkandy's gaze darkened. "Yes."

"What is our situation, then?"

He spoke slowly, as if choosing his words with care. "There are many of them and fewer of us. But we are better fighters and we recover faster. We might have a chance if it wasn't for Anvil." He stretched, rubbing the small of his back. "Muller says the dark mage has no remorse for abusing his gifts."

"None." Chime told him what Anvil had described of his childhood. It was hard even to say the words. "Day after day of that treatment, ending in the death of his family—it burned out his ability to feel."

"So he wants vengeance."

"Yes."

"Why didn't his family leave the village?"

"I've wondered, too." Chime shook her head. "And it is odd they had such powers. I've made inquiries. Stonce is a hamlet in the north, very ingrown. Its people marry one another. If

Anvil's family had gifts, surely others would as well. But apparently no one else there does."

"You were the only mage in Jacob's Vale."

Chime thought of what Muller had told her about his visit to her home. "Some people there showed traces of mage talent, including my brothers and my mother." Now that she knew what to look for, she remembered many other signs as well. "My girlfriend Merry is probably a red mage who can use squares. And Jacob's Vale isn't as ingrown as Stonce."

Arkandy exhaled. "Whatever the truth, Anvil is here now." He stretched his arms, cracking his knuckles. "Shall I walk you back to camp? Then I must return to my rounds."

"If it is all right, I would like to remain here." She glanced at Suncroft, so beautiful in the night.

"We've a good number of sentries here, but best that you don't wander, Lady."

"I won't." She glanced at him. "And Arkandy."

"Aye?"

"Thank you."

He blinked. "It is a small thing to let someone stand under a tree."

Her face gentled. "I meant for your loyalty and friendship to Muller."

"Ah, well." He gave a gruff laugh. "The fellow needs me around, eh? He used to be so accident prone, I had to pick him up half the time."

She wondered what Arkandy would think if he knew the truth about Muller's accidents. "He is a lucky fellow."

Arkandy grinned. "Aye, that he is." With a salute, he sauntered back to his rounds.

Chime stood watching the castle and the countryside for a while. Scattered fires burned on hills to the west and north, where Varqelle's men had hunkered down for the night. Nothing stirred in the battlefields around Suncroft, an eerie contrast to the ferocity that had swept across them earlier today.

The redwings trilled every now and then, but the other birds in the area seemed to have fled, leaving only the chirping of insects. Even they were subdued by the presence of so many warriors. Rustles came from the men on patrol, and a snore here and there.

Chime walked along the edge of the woods, westward toward Suncroft. She soon reached a point where she would have to leave the shelter of the trees to approach the castle any closer. Even knowing she should go back to sleep and conserve her strength, she stayed, lured by the deceptive tranquility of the golden fortress.

She made a decision. Before she could think about it and lose her nerve, she ran out from the forest and down the slope. Her feet thudded on ground packed down by hundreds of booted feet earlier in the day. Racing hard, she imagined herself as a nighthawk soaring across the land. The sleeves of her gray tunic billowed with the wind of her passing. She reached the bottom of the hill and sprinted up the slope toward Suncroft, painfully aware that if any Harsdown sentry looked in this direction, he would see her out in the open.

As she neared the castle, it rose up before her, its walls lit by torches and darkened by shadows. The great entrance was closed, as were the side doors by the gate.

"Saints almighty," a voice whispered. "Lady Chime, here!" A hexa-major stepped out from the shadows, an older man with graying hair.

Chime skidded to a stop next to him, her breath coming in gasps. "Good eve, sir."

He grabbed her arm and pulled her to one of the small doors, into the protection of its recessed doorway. "What the blazes are you doing? It isn't safe to come here."

"Is Prince Muller here?"

The major scowled mightily. "Inside." He unlocked the door with a ten-sided ring of keys. The massive portal creaked opened into a chamber, also ten-sided in shape, where people could leave boots and gear. Two sentries inside watched them, eyebrows raised, and a third stepped outside, taking the place of the man who was bringing in Chime.

"Why didn't King Jarid call us back here?" she asked.

"It isn't safe. Varqelle's mage has breached the castle." The hexa-major shook his head. "No one has found him yet, but the king says his spells are everywhere, interfering, damaging." He led her across the room to a door. "No one has seen him. Perhaps it is his spells."

Chime nodded. If someone caught sight of Anvil, he could make an "overlook" spell that would encourage them to forget his presence, overlook him so to speak. The more they saw of him, the less an overlook spell would work, but if it was only a glimpse, it could succeed.

But no—an overlook spell worked by changing a person's mood, so they remembered an emotion incompatible with whatever the mage wished them to forget. That required the one color Anvil couldn't use.

"He can't hide that way," Chime said. "He can't make green spells."

The major grunted. "Well, no one can find him."

As the major opened the door, Chime focused on the vine carved into its border, a scalloped representation of shape-blossoms. Using its rounded depressions, she made an emotion spell and searched for Anvil, whose signature had become all too familiar to her.

"It is true." She let her spell fade. "He is here."

"You feel it, too?"

"Like oil on water."

"So." The sentry ushered her into the hall. "Your husband will not be pleased you've come, milady."

She gave him one of her quelling looks. "And why is that? I live here."

The major cleared his throat. "Uh, well, ma'am, he says—" He ground to a stop, his cheeks flushed.

"Yes?" Chime asked, all sweetness.

"That, ah..."

"What does he say, Hexa-Major?"

He straightened his back as if he were preparing to face a regiment of Harsdown warriors. "He says, most gracious lady, that you get yourself into all sorts of trouble and he intends to put a stop to that behavior."

"Does he now?" Chime gave the alarmed major her most honeyed smile. "We will see about that. Lead on, sir."

"Ah, yes." His face red, the major led on.

Muller frowned, intent on the plans of the castle. It had been almost a century since these schematics had been recopied; the scrolls had become curled and yellowed from age, with tears in the edges of the parchment. He, Jarid, Fieldson, and Brant had spread them out on a large table in Jarid's Octagon Room, holding them open with statuettes at their corners. Now he and the two advisors stood around the table, leaning over the scrolls, searching for signs of hidden passages or rooms that might shield an unwelcome mage.

He wished they had Della's help; she knew this castle at least as well as he. But she was in charge of the infirmary, helping Skylark tend the wounded—and the dying.

A knock came at the door.

Muller glanced up, puzzled, an odd apprehension tickling his throat. Could some menace await them on the other side of the door?

Cube-General Fieldson straightened, looking at the king. "Shall I answer?"

Jarid continued to study one of the parchments, tracing his finger along lines indicating a corridor. He had an eerie intensity, inwardly focused. Muller suspected his cousin knew far more than the rest of them about finding places he had never seen.

After a while, Muller said, "Jarid?"

"Eh?" The king absently waved his hand at Fieldson. "Go ahead."

As the general crossed the room, Brant pointed out another set of rooms on a scroll of the second level in the castle. "You see that ring of five-sided chambers? They don't fit together. Spaces exist between them."

"Those are broom closets," Muller said.

Jarid spoke mildly, still intent on the map. "She will pulverize you, Mull."

Muller blinked. "She?"

Jarid stood up straight, a smile playing about his lips. "Your wife."

"My wife?"

Brant looked at them, his hand braced against a map. "Lady Chime is safe with the army."

At that moment Fieldson opened the door.

"Good eve, Cube-General," a melodious voice said. A golden vision swept into the room, her disheveled hair tumbling over her wool tunic and leggings. She came forward and stopped across the table from Muller. Her lovely smile did nothing to hide the flash of her eyes.

"My greetings, husband," she said.

Ah, hell. Muller knew the signs. He was in trouble. But he was the lord in their family, a prince of Aronsdale. He refused to be intimidated. Pulling himself up to his full height, he glared at her. "What the blazes are you doing here?"

"I am glad to see you, too," she said sweetly. "So here you are, warm and comfortable in our home while your wife sleeps in the woods and agonizes over your safety."

Muller crossed his arms. "You should be out there with the army. You have no idea what we face in here."

She looked around the Octagon Room, her gaze lingering on the fire in the hearth, the tapestries, the goblets of wine on a nearby octagonal table. Then she gave Muller another of her devastating smiles. "I see your terrible hardship here. My sympathies."

"Chime." He made his voice stern. "You must follow the orders of my officers in the field."

She put her hand on her hip. "Yes, well, you're so convinced you know what is best for me, you are hoisting yourself on your own metaphorical sword."

Muller blinked. "What did you say?" Whoever mistakenly thought his wife didn't have a biting intellect had never faced her in one of these moods.

She made an exasperated noise. "I can help you, my handsome but befuddled husband."

His face flamed with a blush. He saw Fieldson at the end of the table now, holding his chin, his fingers over his mouth as he tried to hide a smile. Brant and Jarid were watching, too. He gave Chime his most formidable stare. "Wife," he thundered. "You will obey me."

"Oh, Mull." Chime sighed. "I didn't come to bedevil you. I really can help."

He could tell she believed it. But that didn't change the necessity that she leave Suncroft as soon as possible. "Your magecraft is a great asset, Chime. But you should be as far away from here as possible. You don't know about the danger."

"You mean Anvil?" she asked.

Saints above. How had she known? It didn't help that Jarid,

the always brooding king, was grinning. At least Fieldson had the discretion to hide his smile. Muller glowered at the king. "You find it amusing that my wife risked her life to come here?"

Jarid waved his hand. "You try telling her she can't do what she wants. See how well it works for you."

Muller frowned at Chime. "You must go back."

"It wouldn't be safe to run around in the dark out there," she said, using her most sensible voice.

Muller slapped his hand on the table. "Then why are you here? It wasn't safe to come, either."

"You need my help."

"I need you to stay put when the army tells you to stay put."

Chime fixed him with a formidable stare. "Do you want me to find Anvil for you or not?"

"No! I don't want you anywhere near him."

"I don't have to go near him."

"How did you know he was here?" Muller meant to be firm, but he sounded bewildered instead.

At the sound of his confusion, her posture eased. "Ah, love." She came around the table, not stopping until she stood right next to him. "Do not worry so."

Seeing her soften relieved him so much that he almost reached for her, wanting her warm and lovely body in his arms. He couldn't do it with his audience, of course. But he did lower his voice. "You sense Anvil?"

"I recognize his emotions."

Jarid spoke. "You can feel his moods?"

She turned to the king. "Yes. His inability to use mood spells doesn't mean other mages can't sense him. I think even he can sense green power. He just can't invoke it." She shuddered, folding her arms for warmth. "His mind is...slippery somehow. Wrong."

"And you believe you have located him?" Fieldson came

around the table to Jarid so she wouldn't have to turn from the king to speak to him.

"Roughly," Chime said. "He is in this wing of the castle."

"That is more than we knew." Muller wanted to be angry with her, and he would be later, when he didn't have an audience. But apparently she did have important help to give them. "We weren't even sure he was here."

Her face paled. "Can't you feel him?"

He froze, afraid Fieldson would understand what she meant. Only another mage would "feel" Anvil's presence.

Jarid answered as if she had spoken to him. "Only in a vague sense. More than that, I cannot say."

"But you wield so much more power than the rest of us," Chime said.

The king shrugged. "We each have our strengths. Green isn't mine. I am less attuned to him than you."

Even knowing his cousin had limitations, it startled Muller to hear him speak of such. "Jarid, do you remember the day Unbent and I found you in the forest? You were sleeping in that hollow."

"I remember. Why?"

"Somehow in your trance you gathered power from the forest, focused through that hollow. The woods seemed…" He struggled for the words. "Alive somehow. I heard a cry from your dream as if it were there, in the forest."

Jarid stiffened. "What cry?"

Muller spoke with the gentleness he usually tried to hide. "Your father. My cousin. Prince Aron."

Jarid rested his fists on the table and leaned forward, staring at the plans of Suncroft, though Muller doubted he saw them. He answered in a low voice. "I had a nightmare about my parents' death."

"I'm sorry," Chime murmured.

Jarid looked up at them. "Why do you mention this?"

"I think you have another ability," Muller said. "In your trances or dreams, your spells fill everything. It happens here, too, I think, because Suncroft has so many shapes, in mosaics, tapestries, engravings, windows, the towers, all of it. Your power fills this castle like wine fills a goblet."

Jarid straightened up. "I've no idea what you mean."

Muller spread his arms out from his sides. "I don't know how else to describe it."

"You believe that if I harness this filling spell, I can locate Anvil?"

"How could you miss him?" Muller hoped he wasn't angering Jarid by asking him to recreate a spell borne within a nightmare. "Your mind will reach everywhere within this castle."

Jarid's face took on a shadowed look. "I was asleep when you felt this spell. I have no idea how I made it."

Chime's melodic voice flowed over them. "Perhaps if you went into a trance?"

"I just meditate." Jarid spoke tightly, obviously discussing part of his life he preferred to keep private. "I've never known it to 'fill' anything."

"You probably don't realize it," Muller said.

"Mull, I don't know." Jarid rubbed the back of his neck, his motions slowed by fatigue. "I doubt it will help."

Fieldson motioned at the plans strewn across the tables. "We've had no other luck in locating Anvil."

"Very well." Jarid exhaled. "I will try."

37

The Chambers

Jarid stood in the circular room atop the Mage Tower. The chamber had no furniture, no paintings, no hangings, nothing but a window that looked east. The candle he had set on the sill gave only dim light, making the pale violet stone of the walls appear white.

As a child, Jarid had often snuck up here. The King's Advisors admonished him, saying he had no business playing in a place reserved for mages. Only his mother understood, recognizing the stirring of his power.

The room fascinated him. A long-ago sculptor had engraved its walls with vines, every blossom a perfect shape: triangles, squares, polygons, circles, polyhedrons, spheres. They curved around the walls in graceful designs. The room drew him even now, when a hostile army waited outside and a deadly mage prowled his home, ready to destroy all he loved, all he had thought he lost forever and then miraculously regained. It would destroy him to lose it again. If he could, he would fill the castle with his mood spell, saturate it, until he flushed out Anvil the Forged.

Jarid sat on the floor, facing the closed door. Gradually his mind relaxed and his power gathered, focused by the engravings, the circular room, the conical turret, the mosaics throughout the castle, the great Shape-Hall, the castle itself.

He became aware of people: Skylark, a blue glow of light, asleep in the Cross Room where she treated the injured; Della snoring in bed, her dreams restless, exhausted from her mage work during the battle; Chime, warmth and fire, vibrant with life, as was the tiny mage daughter she carried; Muller, a blaze of gold light, ragged and unfinished, with a bracing purity.

Jarid could imagine what acerbic comment Brant would have about Muller's "purity," given the way his cousin had wooed Chime. Muller wasn't courting now, though. His mood came through clearly; he was trying to admonish his wife. Jarid took pity on his cousin, who for all his blustering was helpless in the face of Chime's indomitable will, and sent a side spell to sooth their argument.

His main spell continued to expand. He had found many people now, but no trace of Anvil. Could Chime have mistaken his location? He reached beyond Suncroft, across the battlefields and the hills beyond. Such grief, fear, exhaustion. The soldiers wanted to go home, everyone, on both sides. He offered a spell of peace, but it wasn't enough, even with his power. He couldn't counter the years of hostility between Aronsdale and Harsdown with one spell.

A new mood came to him, one full of colors and warmth, deep and wide. Iris. His wife. She slept out there, safe in the woods, protected by his army. During the Tallwalk battle, he had blazed with fear for her life. He would do anything to protect her, even use his gifts in violence. The intensity of his emotions terrified him; what was this fierce, brilliant emotion she evoked?

His temples ached with the strain of his spell. He drew back into the castle and the pain receded. For a while he sat, clearing his mind. When his strength returned, he closed his eyes and filled his mind with images: spheres, rotating, sparkling, spinning. Their beauty saturated his thoughts. Filling. Muller had chosen a good word. So many colors filled the world.

Still he hadn't found Anvil. Chime felt certain she had narrowed the search to this wing, but even in such a limited area, he found nothing of the dark mage.

A green spell shimmered into form around Jarid, sweeping him with emerald mage power like jeweled dust. He stiffened, unfamiliar with this intrusion. But the beauty of the spell drew him, as did the strength that went deep below its glimmering surface.

Chime.

Ah.... His mind relaxed and his spell blended with hers, swelling, expanding. She could find Anvil. They swept through Suncroft, through its halls, floors, walls, ceilings, shapes, and colors—

Darkness.

It hit him like ice. As soon as Jarid identified Anvil, he cut his link with Chime, shielding her from the darkness. He hadn't found Anvil before because the dark mage was a *lack* rather than a presence. Chime had neither Jarid's power nor his reach, but she had a green ability unmatched by anyone he knew, including himself, enough to find Anvil even by his absence.

Jarid tried to brighten the cavity of the dark mage, but it stayed black. His spell glided across it like water on oil. So. Now that he had found what they sought, his advisors would expect him to descend the tower and reveal Anvil's location. But they couldn't fight the dark mage; Anvil could too easily destroy them. Jarid had to face this dark mage on his own.

I am here, Anvil. He poured disdain into the words, goading. *Come, little mage.*

The darkness stirred.

Jarid opened his eyes, aware of how dim the chamber had become, the candle burned to almost nothing. He wove a shield, a gold and sapphire spell made from his abilities to soothe and heal, but directed outward to protect the people of Suncroft against emotions meant to harm. He layered the spell over their sleep and waking.

Then he waited.

The passage of time meant little to Jarid. He had spent so much of his life without reference to day and night, it no longer affected him. Just as he had meditated when he lived with Unbent, so now he sat in a trance. The candle guttered and flickered.

The gold doorknob moved.

Jarid stayed motionless, his shallow breathing the only sign he was human rather than a statue. The door opened, framing a man in its archway, a tall figure with broad shoulders and long legs, his dark hair combed back from his forehead. His black eyes seemed to absorb what little light remained in the room.

Jarid rose to his feet. "Anvil the Forged."

The man regarded him impassively. "King Jarid."

"Why forged?" Jarid asked his enemy.

"By my life. Beaten into the shape I am now." Anvil stepped into the room and closed the door. "Made strong."

Jarid cupped his hand as if he held a sphere. Light glowed within, blue, then indigo.

In response, Anvil folded his hand around the metal sphere that hung on a heavy chain from his belt. He raised his other arm, his palm out toward Jarid. Indigo sparks jumped from his hand, arcing across the space that separated them. Instead of hitting Jarid, the sparks shimmered around him, lighting his body but unable to touch him through his mage shield. The orb of light in his hand glowed, turning an intense violet.

"A violet mage." Anvil stared at him, hatred in his gaze. "It cannot exist."

"He." Jarid's gaze never wavered. "I am no 'it.'"

"Tell me," Anvil said curiously. "Why blind and deafen yourself?" Malice honed his words. "Why no voice? Perhaps the power is too much for you, eh?"

"It will do." Jarid refused to respond to Anvil's provocation, but he felt far less serene than the façade he presented. Although he had the greater power, he lacked Anvil's experience and his ruthless nature. The darkness that scarred the mage went deeper than a lack of green. He was cold, like a windswept plateau high in the mountains where no trees survived.

Jarid focused on the sphere of light in his palm and it began to grow.

"You make spells without shapes," Anvil said. Hard edges brooded beneath his casual words.

"My spell is my shape," Jarid said.

"You cannot use your spell to make your spell."

Jarid shrugged. He couldn't explain. He didn't care how it worked; suffice that it did. His sphere grew until it filled the room with violet light.

Anvil stepped back. "I feel nothing."

"The spell does nothing but drain your power."

"Nay." Anvil's jaw jerked. His hand tightened on his metal ball, his knuckles turning white. Indigo light intensified around him. It couldn't force back Jarid's spell but it stopped its advance.

Then Anvil struck.

Pain shot through Jarid's chest as if he had been stabbed. He lurched back, his light dimming. His anger flared as it had the day Aronsdale soldiers wrested him away from his home with Unbent. But this time he faced a far darker foe. He gathered his power into a bolt and jerked back his arm. He barely regained control in time to stop himself from hurtling the spell at his enemy.

Anvil's lip curled. "Smite me, Mage King."

Jarid ignored the taunt. He brought both hands in front of his body, palms upward, cupping them to hold spheres. Blue light intensified within them until it filled the chamber.

"Stop!" Anvil raised his arm, shielding his eyes.

"It is only light," Jarid said mildly. "It heals."

"I scorn your healing." Anvil clapped his hands and the blue light in Jarid's hands turned red. Heat flared as if Jarid held scorching coals, and he jerked from the pain. In the few seconds it took to douse the spell, his palms burned, real burns, no phantom heat. Then the heat vanished, leaving him with sweat running down his neck and a searing agony in his hands.

"You cannot win," Anvil said. "If you refuse to attack, I triumph. If you attack, it destroys you. Either way, you fail." An oily smile creased his face. "Your name is a lie, Jarid Dawnfield. You are night rather than dawn. You realize this."

Even knowing Anvil was baiting him, he recoiled from the truth in those words. Yes, he was night. He had felt that way since his parents died. It made no difference how many people felt otherwise, how many considered his deed justified and his mage light strong. They didn't live with his memories. But for today, he would be light; for Iris, Muller, Chime, for everyone who depended on him, he could, this one day, be his name. Tomorrow, the next day, each day he overcame his crushing, self-inflicted guilt, he became stronger.

"Even so," Jarid said, "I will not kill you." He made a blue spell and coated his hands with it like a balm. The pain receded.

Anvil raised his arms. "Hear me, Mage King!" Outside, a crack rent the night. The window behind Jarid shattered, raining broken glass over him. His spell of healing deflected most of the shards, but a few sliced his clothes, bringing more pain.

"Stop!" Jarid stretched out his arm, his palm facing Anvil. A wall of purple light rolled out from his hand and swept across the dark mage, making him jerk backward.

"Stop my spells, will you?" Anvil laughed. "All of them! You don't know how to deal with so many at once."

This time thunder rumbled *within* the castle, a rolling crash that shook through a nearby wing. Anvil was attacking Suncroft. Jarid's temper surged. Wind rushed through the shattered window at his back, whipping his hair around his face. Somewhere a woman screamed. Sparks jumped from Anvil to Jarid, searing his skin despite Jarid's protective spells.

"Go ahead!" Anvil shouted above the noise. "Strike me!" His scorn fueled his spells, making flames jump within the chamber.

"Waterfall," Jarid said. Sparkling blue light poured down from nowhere, dousing the flames, healing, calming, cooling his temper.

"Look." Anvil motioned at the window. "See what happens to your home while you play water games." As he spoke, another crack sounded outside.

Jarid whirled—and saw flames. The Starlight Tower, clearly visible from here, roared with fire. Nothing remained of its turreted roof except a jagged border at the top of the burning walls.

"I will bring it down," Anvil grated. "All of it, unless you relinquish to me your life and your kingdom."

Cries came from within the castle, piercing Jarid like a sword. He swung around in time to see Anvil make a light spell, the glowing image of a woman in the palm of his upturned hand—a perfect replica of Iris. She screamed as flames enveloped her body.

"This is what she feels now." Hatred consumed Anvil's voice. "Watch her suffer, you madman."

Jarid's rage leapt. He *felt* Iris's agony—and his capacity for rational thought vanished. Power surged through him, building to an explosive peak.

Anvil kept pushing his spells outward. With a great, thundering crash, part of the wall around them collapsed, destroying the layers of Jarid's spell that drew on the shape of the chamber. No matter. He needed no concrete shapes. He threw his fury into the orbs of light he held, turning them violet. They spun as he raised his arms above his head. Power rolled through him, building, gathering, cresting. Anvil had no idea; Jarid could destroy any spell the dark mage created, shatter it as easily as Anvil had shattered the window. He could kill this monster with one bolt or make him suffer protracted agony. His power flared, raging, and violet flames roared around his body.

"Jarid, no." Muller's shout came from behind Anvil. "Don't do it!" He stood in the doorway, his body bathed in radiance, his gold hair luminous with reflected light.

The king barely heard him. He drew his spell back as if it were a spear he would drive through Anvil. Power coursed within him, wild, fierce, unstoppable.

And in that moment, just before Jarid killed, Muller lunged into the room. He knocked Anvil to the side and stumbled when a backlash of the dark mage's power hit him.

"Muller, stay back, you fool!" Jarid shouted. He was losing control of his spell; his cousin could die here as easily as Anvil.

The dark mage grabbed Muller and swung him around, his arm around Muller's neck. "See your cousin!" he called to Jarid. "Watch him die."

"No." Jarid's voice fell into a deceptive calm. Muller stared at him, gasping for breath as he fought Anvil, his eyes taking a manic light. Erratic power flooded Jarid, an incredible power, untrained, untutored, unleashed for the first time with no restraint. Surely such an immense, indigo strength came from

Anvil—but this magnificent power had a purity the dark mage would never know.

Then, suddenly, Jarid understood; the room's shape had become imperfect when the wall collapsed. Muller was using it to let his full power loose for the first time in his life. His cousin was an *indigo sphere-mage*.

Light flared around Muller like wildfire. His power surged, but instead of striking Anvil, it blasted Jarid. The king was already struggling to hold his killing spell; now, with Muller's spell whirling through him, Jarid lost control. Thunder crashed and light flared until he could see nothing, neither his cousin nor his enemy. In that searing moment, he knew Muller had never plumbed a fraction of his power. Stronger than Anvil, surely one of the most powerful mages ever known, Muller came close to breaking Jarid's killing spell—

But even he couldn't stop the fury Jarid unleashed.

With power coursing through him, Jarid stood, his legs planted wide as he raised his arms to the sky. His spell roared through the broken chamber. Muller's spell coursed through him, melded with his own now, bending the forces Jarid and Anvil had thrown at each other. The roof and remaining walls of the room exploded outward in a rain of debris. Wind rushed across Jarid as he stood, his arms to the sky, his body ablaze like a star.

He was dimly aware that Anvil and Muller had fallen to the ground. Muller was kneeling, staring upward in shock. Jarid fought to regain control of his power before the spell destroyed everything. His light filled the chamber, the tower, the castle, and flooded across the countryside, casting harsh shadows in the night.

All around Suncroft, on the field and hills, in woods and vales, warriors were rising to their feet. Jarid saw them clearly, though they were far away. They stood among trees and by campfires, climbed out of bedrolls, and held restless horses. All stared upward at Jarid, who stood atop the broken tower, his arms raised to the sky, mage light brilliant around the radiant pillar of his body.

Jarid thought he could stand there forever, lost in the magnificence and fury. Time lost meaning. A thousand glorious eons passed.

Only gradually did he become aware that a woman had come to him. She stood within the circle that had been the floor of a chamber and was now the top of the tower. Her hip-length hair whipped in the gales, a curling mane, gold, bronze, amber, brown, red, copper. She was fiercely beautiful, like the warrior queens of legend who blazed across the sky on horses of fire.

She spoke, but in the roar of his power, he heard nothing. As she came closer, her lips formed a word: *Jarid*. He should know that word, but his mind had filled with his spell until he thought he would ignite and be consumed in its fire.

She took another step, closing the space between them—and touched him, laying her palm against his chest. With horror, he knew his spell would incinerate her.

And yet, incredibly, power flowed around and through her, and she absorbed it unharmed, siphoning the energy that streamed off him with such ferocity.

As his spell eased, he remembered his name. Jarid. He dragged in a breath, brought back from the edge of a catastrophe that could have incinerated everything he loved. This warrior mage was his wife. Iris. She stood with her hand against his chest and he could finally, mercifully, let his spell dissipate into the rushing winds.

By the time Jarid came fully to his senses, dawn had turned the sky red. Iris continued to stand with him, her gaze steady. With a groan, he took her into his arms and buried his head against her hair.

"Saints forgive me," he rasped. He had almost destroyed it all—Suncroft, Croft's Vale, everything.

"Such power," she whispered. "A spell created by three sphere mages, two indigos and one violet. And you held it *all* within yourself."

Jarid wasn't ready to consider the magnitude of what he had done. He drew back and lifted her blowing away of her face. "Anvil told me you were burning alive."

"I am not so easy to overcome."

She didn't fool him. Her mood echoed with the agony she had endured from that spell, which had burned her mind rather than her body. "I am glad you are alive." It barely touched what he felt.

"And I you." Her voice caught.

He spoke raggedly. "You are my love. Always."

Moisture gathered in her eyes. "As you are mine."

Jarid became aware of other people. Lifting his head, he saw Muller standing a few paces away, his face pale, his arms hanging at his side, his hair ruffled in the wind. Brant stood behind him with Della and Fieldson. Arkandy waited with Sam Threadman, Muller's valet. Beyond them, across the razed tower, stood the other chamber, the one with imperfect shapes—except it no longer existed. It too had exploded.

Muller followed Jarid's gaze to the blasted chamber. Then he turned back to Jarid. "It magnified my spell."

"Your *what?*" Della asked. The others stared at Muller in bewildered astonishment.

Jarid spoke quietly. "You saved my life, cousin."

"Nay." Muller flushed. "I almost destroyed you."

Jarid shook his head. "You deflected Anvil's spell, so it exploded the room instead of killing anyone."

Muller swallowed. "Quite some luck."

Luck. He wondered if Muller had any idea what he had accomplished. Anvil would have pulled Jarid's spell inside out, turning it to evil, just as he had done to Chime when he attacked her while she rode with the army, or to Muller when

Anvil tricked him into losing his way in the bog. Only this time, the dark mage would have been dealing with a power unlike any other unleashed. If Muller hadn't shunted off Anvil's attack, turning it against the tower, Jarid could have destroyed Suncroft and saints only knew how much of the countryside.

Jarid looked around at them all. "Anvil?"

Iris indicated the ground. "He is gone." Ashes in the shape of a man lay there. Despite the wind lashing the tower, nothing disturbed the remains.

Jarid knelt next to the ashes, but a spell stopped him from touching them. He looked up at Muller. "How?" His voice sounded eerily calm.

"I was trying to protect you." Muller swallowed. "It seems I protected Anvil instead, even in death."

"Nay." Jarid rose to his feet. "You turned his spell back on itself. He tried to make me strike down Suncroft in flames. Instead, he incinerated him." Softly he added, "His hatred finally burned him alive."

Iris spoke to Muller. "Your protection only keeps his ashes here. He died from his own spell."

Muller just shook his head. Jarid didn't know how to make his cousin believe in himself, but this much was clear: Muller needed to master his gifts instead of hiding from their terrible, beautiful power.

Then Jarid realized who was missing.

"Where is Chime?" he asked.

"Just behind—" Iris stopped when she turned and saw no Chime. "She was running to the stairs with me."

Muller's agitation flared. Without a word, he strode to what remained of the landing at the top of the stairs and took off down the steps spiraling into the tower. Jarid followed, a weight descending on his heart. In all that had happened, he hadn't been consciously aware of a lack, but now he felt it clearly. Emptiness existed where Chime's warmth had touched them.

Tonight's cataclysm may have stolen a treasure more precious than any castle—the life of their emerald mage.

38

Burgeoning Sphere

Chime walked through the night, thunder crashing above her, though no clouds darkened the sky. A great, jagged branch of lightning hit the Starlight Tower, exploding the top with a crash. Debris rained down the castle, chunks of rock rebounding off the walls.

She kept walking.

Wind plastered her tunic to her body, wrapping the green and gold silk around her. She walked down the slope from Suncroft on its northern side, putting the castle between her and the woods where she and Iris had been with the King's Army. To her left, the campfires of the Harsdown army flickered on slopes and ridges.

She continued on.

At the bottom of the hill, Chime crossed a field where the fighting hadn't yet reached. Grass brushed her calves and knees, wet with dew, soaking her leggings. She came to the next slope and started hiking up Mount Sky, the highest point in this region of Aronsdale.

Thunder rumbled, followed by an explosion behind her. She stopped and turned to the castle. The top of the Mage Tower had collapsed, leaving Jarid standing in the open, his arms raised to the sky, his body radiant with violet light. His spell roared through Chime and lit the countryside for miles around. Everywhere in the hills, warriors were rising to their feet, their heads turned up to the Mage Tower.

"Be strong, my cousin," she murmured. Then she resumed her climb up the hill.

Chime had felt the power rising in Anvil tonight the instant Jarid had found him, guided by her spell. The king had tried to shield her, but nothing could break the link that had formed between Chime and the dark mage.

When she reached the top of Mount Sky, she turned toward Suncroft, toward the pillar of light that was Jarid. The moon on the horizon had turned a jeweled green, though she had never heard of an Emerald Moon. Then she realized that a sphere of glimmering emerald light surrounded her, coloring the world.

Chime felt Anvil die.

His spirit rose into the sky as his body turned to ash. But he refused to relinquish his hold on this world. She had known he would never give up. The time had come for her to face him. He came toward her, and she stood firm within the glistening light of her enchanted sphere, the wind swirling her hair around her body.

Suddenly Anvil's spirit rushed through the air above her. He was all around, encompassing her spell, closing his sphere of emptiness around her light.

Chime pulled off the gold chain around her neck and clasped her fingers around the emerald orb. It glowed within her hand, casting light as rich as new leaves in spring.

You cannot stay, she thought to Anvil. *Your spirit must pass on from this, the land of the living.*

Come to me, he answered. *Come to me.*

He filled her mind, drawing the essence of her spirit to him. More than any other mage, any human alive, she had what he lacked, the green of empathy, of compassion, of moods felt and understood. It was the color of new life, of burgeoning fields and deep lakes. He filled himself with her spells like a man dying of thirst suddenly given a lake of clear, fresh water. He drowned himself in the empathy that life had burnt out of him, that he no longer had—*because he had felt emotions too much.*

"No," Chime whispered.

"Become me." Anvil's ghostly voice drifted on the wind. "And I will become you."

She tried to pull away, but she couldn't break their link. He would fill her with himself and she would become the dark mage, giving him a body to strike at Aronsdale, not only possessing her but also her unborn child, and through her, Muller, perhaps even Jarid. He would triumph now, when they thought him defeated, and he would do it by using her.

You cannot, Chime thought. *I am too strong.*

You are only a tender green mage, he answered. *Unlike any other, but no match for me.*

Strength comes in many ways, Anvil the Forged.

And I have them all. His spirit saturated her mind.

Fear sparked within Chime, but she didn't flinch. She accepted now that she had more within her than she had been willing to admit for so many years. Mage. Green mage. No longer would she deny her gifts, letting her doubts weaken her power.

Suddenly she remembered the incantation. Sphere-inside-out. She had used it to free herself from Anvil before. She would do it again.

No. His thought rumbled within her.

Yes. Chime prepared to speak the words.

Then she paused. The first time she had used the spell, it

had left her nauseated, weakened with a darkness that she had abhorred.

But it had worked.

Perhaps she had to suffer its darkness to achieve the greater good.

No, Anvil thought. *Do not.*

Chime felt his mood. He projected fear. But she didn't believe it. He wanted her to think he was afraid that she would use the incantation. But why did she know it? She had dreamed the words while he tormented her nights.

Desperation tugged at her. Sphere-inside-out. *Allar nellari remalla.* Was he maneuvering her into speaking those words? He reversed spells: the incantation reversed spells. It had seemed to work for her before, but doubt assailed her. Had it been a trick? The incantation might be her only hope of escaping his spirit or it might bind her to him forever.

She didn't have the mage power to overcome him. But if she didn't stop him, he would take all that mattered to her, to the people she loved, to Aronsdale.

She made her decision.

Chime lifted her arm into the air, her hand fisted around her emerald pendant, its gold chain hanging down her arm. The wind whipped down at her sleeve, leaving her arm pale and bare in the night. Lifting her chin, she spoke the incantation—backward:

Allamer irallen ralla.

Reversed, the ancient words poured into the world with clarity and light. Brilliant. Anvil's spirit cried out in horrified fury. He had never expected her to reverse a spell of reversal. His spirit whirled in the wind—and fled from her mind like a bird arrowing into the heavens.

Chime followed.

He plummeted through the clouds of death as if he had been

struck by an arrow. Chime caught his spirit in her mage hands, cupping them around the fading essence that had been Anvil the Forged. Within that spirit, she found his life—the truth of his life. Mourning for the child he had once been, she drifted down to an endless ocean that filled her magescape from horizon to horizon.

Colors swirled: the red of an apple, streaming gold sunlight, the yellowing green of a leaf at summer's end, the sparkle of emerald, a forever sky, the indigo ink of a pen, the violet of night. They blended into a haze. She floated within them like a cork on the sea, drifting father from shore. A burial craft bobbed next to her, the ashes within it lifting on the wind and wafting into an endless clouded sky.

Chime drifted into the wind, spreading out, as free as light and air. Lovely music tugged her mind. It receded and she began to fade. Then it began again, pulling her back, back, *back*...

"...back, please." The voice, the music, became words. "Please come back to me."

She couldn't bear the grief that drenched that beautiful voice. With a silent farewell to the floating pyre, she let the voice pull her back...

Chime opened her eyes. Muller was kneeling next to her, his face drawn. "Please come back." Tears slid down his face. "Chime, I cannot be without you. Come back."

The sun had risen. She was lying on her side at the top of Mount Sky, her cheek against grass drenched with dew. The light of the rising sun slanted across her face.

She answered in a whisper. "Don't weep, my love."

"Gracious Saints." Muller pulled her into his arms, leaning over her, his body shaking. He kept saying her name over and over, rocking back and forth.

Sitting up, holding him close, Chime laid her head on his

shoulder. The funeral pyre had been Anvil's spirit, shepherded to its final rest, gone forever from their world, freeing them from his rage, his cruelty——and his agony.

"I thought you were gone,' Muller whispered.

Pulling back, she touched his beloved face. "I cannot leave, dear Muller." A tear ran down her cheek. "Then who would scold you for worrying too much about your clothes?"

He laughed unsteadily. "We mustn't let that happen."

She cupped her palms around his face. "I am so glad to see you."

Muller kissed her. "Why did you come out here?"

"Anvil——"

"No!" He grasped her shoulders. "What did he——"

Chime laid her fingers on his lips, stopping his words. "I came here to meet him. We had to finish our business, he and I. He wouldn't leave this world until we did. I caught his spirit and sent it home."

He searched her face. "Are you hurt?"

"Nay, love." She touched his temple and traced the line of his cheek. "He was kin to you and Jarid."

He stared at her. "Impossible."

A voice rumbled behind them. "That cannot be."

Startled, Chime looked up. Jarid, Iris, Arkandy, Sam Thread-man, and several military officers were gathered around on the grass. It was Jarid who had spoken.

Chime and Muller rose to their feet. Although they let go of each other then, Chime felt as if his arms were still around her.

"It is true," she told the king.

Jarid's voice darkened. "It cannot be."

"It would explain his power," Iris said.

Muller shook his head. "But we have no kin in Stonce."

"I don't know how you are related." Chime recalled Anvil's mind as it drifted into oblivion. "He genuinely believed what he told us about his family, how they died."

Muller spoke quietly. "You speak as if you no longer do."

"I saw it all. His life. It was nothing like what he describes. His friends, family, the villagers, they all treated him well. His mind, it—it buckled." She struggled to express what she had felt in his dying, as he escaped the insanity that had tortured his life. "He was a mutant."

"He was born without green ability?" Della asked.

"No. The opposite." Chime spoke in a subdued voice. "He had too much. He lived in a constant mood spell. It all poured into him." Her voice caught. "He was just a little boy. Every pain, agony, torment anyone suffered, he suffered, too. It was a nightmare that never ended. He didn't understand. Neither did his parents; they only saw him become more and more withdrawn." She folded her arms around herself, feeling cold. "He burned out the green within himself so he could bear to live. Then he never had to feel again. Nothing. But it drove him insane. He ran away when he was eleven, convinced he had lost his family. They probably never knew what happened."

"Saints almighty." Muller's face paled.

Iris came forward. "It took compassion for you to guide his spirit on its last journey. Not many would have done such."

"I wouldn't call it compassion. I wanted to make sure he left." After a pause, she added, "But even the darkest soul deserves to rest from a life that devastated." She grieved for the child Anvil had been, a mage of unimaginable sensitivity destroyed by his own gifts.

"I have no compassion for this man," Muller said. "He would have destroyed my country, killed my king and cousin, and stolen my wife and unborn child."

Jarid's voice rumbled. "He gravitated toward Chime."

"Of course he did," Muller said. "She's an angel."

Chime smiled, tears in her eyes. "Not that you're biased."

Iris spoke gently. "Anvil knew you could help him."

"I don't know that anyone could have helped him," she said. "Perhaps I am sorry for him. But I cannot regret his passing. He would never have rested, no matter how much he destroyed. His inner demons drove him too hard."

The clank of mail came from behind them. As Jarid and the others turned, Archer and a hexahedron-major approached them, climbing the hill. They stopped and bowed to Jarid.

"What is the situation?" Jarid asked.

Archer answered. "King Varqelle wishes to meet with you, Your Majesty."

Jarid tensed. "Did he say why?"

"His emissaries chose their words carefully." Archer gave a grim smile. "But I think he wishes to surrender."

"After what happened this morning," Fieldson said, "I would be surprised if he felt otherwise."

"Very well." Jarid spoke quietly. "Tell King Varqelle I will meet with him."

Chime stood in an alcove of the Starlight Wing in the castle, looking out the window there, up at the nearby Starlight Tower. The top chamber had ceased to exist last night, blasted into rubble. Fortunately they could rebuild it. The tower had sound construction and the rest of it remained firm, including the portion of the Star Walk that led to its upper level.

The Mage Tower had fared less well; the collapse of the upper level had also weakened the lower levels. Chime could see across Suncroft to its remains, jagged and black in the daylight. But rebuild they would, including the two rooms at the top, both the chamber of perfect shapes and the chamber of flawed shapes.

In the fields below the castle, the Harsdown army was

preparing for their journey home, guarded now by the Aronsdale army. Everyone had a subdued quality. She felt it herself, though she was among the victors in this unwanted war. It would take a long time for their countries to heal from the powers unleashed here.

A rustle sounded behind her. Turning, she saw Jarid in the arched entrance to the alcove.

"Your Majesty." Chime bowed.

"Jarid," he reminded her. "We are kin. You must learn to treat me as such."

She wondered if either of them would ever feel comfortable with court protocols. "I thank you. But I also wish to show respect for your title."

"And yours." He came forward.

"Mine?" She couldn't imagine answering to Princess Chime. She grinned. "Tree Climber, perhaps?"

He laughed gruffly. "Perhaps."

She wasn't sure how to interpret his mood. "Will you speak with King Varqelle soon?"

"I just finished."

"Already?"

"At his wish, yes." Jarid indicated the Harsdown warriors outside. "He didn't want me to attack his army as I did Anvil."

"But you didn't attack Anvil."

Jarid shrugged. "He thinks I did."

"And you let him believe it."

"Yes."

"So he surrendered."

"I would have, too, in his place." His gaze seemed to turn inward. "Nor am I sure I wouldn't have done exactly what he feared. I have too little control."

"You have more than you know."

Jarid shook his head. He stared out at the hills beyond the castle, his silence her only answer.

After a moment, Chime said, "Did you want to see me?"

He glanced at her. "I came to talk about Muller."

It didn't surprise her. The news had traveled like wildfire this morning; *Muller Dawnfield is a mage.* Astonishment rippled through the castle, tangible to Chime. Muller would spend the rest of his life learning to deal with that truth.

"I thought he was with you," she said.

"He was. He went to the stables, to see his horse."

"Then Windstrider is all right?"

"Yes. Fine. Anvil left him with Varqelle's men." He sounded odd, as if he were taking great care with his words.

"Is he still at the stables?" Chime asked.

"No." It seemed Jarid would say no more. But then he added, "Now Muller speaks with Brant, Della, and Fieldson."

"Your advisors." She wondered why.

"Yes. Also his, for the next few months."

"His?" She stared at him, dismayed, able to think of only one reason the King's Advisors would suddenly answer to Muller. "No! You must not leave! We need—"

"Chime, wait." His face lit with a smile, his teeth bright against his sun-roughened skin. Suddenly he looked his age, barely a youth of twenty. "I am going nowhere."

"But why...?"

His smile faded. "Varqelle attacked my realms. He lost. I won."

"Yes." Her voice hardened. "I am glad he lost."

"I also."

She searched his face, trying to understand. "He will leave with his army, yes? He will bother us no more?"

His voice had a shadowed sound. "You see the world in so much purer terms than the rest of us."

She flushed. "I don't understand."

"Varqelle tried to conquer Aronsdale and kill me. I cannot let him go."

It was a truth that nothing would change. "Will you execute him?"

"Brant and Fieldson wish so. Muller says no." Jarid rubbed his eyes, then dropped his arm. "I can imprison him. I could send him to a holding in the north, in the Barrens. With guards. He could never leave."

"It seems the compassionate choice."

"Or the foolish one." He sounded tired. "As long as Varqelle lives, he may escape and rise against me again."

"Hai, Jarid." Chime didn't envy him the decision. "What will happen to Harsdown?"

When he didn't answer, she wondered what she had said wrong. It seemed she would forever stumble over her words and offend people. She resisted the urge to make a mood spell using the wall mosaics; she wouldn't intrude on her king and kin that way.

Then, unexpectedly, he said, "That is why I speak with you now and why Muller is with my advisors."

She didn't see what he was trying to say. "I know nothing of Harsdown."

His mood was quiet today. "I would like you and Muller to be my representatives there. To rule Harsdown."

She stared at him. Lead a country that size? "No! Muller maybe, but I could never do such a thing."

He smiled. "You sound like your husband. And like him, you do sorely underestimate yourself."

She didn't know where to put the immensity of what he asked. It would make ruling Aronsdale seem easy, and she had never believed herself up to that responsibility. To take on a country with so many problems would be an insurmountable challenge. "I cannot."

His voice cooled. "And yet I, after fourteen years in isolation, with no preparation, am to lead Aronsdale?"

Her face heated. "I am sorry. I don't mean to shirk my duties. But I am not you. I cannot do this." The obstacles were too great.

"You misjudge yourself. You can surmount much greater obstacles than you believe."

Chime regarded him warily. "Are you putting mood spells on me?"

"I need no spell," he said dryly. "Your face tells me your thoughts."

She put one hand on her hip. "Then it must be yelling that I cannot be queen of Harsdown."

Jarid motioned to the window, indicating the armies. "Fieldson is taking a contingent of the King's Army to Harsdown. He will govern there during the transition. Muller has said that if you agree, the two of you can join Fieldson after preparing here with Brant and Della."

She slid her hand over her abdomen, which had yet to begin swelling. "My child isn't due for seven months."

"The transition would take at least a year." His violet eyes were vivid in the sunlight. "I need people I trust in Harsdown. And its people need to learn better uses of their land. Schooling in agriculture and animal husbandry could go a long way toward ending their poverty. Varqelle hasn't given them that." He regarded her steadily. "I think you and Muller could. You both have the background and a love of the land."

It was true she had always wanted to run the orchards. Muller came from an estate that took its prosperity from farming. But loving such a life and being able to guide a country were two very different prospects.

"Would Brant and Della come with us?" she asked.

"I'm afraid I need them here. But Fieldson will be there. Skylark has also offered to go, since Iris can be healer at Suncroft."

"Iris is sapphire?" Chime's mood lightened. "It is hard to understand her talent. I don't know what it means to be a rainbow mage."

He hesitated, thoughtful. Then he said, "When you make a spell, it uses one color, yes?"

"Always."

"She uses more." He ran his finger along the mosaics that bordered the window, tracing out a design that were mostly blue, but with accents of other colors. "Her spells are like this. They depend mainly on one hue but include some of all. When she makes a healing spell, she soothes a little, feels her patient's mood, gives a bit light. Her healing may have less power because of that, but she adds nuances we cannot achieve."

"It sounds lovely."

His face softened. "Aye. She is."

She smiled at his besotted expression. "We all have much to learn about our gifts."

"So Muller says." The king shook his head. "He believes he is cursed."

"Jarid, he is wrong. I have looked through many histories, trying to understand."

Curiosity flashed in his gaze. "You have an idea?"

She hesitated, afraid to sound foolish. But she had to learn to express herself better, with more confidence. "I might. I believe some ancient mages used that room in the Mage Tower to concentrate their power."

"Many of us did. But Muller never could focus through that room."

"I didn't mean the one you used. The other."

"With the flawed shapes?" When she nodded, he said, "I hadn't realized our histories recorded mages using that one."

"Often they just say 'the chamber.' We've assumed it meant the one with perfect shapes." She paused. "But I've found mentions of a view from the window that make it sound like the chamber of flawed shapes."

He considered her words. "You think that room existed because other Dawnfields had powers such as Muller?"

"Yes." She paused, seeking to speak well instead of stumbling. "I think long ago, your ancestors tried to breed Dawnfield mages who didn't need actual physical shapes to focus their power. Instead they ended up with mages who used imperfect shapes. Like Muller. War mages. Perhaps that is why Anvil had an imperfect green power."

Jarid stiffened. "No comparison exists between Muller and Anvil."

Her voice softened. "Muller is light. Anvil is dark. I meant Anvil's gifts were skewed. Perhaps those traits our ancestors explored can show up many generations later, changed by the passage of centuries, even millennia." She had seen another truth in Anvil's spirit. "Do you recall the incantation I dreamed?"

"*Allar*—" He stopped. "I dislike the words."

"I also."

"'Sphere-inside-out.'"

"Anvil used it to reverse spells. Perhaps it spoke to him because he was a throwback to those ancient mages."

Jarid grimaced. "He should have left it in oblivion."

"Aye," she murmured. "Muller's spells are different. They often do achieve good, but in strange ways."

A smile eased the severity of the king's face. "That cousin of mine is incapable of cruelty."

It gratified her that he understood. "His spells go awry because he can't control them. No one knows how to teach him."

"He has learned some. He was so accident prone when I was little. Now he has less trouble."

"Jarid—"

"Yes?"

She spoke quietly. "You make spells without shapes."

"I always use shapes."

"But you imagine them. They don't have to be real."

"Real shapes strengthen my spells."

"Yes. But if your ancestors did try to breed mages who didn't need real shapes, you are what they hoped for."

He gazed out at the countryside, becoming distant. "I had little to do all those years except meditate."

Chime couldn't imagine the loneliness. She wanted to hate Unbent, but he had given Jarid unconditional love, making those years bearable. Without that, Jarid probably wouldn't have survived.

"You refined your gift," she said. "Purified it until you could tap into your power."

He turned back to her, his gaze intent. "I need a magic now that only you can provide. Say yes. Say you will go to Harsdown."

She twisted the cloth belt of her tunic. "I must talk to Muller."

"All right. Do that." He grinned. "Then say yes."

She couldn't help but smile. "You are incorrigible."

Mischief lit his eyes. "Perhaps I am."

She hesitated. "I heard you sent emissaries to Stonce."

"To find Anvil's family, if they live."

"I will weep for them."

His jaw stiffened. "But not for him."

Chime lifted her palm outward as if to splay it on his chest, but she held it a finger-span away from touching him, though no spell stopped her. She was too aware of the invisible shield he used to isolate himself.

Softly she said, "You must first learn to forgive yourself."

True to his name, Varqelle the Cowled wore a dark robe this night, its hood pulled up to shade his deep-set eyes. He stood at the barred window of his room and let gusts of wind ripple over his face. They had imprisoned him in an upper room of the Starlight Wing, one well appointed with heavy gold drapes and gilded furniture upholstered in wine-red brocade. Chandeliers glittered above, and urns painted with geometric patterns held sprays of ferns. An echo-dove harp with gold strings stood in one corner.

It was still a cell.

The door rattled behind him. He turned to see its ornate gold knob turn. The door opened, leaving a tall, dark-haired man with a scar on his neck framed in its archway.

Jarid. The mad king.

He walked into the room, the gusts from the window molding his violet shirt to his muscular torso. Six guards came with him, a hexagon. He stopped a few paces from Varqelle and they stood taking each other's measure, both of them the same height, their gazes level.

Varqelle pushed back his hood, letting the wind pull at the gray-streaked hair he had tied in a warrior's knot on his neck. He felt darkness closing around him. Soon he would die. But he would go to his execution with his pride intact.

His gaze remained firm. "My greetings, Your Majesty."

"And to you, Your Majesty," Jarid rumbled.

Varqelle had no desire to exchange pleasantries with his captor. "Then it is time for the execution?"

For a long moment Jarid watched him. Finally he spoke in a dusky voice. "My men will take you to a holding in the Barrens. You will spend your life as a prisoner there."

He knew then that Jarid Dawnfield truly was mad. But he said only, "You are generous."

"Perhaps," Jarid said. "If you give me cause to reconsider, you will die."

"I shall give you no such reason," Varqelle lied. Jarid seemed painfully young.

The king inclined his head. "Good eve, Your Majesty."

"And to you, Your Majesty."

After Jarid took his leave, Varqelle went to the window and resumed studying the countryside around Aronsdale. For the first time since yesterday morning, when Jarid had brought down the castle towers with the sheer force of his mage power, he felt hope.

Varqelle had wrestled with escape plans, but none had offered any realistic chance of success. Now Jarid had changed all that. The boy was compassionate, yes. He was also a fool. Compassion weakened a person. Varqelle would never have let his enemy live. He had no doubt he would be imprisoned and well guarded, with no means of escape, especially in the desolate reaches of the northern Barrens.

But nothing was impossible, not as long as he lived.

He put his hand on the bars of his prison. Someday, somehow, even if it took decades, he would regain Harsdown, if not for himself, then for his son.

The morning of the memorial service dawned cold and gray. Chime and Muller stood at the peak of Mount Sky with Jarid, Iris, the King's Advisors, Chime's maids, Aria and Reed, and Muller's valet, Sam. King Varqelle stood in the midst of eight guards, his face somber.

They had waited ten days for the emissaries to return from Stonce. Anvil's parents came with them, an elderly couple. They did have a relation to the Dawnfield line, though they hadn't known; the names on their family tree suggested Anvil's great-grandfather had been the brother of Jarid's great-grandmother. The man had dallied with a girl in Stonce and a child came of that union. The mother knew too little about the father to find him, but they had recorded him in their family scroll, Seaborn Knoll, a name rare enough in landlocked Aronsdale to have been Jarid's forbearer. Mage gifts could remain latent for decades, even centuries, before they manifested again.

Anvil's parents had searched for years, praying they would find him or that he would return. Mercifully none of their other children had suffered as Anvil. Several showed signs of mage ability, but no full-fledged gifts.

Muller had unlocked the spell binding the ashes, and now Anvil's father held the urn that housed them. They wept for his loss, but Chime also felt their closure; finally, after twenty years, they knew what had happened and could properly mourn their son.

When the service ended, Chime had a sense of release. They had survived this war. The recovery wouldn't be easy. She couldn't imagine governing Harsdown, but Jarid's confidence buoyed her. Even more startling, his advisors agreed with him that she and Muller should go to Harsdown.

So much had changed in her life. Yet she regretted none of it. The morning had come.

39

Epilogue

Chime sat at an octagonal table on the veranda of her home, going over the newly inked scrolls with Quill, her Pyramid-Secretary. She practiced the words of her speech. "Creating Guilds here, as we have in Aronsdale, will help establish more reasonable wages for everyone."

"They surely need some standard," Quill said. "They pay almost as much in taxes as they earn."

"Aye. They must be lowered." They couldn't keep taxing the people at this rate, but the treasury was empty, drained by the war. "All these changes will take time."

"I do think so." Quill continued working on the parchment, inking the words Chime had given her. This evening, Chime would go over the speech, preparing for her meeting tomorrow with leaders from the surrounding towns.

She gazed past the porch columns to the gardens and beyond those to the orchards. Two sphere-lieutenants patrolled the gardens; another stood at the other end of the veranda, tall and strong in his uniform. She was becoming used to them. Before going to Suncroft, she had never realized how much privacy a sovereign relinquished.

Had someone asked the carefree girl dashing through the orchard a few years ago if she could imagine herself leading a country, Chime would have laughed and run on her way. She missed those days; they warmed her memories like sun on a field of wheat. She had enjoyed her childhood—but now she wanted purpose to her life. She wouldn't give up this life. Even more astonishing, she was finding resources within herself to achieve goals she had once believed far beyond her abilities.

A door creaked behind her. She turned to see Muller walk out onto the veranda, carrying Melody, their daughter. The baby was fast asleep, snug in a white gown and knitted white socks with blue ribbons. Muller settled on the wicker swing and beckoned to his wife.

Glancing up, Quill saw Muller. She smiled at Chime. "It will take me a while to copy your report."

"Thank you, Quill." Chime went to Muller, settling next to him on the swing. As it rocked back and forth, he handed her the sleeping baby, who was barely five months old. Melody stirred in her arms, her eyes closed, her face turning toward her mother. She rubbed her lips against Chime's tunic, searching out her breast.

"Little beauty," Chime cooed as she opened her tunic and began to nurse. She drew her scarf around over her arms, veiling the suckling baby.

"Her mother is a beauty, too," Muller murmured. "But you look pensive today."

"We so rarely get to rest." She cradled Melody. "Times like these are precious."

He touched the baby's head with that tenderness he showed only her and their child. "Yes."

For a while they sat, enjoying the moment. They had moved their household to Harsdown three months ago, two months after the birth of their daughter, a girl with wisps of gold hair. Neither Chime nor Muller had wished to live in the stark halls of Castle Escar; instead, they had come here, to a southern estate with farmlands and orchards.

Aided by advisors and assistants, they spent their days learning Harsdown. It caught Chime by surprise when Varqelle's staff began to help them. She had expected resentment, even hatred. And some reacted that way. But Varqelle had been a hard master, unforgiving and unrelenting in his ruthless drive, a king who followed the ways of his predecessors, driving the country further into poverty. Some of his staff welcomed the change.

They were establishing a program to help farmers improve crop yields. Muller was training and recruiting a new army, one led by Aronsdale officers. Chime would establish Guilds and schools. So much had to be done.

But for these few moments, they could relax.

Muller pulled out the cord with the dented ring from under his vest. "We must visit your family so I can return this to Drummer."

"Knowing it saved your life has meant so much to him." Chime thought fondly of her brothers and grinned. "Apparently he hasn't let Hunter hear the end of it."

"You don't think it bothers them to know I am a mage?"

"Not at all."

"Perhaps someday I will become used to it." He paused. "I started a fire in the hearth today."

Chime recognized his hesitation. "Was that what you intended?"

He reddened. "Actually, no. I wanted light. But at least this time I didn't damage anything."

"I'm glad."

"So was Skylark. Relieved, anyway." His lashes lowered halfway as he regarded her. "You look lovely, sitting there."

"So do you." She did truly enjoy the sight of him, dapper in gold and russet silk, his long legs clad in fine leggings, his white silk shirt covered by a brocaded gold vest. Sam Threadman had come with them, as dedicated as ever to fussing over Muller. Her husband had changed a great deal, but he was still the best dressed man she knew.

"Why are you looking at me like that?" he asked.

"Like what?"

"As if I am a delectable morsel you plan to eat."

Chime laughed softly. "Ah, Muller, you do truly fill my days full of charmed light."

His face gentled. "And you heal my shapes, love."

So they sat together. The future they faced wouldn't be easy, setting a course for a restive, impoverished country. But whatever labors lay ahead, their intertwined lives and love would make it worthwhile.

LUNA

In Camelot's Shadow

An Arthurian tale comes to life....

From the wilds of Moreland to the court of Camelot, a woman searches for her true powers....

Risa of the Morelands refuses to be a sacrifice. Promised to the evil Euberacon, the infamous sorcerer, Risa flees armed only with her strong will and bow. When Risa stumbles upon Sir Gawain returning to Camelot, she believes she has discovered the perfect refuge: Camelot, noble Arthur's court. The sorcerer would never dare to come after her while she was under the protection of the Knights of the Round Table! Clearly, Risa has underestimated Euberacon's desire to have her as his wife.

On sale February 24. Visit your local bookseller.